WILD FOR HIM

"I was right, girl," he said. "You are mad."

She flinched. "I am *not* mad."

Good sense said Meg would pull away. She had taken offense before, but this time she did not retreat. Her fingertips curled into the muscles of his chest and scored him with blunt fingernails. Tipping up her chin, she brought her mouth closer. Their breath mingled, the only heat in the forest, until she claimed Will Scarlet with a kiss.

BOOK YOUR PLACE ON OUR WEBSITE AND MAKE THE READING CONNECTION!

We've created a customized website just for our very special readers, where you can get the inside scoop on everything that's going on with Zebra, Pinnacle and Kensington books.

When you come online, you'll have the exciting opportunity to:

- View covers of upcoming books
- Read sample chapters
- Learn about our future publishing schedule (listed by publication month *and author*)
- Find out when your favorite authors will be visiting a city near you
- Search for and order backlist books from our online catalog
- Check out author bios and background information
- Send e-mail to your favorite authors
- Meet the Kensington staff online
- Join us in weekly chats with authors, readers and other guests
- Get writing guidelines
- AND MUCH MORE!

**Visit our website at
http://www.kensingtonbooks.com**

WHAT A SCOUNDREL WANTS

CARRIE LOFTY

ZEBRA BOOKS
Kensington Publishing Corp.
www.kensingtonbooks.com

ZEBRA BOOKS are published by

Kensington Publishing Corp.
850 Third Avenue
New York, NY 10022

All Kensington titles, imprints, and distributed lines are available at special quantity discounts for bulk purchases for sales promotion, premiums, fund-raising, educational, or institutional use.

Special book excerpts or customized printings can also be created to fit specific needs. For details, write or phone the office of the Kensington Special Sales Manager: Attn. Special Sales Department. Kensington Publishing Corp., 850 Third Avenue, New York, NY 10022. Phone: 1-800-221-2647.

Zebra and the Z logo Reg. U.S. Pat. & TM Off.

ISBN-13: 978-1-4201-0475-2
ISBN-10: 1-4201-0475-6

First Printing: December 2008
10 9 8 7 6 5 4 3 2 1

Printed in the United States of America

To Keven

Acknowledgments

Thanks to Kelly Schaub, Patti Ann Colt, Lindsey Sodano, and the other Circle ladies for helping make my manuscript shine; to Casey Stone and Pete Brooks for brainstorming; to Jenn Ritzema, Liz Powell, and Karen Martin for endless friendship; to Ann Aguirre for being right about everything, especially this story; to Kate Rothwell for being my first fangirl; to Chicago North for accepting me with open arms; and to my family for their enduring love and support.

My special thanks to Hilary Sares and Caren Johnson for making this book possible.

Will you hear a tale of Robin Hood,
Will Scarlet, and Little John?
Now listen awhile, it will make you smile,
As before it hath many a one.

"Robin Hood and the Peddlers"
Folk ballad, nineteenth century

Chapter One

"You, Scarlet, you are always moody here."
—Robin Hood

The Foresters: Robin Hood and Maid Marian
Alfred Lord Tennyson, 1892

Near Melton Mowbray, England
Autumn, 1199

Will Scarlet hated trees. Any trees.

Woods. Holts. And Sherwood Forest, most of anything.

Although Sherwood lurked at the end of a long day's ride to the northwest, Charnwood Forest taunted him with its resemblance. The stink of rotting leaves crawled into his nose. Noises like chattering goblins sounded through the ever-moving branches. Even at noontide, details hid within clusters of shadow.

A shiver skimmed his backbone. Crouched in the ferns, he glanced to see if the other dozen men working for Sheriff Finch noticed his nerves, but they remained intent on their task.

"God grant me leave from this hell pit," he muttered, crossing himself.

Sinking a knee-guard into the loam, he leaned forward along

the road to Nottingham. Four warhorses slowly approached, riding out of Melton. Struggling fingers of sunshine burnished the mail of the foremost riders. One's lax posture suggested a light sleep, while another carelessly held the reins of his plodding mount. Slender-bodied horses followed, bearing riders in stately dress and the crest of the Earl of Whitstowe.

Will's superior, Roger of Carlisle, a close confederate of the Sheriff of Nottingham, stepped from the cover of brush. The nearest horses snorted and shied. Riders jerked to attention, raising flattop shields and unsheathing swords in a cold song of steel sliding along steel.

The earl's foremost guard, a gaunt man with ruddy cheeks, raised a gloved hand and brought the procession to an abrupt halt. "Who goes? Away now, man."

"No." Carlisle crossed thick arms across his chest. The boiled leather he wore made his stout, muscular body appear even more formidable. "I shall speak to Lord Whitstowe."

The earl himself nudged his horse forward. "What's the meaning of this?"

"I am Roger of Carlisle. I represent the Sheriff of Nottingham, Peter Finch."

Lord Whitstowe pushed back the hood of his embroidered surcoat, scowling. "My party has not reached the Nottinghamshire boundary. What business have you here?"

"Milord, you hold lands in both shires. Your obligation to King John is to protect these forests from poachers and itinerants."

Whitstowe's face darkened. "You lark about in the road and dare remind me of my duty to His Majesty?"

"I do, milord, on behalf of the sheriff, because you've failed to obey that duty."

Holding his balance, Will flexed his feet. Reputation held Whitstowe to be a man with sense as good as his breeding, but with a history of defying royal edicts regarding quitrents and armies. He deemed a number of royal demands wasteful and, on that excuse, disregarded them.

Hiding in trees usually meant trouble. But perhaps dealing with stubborn nobles required Carlisle's dramatic methods— forcing an audience in the road like a highwayman. A recollection of the wage Will stood to earn smoothed his sudden unease.

The second of the two lead sentries wore a conical steel cap, a nosepiece obscuring his face. He guided his warhorse between Carlisle and the nobleman. "You dare speak to Lord Whitstowe thus? Show respect, man!"

"Settle your temper, Hendon."

"Milord, I will not," said Hendon. "His insolence cannot be borne. You there, clear out of the way!"

Carlisle grinned. "You clear out. I have matters to discuss with your liege, gelding."

"Knave!"

Hendon hoisted his massive sword and charged.

From all around, Carlisle's men jumped from their cover and rushed the procession. Cries and scorns slit the air as the two factions brought to blows. Swords bashed together with force enough to loosen teeth. Horses reared high. Arrows flew. A masterful shot pierced the neck of the first, ruddy-faced guard, dropping him dead at the hooves of the earl's horse.

Will watched in mute horror. Time blurred into a chaos of motion and violence. He should move. He should fight. But motives and meaning escaped him. How could he know which side to take if he hardly understood what sparked the fray?

A scream ripped through the impassive trees.

A woman? By the best!

Before he could deliberate, he leapt from his scrubby cover. No woman deserved to be caught out when men met with flaying swords.

He trained in on the echo of her distress and sped through a tangle of struggling bodies and deadly armaments. When he could evade direct conflict, he parried or ducked. But when he faced one of Lord Whitstowe's men in an unavoidable duel, he lunged.

Fully a hand taller, the challenger pivoted and swung his

sword. The long, deadly blade caught Will on the left arm, imbedding in muscle and leather-lined mail. Pain surged at his shoulder. He cursed, twisting and setting the other man off kilter.

Despite the torture of his injury at every flex and move, he gripped the sword with both hands. Again he lunged, pushing and attacking. The demand for survival and that ancient need to aid a woman in distress inflamed his assault. His physical responses slowed, but his mental acuity quickened. He waited for any misstep. When the man briefly exposed his neck, Will hacked through flesh with a sickening chop of steel.

The soldier gurgled and paled. Will wrenched his blade free, snaking from under the flaccid corpse as it collapsed. Blood coated his gloves and bile filled his mouth.

He spat, turning to behold another slaying—a slaying that turned his stomach more cruelly than the wound he suffered. Hendon, the earl's guard whose charge had sparked the fight, pulled his liege to the ground and bared his throat. The single slice of a dagger ended Whitstowe's life.

Stance relaxed, weapons lowered, Roger of Carlisle looked on. A grin stretched the weathered skin of his face.

They are in league?

When he met Carlisle's eyes, a cold sluice of understanding slid down Will's back. Treason. A plot. And he was stuck in its midst.

Another scream sprouted goose bumps on his neck.

He wheeled from the duplicitous butchery to find a woman in blue seized by Dawes and Munro, two of Carlisle's men. Dark stains of anonymous blood discolored their hands and tunics. The woman thrashed, whipping her head free of attempts to stifle her hysterics.

Distracted by their writhing quarry, the pair did not see Will's furtive advance. He sliced Munro's calf—a man who, minutes before, had hidden in the roadside bushes beside him, both in the employ of Sheriff Finch. Munro screeched and rolled, clutching a hunk of ruined muscle.

Dawes hauled the woman in front of his body, using her as a slender and uncooperative shield. A blade pressed to her neck calmed her struggles. "Stay where you are, Scarlet, or I'll kill this comely prize."

Will sheathed his sword and held bloodstained gloves face-up.

"No draft, Dawes," he said. "I killed one of the earl's men, same as you." He stepped closer—once, twice. With a wink, he unceremoniously hiked his tunic and began to unfasten his breeches. "She'll be reward enough for both of us."

Dawes blinked, a moment of hesitation. From a fold at his waist, Will retrieved an anlace and leapt. He drove the petite dagger up and into the soft flesh beneath Dawes's chin.

Only when his opponent fell did Will look at the woman. She knelt, her eyes downcast. An outmoded, saffron-colored cowl covered her head and draped around her face. Recognition pounced on him.

But I arrested her in Nottingham.

Plots and double crosses teased just beyond his understanding. He felt like the only reveler left without a partner at the beginning of a dance.

He touched her. Flinching and screaming again, she pitched and drove her shoulder into his gut. The unexpected assault upset his balance, toppling him to the ground. Breath erupted from his lungs. The woman landed astride his torso and slammed a fist into his ear. He grunted, then roared when another flailing fist connected with his wound. Catching hold of her slender waist, he flipped her away.

Carlisle's shouts to his men thundered in his brain, banishing thought. Only instinct remained. He claimed the woman's wrists and dragged her to the nearest horse. The agonizing ache of his injury made him clumsy, but dread pumped strength into every movement.

"Let me go!"

"Without lies, I mean you no harm."

He propelled the woman and her entangling skirts into the saddle and mounted behind her. Dark, curled hair made untidy by rough treatment poked from the cowl, tickling his nose. She smelled of damp leaves, sunshine . . . and vinegar?

Will gouged the horse with his heels and made their escape.

The horse charged and wove through Charnwood Forest. Leaves and twigs like whips scored Meg's face, tugging her hair, and every lash stung anew. She burrowed her head into the hard solace of her captor's chest. Leather overlaid with iron rings bit into her cheek. For whatever mindless moments of flight remained, her safety atop that breakneck mount depended on his skill—no matter whether he proved a champion or a villain.

But no fate could match the woe she nearly suffered. Never had she known a fear as deep and sharp as being wrenched between those grasping male beasts. Faring against a lone opponent worried her less.

He flexed, ducking low over the animal's neck. Balancing in opposition to quick cuts and jumps, he shielded her from the worst of the battering branches. His breath came in grunting exhales, urging their dreadless pace. Minutes passed as slowly as sleepless nights.

When the horse began to tire, the man straightened and pulled the reins. Meg emerged from the shelter of his body. "Why did we stop?"

"The horse is easily traced."

Exertion roughened his voice to a gravely rasp. Or, remembering Hugo, she hoped it was exertion. That foul thief had sounded similarly winded when thrusting into her. But then, she had as well.

Suddenly aware of her position on the stranger's lap, she pushed to loosen his firm hold. "What will you do?"

"Calm yourself. I mean you no bale." His breathing slowly regained a usual cadence. "With mine, your account will establish the circumstances of the ambush. I'll not be held answerable for that disorder."

Meg rubbed a thumb against her lower lip. He must have

given the attack a great deal of consideration, studying facts while navigating the forested terrain. By contrast, the wild ride had concealed her logic in a mist of dread and frustration. She swallowed the mineral taste of fear and collected her scattered reason.

He swung from the fatigued horse and pulled her to the safety of still, sure earth. "Will you help me, woman?"

She kept her head bowed. Her captor had brought low two men, perhaps more. To save himself from hanging, he would protect her.

The lie came easily. As always.

"I will."

"Good."

She could not see his reaction. In truth, she had not seen a moment of the carnage on the road—nor anything else for five long years.

But the truth mattered not at all. As long as he believed her testimony valuable, he might keep her from harm. Lord Whitstowe and his knights would lay hold of them soon. She only needed to disguise her impairment until their arrival.

Straightening her skirts, she ran a hand over the alms-bag at her waist. She smiled to herself, reassured, for she could always resort to other means if her deception failed.

"Where shall we go?"

He did not answer.

"At least tell me your name, good man."

"I'm called Will Scarlet."

Again she waited, resisting the urge to fidget. He must be watching her, and she hated the sensation of a prying gaze on her face, her body. Eyes tenaciously downcast, she could do nothing but suffer the examination and imagine the worst. Apprehension blossomed into spite.

"Will Scarlet," she said. "That's an unusual name."

"You've not heard of me?"

A glimmer of emotion peeked through. At last. Her thoughts bounced in busy circles. She searched for a hint, traveling along a tally of pikers and sharps she knew, but found nothing.

"Should I have?"

"We waste time," he said. "Anyone can catch us out in this clearing."

Navigating Charnwood's uneven terrain required her entire notice. Breaks in Scarlet's steady gait helped her anticipate logs and brush. Scuffing through the autumn leaves, his footfalls became her guide, even as she grew resentful of his sure-footed grace.

Brambles snagged her skirts again. She stumbled and tripped.

"Keep up."

"I'm exhausted."

"Keep up, or I'll abandon you to the sheriff's men."

A shiver dusted her skin. "But you're one of them, I know. You were not among Whitstowe's party, and that man you killed—he knew your name."

He stopped short. Even near enough to touch, he revealed little. The insulating leather he wore concealed any body heat. His respiration and heartbeat escaped detection. He hovered within her awareness like a menacing wraith, bristling the delicate hairs at her nape.

"For the moment, accept that I've renounced my association."

Surprise of surprises, he talked. She needed to define the hazy line between fostering a useful conversation and provoking him too greatly.

"I appreciate what you've wrought on my behalf. I prefer to stay in your keeping."

"Then do as I say," he said, his voice low and close. "I've no need for your questions."

Banking her defiance, nurturing her dislike, she nodded. "I understand."

He turned and resumed their trudge. Meg stumbled nearly as often as she stepped. Without great success, she attempted to solve the basic problems of poise and motion.

For his part, Scarlet muttered useless orders. Pick up your feet. Mind that branch.

With each brusque sentence, she studied his words. Edgy impatience could not disguise the melody of cultured speech. No matter his posturing, he was no brute. The vice of fear that squeezed her since the ambush loosened. Mindless men could behave as animals, but she might appeal to one accustomed to reason and rules.

Apparently tired of issuing orders without results, Scarlet lapsed into silence. Meg's isolation returned, blanketing her like a thick fog. That she was so lonely for companionship, craving even the random commands of her murderous captor, galled her.

And she missed Ada. What an irritating turn of events.

Only the sounds of snapping branches, halting steps, and their matched respiration intruded on the heavy quiet of the wide woods.

But the menacing rush of a river stopped her heart.

Fear snaked a crooked path through her insides. Old terrors burgeoned. Sliding below the surface. Losing the hard thump of earth beneath her feet. Clutching at a liquid void, deafened by the gurgle of water. Only one terrible sense would remain: She would learn the river's taste as it filled her mouth.

Panic gorged on the calm she had barely maintained. She pulled free of his hold and stumbled, grasping the nearest means of support: Scarlet's upper arm. He cried out. Lashing against the creature causing his anguish, he yanked her cowl. Her skull snapped back, dragged by his grip on a handful of cloth and hair.

"Let go!"

His gravelly voice hissed near her ear. "You first."

She did. He flung her away, disorienting her. She landed on her knees with a splash. A scream burst forth, certain the water would consume her. But her frightened brain identified the mud slinking between her fingers at the river's shallow edge. With an exhausted gesture of good sense, she shoved the alms-bag behind her back, keeping it dry.

"You said nothing of your injury," she said. "I didn't intend to cause you more hurt." When silence answered, she sat on her heels and turned to Scarlet. "Hello?"

"Telling you shouldn't have been necessary."

Anxiety crumpled her weary body. He was farther down-river than she guessed. Pain laced his words, conjuring an assortment of ghastly images. How much of that stench had been *his* blood?

"This wound should be obvious to anyone who can see. But you cannot see, can you?"

Trees creaking, birds singing—the river's vigor obliterated every noise in the forest. All that remained was the sound of her pumping blood.

"No. I cannot."

Chapter Two

We cannot bid our dim eyes see
Things as bright as ever;
Nor tell our friends, though friends from youth,
That they'll forsake us never . . .

"Robin Hood, An Outlaw"
Leigh Hunt, 1820

A deep scowl pinched between his brows. Disbelief and anger warred for supremacy, with utter foolishness tagging closely behind. Will had been determined to outrun Carlisle and the earl's traitorous men, all the while loathing his return to woodsy exile. That he dragged a blind woman through those same woods escaped him entirely.

Tripping, grabbing his injured arm for support, struggling to pick her way across the cluttered forest—she could not see. The simple and blatant truth mocked him.

Life ambling through various noble houses had softened his skills, true, but this error was unconscionable. He stood little chance of escaping blame for Whitstowe's murder if he failed to detect something that obvious.

Failure inevitably led him to thoughts of his uncle. Robin, Earl of Loxley, the famed outlaw Robin Hood, would have handled the situation differently. To start, he would not have crouched at the roadside, ready to do the sheriff's dirty bidding.

His injury throbbed. What manner of devilish day had he yet to endure?

Kneeling on the shore, water seeping into the ruined soles of his boots, he faced her. "What is your name?"

"Now you think to ask."

Rubbing the stubble along his jaw, he wanted to shake her until answers fell like rain. He yanked her up and stepped away before she became a target for his strengthening anger.

"In lieu of manners, you'll have to make do with my rescue," he said. "What is your name?"

She removed her skewed cowl and shook a tousled plait of dark, waist-length hair dampened by river water. Her face was long and thin. Graceful lips turned upward at the corners, giving her the appearance of smiling.

But what she had to smile about, he had no idea.

"I am Meg," she said at last.

"Nothing more? Where do you come from, then?"

"First Keyworth. Near Broughton, at present."

He studied her face, now unfettered of the cowl's saffron folds, and wondered again at his shoddy handling of their situation. Coated with a pale, silvery film, her sightless eyes shifted constantly and focused on nothing distinct. He found no soul in those icy blue depths, no indication of personality or presence.

A chill of revulsion shook him.

"A fine witness you would've been. When did you intend to tell me?"

"I had no such intention."

"I suppose you awaited an opportunity to make your escape?"

"Or a rescue. Earl Whitstowe and his son offered me aid," she said. "Surely they'll send a search party."

Molded to her body from bust to hips, her woad gown was wet, filthy, and easily older than either of them. An alms-bag hung from the inward flare of her waist. He almost pitied the disheveled wench, but no amount of pity ebbed his frustrations.

"You wait in vain. The earl is dead."

"You lie."

"Why would I?"

Dark brows pulled together. She seemed to absorb the question, testing it for truthfulness. "I can't think of a reason."

"And I can't think of a reason to escort a blind witness through the forest."

"But my home is miles from here!"

A twitch of chivalry grated his conscience, taunting him with images of the poor woman in six hours' time, wet and stranded in the evening chill. Already the air cooled his skin, or was that the onset of a fever? He shivered uncontrollably. The quicker he abandoned his burdensome obligation, the quicker he could tend his arm.

But where would he go? None of his acquaintances would offer lodging to one of Nottingham's men. Will's work for the sheriff had alienated his few friendships.

And as for Marian, he refused to ask her for help—not after his promise. Especially not with Robin likely to return from Châlus.

No. He simply needed to be gone.

"My apologies, miss."

"Please! I can tend your injury."

She reached forward, searching for him. Will took hold of her arms; some maddening part of him cringed at the prospect of seeing her fall again.

"You are a physic? A healer?"

She pressed her lips into a line as thin as thread. "Of sorts. My sister helped me."

"Helped?"

"*Helps.* If I doubted she yet lives, I wouldn't be stranded here."

Suspicions sounded a heralding call. With his thumbnail, he picked at the old scar on his palm. "Where is she?"

"I know not. Ada's been gone these two weeks."

Ada. That was her name. During the ambush, he had

mistaken Meg for that brazen cheat at the Nottingham market. But closer inspection revealed differences. Meg was thinner in both form and face, with an angular chin and that quirky, smiling mouth. And those glassy blue eyes.

Had Will required a more convincing reason to forsake his burden, he found one: He had arrested her sister.

He untangled their fingers, their destinies. "Consider our ride all the gallantry I can muster today."

"You've shone no gallantry!" Her cheeks colored with uneven splotches of pink. "You thought to use me, that I might hold Finch's hangman at bay."

Will bit back a protest. He had not flown into the fray to pursue selfish ends. How could he explain those moments of confusion by the roadside? Ally and villain had intertwined in a gruesome dance, exchanging places, until her terror cut through the confusion. Pure, hard, and desperate, her scream had ripped into being without artifice or ambition.

And like it or not, his body responded. His soul. With the cleanest part of himself, with the most honest of intentions, he had rescued her—the opposite of his behavior toward her sister. He could no more understand the primal motives for one than he could excuse his greedy designs for the other. Saving her had been his most selfless act since leaving Marian.

He expected gratitude, but he better deserved what Meg offered: She spat near his feet.

"That's enough," he said. "I'm going."

"And you'll bleed a trail for anyone to follow."

"Even a blind woman?"

Outward signs of anger faded at his taunt. She smiled, cold and tight and controlled. "Those brutes will find either a dead man or one too weak to defend himself."

A mean temper burst his patience like a blister. "On God's half, woman, I'm not helping you! I cannot. The odd man out takes the blame, and everyone but me knew what awaited Whitstowe."

"I don't believe you."

"Believe it. Otherwise, I wouldn't have risked rescuing you." Chills doubled and trebled, leaving him breathless and dizzy. He glanced at his mangled shoulder. "I am beset with difficulties and have no need of another. Your family has caused me enough misery."

Sightless eyes widened to the size of eggs. "What of my family? What do you know?"

Will railed against saints, devils, and his own careless tongue. But deserting a furious woman would be easier than turning his back on a pleading one.

"Your sister—Ada, was it? I arrested her in Nottingham."

"You spineless bastard!"

"Perhaps," he said. "Such a pity no man of quality dared save your skin."

"I'll slit your throat!"

"I await the attempt, if you can find me."

He turned and took a step toward freedom. The heels of two feminine hands drove into his upper back, pitching him face-first into the leaves. Air slipped from his lungs. Pain exploded in his shoulder. She landed on his back, her forehead smashing the base of his skull and driving his mouth into the mud. Dirt painted his tongue.

He shrugged free of her weight, turning his fouled face to the sky, but she attacked anew. An armful of female scrambled astride his chest. She crushed his neck, forearm grinding against his windpipe.

"Found you, wastrel," she said with a snarl.

Will gagged. Hot blazes of color marred his vision, blending to livid streaks. He surged, rolling until he pinned her with the length of his body. "For grace! Enough!"

"Hardly." Winding a hand between their bodies, she grabbed a handful of bullocks and twisted.

"Foul bitch!"

He crushed an elbow into her upper arm, grinding the muscle until her hand spasmed, freeing him. Catching slender wrists, he fought the base impulse to harm his slight attacker. "I say again—enough."

She calmed, but harsh breaths shoved her breasts against his armor. With a grim smirk, she bucked her hips. Arched her back. Wiggled.

He gasped. Blood spun from his head to his groin. "What manner of woman are you?"

She laughed. "One you enjoy pinning, coward. Either prick me with that rod of yours or release me."

Will jumped free as if burned by fire. He would have eyed a snake with less suspicion. "If you reach between my legs again with less than friendly intentions, I'll cut off your hand."

"Unwise, Scarlet, because I'd still have hold of your bullocks." Sitting up, she delicately arranged her skirts. Her voice was sweet, nearly careless, but her loathing swelled against him like a solid fog. "Regardless of who murdered the earl, if he is dead, you killed the sheriff's men. You are a wounded, hunted man. No one will take you in."

He wanted to protest. He wanted to recite an impressive list of good families—maybe his own family—ready to welcome him in a time of need. He wanted to prove her wrong.

But he could not.

All he could do was walk away.

Ada opened her eyes to complete darkness and panicked. She circled her gaze in search of any flicker of light, any ebb. Blackness swirled without limit, a taunting reminder of her most profound fear: losing her sight. Like Meg.

A shadow. She found the barest difference between a wall and the gloom along the floor. As her eyes adjusted to the nearly impenetrable black, she sucked in hasty, thankful gulps.

Stiff, weak, she crawled along the cold dirt to the opposing wall, outlining the contours of her confines. No wider or longer than two lengths of Ada's body, the cell barely allowed room enough to stand. Cracks between the bricks wept a dank wetness.

In the two weeks since being arrested by the sheriff's men—Will Scarlet and that ogre, Carlisle—she should have been fined or hanged or released. But unknown captors still held her, moving her from location to location.

Would Meg find a way to locate her? Perhaps she would enlist the aid of Lord Whitstowe. And if the earl refused, she could seek Asher ha-Rophe or his son, Jacob. Maybe even Hugo.

No, she would never ask Hugo.

Whether she would bother searching at all teased and niggled Ada's conscience. Meg had yet to forgive her, a knowledge they shared as intimately as the isolated cabin they called home.

Footsteps sounded along a corridor, muffled by thick walls. The cell door swung open with a fantastic creak, torchlight flooding into the dim space. Ada blinked furiously and squinted against the sudden brightness.

Anger and fatigue gnawed away at caution. "I need food," she said sharply.

"And I need answers."

She could not tell which of the four silhouetted men had spoken. His curt sentence reverberated in the tiny space, quiet but unchallenged.

"Who are you to hold me?"

"I'm Peter Finch, High Sheriff of Nottinghamshire." The man stepped through the squat doorway. "What are you called?"

"Ada, my lord sheriff."

"Now, Ada, you will answer my inquiries."

Scrutinizing her foe, she searched for any obvious physical marker, but an inexplicable plainness defined Finch. His mundane features formed a common appearance. He was of medium height and build. His hair, neither long nor short, was an ordinary shade of brown.

Had he been dressed in silks and layers of embroidered

finery, he would have passed as a nobleman. Dressed in an apron and covered with grimy sweat, he would have looked the part of an able blacksmith. But clad in nondescript black garments, he blended with neither profession—only with the shadows.

Finch squatted within arm's reach and Ada edged away, pressing her back to the wall. Weakness and hunger sapped her strength, melting her brain into a fuzzy mass of impulses. She wanted water, clean air, food. Freedom.

"You tried to sell counterfeit emeralds to a merchant in my city," Finch said. "And I wager you've succeeded in other markets."

Modulating his words with slow precision, he sounded lazy, almost tired, but Ada recognized the truth. He used his bland appearance and calm demeanor to dull his opponents' wits—in this case, hers.

"I want you to tell me the origins of those imitations." He pitched his voice lower, a man whose patience was thinning. "The nature of your captivity will depend on your cooperation."

Her mind swirled through and around a host of inappropriate replies. She could not refuse him, but neither could she reveal Meg's role in the plot.

Or could she?

Ada blinked, trying to find a way free of the hypnotic cadence of his words. The monotonous parade of syllables lulled her senses. Weakly, she said, "I'm hungry."

Finch snapped his fingers. Two men stepped through the small door and took hold of Ada's arms and ankles, pinning her. Terror lodged in her throat. A third guard jammed his torch into a sconce, the flames casting a wobbly pattern across damp walls.

Rational thought rejected the scene as too strange, too impossible to be real. Just as she had blinked past the temporary blindness, she willed her nightmare to end. But nothing altered. No manner of wail or wish expelled those brutal men or flung away their hands. Panic filled her mouth, like trying to breathe while submerged in sap.

Finch removed a dagger from his belt. Jewels glinted on its handle, the hectic torchlight scattering colors around the cell. He drew the weapon nearer. The threat of that blade pressed on Ada's mind until her entire world reflected in its gleam.

"These are real emeralds, Ada, my dear." He lifted the dagger's handle to the light. The green gems lit with a clear fire, glowing like sunshine through summer leaves. He brought the blade low, softly sliding the cool metal along her bare sole. "And you try my patience."

"Please, I'll tell you."

"Yes." He smiled as if sharing a jest, the most emotion he had yet displayed. "If you want bandages, you'll tell me everything."

Before the words registered, a sharp, unearthly pain sliced through Ada's foot. He cut her. From heel to toe, hot blood rushed past disoriented nerves. She screamed, the whirling echoes of her agony creating clouds of sound. Pinned by the unflinching guards, she thrashed and kicked to no avail. Tears flowed, drenching her cheeks.

Finch wiped the knife along the hem of her dress. His blandness transformed into resolve as hard as his dagger's steel. "Talk."

Her panting sobs bubbled into the air. "My father was an alchemist. He made the imitations. When he died, he left them to sell if I needed to."

"Are there more? Can you make more?"

Even through the pain, she recognized much. There would be no trial, no fine. And Meg was in terrible danger.

"I can," she said. "But the process takes time. You must secure a supply of Cyprian copper. It has to be Cyprian."

"You'll have it."

Ada suppressed the hysterical hiccup of laughter. He had not blinked. He had not asked for an explanation. He had merely consented.

The sheriff stood and tossed a ball of linen strips into her lap. "You'll cooperate, unless you want a matching wound on your other foot."

Ada bowed her head and nodded, a shudder engulfing her body. Her pride balked, and again she thought of Meg—always relenting, always dipping her eyes when a lie demanded it.

How do you do it?

Finch nodded for the guards to release her. "Until you buy your freedom by providing that recipe, consider this your home."

The men withdrew. A third guard deposited food, ale, a blanket, and a fresh chamber pot before locking the door.

Cold from the floor seeped into her legs, stealing grace and power from her muscles. The sound of scattering feet revived her. Ada shrieked and lunged at eager rodents, slapping them across the floor. Like an animal, she hunched over the food and ate greedily.

Hunger sated, she crept nearer the dwindling torch and examined her foot. Fresh blood and dirt mottled the wound, and its smooth edges would be long to mend. She worked quickly to clean the twitching limb with ale and dress it, an agonizing fire nestling along her sole.

She sank into fresh straw and tugged the blanket over her trembling legs. Fear dyed her thoughts with ugly colors. She was a scholar and, despite how poorly she had handled Finch, she had faith in her ability to maneuver people.

Meg, however, made the emeralds.

Hurry, Meg.

But memories of Hugo forced her to alter the plea.

Please hurry—if you're coming.

Chapter Three

And Scarlet he was flying a-foot,
Fast over stock and stone,
For the proud sheriff with seven score men
Fast after him is gone.

"Robin Hood and Guy of Gisborne"
Folk ballad, fifteenth century

Meg walked into the copse and struck a tree with out-stretched hands. Kneeling, she rummaged amongst the leaf-strewn forest floor and found a branch as long as a half-grown child. She made short work of its leaves and twigs to form a crude walking stick. She turned into the black woods and cursed Will Scarlet with every faltering step.

Regarding Scarlet as she would any other mystery, she broached an escalating wall of anger to mull her findings. He had reeked of blood. His guiding hold could have been that of any grown man, reserved and impersonal. He refused more than a handful of words, but he sounded educated.

And she could not very well taste him.

Her senses exhausted, she discovered nothing to compensate for the simple task of seeing. Awaiting the results of her experiments vexed her none, and her schemes only bore fruit after patient planning, but that afternoon had moved faster than any in her life. She wanted explanations with equal haste.

Such human fickleness! He risked his life to save her from ravishment, only to abandon her to the whim of the woodlands. He seemed distraught about the ambush, but he admitted to working for the sheriff and arresting Ada.

An unpleasant guilt trudged with her through the forest. She should have known such a fate awaited them. No swindle, no matter how clever, could go unpunished forever. But two years of successes lulled them into complacence.

Worse still, even if she managed to secure her sister's release, she would have to rely on selling fertilizers, not forged emeralds. The gemstones traded for more gold than did the potash, and without that gold, she would have to abandon her experiments. And Ada would likely get married, eager for a better life—or at least a life of her own.

Her jaw turned to stone. Hers had been a fool's errand from the start, and now she was lost in Charnwood, miles from home. Pursuing her deceitful sister made as little sense as forgiving her, a chore Meg left stubbornly unfinished. But she loathed the idea of losing Ada.

Her distracted thoughts proved hazardous when she kicked a rock. Agony sparked from toe to kneecap, like a carnivorous animal clamping sharp teeth through her boot.

Tears burned and she cursed her useless eyes. She swallowed grief and frustration like unripe fruit, bitter but vital. She played at eliciting sympathy from gullible people, but she would not succumb to genuine self-pity. Not again. That way led to madness.

She knelt and massaged her aching toe. With perceptive fingers, she found the palm-sized rock and flung it into the woods. A rustle of leaves and squawking birds split the forest calm. Another rustle followed. And another.

She straightened. "Who—?"

Large hands clamped onto her face and around her arms, smothering her in a wash of foul-smelling terror. When a scream tried to escape, fingers clad in leather filled her mouth.

Scarlet?

But no. Pressing close, the man was shorter and smelled foul. His nasal voice confirmed her assessment. "Hold fast, miss. You need to come with us."

Surprise ceded to anger. For heaven's love, she wanted to be a man—a brawny man with perfect vision and a pikestaff like a small tree. She would beat every brigand witless.

Instead, she clipped the back of her captor's calf with her heel. Biting hard on a mouthful of leather, she heaved and struck. The skin of his lips gave way beneath her knuckles. The man yelped but held fast no matter how she wrestled.

A second man with lean, bare fingers lashed her hands. Rough rope chewed the thin skin at her wrists. "There's a girl."

They released her body but held tight to the rope, tugging her like a leashed animal. "You have no right to detain me. I have done nothing!"

"We'll let Hendon decide that, miss," said the nasal one.

Hendon? As a man-at-arms for Lord Whitstowe, he should be protecting her, but if Scarlet was right and the earl had been murdered, Hendon must have played a role. Still, she could no more trust Scarlet's tales than she trusted the twin boars pulling her through Charnwood Forest.

She tried to catch the looping laces of her alms-bag, to no avail. She tripped. Two clumsy hands yanked her from the sodden ground.

"Let me go, please," she said. The sulfur sting of fear gathered at the back of her tongue. "I can tell you which way Will Scarlet went."

The second man laughed like a donkey's bray. "You're a helpful miss. But no need—we have him already."

Lashed to a tree, Will wondered why his reward for chivalrous deeds had been a spiteful, vicious day. And two or three hours remained before sunset. Plenty of time for a plague of locusts or death by torture. But at least the soldiers showed no intention of killing him. Not yet. He might have time enough to survive the situation.

He eyed Earl Whitstowe's traitorous guard, Hendon, as he stalked the clearing and ordered his men to prepare for nightfall. Two other soldiers continued upriver in search of Meg. Will had surrendered in hopes she might delve deeper into the forest. Her assault on his bullocks was no reason to wish her harm at the hands of these villains.

Hendon stalked to the oak and knelt beside him. "Comfortable?"

"I assume you're under orders to take me back to Nottingham?"

"Of course." Hendon pulled a dagger from his waist and twirled it over his fingers, spun it, then caught it. Heavenly justice would ensure that he slipped and sliced off a thumb, but he continued the tricks without flaw. "Otherwise I would've killed you already."

"You would've tried."

Hendon exhaled, almost a chuckle. "Where'd the girl go, Scarlet?"

"You sniff her out." He yawned and closed his eyes, leaning against tree bark as jagged as shattered glass. "She's not my concern."

"But I can make her your concern."

Something about Hendon's stony voice and the sharp menace behind his words set his nerves alight. He peered at his captor. "How so?"

"I would hate to see anything happen to Lady Marian, not with her husband out of the country. And they have a son, am I right?"

A mist flowed over Will's skin, enshrouding him in outward composure. But fury surged. "If you harm his family, Robin will hunt you to the ends of Christendom."

"Perhaps." Hendon grinned at last, a dog baring his yellowed teeth. "But she's rather vulnerable at Loxley Manor, is she not? Without you there to protect her? I wonder which of us he would hate more: me for raping and murdering his wife, killing his little boy, or you, his dear nephew, for leaving them to die?"

Will yanked the ropes. The wound at his shoulder screeched in protest, agony casting his vision in a haze of red.

Hendon only widened his canine grin. "Does that hurt? Because I can make your imprisonment less enjoyable." He grabbed a blunt stick from the forest floor and jabbed it into Will's wound. Wood splintered in the mangled flesh. He yelled as pain exploded, like dipping his arm in fire. "Are you paying me mind, Scarlet?"

He hissed through clamped teeth. "Toss the stick away and we'll talk."

"Making demands of me? My, you have chops." Hendon waved the piece of wood nearer to Will's shoulder, teasing, before pitching it into fallen leaves. "Will Scarlet, man of legend—afraid of a twig. Next time I'll use the dagger so you won't lose face."

"If I cooperate?"

"Marian sleeps safely."

"And if I kill you first?"

"Unlikely, but what does it matter? Carlisle will have as much fun pricking her, I'm sure. Think on it, Scarlet," he said, standing and dusting leaves from his quilted leather breeches. "A few hours of light remain. We can still catch up to her."

Will closed his eyes as Hendon walked away. The biting bark, the pain like flames—none of it mattered. Marian would suffer because of him. Young Robert was in danger.

And Robin.

He shuddered to think how his actions would appear. He had abandoned Loxley Manor without explanation, a purposeful decision his uncle had yet to forgive. Robin would never know his motives for leaving, not if Will had breath left to honor his promise to Marian.

But how would he explain taking service with the new sheriff? No excuses would make it right if harm came to their family. The rift between them would become a killing feud, and he would go to his grave by his uncle's hand. Robin would forever believe Will had abandoned Loxley Manor for the worst, most selfish ends.

Unacceptable.

He pushed one heel against his shin. The damp sole of his boot stretched and bulged until the leather gave way at a patched seam. Iron caught the waning daylight and glinted a dull gray. Bending over, lifting his leg, he caught the sliver of metal in his teeth. He twisted and dropped it near his hip. Stretching, arching, he loosened the ropes just enough to pick up the shard.

Distant shouts roused Hendon's attention. He and a second soldier grabbed their weapons and rushed into the woods.

Will seized his opportunity. He quickly carved the iron shard into the hemp until the ropes twitched, eased. An incautious slice against his skin caused him to jerk. The hard, reflexive jolt of muscle broke through the last of his restraints.

He leapt free of the tree and snatched his sword. Confronting the only remaining guard, he swung the blade down. The man dropped with a strangled cry, gripping the horde of mangled muscles at his hip.

Male voices emerged from the woods. The two soldiers who had broken from Hendon's group dragged Meg between them, ropes encircling her wrists.

Will attacked. He kicked the taller man's weapon into the air and caught it, leveling two blades at his bleary opponents. "You, drop it. Good. Now lie on the ground."

The shorter soldier sported a bloodied lip. His helmet was nowhere to be seen. At his right temple, a hunk of hair was missing.

Will flicked his gaze to Meg, unable to suppress his approval. Long hair framed her face like a dark veil, and she flaunted that strange little smile. Slumped shoulders and a lowered chin suggested deference, but readiness coiled in her muscles. She balanced on the balls of her feet.

Unpredictable, dangerous—that much he knew. But Finch's men believed her valuable. He wanted to know why.

"Meg, are you injured at all?"

"No."

"Staying here or coming with me?"

He would drag her to Nottingham if he must, but he preferred her cooperation. Defending them both would be more difficult if he also had to watch his back.

"I'll stay with you."

As if accepting a dare, she offered her wrists. Will sliced through the ropes.

Icy water splashed and soaked her gown, weighing her skirts. Boots found traction on the slippery stones through force of will alone. Her fight for air became a losing battle, but on she ran through the shallows.

At some point, Scarlet had abandoned his leather gauntlets. Bare fingers enveloped hers. Abruptly, he wrestled her into a clump of forest shrubbery and pinned her. "Hendon's right behind us."

A parade of heartbeats passed before he eased his grip. His thigh settled between hers. She shifted, a startling awareness streaking through her limbs. "Did you have to manhandle me?"

"They would've seen us. And I cannot fight them."

"Your arm?"

Defeat colored his voice. "'Tis foul."

"May I touch it?" He stilled, hair tickling her forehead when he nodded. "If we weren't this close," she said, "I wouldn't know a nod from a blink."

"Do what you must."

She traced the wound, striving for gentleness. The gash was relatively shallow but longer than her palm, extending from his collarbone to the thick muscle of his upper arm. Splinters of ruined mail peppered hot flesh. Warm fluid slicked his skin. He hissed despite her caution.

"You won't be conscious in an hour," she said. "Already, you have a fever."

The sound of snapping branches and rough steps interrupted. She held still, imagining herself a rabbit. What that made the man sprawled on top of her—she could not decide.

"Surrender, Scarlet, or we'll ravish the girl."

Hendon.

"I assume you have eyes," she whispered, her lips pressed against the coarse stubble of Scarlet's jaw. "Eyes that work?"

"Yes."

"Then your choice of hiding places disappoints me."

"You choose next time."

"Can you handle your sword?"

His hair fell across her face again, teasing her with their intimacy. "I said I cannot fight, woman. I am . . . blast, but I'm dizzy."

"I said nothing of fighting. Can you *stab*? And be my eyes?"

"I don't understand."

She loosened the laces of her alms-bag and retrieved the small copper vial it contained. A tiny bubble of laughter wiggled free. "No thinking, Scarlet. Follow my lead."

She shoved the hard wall of his body until he relented and rolled aside, leaving behind an unsettling sense of disappointment. Standing side by side, she groped for his bare hand and clasped it tightly. The frustrating tremor in her limbs eased, ushering a return of clear thought.

Strange, that rush of calm. Simply holding his hand. Hours earlier, she would have fought the Devil's own army for the right to gut him.

And she might again, as soon as they killed Hendon.

Chapter Four

"No, no; it can never be—
I'll not believe she so could cheat our eyes,
To make us think, while we all look'd on her,
We only saw a weak and timorous hare."
—Will Scarlet

Continuation of Ben Jonson's *Sad Shepherd*
F. G. Waldron, 1783

"Good fellows, you lack manners," Meg said. "If you wish a turn, I ask that you wait."

Scarlet strangled on a grunt of surprise. Hendon snickered and so did his accomplice. "We don't need your permission, strumpet."

She tipped her head to the side. "Do you mean to imprison him or kill him?"

"He murdered Whitstowe," Hendon said. "We're taking him to Nottingham."

Scarlet tensed. "You did him treason, butcher!"

She placed a hand on his abdomen, stilling his surge of candid anger. He had told the truth; the earl was dead, and these men intended a more public form of execution. That left Meg for their sport and Scarlet her only ally. Fever ravaged his body, adding urgency to her gambit.

"Why to Nottingham?" she asked. "Surely his son will want him hanged at Bainbridge Castle."

"I'm not going to hang!"

"Quiet, Scarlet," Hendon said. "How would you know what he wants?"

"Why else would I ride with Whitstowe's party?" She smiled, keeping her eyes low. The woman she heard sounded distinctly like Ada. "His son and I were well . . . acquainted. You'll be rewarded if you return me to his safe keeping."

"Whore."

She shrugged. "All the better for you, I should think." Sliding her hand down Scarlet's body, she reached his groin and offered a quick squeeze. He groaned, a most convincing performer. "But this one will prove a calmer prisoner if you allow us another moment alone."

"Come here, woman." Hendon sheathed his sword. Breathless impatience colored his command. Both sounds encouraged her; she had his full attention.

Scarlet's grip tightened around her waist, his wounded arm surprisingly strong. "Don't, Meg."

"I must." She clenched the copper vial and smiled. "They outnumber you, although I doubt their swords are larger."

Hendon ripped her from Scarlet and into hard, unkind arms. The soldier clamped his mouth on hers, the sour tang of it balling her stomach. She fought the instinctive need to cry out, to fight and kick.

Instead, focusing on her dodge, she submitted to Hendon's brutal hold. Deep beneath her disgust, she reveled in the game, eager for the chance to bring low those who underestimated her. She returned his rough kiss, enthusiastically wetting his lips with her tongue.

But when a greedy hand clutched her breast, her tolerance splintered.

"Scarlet!"

She pushed back and dashed the contents of the copper vial at Hendon's face. He roared in anguish, flinging her. Meg scrambled from his shrieks. She feared another pair of coarse arms encircling her, any moment dragging her back to that grasping hold.

But Scarlet dispatched them. The swift play of swords rang over the rush of blood in her ears. "Meg, wait! They're dead. Meg!"

Arms encircled her, yes, but she gave herself over to relief. Scarlet held her. They trembled, panting, holding each other on the forest floor.

He pulled away first. "Explain."

An uncomfortable flush warmed her nape, like too much time spent in the sun. She retreated from the lap of the man who had imprisoned Ada.

"I know you're unwell," she said. "But these thoughts of yours—a single word isn't enough to help me read you."

"What did you do? Why'd he cry out?"

"Pain will do that." She opened her hand and showed him the emptied copper vial. "Lye's exceedingly painful when it burns wet skin."

"Wet?"

She kissed the air to demonstrate. "A means to an end."

"Would you've used it on me?"

"Had you given me reason, yes."

"Are you a witch?"

"Certainly not. Any soap-maker will agree that lye is the most dangerous part of their trade." She placed a hand to his forehead. Fever flared beneath her skin. "We must seek shelter. And I have an idea to help your arm."

Will gnawed on a strip of dried mutton. "You want to do what?"

He had tugged Meg through the surrounding holt to a patch of dry ground beneath an outcropping. After an arduous struggle with his tunic and mail, he sat bare-chested before a tiny fire. She slid delicate fingers over his skin and pulled coils of warped metal from the wretched gash. That she carried flint and a piece of dried meat in her bag . . . he could hardly muster a hint of surprise.

But this—he could not accept what she proposed.

"I told you," she said. "I'll use the lye on your arm."

"That man would yet scream if I hadn't sliced him open."

She nodded. "You did him a better end, actually."

"You didn't see his face!" Recalling the hideous, bubbling skin of Hendon's mouth and his twisted grimace, he shuddered.

"Hold still."

"And you want to do the same to me?"

"To help you."

"How? How will this help me?"

"Lye will seal the wound and allay the bleeding. But more than that, when your body does not have to fight the fever, the wound will heal faster." Her forthright, reasoned explanation echoed quietly around the shelter, a sentence just short of death.

The spiraling flames cast a flickering play of light across her intent face. While he enjoyed the candor of observing a woman without having to check his stare, he could not settle. The memory of her body struggling under his collided with the feel of her hand clenching his shaft. He shifted uncomfortably on his seat made of rock.

"No, I don't believe you," he said, honing his frustrations into a weapon. "You're aggrieved because of your sister and because I left you by the river. Now you want revenge."

"I did when you left me. Had the Devil provided me a club, I would've beaten you and fed you to his hounds."

"You harbor those ill thoughts in your skull, woman?"

She laughed like bell chimes. "You believed me a simple, infirmed girl made of sugar?"

"Yes. And I would've agreed to a large and foolish wager that you're more naïve than your boldness implies."

"Do you make such wagers often?"

"No," he said. "Gambling is a harder means of living than swordsmanship."

"Good. Never wager on what you know of me."

"As ever I ate bread, you're a madwoman."

She pulled hard at an iron coil. "I'm *not* mad."

Will flinched. He could all but see anger in her sightless eyes.

Saints be, none of it mattered. Hendon was dead, but Carlisle would take word of the successful ambush back to the sheriff. Marian was still in danger. If Meg was important enough for Finch's men to threaten a nobleman's family, she was still useful. Instead of offering the truth about Whitstowe's murder, hoping to be believed, he would trade her for a pardon and a guarantee of Marian's safety.

A surge of pain twisted his gut. He should not have eaten the dried meat.

"And what do you want from me in return for this—well, I hesitate to call it a kindness."

She tucked her bottom lip into her mouth. "Deliver me to a safe destination."

"Your cabin?"

"No. My cabin is five miles distant, but Asher ha-Rophe lives only a mile north of Asfordby. He and his son will see me home."

"Jews?"

"My father's friends, yes." Her face turned to moonstone, hard and unreadable. "After the wrong you did Ada, I've no wish to prolong our association."

He no more trusted her motives than she should trust his. But though he might be a fool to agree to her strange medicine, his wound already ached and throbbed. She might accidentally do him a sympathy if she settled on revenge and killed him.

"Tell me more," he said.

"The treatment will be painful, yes, but you'll not suffer as Hendon did." She pulled a glass vial from her bag. "This is vinegar. When applied to the lye, the burning stops."

"How?"

"I—" She hesitated, frowning. A childish splash of satisfaction washed over him when she faltered. "I know not. No one does. But lye and vinegar counter each other."

"And you carry them with you?"

"I make a habit of carrying items for many possible events." She eased the last ring of steel from his shoulder and pressed a strip of her kirtle to the bleeding flesh. "How else would I protect myself?"

"At least that explains the smell."

"What smell?"

"You, your hair and clothes. You smell of vinegar."

She scowled and withdrew, wrapping slender arms around her middle. "I have wolfsbane to ease the pain, but if you'd rather, I can toss it into the fire."

Spiteful witch.

But resignation and a sick helplessness smoothed his internal struggle. He only wanted to succumb to the lassitude stealing beneath his skin, lulling him despite the pain.

"I'll see you to the Jew's cabin," he said, his words slurring. "Do what you must."

Drowsy and disoriented, Meg awoke to a familiar darkness and unfamiliar surroundings. Caution froze her limbs like the earth in midwinter. It may as well have been winter for the chill permeating her body. The moist cool of an autumn night crawled through her clothes, which were still clammy from the river.

Only a few feet away in the crude shelter, Will Scarlet lay still. His even breathing rasped. He moaned from beyond the veil of sleep, a sound like laughter compared to his agonized cry at the first touch of lye. But he had endured, even steadying his right hand to help aim the neutralizing vinegar.

That he promptly collapsed into unconsciousness had not surprised her. That she was relieved at the end of his suffering had.

But her concern was born of necessity, nothing more. She needed his eyes.

She rubbed her hands together, working to banish the cold

numbness, and crawled to his side. Gently, she skimmed shivering fingertips along the dressing. Sticky blood soaked the fabric, but none of it felt fresh. She would wait until he awakened before changing the bandage.

If he awakens.

Through the perpetual black, she found his forehead and slid her hand to the base of his skull. While he did not burn with the blistering vigor of a body gripped by fever, his skin pulsed with heat. He did not sweat or shiver—although, as the cold bored into her bones, she would not have begrudged him the latter.

Despite having appeased her concern for his well-being, she lingered. Her hands still cupped the back of his neck, fingers woven down to his scalp. Had she been able to see, she would have been acquainted with his appearance for hours. But she knew only impressions formed by his words and mannerisms. Curiosity urged a brief exploration.

She lightly mapped the contours of his face. Above sloping cheekbones, closely set eyes crowned by thin, arched brows created the impression of a wolfish look. Scant wrinkles radiated from the corners of his eyes. Lines drawn from his straight nose wrapped around firm lips that kindled dark imaginings.

He's beautiful.

If not for Will Scarlet, none of the day's horrors would have happened. She would be at home, safe, as would Ada. She should hate him for reasons of prudence alone. But he had saved her life. Twice. And the more she discovered, the more she wanted to know. Hunger compelled her, the elemental yearning for human contact—a contact long denied her.

She smoothed her hands along his strong jaw to the hollow at the base of his neck. Stubble scored the pads of her fingers. She shivered. Like an explorer, she found the muscled cap of his good shoulder, the firm resilience of his bare chest, and the flat, taut wall of his abdomen. The lightest dusting of curled hair tickled her sensitive skin.

A restless ache pressed against her lungs, flowed between her thighs. The call of desire. Her body responded to its insistent push, urging her closer to the man lying defenseless before her. The feel of him—polished and hard like a gemstone, warm like a beckoning fire—tempted her with the thrill of knowing more.

Long accustomed to drawing from her other senses, she found no satisfaction in mere touching. She inhaled the masculine power of him, her nose mere inches from his naked skin. The river had not completely cleansed the primal tang of blood, metal, and sweat, but she reveled in the heady scent. Fascination washed across her like a waterfall, drowning her in a bright, hot world of sensation.

Bracing her hands on either side of his torso, she parted her lips, breathing against his bare flesh, hoping each draw of air would satisfy her strong and desperate impulses. She damned herself for the lonely, desolate creature she had become, but no measure of damnation, no press of fear, could dissuade her. Fear, in fact, mingled with the power to determine every move, urging her on. She wanted to search and push and be the bold one.

That she wanted these things with the man who had jailed Ada—a spiteful part of her reveled in the danger, the sick game of it.

As when the scent of food only whets a hungry appetite, Meg wanted to feast. She pressed the sensitive tip of her tongue to his skin. Salt and spice enveloped her tongue, soaking her senses in raw male essence. A steady, wicked fire gathered in her blood. She shifted against the wet pleasure of her arousal, ready to take more.

Strong fingers clutched her backside, squeezing her flesh. She moaned.

So did he.

"Stop now, Meg, or I'll slide into you without one regret."

Chapter Five

Stay thee, Will Scarlet, man, stay awhile;
And kindle a fire for me.

"Robin Hood's Flight"
Leigh Hunt, 1820

Meg raised her mouth from his belly. Lips swollen and parted, eyes lowered and in shadow, her expression rushed between surprise and smug control. She smiled and licked those lips, her mouth forming its customary half smirk. An enigma. Frustrating and tempting.

"I have no intention of stopping," she said, her voice husky.

Blood raced wild circles through Will's body and hardened his shaft. He wanted inside this strange woman—either that or oblivion. That he might find such oblivion between her thighs taunted him and kindled a swift need. His shoulder blazed like dancing in a bonfire, but the rest of his body hummed, aching with anticipation. Waking to such confusion mashed his brain.

Illuminated by pale remains of the fire, Meg sat and straddled him like a wanton goddess. Dark curls splayed over her shoulders, her bold hands still moving, still scraping his skin. Panting breaths puffed into the frigid night air.

He tightened his grip on her thighs, enjoying the firm

female flesh yielding to his touch. She gasped and arched, but he wanted more. He wanted to climb into her mind and keep searching until he learned her secrets. He wanted to intimidate her, to dominate the implacable girl, but he could not find a chink in her armor. Greedy, mindless, he settled for her body.

He stroked a finger along her jaw and gratified in her sharp gasp. She leaned into his hand, her eyes closed. An unknowable expression replaced her smirk, enshrouding her pale features in an arousing mystery.

"Kiss me," he said, hearing a plea buried in his command.

"Where?"

"By the saints."

He closed his eyes, hammered by the thrill of her question. A shuddering breath did not douse his ardor. Pain and pleasure blurred the boundary between waking and dreaming, but the idea of Meg's teasing, smiling mouth on his shaft cut through the confusion.

"I was right, girl," he said. "You are mad."

She flinched. "I am *not* mad."

Good sense said she would pull away. She had taken offense before, and the tight, bunching tension in her body revealed as much again. But she did not retreat. Her fingertips curled into the muscles of his chest and scored him with blunt fingernails. Tipping up her chin, she brought her mouth closer. Their breath mingled, the only heat in the forest, until she claimed him with a brutal kiss.

He intended to absorb the drunken sensation of her mouth on his, slowly, but a rush of need urged complete surrender. His and hers. Will abandoned his useless qualms and gave himself to the surprise of their joined lips. She opened her mouth and invited him deeper. Tongues touched in an exploratory dance. She tugged his lower lip with her teeth, soothing the sharp sting of her bite with another sweep of her tongue.

Power surged through him. He used his good arm to pull her into a full embrace. Belly to belly, legs layered over legs, she nestled her pelvis into the valley of his hips. She rocked against his straining erection. Their groans vibrated together. He returned her thrusts, demanding the release she promised.

When Meg threaded slender arms around him, grasping his arse, he could take no more. He grabbed at the fabric of her skirts. She lifted her hips and took hold of his hard rod, guiding him inside without hesitation. The swift shock of their joining ripped a cry from them both.

He sank his head into the loamy earth, thrusting his hips. Pleasure tensed his muscles but melted his bones. He gloried in the slippery heat of her sex. Every sliding plunge jammed bright sensation into his brain, setting his skin alight. He found no breath, only a choking hunger for more. *More.*

Opening his eyes—when had he closed them?—Will clasped the back of her neck and dragged her down for another stinging kiss. She tasted of salt and sugar, both. Her tongue swirled over his, fighting for control. Unappeased passion made him rough, and he indulged in his dark violence. He pushed his mouth against her neck and kissed, bit, sucked. He tightened restless fingers into her hair and tugged. She hissed, arching, crushing ripe breasts to his chest.

The fabric of her bodice frustrated him. He groaned, wanting her breasts stripped bare, her stiff nipples pushed against his skin. The thought rocked his tenuous self-control. He wanted her naked, but the fervor of their coupling demanded release, not delays.

She grabbed his hips and urged him to take more, give more. Her rasping moans patterned the air with a cadence to match their slapping bodies. She cried out and threw her head back. Eyes clenched, her face melted into a picture of happy agony. The muscles of her sex clamped around his aching flesh. Her slick sheath became tighter still.

Doubling the speed of his hips, Will pumped into her hot softness. He dug his fingers into her backside. Pain ricocheted from his wounded shoulder, but he gripped harder still. His mind spun. And his release, when it came, hit him with the force of a blow.

* * *

Lightheaded and spent, Meg struggled to catch her breath. She lay sprawled across Scarlet's heaving body. Echoes of pleasure pulsed between her thighs. She pressed trembling lips to his neck, his collarbone. He shuddered and closed his arms more tightly across her back. She enjoyed the reaction, both submissive and protective.

She shifted her hips and he slid free. A whimper climbed from her mouth. His withdrawal and her gradual, reluctant return to Earth seemed a reality too terrible to endure.

I'm not ready. Not yet.

She curled around him, resting on his good shoulder. The autumn evening chill was a distant memory. Fires could not match the warmth he stoked in her blood.

"What were you doing to me?" Scarlet's gravel voice rumbled against her cheek.

"I wanted to know how you look."

"Why? You're blind."

"And?"

"Why would a blind woman need to know a man's appearance?"

His condescending tone froze her from the inside out. She straightened and put a sliver of distance between them, shivering. "I didn't say I needed to. I wanted to."

"And what if your search revealed that I have pox scars, no hair, and a single tooth?"

"I wouldn't have kissed you."

"You find me attractive."

The base truth of her actions left her vulnerable and stripped. He could have been anyone—any man with half an interest in her body, any man with a body she found exciting. The extent of her eager desperation made her nauseous. But she could not bear his conceit.

"You portray my curiosity like an absurdity, but you lie there and watch me."

"But why do it in my sleep? Without my permission?"

"Because taking is more enjoyable than asking."

Scarlet tensed, his breath rasping. "I'm certain those men on the road thought the same of your struggles."

She licked her lips. "Hardly the same instance."

"You touched me for your pleasure, without my consent. Explain the difference."

Meg bumbled and bumped against her growing aggravation. They had both enjoyed the unexpected tryst, yet he insisted on reminding her of her sordid behavior. She needed no reminders, but neither would she offer apologies.

"You were asleep."

He laughed, a warm and throaty chuckle that dove into her blood. "A clever excuse. You implicate me, an injured man at rest. Part of the blame is mine, then?"

"Nonsense."

He sat up. The full brunt of his spicy masculine scent assaulted her. Memories of his kiss and his groaning release would not let her think. "Do you hear me, Meg?"

"Of course, you dullard."

"No, listen to me." He gripped her chin, his thumb swiping across her lower lip. "If you could see, I'd ask you to look in my eyes. I want you to know the truth of what I say."

"I hear you."

"Had I been dead and cold, your lips on my chest would have brought me back to life."

Heat shot from her lips to the apex of her thighs. He brushed his mouth against hers, peppering her with the softest kisses. Another. And another. He released her chin and cupped the base of her head, weaving agile fingers through her hair, holding her fast.

The man made her senseless. She hated him for that.

And no matter her determination to keep shame at bay, the slinking, slimy touch of regret crept up to her. She was lost in the woods, in pursuit of her missing sister—all because of him. She had no right to find pleasure in his arms, no right to want him still. Her wanton behavior was as selfish as Ada's betrayal, maybe more so, and her disloyalty twisted beneath her skin.

A burgeoning hate for Will Scarlet joined forces with self-loathing. He made her vulnerable, made her weak, and she resented nothing more than her galling weakness.

To regain the upper hand, Meg kissed him more deeply. She distanced her mind from the physical act of kissing, as she had when kissing Hendon. And like that man, Scarlet yielded to her summons. He leaned into her body, relaxing. His tongue played tempting games, but she remained resolute, denying her body and her lonely heart the enjoyment they craved.

She broke the kiss and smoothed a palm over his cheek, ignoring how she trembled. "I want to check your shoulder," she said. "You've probably undone all that we accomplished with the lye. Can you see how it looks?"

He sighed heavily. "Let me aid this fire."

When the comforting crackle of flames filled their tiny shelter, Scarlet reclined. He winced as she unwound his bandage.

"How does it appear?"

"Raw, rather jagged," he said. Despite his cold assessment, he sounded unsteady. "But there is no new blood."

"Good. What color is it?"

"You know colors?"

She stilled, her pulse hammering. Surely, so close to her body, he could hear the pounding like hooves against stone. "I have known color, just as I know its absence. The color scarlet, for instance."

"The wound is red," he said after a pause. "No shade of bile or sickness." He pushed a strand of hair away from her cheek. She flinched from that gentleness. "You are a strange one."

"And you have no call to be particular." She wrapped the deep cut with another strip of her kirtle. Sinuous muscles jumped and flexed beneath hands she fought to keep steady. "But by all means, if you have another physic ready to tend you . . ."

He closed his good hand over hers, gave a little squeeze. "I thank you for this, Meg."

Stop it!

Upon urging her patient to lie back, she petted the sharp lines of his face. The hideous trek back to Broughton loomed like a nightmare. And then Ada? The idea of beginning her search anew, this time without the earl, sunk her spirits.

No matter the future, the sooner she was free of Will Scarlet's maddening influence, the better. But for the moments remaining between them, she permitted herself the tiny luxury of memorizing his features. Isolation stretched ahead of her, longer and colder than the years since her illness. The greedy part of her that had taken Scarlet as her lover demanded a few more forbidden memories, hoarding them against a dark future.

His wicked, teasing eyebrows arched over closed eyes. Rasping breaths evened and slowed. His full lips grew slack. Meg touched her mouth to his, lingering over a final kiss.

Then she set about mixing the wolfsbane.

Dawn in the woods was a repulsive enough prospect without awakening alone to a useless fire. Will shivered, bare from the waist up except for the bandage covering his aching shoulder. Cool dew invaded every fold of his breeches. Fog hovered over the land, shrouding every tree and shrub in pale gray. Hoping the pathetic little misfit of a fire would banish his chill, he nettled it with a damp twig. The embers merely spit and waned.

His senses felt submerged in water or stuffed with flax. Soft and hazy. And his head—his head pounded with an unnatural lightheadedness and pain. A thousand grinning witches danced a wild pattern in his skull, but he blamed a particular witch.

Meg.

Flashing memories of the previous night piled one over the other, dreamlike: Meg straddling his eager body, illuminated by deep amber flames and haloed by rivers of dark hair. She had behaved like the lowest strumpet. He had pricked her like a rutting animal. But the wonder of their encounter retained power enough to light his body anew. Pure fire. They had produced heat enough to scorch the leaves from every branch in the forest.

But where was she?

He looked around and groaned, a clench of nausea swirling through his gut. His head swam in thick mists. He felt no particular signs of fever, not as he had suffered the day before. Pain like gripping talons lodged in his shoulder, but the injury lay modestly beneath its linen dressing, a strip from Meg's kirtle. No blood stained the saffron-colored fabric.

But something was amiss. His mind and body were in dispute, neither willing to cooperate. A worrying numbness crept down his injured arm. He clenched his fingers and urged them to function. The best he managed was a halfhearted fist. Had the lye treatment done an even greater damage?

Dread burst to life. The lye had been excruciating, a pain greater than any wound he ever suffered. Only stubborn pride kept him from crying and begging like a child for mercy.

He exhaled slowly, quelling the nausea and focusing on the cold emptiness of the shelter. The scattered patches of loam and rock beneath the outcropping revealed no other human presence. Meg was gone, as were her alms-bag and walking stick. Birds and chipper forest pests split the air with their morning songs, but Will was on his own.

Shrugging into his banded mail proved both difficult and tedious, arms shaking from the cold and the residual shock of his injury. The numbness did not relent. No number of deep breaths assuaged the pulse of anxiety.

And Meg of Keyworth did little to make the fundamental task of breathing any easier. Memory of her little cries of pleasure taunted him. Signs of her bewildering arrogance had disappeared as their passion intensified. Her mysterious smile slipped away, leaving behind a woman in the throes of bliss. He enjoyed knowing he could affect her that way, even if her depravity suggested he was not alone in having pleasured her.

Perhaps the earl's son, as she had implied to Hendon? No, he refused to pay her any more mind than was necessary.

But maybe "refused" was unrealistic. He endeavored. Hoped. Yes, he hoped to pay her no more mind. The encounter had been too memorable and the woman too strange to ignore completely. She was fickle, unstable, and certainly no ideal of decent womanhood, certainly nothing like Marian.

That name lanced through his foggy thoughts.

Marian was in danger. And no matter how much he wanted to forget about Meg, their tryst, and everything about the day before, he remained a wanted man. Sheriff Finch and his thug Carlisle would not relent in whatever scheme they planned. The roadside ambush was no mishap, nor was it likely to stand as the last of their violence. The haze of his bizarre awakening had briefly erased Will's resolve: He would take Meg to Nottingham.

He just had to find her. Again.

Overcast and gray, the sky provided no relief to his sunken mood. He trudged through the forest with the finesse of an ox. Every step, every motion belonged to some other body. His mind wavered above the cracking branches and stumbling footfalls, a helpless observer. Knees like water warped under his weight. He fell to the forest floor, needing sleep more than he needed air.

Yes, sleep. He had slept beside Meg. She had taken care of him in the moments after their joining, changing his bandages and soothing his brow. He could still taste a bitter twinge on his tongue, the remedy she provided to ease the pain.

His eyes opened, working independently of his drowsy thoughts. Realization pounced on him. He struggled to pull upright. He had been wrong to blame the lye treatment for his muddled thoughts and rebelliously inept body. The lye did its job, despite the freakish pain he endured.

No, Meg had waited until he was relatively whole. She stopped the bleeding, cured him, bandaged his wound. Then she took her pleasure. Only when she was well and truly through with him did she flee, ensuring her escape by poisoning him.

Chapter Six

Then, as near a brook his journey he took,
A stranger he chanced to espy.

"Robin Hood and Little John"
Folk ballad, seventeenth century

She poisoned me.

Over and over, Will repeated that incredulous phrase. He cinched numb fingers around the width of leather at his waist. Every step along the river's edge jarred his molars in an angry clench. The ominous woods helped diffuse his foul mood not at all. He wanted to kick every menacing tree and curse each spray of autumn leaves.

He had once kissed Marian against her will, and the consequences of that impulsive deed echoed into the present. But he had never hit a woman. Ever. The very notion of inflicting one with physical pain set his gut on its side.

But when he found Meg of Keyworth, he would need to tether his hands to his belt—as far from her as the ground was from the heavens. When she smirked and jeered and transformed his blood to flame, he simply did not trust himself. His anger conjured a potion strong enough to disease his few remaining principles.

She poisoned me.

To the west, a noise in the forest dragged Will from his fuming reverie. He jerked to vigilance and cursed his inattention. Trudging in search of Meg while distracted by thoughts of her would produce no good end. And Marian would suffer if he failed.

Picking across a skittering pile of rocks at the base of an oak, he slowly, almost silently, drew his sword from its scabbard. He hardened his nerves, but with more difficulty, he urged the throbbing, fiery ache in his left shoulder to subside. Dizziness snaked into his bones. His left arm trembled, and his hand grew increasingly numb.

An armored man strode along the river. Over a hauberk of mail, he wore a soiled, knee-length surcoat of black wool. A sword hung from the ornate girdle at his waist, a shield covered his left arm, and a steel casque obscured his face entirely. If his armaments were any indication, he came from a wealthy background, despite how he was nearly as filthy and trail-worn as Will.

Battling such a swordsman daunted him in the most ideal circumstances—healthy, well rested, and backed by armed companions. He silently urged the man to continue his purposeful walk along the river's edge.

He did not.

Noticing where Will's footprints emerged from the shallow banks, he spun toward the oak and drew his sword in a fluid movement.

Will cursed silently. His mind, trapped and weary, let slip a thought as distracting and infuriating as it was treacherous.

I wish Robin were here.

He peeked from behind the tree.

With a quick trio of steps, the stranger attacked. Boots covered by mail found no easy traction, and he slipped on the pile of rounded stones. He slid to his knees, gripping his sword and bracing his body with one hand.

Will jumped backward. Circling into a small clearing, he

sought level ground. His boots, however abused and tattered, provided better traction on the cobbled mud. His attacker stumbled clear of the oak and its skirt of dislodged stones, pursuing until Will had no choice but to turn and raise his weapon.

Swords clashed. Will shrank from the ferocious strength of the blow. The impact rattled his joints. He ground his teeth together against the effort of each successive strike. With gratifyingly efficient speed, he parried. He welcomed the oblivious state of bliss when pain and his rational, fearful mind relented to the firm command of reflex and experience. Composure and technique returned, as did power fueled by the immediacy of combat.

He took the swordsman's well-struck blows but found no purchase against his blade and shield. Will may as well have been striking a stone wall, except a wall would not thrust and hack with deadly, unrelenting intent. His breath stabbed tiny needles in his throat, and his hearing degenerated into a continuous pulse of fatigued blood.

Hoping to regain an advantage of position, he cut back to the river and skittered across the slippery rocks. His opponent followed, suddenly hesitant. Will surged anew, forcing his left hand to cooperate. He clutched the hilt of his sword in a sure two-fisted grip. Metal clanged against metal. The shield strapped to his foe's arm would not budge, but the full power of Will's attack chopped the sword from his hand. The man caught the blows against his trident until he stumbled and took a knee.

Too lightheaded to press his advantage, Will asked, "Do you yield?"

The challenger's accelerated breathing echoed from within his metal helmet. "I will run you through, brigand."

"Not the answer I was seeking, I admit."

"These woods are not yours."

Will raised his sword and compelled his uncooperative body into a fighting stance. His opponent was not beaten. "And neither are they yours."

"I am heir to the Earl of Whitstowe, you ramskit filth. These *are* my woods."

He slammed his trident into Will's chest, attacking with renewed force. Air fled in a dazzling rush. The muscles around his heart seized and clenched. His shoulder exploded in a burst of white heat. Raising his sword in self-defense went from improbable to impossible. He lost his footing in the shallow water and flailed, edging away from his attacker—a man armed once again, recovered, with sword in hand.

He crawled backward, wheezing. "Will you let me explain?"

"You presume to do me harm on my own lands, and I'm to let you speak?" The man offered an unkind chuckle and raised his blade. "Hardly."

Will kept his sights on the man's shadowed eyes, not the deadly edge of steel he held. "I was at the ambush where your father was killed. I can provide an account."

The sword wavered and dipped. "I doubt it not. You were likely in the sheriff's employ."

"Was."

"What are you called?"

"His name is Will Scarlet, and he's ours. Lay down your weapons."

A dozen woodsmen emerged from the shadowy thicket. Armed with bows, clubs, and daggers, they stalked forth to form a half circle against the river, surrounding the pair. Will took the occasion to leap from the water, sword poised in his good hand.

"I said lay down your weapon, Scarlet," a rakish woodsman said.

"Do I know you?"

The stranger stepped closer, sleek and dark-haired like a wild cat. By his assertive stance and role as the rabble's voice, the man likely held sway even if he did not lead them outright. He wore well-kept garments, a belt lined with four daggers, and a disarming smile.

A length of hemp rope coiled around his left arm.

"No, Scarlet, but we know you. And we're here to stretch your neck."

Meg knelt on a shallow bank at the river's edge. She ripped another length of cloth from her kirtle, leaving the hem ragged and dangling above her knees. After dipping the scrap into the water, she returned to the cover of trees and began to wash. No matter who pursued her, no matter how far she had yet to travel before finding a landmark, she could not take another step while reeking of Will Scarlet. The scent of him—of them together—pushed into her nostrils.

She shoved the wet rag into each sleeve and cleaned beneath her arms, then down the front of her bodice. Her nipples tightened. He had not touched her there, but her body, already sensitized by the recent memory of him, imagined for her. She hiccuped at the sudden thought of his mouth covering each nipple, laving and caressing with his hot tongue. She snatched the rag from her bodice.

Unsteadily, she scrubbed the warmed cloth on the insides of her thighs. Rough strokes, detached and cursory, still ignited the trembling flesh between her legs. She scrubbed harder until the slick aftermath of their union was rinsed clean, tossing the scrap of wool to the ground. She spun with a dizziness that started and ended with him.

But the fault was hers. She had explored and touched and kissed. She had crawled atop him. She should have anticipated this sickening argument between desire and pride. After all, each encounter with Hugo had left her similarly debased, unforgivably hopeful that his enjoyment of her body would mean enjoying *her.*

Bastards. Both of them.

She banished both shame and pleasure. Only an indistinct anger remained—at him for making her vulnerable, at herself for desiring their brief connection. If she gave Scarlet a little too much wolfsbane and he slept for a week, she would have no regrets. The bugger deserved worse for putting Ada in jail. And he deserved worse still for making Meg weak.

The swishing of footfalls grabbed her attention. She pushed against a tree and crouched low, only half hoping her cover would prevent detection. Her luck had been too poor to wish for a better outcome. To her advantage, she did not hear the metal clang of armaments, but she did detect . . . sniffing?

A sharp howl split the midday air. Her heart leapt. Before she could decide what to do, she cringed at the wet slop of a canine tongue. She yelped.

A call rang through the oaks and birches. "Asem! Heel!"

She raised both hands to fend off the dog. The massive animal anointed her face with countless panting licks. "Jacob? I'm here!"

"Meg? Such a! What are you doing here?"

"Surviving Asem's affections. Get me clear!"

Asher ha-Rophe's only son whistled sharply, grabbing the mastiff and dragging him away. He took her arm and urged her from the ground. Her knees shook with relief.

"Forgive his behavior," Jacob said, his crystalline voice soothing her uneven heartbeat. "He must have caught your scent because he dragged me across a mile, at least."

"I'm glad of his persistence."

"But Meg, I left you at Bainbridge Castle. How did you come to be here?"

Weariness pressed behind her eyes. The night before, when she should have been resting, she was busy seducing an injured man. At every opportunity, her mind and her body found cause to remember.

"The last day has been eventful."

Jacob tucked her arm through his and directed her back the way she came. "You can tell me as we return to Father's cabin."

"Back? I thought I was going the right way."

"You are two miles distant."

Frustration surged. She had not been lost in Charnwood

since the initial onset of her blindness. Scarlet muddied her senses to the point of uselessness.

Tensing her fingers around the walking stick, she wanted to smash the thing against a tree. "I have been checking, but still . . ."

"You've fared better than would most," Jacob said, unwilling or unable to hide a quiver of condescension. "What happened?"

For a few moments, she allowed the young man to guide her steps. She leaned into his wiry frame and described the previous day's events. The more difficult task was expunging emotion from her tale. As for the night with Scarlet, she avoided it entirely.

"Meg, I am at a loss. I apologize."

"There is no need for an apology," she said. "You left me at the castle under the protection of our liege. How could we know his protection would not be sufficient, or that the sheriff could be so bold?"

"Why do you believe the sheriff was to blame?"

She suppressed the urge to rub the tingling skin at the nape of her neck. "The man who rescued me worked for the sheriff. I believe he underwent a change of heart once the fighting began. He said that the leader, Carlisle, is Finch's closest associate."

"Who was the man? Do you know?"

"Have you heard of Will Scarlet?"

"Will Scarlet?" Jacob laughed, a quick and merry sound. "Of course."

While she hoped for details, she had not expected immediate recognition. "Who is he?"

"He is nephew to Robin of Loxley. Robin Hood."

"*The* Robin Hood?"

"Yes. Son of Loxley's elder sister."

Scarlet's behavior seemed like that of two different people—careless and selfish, reasoned and chivalrous. This new information did little to unravel his mysteries. Given the least opportunity, most men would have boasted of a connection to

Robin Hood. But not Scarlet. He fought his conscience like a demon come to claim his soul and made no mention of the famous outlaw.

Puzzles she thought herself capable of solving flew apart.

"They fought with King Richard against John's uprising five years ago," Jacob said. "Do you remember?"

"Five years ago? No."

"Ah, your illness. Forgive me." He cleared his throat, sounding embarrassed. "But Scarlet was working for the sheriff? That seems odd, considering his past. Did he offer an explanation?"

"No, nor did I ask."

"And yet you are here by yourself."

Ahead in the forest, bounding through the fallen leaves, Asem provided a few moments of distraction. Meg was gratified by her body's response. Her pulse did not accelerate. Her stomach did not constrict. Only her hands proved wayward, tightening, relishing the memory of Scarlet's flesh beneath her fingers.

"We parted ways," she said, appreciating her flat tone.

"You must have disliked him a great deal to favor this over his company."

"He was the man who arrested Ada." Repeating the truth aloud banished the new, raw memories of pleasure.

"Because of the emeralds, as we feared?"

"Yes. And now I simply want to go home."

Jacob stopped short, his body rigid. "What about Ada?"

"What about her?"

"You cannot leave her in prison!"

"I can." Cold anger stiffened her jaw, honing each word into a sharp lance. "She'll be tried and fined, nothing more. Pursuing her was a mistake from the start."

He firmly unlinked their arms. "This isn't right, Meg."

"You love her; you go find her!" Hostility simmered under her skin, even though Jacob was not her enemy of choice. But his pining loyalty to Ada never failed to stoke her temper. He stubbornly failed to see her sister for what she was. "You know why I cannot trust her, and she holds no affection for me."

"That's not true."

"Enough, please. Will you lead me home or not?"

Jacob's decision remained unvoiced as wild shouts echoed from a nearby clearing. He called to Asem before fleeing in pursuit, footsteps and excited voices and dog barks creating an unnatural cacophony in the deep woods.

"Jacob, wait!"

Alone again, Meg permitted fatigue to slump her shoulders. She gripped her walking stick and dipped her forehead to the ground.

Minutes passed and she forced her unruly body to straighten. She shook free of weakness like shrugging a wet blanket from her back. Despite her disorientation that morning, she knew Charnwood Forest, especially near to landmarks such as Jacob's cabin.

But better than the trees and swamps, she knew the unpredictable woodsmen who lived within its sheltering branches. No matter the giant mastiff ready to do his bidding, Jacob, a lone Jew, stood little chance against Hugo and his rabble.

Chapter Seven

But back again he shall be led,
And fast bound shall he be,
To see if you will have him slain,
Or hanged on a tree.

"Robin Hood and the Beggar, II"
Folk ballad, seventeenth century

Buzzing, angry voices like a nest of hornets pricked at Will's ears, each calling for his head. Unarmed, tugged by the rope around his neck, he trudged across the small clearing known as Rutfield Glade. Clusters of peasants dotted the open space, gathered around fires, belongings, and crude shelters constructed of sticks, waddle, and draped blankets. Younger children chased each other in wild games, oblivious to the parade of woodsmen dragging two prisoners toward their deaths.

"This is *your* doing," snarled the armored man, bound and stripped of his helmet.

"You're supposed to be the Earl of Whitstowe's son. Get us clear of this."

"Enough, both of you," said their leader, the man named Hugo. "You there, bring that log around."

David Fuller, an ally from outlaw days with Robin, helped angle a substantial log to rest under a bare birch tree. Betrayal pinched at Will's temples, bringing a ferocious headache. "Fuller! You're helping him do this? I've done nothing wrong!"

The short, thickset farmer shook his head against Will's outrage. "It matters not. Nottingham's soldiers have been searching the forest for you, bullying and making arrests. We'll not go back to the days when the sheriff can toss apart our homes, when Robin isn't here to stand for us."

His pride shriveled like an apple left in the sun. Shortcomings dogged his every step, especially when faced with men who yet compared him to Robin. He needed no such reminders.

"And we know of your work for the sheriff, arresting simple folk in the markets," said Hugo. "Most of us have been itching to get a rope around your neck for weeks."

He yanked hard. Will lunged forward and caught his balance, coughing as the noose bit into his windpipe. Bright stars flashed across his line of sight.

"But I have done nothing," said the captive swordsman. "I am Geoffrey Dryden, heir to the Earl of Whitstowe. I demand you release me at once."

Some in the glade exchanged worried glances, and although it did him little good, Will relished their hesitation. He saw reflected in their expressions the same uncertainty he had known at the roadside, faced with the prospect of doing murder. But Hugo persisted, stringing both ropes over a low-hanging branch. A sword at Will's back urged him to step onto the log. Dryden joined him.

"We don't know you, milord." Hugo's oily voice and patronizing smile spoiled his dashing looks. "Nor do we trust you. A shame we found you in this one's company."

"I was fighting him!"

"You should've let me win," said Will, grinning. "Though beaten and humiliated, you would've been safe from my taint."

"Quiet, you!"

"Or what, Hugo? You'll hang him?"

Heads turned toward the far edge of the glade, searching for the robust woman who dared mock the proceedings and

Hugo in particular. Meg stood holding a walking stick and the arm of a young man with black hair. At his feet sat a massive dog, restrained only by a cord of braided leather that did not appear up to its task.

The sarcastic grin he offered Dryden stretched wider across Will's face. Never had he been on the receiving end of such a strange and fortuitous distraction. But his initial reaction was quickly supplanted by conflicting torments: She had healed him, seduced him, poisoned him. Although he had not been prepared to die by hanging, he craved his freedom all the more, if only to confront Meg and wring from her an explanation.

She released the young man's arm and walked into the clearing. The foremost folk backed away in concert with her steps, once, and again, while behind his back, Will worked to loosen the length of hide at his wrists. He concentrated on Hugo's distracted smirk to judge the remaining moments of opportunity.

A wind blustered through the trees, sending a scatter of autumn gold into the assembly. Bowing her head, Meg tipped an ear to the ground and angled the other to the thinning canopy of leaves lining the sky. Listening, perhaps. Divining the wind.

From that odd pose, she addressed the group. "I seek Hugo."

A ripple of tense murmurs crossed the peasantry. From here, from there, whispers moved over the glade.

Mad Meg. Mad Meg.

Will's heart shuddered, skipping its usual rhythm in favor of one that loped and hesitated. He flinched when Dryden's hands joined his, back to back and tugging the rawhide bindings. He glanced over his shoulder and raised a questioning eyebrow.

"I've no intention of dying here," Dryden whispered.

Beneath the haze of overcast clouds and dancing tree limbs, the man's face shone unnaturally red, either from anger or a lack of air. He appeared unusually young without his helmet. Not even his dark, closely trimmed beard added clout to his smooth features. Across his brow, sweat collected like dew on grass. Lacking armaments, in the midst of a situation he could not control, Dryden appeared . . . *frightened.*

"I'm waiting, Hugo." Meg raised her hands, a witch casting a spell, and confronted the gathering with an utterly blank gaze. Those who had not yet receded stepped back. Two women crossed themselves.

Parting the sea of anticipating faces, Hugo strode forth. His swagger spoke of authority, and on his face he wore an expression of loathing. Although Will did not savor finding anything in common with the man who would be his executioner, he shared that antagonism toward Meg.

"How good to—well, to *see* you, Meg."

She lifted her eyes, almost where she would have met his gaze. "Release them."

"You always did have a curious sense of humor."

"With you, I have none. Let them go."

Will flexed his freed hands, urging sensation into deadened fingertips. At last, a slow trickle of warmth banished the numbness. He eased from the left foot to the right, minutely, in a cadence with his mounting anxiety. He held his body ready atop the log, unsure of what to do. No. Surrounded, without weapons, he was simply out of choices. Whatever game Meg set in motion, he had no choice but to let her play.

She closed the distance separating her from Hugo, smacking him on the shin. He kicked the walking stick away, but she shifted her weight and pulled it near. Her poise never faltered. They moved in a dance, as if they had rehearsed the meeting long before. Whatever their connection, they shared a long history—that much was clear. The entire glade held its breath.

"You defend Will Scarlet?"

Her answering hesitation revealed the smallest flicker of emotion. "'Tis Dryden I want. When he claimed to be the Earl of Whitstowe's son, he spoke truthfully."

"They are ours to do with as we please. What would please me is a pair of hangings, and one fewer witch in our midst."

"Are you ready to challenge me on this?"

Energy and expectation crackled between them. Hugo traced the length of her jaw with a forefinger, from ear to chin and around to the other ear. The caress was intimate, like that of a lover, but she remained a statue. Will looked for any indication that she even felt the man's touch, but he found only resolve, as unmoving as rock.

"I dare," Hugo said.

She stepped back and snapped the walking stick across her knee. The wood split into ragged halves. She flung the fractured pieces toward the hanging birch. The gigantic mastiff at the young man's feet sprang in pursuit, barking, bounding with long, powerful strides.

A tremendous crack threw the peasants into confusion. Grizzled faces and wide eyes whipped back to Meg. Among a haze of smoke, she flung a handful of tiny white bundles at a nearby boulder, birthing another jagged crash of sound. Screams and terrified prayers climbed through the trees as the woodsmen and their families shrank away, abandoning their leader.

Will jumped off the log and snatched a man's short sword. Dryden joined him, brandishing a makeshift club. They turned to face the charging dog, but the animal only sought the broken stick. It poked from either side of slobbery jowls. A great, shaggy tail wagged in apparent contentment.

But its master was far more dangerous. The youth who had guided Meg out of the copse leveled a crossbow at Hugo and strode to her side. He casually angled a hand within easy distance of a dagger at his belt. Will liked the fellow already.

The smoke surrounding Meg in a devilish cloud began to thin. "Release the prisoners," she said.

Her cold voice lifted the hairs on his arms. That she could sound and appear so altered from the previous night made him wonder what manner of woman he had bedded—or had bedded him. Could she really be the same woman who had scored his chest with her teeth?

Then again, her bite had been none too gentle.

But for the moment, he was content. A gratifying fear rippled across Hugo's lean face. The worrying numbness had dispersed. And for the first time in hours, no one stood ready to do him harm.

Dryden ran fingers through close-cropped hair. "We're free."

"Good." She smiled with all the sweetness of newly-sharpened daggers. "Hugo, you will permit us to stay in these woods unmolested."

"If you can pay."

She frowned. "Pay with what?"

"The emeralds."

"Still pining after a few worthless rocks?"

"They're not useless to me," the woodsman said. "I know you can make more."

She made the emeralds?

Meg tensed. Her face blanched as white as almond milk, silently confirming the truth.

The headache at Will's temples spread across his scalp, festering at the base of his skull. He had arrested Ada because she tried to sell replicas. Knowing the sheriff sought an alchemist, thinking Ada might reveal her source, he relinquished her to Finch.

The lye, the smoke, the tiny exploding bundles—proof of Meg's understanding of alchemy lined up like stalls at a market. She created the emeralds, and she had survived the ambush on the earl. Little wonder the sheriff's men pursued her with such dogged mania.

And if he learned the extent of Meg's value, Hugo would not settle for counterfeit gems.

Dryden slid Will a frowning glance. The nobleman, it seemed, had pushed the same pieces into place. He positioned himself between Meg and her smooth adversary. "You'll do well to remember who I am," he said. "Permit us refuge and I shall disregard your transgressions."

Hugo flicked a quick, animal gaze across the glade, recognizing his loss of support. But he did not cower. Eschewing the chance to beg Dryden's forgiveness, he turned to Will with a nasty sneer. "Maybe a hanging was not the best choice for you. We should've simply left you to the fine company of this witch and her Jew boy."

Will gripped the short sword, not at all surprised by the intensity of his dislike. "I should run you through."

Meg rolled her blank eyes heavenward. "Do not ruin this, Scarlet."

"Why, are these his woods?"

"There are no laws here, hardly even noble titles." The faint lines between her nose and mouth pinched into deep grooves. "Hugo has many allies whereas you have none, no matter that he is a thief and a churl."

If anyone knew the unwritten laws that governed outlaw assemblies, Will did. He had lived by the edicts of the forest, the foremost of which designated the man with the ablest skill and the readiest followers as the leader. Robin had been such a man, unswervingly in command no matter the moniker of outlaw.

But he also knew that no interloper, no newcomer to Sherwood, would have been able to wrest power from his uncle. With whatever magic she wielded, Meg had stolen Hugo's authority, leaving only foul words and a tetchy temper in its place.

He swiveled the stiff muscles of his shoulder and glared at her. Thinking well of Meg and Robin could not become habit. He had to get her to Nottingham. Soon.

Chapter Eight

The trees in Sherwood forest are old and good,
The grass beneath them now is dimly green;
Are they deserted all?

"Sonnet on Robin Hood I"
John Hamilton Reynolds, 1847

Like air pushed from shuddering lungs, the tension dispersed. Meg expected one of the men to retaliate, but none fractured the uncomfortable accord. Hostility eased into awkward acceptance. Night would bring the uncertainties of the forest, and everyone seemed to prefer tasks of survival to facing the nobleman they had nearly murdered.

She wanted to collapse. She wanted her own bed. But the infuriating people who insisted on abrading her peace would not let her be. Scarlet, Hugo, Ada, young Jacob and his lovesick notions. She found no distance from any of them.

Even Dryden would not let her be. "My thanks, Meg."

"Yes, milord."

"Your arrival was most timely."

She nodded. "You should know I acted in hopes of receiving a favor in return."

"Of course. I haven't forgotten your sister," he said. "My

father made a promise to you, and I renew his pledge. We shall find her."

Despite his claim, Dryden's intonations were flat and passive. His voice suggested a dark sort of regret, although she could only guess at its origins. Grief? Shame for having survived the ambush while his father lay dead, or for having run away?

No matter. She would do well with the nobleman as an ally.

"I'm grateful, sire. How did you come to be paired with Scarlet?"

"We clashed by the river. I mistook him for an enemy."

"Your pardon, but you make a mistake when you assume him anything else."

Scarlet's words laced between them. "Meg would have preferred rescuing you but leaving me to hang."

She flinched, feeling him as intimately as if his mouth had brushed hers. His low voice sounded impossibly close, confirmed by the sudden touch of heat from his body.

Damn you.

He had returned to her like a guilty thought. Consequences clung to him like honey, sticky and sweet and dangerous. She licked her lips, half expecting to taste him. The salty tang of his skin stayed with her, remembering him as accurately, as painfully as the yellow brilliance of sunshine.

Damn us both.

"Sometimes the bad comes with good," she said.

Scarlet chuckled. "I've recent experience with that, yes."

"You fared better today than you deserve."

"Recompense for a very poor morning."

"Meg, you would have let him hang?" Dryden sounded surprisingly eager, like a half-grown boy enjoying tales of a hunt.

"Of course not. I never give Hugo what he wants, not purposely."

"Who is he?" Scarlet asked.

She rubbed the hollow below the right side of her jaw. Grinding her teeth left the tendons sore. "A thief and a liar. Nothing more."

"Too bad about the noose, then. We could have been friends. Are you going to tell us what you used to scare these peasants half witless?"

"Witches use magic."

"But you use potions," he said with quiet menace. "I know firsthand."

Meg suppressed a weary sigh. For a few moments, she had been proud of herself. She had trampled painful memories of her desire for Hugo, able to challenge him in the face of his loyal followers. But braving him had been a slight victory compared to the grit she needed to endure Scarlet's anger. She would not retreat, could not, unless she wanted him to know how terribly their encounter continued to afflict her.

Instead, she lifted her eyes, eyes many people found dreadful—anything to guard against the palpable waves of his ire. "I used niter, sulfur, charcoal, sugar, and a little friction," she said. "The tricks of my trade."

"A blind alchemist." He snorted. "And a woman."

She could have spit. She would have, had she been sure of splattering it between his eyes. "My blindness and my sex do not limit my pursuits."

"Enough, please," said Dryden. "Tell me what happened on the roadside. I care to know your perspective, Scarlet."

"If you mislike my answer, must we fight again?"

"Only if you killed my father."

"That I did not do."

Meg commanded her eyes to miraculously resume their usefulness. She wanted to see their expressions, any clue as to how these men might be maneuvered. But the blackness remained. She found herself lulled by the rasping cadence of Scarlet's words as he described the roadside ambush. She shuddered, recalling that cold wash of fear. Helplessness and disorientation threatened to overcome her once again, and renewed gratitude left her flustered. She did not enjoy being beholden to this man.

"We fled into the woods to evade their pursuit," he said.

Holding her breath, clutching the new walking stick Jacob had provided, she waited for what Scarlet might say about their night together. But Dryden interjected, his grief-stricken tone as raw as an open sore. "Forgive me, please. I should have been the man to protect you."

The details of Scarlet's face—smooth skin and rough stubble, hollows and lines and firm lips—made her fingertips itch.

Yes, you should have been there. Maybe then I wouldn't be feeling such a fool.

"My apologies, Will."

He turned to find David Fuller standing with him at the edge of the glade. The man pushed a tattered hood away from his face, looking sheepish and a little fearful. Although stout of body and built for hard labor, he had grown thin. A fresh scar stood in pale pink relief on his left cheek.

"Let the past lie," Will found himself saying. Pity, not vengeance, had taken hold of his tongue. "What are you doing here, Fuller?"

"We've been driven out of Nottingham by another blasted sheriff."

Walk away. *Walk away.*

He had managed that simple act of self-preservation regardless of Meg's pleas, and he could do it again. These ragged, lost people were not his concern, allies though they had once been. They were nothing but a hindrance, a danger to his plans and his duty to Marian.

But curiosity and some nastier impulse made him ask another question. "What has Finch done to you?"

"You worked for the man." Wariness hunched the peasant's shoulders, but Will recognized resentment as well. "D'you mean to say you've no notion of what's happened?"

"Apparently not."

"He sides with the Normans on every dispute," Fuller said. Dark circles rested beneath watery gray eyes that would not hold still. "Unless you live within the shadow of the castle or speak French, you may's well be outlawed. He imprisons everyone caught bartering or using chits instead of gold. No gold means no taxes, and he wants every penny."

"But to live here?" He moved a critical gaze over the clearing. The outcast peasants gathered around a half dozen cook fires and meager shelters, preparing to sup. A pair of women removed dried clothes from where they hung in the trees. "How dreadful could it have been?"

Fuller looked across the same scene, but he managed a tight smile. "Not everyone shares your loathing of the woods."

"Many hated it worse but said naught."

"But of those who groused, none did so louder than you."

"I would do now, Fuller, but no one has the good sense to listen."

When the older man laughed, Will checked his humor. Indulging an old feeling of camaraderie with a peasant who would have hanged him did naught to advance his purposes.

"We took our chances coming back to the woods, like last time," Fuller said. "Surely you can understand the appeal."

"We both know why it worked last time, and he's in France."

"Then we'll do it for ourselves."

Will shook his head. "That thief, Hugo—he's not the man to lead you."

Those watery eyes narrowed. "No one else seems game for the task."

Although the years had taken a physical toll on him, Fuller walked away with calm grace. He smiled at his companions when he reached the campfires. A thin woman of indeterminate age rubbed between his shoulder blades and handed him a cask of ale. He almost looked pleased within the confines of that scant life.

And why shouldn't he?

Fuller lived quietly, in hiding, but he lived amongst friends—friends who would likely share the last of their food or die to defend him. Once, Will had been accepted with open arms. He had laughed and loved and fought with purpose. The trees had not seemed as loathsome then.

Impossible longings hollowed his chest, and traitorous thoughts augmented his headache.

"Will Scarlet?"

He spun to face the young fellow who had accompanied Meg. "What do you want?"

"To introduce myself." No older than fourteen, the lad offered his hand. Curly black hair trailed over his ears and nearly past his eyebrows. "I'm called Jacob ben Asher, milord."

"I am no one's lord," he said, exhaling his frustration. "Use some manner of my name and we'll get along happily."

Jacob shuffled his feet and offered an impish grin. "I know who you are. I've heard much of your exploits. 'Tis like meeting a woodland fairy in the flesh. Hardly to be believed."

"Indulge in that bunch of nonsense, if you wish, but I would not repeat such falsehoods."

The boy shrugged. Impenetrable black eyes defended his thoughts as well as a lowered portcullis. "My apologies."

"You are a friend of Meg's?"

"A friend? No. I am better acquainted with her sister. Their father worked with mine, alchemy and the like." He cast black eyes around the clearing before leaning closer, whispering, "In truth, Meg frightens me."

"You and everyone else here." The lad never permitted his hands to stray far from the weapons he wore. He exuded an agile combination of suspicion and readiness. "Are you as good with that crossbow as you appear?"

Jacob did not blink. "Yes."

"I'll do well to remember that. And you'll do well to learn the difference between ballads and the truth."

The pungent smell of tiny fires consuming damp leaves raked across the clearing. Meg sat alone. Her knees rattled together beneath her kirtle, reacting to a combination of cold, fatigue, and frustration. She stretched stiff arms, cowering from how dreadful she must appear. Her skin itched. Her hair was a mass of snarls. Despite the river water, her skin still smelled of sex and sweat, a constant and maddening reminder of her tryst with Scarlet.

Squeals from bats and a hooting owl signaled the onset of night, and somewhere in the black, Scarlet watched and waited. Discerning his location was impossible, like listening for the silent wings of a butterfly, but neither had he abandoned her. He had yet to confront her about the wolfsbane, a conversation she could only avoid by escaping the clearing altogether—and she would not leave without Dryden, her last, best chance for Ada's freedom.

She cursed herself almost as vigorously as she did Will Scarlet.

"Hello, Meg."

Cold muscles jerked. "Hugo."

Like studying the details of an experiment, she recognized the effect of his glassy voice on her body. Rapid breaths. Trembling fingers. Busy eddies of blood beating a heavy measure at her temples. The earlier bravado she mustered, knowing dozens of expectant eyes scrutinized their verbal advances and deflections, dwindled to dangerously low stores.

Weariness remained, along with a snaking fear of her own weak resolve. She had once loved Hugo, the thief of Tunneley Wood, desiring him beyond reason. The prospect of drowning beneath those sordid sensations frightened her like the river's rush. She could imagine nothing more humiliating than being his fool again.

She stood with deliberate slowness, refusing to remain seated when he loomed over her, looking down on her. "What do you want?"

"To offer you a warning," he said. "You knew no one would turn you away, mad witch that you are. But try your tricks on me again and you'll have to sleep with your eyes—no, your ears open." Moving closer, his quiet breathing filled the scant

distance between them. "Unless you'd rather take shelter in
my bed."

"Hardly."

He laughed, cold and pitiless. "Where's your sister?"

"She's gone missing," she said, her features feeling numb.
"But likely you knew that."

"I suppose I did. Surprised you haven't accused me of
some offense."

"You're guilty of much, but nothing to do with her disap-
pearance."

"Warms my heart, Meg, your faith." He stroked her from
shoulder to elbow, tugging her near. She entered enemy terri-
tory. "Come now, warm the rest of me."

She tensed and shivered. "Let me go."

Lean arms wrapped her into a compromising hold, banding her upper back. He smelled of wood fire and ale. His lips
brushed hers, tempting her to taste. Memories of passion
mingled with an acid streak of shame. She should hit him.
Kick him. Hate him.

But, for the moment, someone held her in the dark. And
she hated only her isolation. Her body molded to his, heat
against heat.

"Without Ada to consider, I thought you'd welcome me."

An old and bubbling pain threatened to burst. Regret and
a distant betrayal pressed the backs of her eyes and scraped
her throat raw.

"Welcome you to crawl into me again? I am not you, nor
am I Ada. Do you believe me so disloyal?"

"No," he whispered, claiming another nipping kiss. "I believe you so reckless."

"Mongrel."

"Perhaps Scarlet sees to you now. Are you grateful I broke
you in?"

"I'm only grateful that our encounters never resulted in a
child."

"Meg, Meg, Meg." A sure hand slid down her spine and

grasped her backside. He pulled her pelvis flush to his. "You write history anew if you deny how you enjoyed me."

Her limbs, brain, and pride finally cooperated. She smacked at his arms, hitting him until he released her—until she was alone in the blackness. "Get away from me."

"No more for tonight, then?"

"Kiss him again, Meg." Scarlet's sharp command punctured the night air with the precision of an arrow. "But only if you have more lye."

Chapter Nine

Villain, I'll plague thee for abusing me.

The Downfall of Robert, Earl of Huntington
Anthony Munday, 1601

She wanted to grow thinner and thinner until no one could see her. Especially not Will Scarlet. Transparent, she could fade into the forest and escape with the animals. She would not suffer the embarrassment of being revealed for such a needy creature. Whatever passion she felt for Hugo—craving, hatred, and an abiding fear—she felt for Scarlet tenfold.

"This isn't your concern," Hugo said.

"What say you, Meg?" The sound of a sword pulled from its scabbard slipped through the night, as chill as death.

"Enough. Hugo, I see no reason to continue our . . . our conversation." She hated the break in her voice.

"No worry," Hugo said. "I'm not missing much when you refuse me your filthy company."

The distant noises of supper and evening songs mumbled together, a quiet backdrop to their drama. Scarlet walked closer, his footsteps the loudest sound in the forest. "Leave."

Hugo snickered. "I wonder if all this fuss means you've discovered the truth about her."

"Which is?"

"When you touch that lovely flesh, she hasn't a shred of pride."

Kicked by his words, Meg struggled to breathe. Humiliation squeezed her neck like clenching hands. Over a distracting pulse in her ears, she heard the two adversaries circling. Feet shuffled through the leaves. A branch cracked. Their grunts and hisses punctuated the night air. Had Hugo drawn a weapon?

"Back away, Meg. About five paces."

She followed Scarlet's instructions without protest. Her bearings—any tenuous mental hold on direction—had spun loose. Only the disorientation of fear remained. "Don't do this."

"I've been in a foul mood all day," Scarlet said. "You'll be just the man to take the brunt of my blows."

"I'd rather best your uncle."

"That makes two of us. Alas, we have but each other."

Steel crashed, breaking the night like glass. Meg flinched. She stumbled backward and found a tree. Chunks of bark chewed her fingertips. Masculine grunts volleyed. Lunges and strikes and evasions wrote a ballad of conflict. Unable to see the precision of any given blow, she could only wait for the sound of agony should a sword meet flesh. With every mortal clang, she held her breath.

One of them stumbled and thudded into something hard. A tree trunk? A fallen log? Hugo groaned on a painful exhale. A sword clanked to the ground, muffled by the forest refuse.

"I'll tell you again," Scarlet said. "Leave now."

"Have it your way." Hugo spat and groaned. "I simply cannot understand the bother in fighting for Mad Meg."

Scarlet growled, a feral beast. "Go!"

She could no longer stand there. Running headlong into an oak held more appeal than waiting between those men for another moment. She turned and stumbled deeper into the woods.

* * *

Despite his defeat, Hugo turned and sauntered away like a man without worries.

Sweat slicked Will's palms. He wanted nothing more than to bury his sword between the cagey thief's eyes. But standing there, alone at the edge of the clearing, he had no choice but to follow Meg. He scowled after her in the darkness. Potent resentment boiled his blood.

And by the saints, his shoulder left him careworn.

Before knowing his own mind, his sword had jumped from its scabbard when he saw them kissing. The need to take umbrage with Hugo's glib advances and crass remarks had propelled him like the wind at his back. But he acknowledged the truth behind his fury. Using the excuse of Hugo's insults was exactly that. An excuse. He longed for a fight. Any fight. He needed to slake the frustrations that had been festering for what felt like years. Meg made him need to pummel something. Anything.

A tree. Her. Hugo.

Yes, Hugo would have done nicely. The man was a thief, however, not a fighter, and the brief duel provided no satisfaction. The passing moments of freedom he had discovered during the fight only whetted his need for a stronger release. But then, he could imagine no amount of violence to satisfy him now. His exasperation loomed too large—or too small, more like, standing in the gray grass with her shoulders hunched forward.

"What do you want from me, Scarlet?" Her wintry question offered no welcome.

"How did you know it was me?"

She kept her head low, her face obscured by a curtain of disheveled hair. "I heard Hugo fall. Did you wound him?"

Not enough.

"Would you care if I had?"

"Of course," she said. "We would have to flee again, and I am much fatigued by today."

"He will live. I did him no great harm, not even to his pride it seemed."

"I would've thought the pair of you better suited to swapping braggart's stories than fighting, at any rate."

He walked to her. "You think me like him?"

"No, you're worse." Restless fingers knotted the fabric of her shabby skirts, wrinkling woad blue wool made black in the nighttime shadows. "You're self-serving and deceitful, yet you mock me with chivalry. At least I know what Hugo is."

"A right pig."

A quiet burst of laughter brought her head high. "Yes."

"And what am I?"

"A confusion." Sobering, she reached for his wounded shoulder. "A weight on me."

He recoiled at the hot tingle of her fingers, but the touch was like that of a stranger. The woman who had stroked his skin, tasted him, stood mere inches away, but she huddled so deeply inside herself that he might have dreamed their nighttime tryst. Every battlement was in place, ready to fight and kick, yet she still inquired after his injury.

Holding on to his resentment was a trial. But he managed.

"How greatly does it hurt?" she asked.

"Less than the lye did."

"If you'll keep from grousing about the pain of healing, the lye worked more than one miracle."

"You poisoned me."

Her features tightened like pond water freezing into ice. "I eased your pain."

"I've heard the hereafter will do that for a body."

"If I wanted you dead, you'd be dead."

"Forgive my confusion," he said, flexing and releasing his hands. Left then right. And again. "I was on the receiving end of a good many contradictory messages last night. What, exactly, did you want?"

"You. Banished from my head." She spat the words, exorcising demons.

"If it was as terrible as that, why did you tumble with me?"

"I liked how you smell."

Will snorted. "That's all you required?"

"Consider yourself irresistible or me desperate. I care not. But I wager you had no higher reason."

"I had little choice with you atop me."

"The remedy for such a situation is short and easily formed: *no*. But I heard nothing of the sort last night." She smirked, making him feel inexplicably foolish. "Now leave me be."

He wanted to laugh. Two hands shorter, blind, hated and feared by the peasants who had grudgingly taken her in— and she was dismissing him. Yes, he wanted to laugh, but he was too busy defending against the nettling sticks she poked at his pride.

A fragment of memory slid forward. He remembered when she baited Hendon, claiming an association with the earl's heir. An uncomfortable stab of jealousy prodded him at the thought of Meg and the nobleman together.

No. He could not afford to think that way. Marian. Safety. Clearing his name. He had squandered too much time already. Nothing else concerned him, not even the strange blind woman he would turn over to Finch.

"I suppose you have no need of me, not when you have Dryden."

The unhurried rise and fall of her bodice seized. "Pardon me?"

"You said as much to Hendon, that you knew the earl's son intimately."

"I lied."

"Is that the truth?"

Her unreadable face provided no clues. "You seem to have missed how I say what I must to get my way."

"That's no answer."

"No. 'Tis a judgment on your powers of perception. He's the earl's heir and will help me in his father's stead."

"I don't trust him."

"Oh, that is rich, Scarlet. He bests you in combat, which makes him untrustworthy."

She raised those empty eyes, blatantly confronting him with the uncomfortable proof of blindness. He was beginning to interpret the action as a challenge; she only used it after exhausting deceptive options, or when emotion got the better of her.

"He ran away from the ambush," he said. "His father was slaughtered, but he didn't stay to fight."

"Shock. Fear. I'm sure you've felt both."

He had attacked out of fear, admittedly, but Will had never run from a fight, not when running meant abandoning fellow men-at-arms. He stared at Meg's lips, hating the sudden need to prove his worth to her, if only in words. But the subject of worth and valor and courage skirted too near unwanted memories. Pressing his tongue to the craggy roof of his mouth, he ran the sharp edge of his thumbnail over the long-healed scar on his palm, picking at the lump of flesh.

"You don't trust him either," he said.

"How do you figure?"

"Why did you keep the truth of my role in Ada's arrest a secret from him?"

She pinched her lips into a scowl. "He doesn't need to know."

"Because you don't trust him."

"Stop it!"

She balled both hands and lunged. Perhaps she moved more slowly because of fatigue, or perhaps he knew better to guard against the angered assaults she was quick to use. Wheedle. Confront. Attack. The pattern of her behavior was becoming clear. Catching slender wrists, he absorbed every twist and thrust. He spun her twice, shoved her away. Meg stumbled and fell into the leaves.

She scrambled to her feet, angled away from him. Will felt a childish urge to hold his breath and stay hidden from her keen ears, but a swift flash of lust made that a difficult task. Sparring with her played unconscionable games with his control.

"You still need me," he said, his claim scratching free of a tight throat.

Meg whipped her head around. "Ridiculous."

"Do you know Nottingham? Or that castle? No."

"And I suppose you do."

He scowled. "Like I'd know my own father."

"No, no," she said. "You've more reason to sabotage me than help me."

"How so?"

"If you bend the sheriff's ear, maybe reveal me as the real alchemist, then life becomes easier for Will Scarlet."

Her blindness had caused him nothing but trouble. She could have cleared his name. She could have made their flights through the forest easier to navigate. But at that moment, he was glad for her impairment. Although prepared to deflect a physical assault, he had not expected her flawless assessment of the stakes. He felt his surprise slash across his face in bold strokes.

"That may be true, but I need Dryden as much as you do," he said. "He's the only one who can help clear my name. If nothing else, I can prove my good worth by coming to your aid."

"I knew you had ulterior motives."

"You wounded me."

"No, I cured you."

He crossed his arms. "Based on our association, I see little difference."

"You suggest that if we share Dryden's influence, in a way, you'll have no cause to betray me?"

Suspicion yet swam through her voice like fish in a stream. To get Meg to Nottingham, he needed to secure her full cooperation. No potions, no tricks, no reason to abandon him for Dryden's convenient status and fickle bravery. She had to come willingly, if only for his own health and sanity.

But how to convince her? The truth was obviously impossible; it resembled his misdeeds too closely, no matter his concern for the safety of Robin's family. And if Hugo were any example of her associations, she would never accept altruism.

Deceitful, lascivious, *greedy* Hugo.

He grinned. "And if you offered a few of those counterfeit emeralds, I'd appreciate it."

"You low, slimy dunghill." She closed the distance between them and jabbed a precise finger into the leather mail he wore. "You arrested my sister. You should be begging for my forgiveness, not offering your services for a price."

"Truth be told, 'tis an inexpensive price," he said. "What sacrifice is it to part with shoddy rocks? Rocks you can conjure?"

"The sacrifice is in giving you what you want."

He stroked a thumb along her bottom lip, feeling powerful when she flinched. A wayward, lustful part of him anticipated the sweet sting of her teeth, fighting, biting him again. "I've already had from you what any man wants from a woman."

She slapped his hand away. "Gelded bastard."

"If I were a gelding, you would've discovered as much."

"You're no better than Hugo."

Good girl.

"Two men working on your behalf will be better than one. Your unscrupulous soul knows as much."

"The Devil take your offer," she said.

"No, the Devil just made you an offer. Let me escort you to Nottingham."

Chapter Ten

"They call her a wise-woman,
but I think her an arrant witch."
—Will Scarlet

The Sad Shepherd: Or, a Tale of Robin Hood
Ben Jonson, 1641

Meg rubbed eyes irritated by a profound lack of sleep. A second night's exposure to the eventide air, lying vulnerable to a host of strangers and adversaries, made sleeping on the forest floor hopeless. Although a reprieve from the late-autumn chill might prove impossible, she waited for the sun to find her skin and mark the end of her terrible night.

She would give every drop of blood to return to dreams of fire, anything but the nightmarish visions she endured. Visions of Will Scarlet.

Since contracting her illness, she had dreamt of nothing but fire, a nightly pattern that comforted her with its consistency and rhythm. By day, she endured an endless, deep well of black, but in her dreams, she saw gold, amber, honey, and russet. Flashes of blues. Streaks of white. The colors of fire.

Never once had she dreamed of a man. Not even Hugo.

What she could not see of Scarlet in waking hours, her sleeping mind imagined with stunning clarity. The angular lines of his face. The arrogant tilt of his lips when he teased, when he kissed. The dusting of springy hair across his chest, tapering like a path to his rigid shaft. She had straddled him that night, but in dream, he was above her, covering her with the startling resilience and power of hard male muscle.

She wanted more, to know more. She knew nothing of his coloring. Brown hair or blond? Dark eyes? Fair skin? The combinations tantalized her as she fanned through endless possibilities. And all the while, the feel of his tongue ravaging her mouth and echoes of his sinuous voice pooled a delicious, maddening heat between her thighs.

She dug her forefingers into her eye sockets. Had she any courage, any dignity, she would dig deeper and gouge him from her thoughts. But she had neither, only a covetous need to hold fast to every forbidden memory.

Rubbing her hands, holding them over the fire, she waited for sensation to return to frozen fingers. The familiar crackle of the blaze soothed her, lulling her. It heated her legs through the fabric of her gown, tempting her with its familiar and dangerous call.

Fire—welcoming, dependable, and far safer than thoughts of Will Scarlet.

She used to appease the fires by feeding wood, wax, and cloth to open flames. As her curiosity developed, she tested a greater range of fodder. Practice and repetition yielded the results she found described in her father's ancient book. Heating bitumen produced tar. Roasting vermillion rocks resulted in quicksilver, the strange liquid metal. Scalding seawater in the presence of clay created salt acid. She repeated them, glorying in the predictable pattern of nature responding to fire, especially when nature had played such an unpredictable trick on her.

Seated in the glade, she would have played with those flames had she been alone. But countless eyes likely followed her actions—Jacob next to her, Hugo skulking somewhere in the camp. And Scarlet watched her, she knew. His eyes touched her neck, her face, reminding her that the heat she had experienced with her enigmatic protector was more dangerous than any beckoning blaze.

And his offer still hung between them.

"We're going to my cabin," she said.

Across the fire, Will shifted and yawned. "No. To Nottingham."

She wound her hands around a leather flagon of ale and drank, hoping he tolerated the night as poorly as she had. "My cabin first."

He swore, his voice sluggish. "Your sister is in the city. Dryden can ease our meeting with the sheriff. Why delay? What need have we for an out-of-the-way dwelling?"

Once Jacob took the flagon, she aimlessly shredded dry leaves and fed them to the fire. "The person who will do best by my sister is me, and I won't go into the city without supplies."

"And a change of clothes," Jacob said.

"Oh, and Jacob is coming too, even with his smart mouth."

"Why?"

"He maintains a baffling affection for Ada, which is something we hold in common."

The younger man spoke past a mouthful of food. "That and a fondness for explosions."

"Asem is an asset too."

"All I've seen Asem do is fetch," Scarlet said. "They'll only be a nuisance."

He spoke in that tight way he did when he became angry, forcing words past a locked jaw. Making him angry fueled her confidence and helped banish disconcerting fantasies. She lifted her face to the sky. Still no sunshine.

"Jacob knows all of Charnwood," she said. "He can show us the fastest way to my cabin and on to Nottingham, unless you'd rather spend more time in these woods you find detestable."

His answering silence provided no clues to his thoughts. The long pause brought her attention back to the flames. Having incinerated everything within easy reach, the dearth of nearby leaves left her restless fingers without a diversion.

She fished a piece of dried venison from her alms-bag and picked at its stringy grain. For each piece she ate, she tossed another into the fire.

"Fine. Jacob can come."

She stood and stretched. "Will Scarlet makes a decision, and all without sainted Uncle Robin Hood."

Scarlet followed. She checked the need to step away from the ripple of frustration radiating from the red center of his bones. "False gems be damned, I'm ready to risk the consequences to see you fail," he said.

Irritation spoiled his speech, leaving her to wonder again at his strife with Robin Hood.

She smiled. "Go ahead and leave for Nottingham, if you wish."

"And where will you be?"

She gripped his forearms, nearly standing on tiptoe to find the privacy of his ear. "I'll be here. In the forest. With two dozen peasants who believe me a witch. And Hugo as their leader."

He laced his fingers through the hair at the base of her neck, clutching, pulling her close. Quick breaths fanned across her forehead and nose. "You're using last night's bit of chivalry against me."

"And your conscience, Scarlet. Don't forget that. It really does work contrary to your ambitions." She gave the muscled ropes of his forearms an appreciative squeeze. She exhaled, something too near a sigh. "Lovely."

"Stop it."

"What?"

"You say what you must to get what you want."

He released her, like flinging a dangerous animal into the brush. Oh, but she could come to enjoy his lack of control.

"You believe my appreciation for your physique might be such a deception?"

"Is my conclusion absurd?"

She laughed. "If I can navigate a situation without the need for lies, I make do with the truth. No sense muddying clear waters."

"Witch," he said. "I can think of another word for you."

"One lacking in originality, I'd wager."

Hugo would have hit her, had she dared speak to him that way. Scarlet, however—she could almost hear him gnashing his teeth. She pushed, she pushed again, and still he refrained from violence. But the careening sensations he nurtured in her blood terrified her in new and unpredictable ways, tempting her to take ever-greater chances.

The Devil's own offer, indeed.

Asem's sharp bark snapped everyone to attention. "What is it, Jacob?"

But Meg's question went unanswered. Jacob gripped his dog's leash, barely restraining the massive animal. With his nose pointed into a thicket made ghoulish by the lingering dawn fog, Asem snarled and strained for release.

Will tightened his hand on Meg's upper arm, not knowing when he had reached for her. "Get your things. Quickly."

She turned without question or argument, retrieving nothing but her new walking stick. "Who comes?"

"I don't want to chance learning, do you?"

"Me? Take chances?"

"Dryden, come. Let's have done."

With the suddenness of a spring shower, a trio of men burst from the thicket. Their scabbards rattled, empty and useless. Barren fists held neither sword nor shield but pumped vigorously, propelling the men across the clearing at a full run. Handsomely decorated surcoats flew behind them, but fright and sweat covered their faces.

Confusion enveloped the clearing. Peasants who had lingered over their midmorning meal scrambled and shouted, retrieving weapons, diving clear of the men.

Dryden collected his belongings and stood beside Will and Meg. Beneath his beard, his face told a story of surprise and concern. "What is this? Monthemer!"

From among the trio, a blond man spun and called Dryden's name. He urged his two companions to circle back. "Cousin! Behind us! They are intent on murder!"

A dozen marauders wearing masks tore into the clearing. Slicing blades cleaved through shelters, and bows littered the air with deadly arrows.

Asem broke free and barreled into the nest of intruders. Although Jacob called his dog's name, he did not appear ready to sacrifice his life in pursuit. He edged closer to their little band and loaded his crossbow. Dryden's cousin retrieved a dagger, determination replacing panic on his face. Leaner, shorter, he seemed a pale pretender to Dryden's dark looks and muscular build.

Meg frowned. "They're wearing mail. Are they soldiers?"

"She's right," said Dryden, pulling on his helmet. "I can hear the metal."

Fear leaked from Dryden's skin like sweat. What happened to the vengeful warrior Will had fought by the riverside?

Tattered homespun garments disguised full coats of mail. The attackers scattered before Asem's charge, only to fan across the clearing with the precision of a trained army, surrounding everyone. These were no ordinary highwaymen.

But Will did not intend to make sense of the violence. "They're trying hard to appear otherwise. Anything in that alms-bag, Meg?"

"I used the last of it yesterday."

"We'll have to fight our way free."

"Lead the way."

"Oh, no," he said. "Soldiers, danger, blind girl. These things don't mix. And you cannot help your sister if you're dead." Without grace or care, he shoved her into a dense patch of shrubbery. "You stay hidden until we can get clear. Promise me."

She smiled sweetly, said nothing, and burrowed deeper into the cover of foliage.

A man assaulted him from behind. He leapt aside to get

clear of a broadsword's downward arc, rushing away from Meg's hiding place. His opponent followed. Will ducked and drew his own weapon. Catching each blow, he shambled toward where Dryden and the others confronted another pair of soldiers in disguise. He caught his foot on a gnarled tree root and landed awkwardly, his sword flying free.

When his opponent reared for a killing strike, Will swept his right leg, buckling the man's knees and pulling him forward. The sword drove into the ground near Will's head. He wrenched a dagger from the fallen man's belt, driving it between his shoulder blades.

Retrieving his sword, he turned to see Jacob plant an arrow between the eyes of a man bearing down on them. "Gramercy," he said.

The lad exchanged his empty crossbow for a pair of exotic curved knives. "If we can get north, the swamps will aid our escape."

"Swamps? I think I prefer the trees."

"Anything is preferable to this place."

Will clambered to a nearby shelter and scooped up a dead woodman's bow. Drawing three arrows from a quiver, he stabbed them into the yielding earth and took a knee. With more haste than precision, he fired each in quick succession. A blaze of pain in his shoulder ruined his accuracy, but he managed to clip two marauders. The first tumbled and rolled, clutching his upper thigh. The other arched and collapsed, an arrow protruding from his gut.

Looking across the picture of chaos, he searched for allies. Hugo, Fuller, and the other peasants stood their ground, armed and ready in little clumps around their shelters, but the peculiar highwaymen no longer paid them any mind. The trio of running men fighting alongside Jacob and Dryden seemed their only intent.

And then he found Meg.

Nearly concealed from the chaos, she knelt behind the largest structure in the glade, a makeshift waddle-and-daub shelter suitable for four people. She cut off a hank of her hair with a dagger and piled loose, dark locks atop a small stack of kindling.

His brain registered her intent even before she pulled a wedge of flint from her alms-bag. He tossed the bow and quiver and broke into a run, dodging skirmishes and jumping over bodies, but the first spark proved all she needed. Hair and kindling transformed into flames, engulfing the shelter. Meg sat before that ever-strengthening bonfire like a parish-ioner at Mass, penitent, reverential. She lifted her hands and her eyes to the gathering heat.

Will slipped on a slick patch of grass and skidded, landing next to her. Searing smoke slipped into his mouth; he doubled over and coughed. Eyes closed, he tugged on her wrists and pulled her from the flames. Only when they reached a safe distance did he turn and catch her face between his hands, pushing wild curls back.

"Are you injured?"

That reverential expression did not change. Her lips turned upward in a private smile. Her nostrils flared, dragging in deep breaths of smoke-tainted air. "Tell me how it looks."

His jaw fell open. "What?"

"Describe it to me. The fire."

She pointed her face to the inferno but saw none of its de-struction. Yellow and gold flames leapt into the sky, sending showers of hot rain over the dell. Mischievous winds passed the fire from shelter to shelter until half of the clearing glowed and throbbed with menacing heat. People who started their day from within those crude structures screamed and ran for safety, collecting loved ones and scant possessions, the blaze at their backs.

"You don't want to know what I see."

"That's not true," she said harshly. "Show me filth and pestilence, and I'd be happy to look upon it."

Will clasped her upper arm and hauled her into the thick of

the woods. She tripped. And again. "I half believe you drag your feet purposefully," he said.

"I half believe you enjoy it."

"What? Your clumsy bearing?"

"No, having an excuse to be angry with me."

He whirled, flinging her arm away. Outrage and anger bubbled in his chest. Her ability to send him careening from enemy to protector, from lunatic to sage, left him reeling. "You set half the grove on fire!"

"I saved our lives."

"Those people—that was likely all they owned in the world."

"Of all the double-minded tripe," she said, her lips curled into a nasty sneer. "They would've hanged you without me. You're only upset because I saved you again."

"I'm upset because you seem completely unaffected by the damage you do!"

"You're allowing a few scruples to take precedent over our survival. I won't stand for it."

"It was unnecessary, Meg." He furrowed restless fingers through his hair. The tart stink of smoke clung to him. "Those men were soldiers in disguise, like you said. But they weren't engaging the woodsmen."

The man with silvery blond hair emerged from the thicket, Dryden and Jacob right behind him. His fair skin appeared ghostlike in the gauzy webs of smoke. "You're right, Scarlet," the pale man said. "They were after me."

Chapter Eleven

[He took] it for granted that his offence was past remission, determined on joining Robin Hood, and accompanied him to the forest, where it was deemed expedient that he should change his name; and he was rechristened without a priest, and with wine instead of water, by the immortal name of Scarlet.

Maid Marian
Thomas Love Peacock, 1822

The group turned north and hastened through the forest, with Dryden introducing his younger cousin, Stephen, Baron of Monthemer. The two other men, Monthemer's companions, were nowhere to be found. Having lost a second walking stick during the skirmish, Meg held on to Jacob's arm for support. Asem lumbered behind them, panting and apparently unharmed.

"What happened back there?" Dryden asked.

Monthemer's tinny voice was a hollow void of fatigue and sorrow. "My father and I traveled on the Leicester Road from Uppingham. Those highwaymen slaughtered him. My men and I have been in flight since yesterday evening."

Meg shivered. Her sister had gone missing—that was all, but it was dreadful enough. And yet she trampled through the woods with a pair of noblemen whose fathers had been murdered. Troubles piled on troubles, adding to her sense of foreboding. "Were they Finch's men, milord?"

"I haven't a notion."

"But that makes two Whitstowe men dead in as many days," Dryden said, sounding as weary as his kin.

"Two, cousin?"

"My father's party was also ambushed. Finch's man, Carlisle, led the assault."

"Saints be," Monthemer said quietly. "My condolences."

Scarlet hacked through brush with his blade. "Is it safe to say my account of the attack is gaining validity?"

"I admit that it does," Dryden said. "What do you suspect?"

"I suspect we need a safe place to recuperate." He called a halt to their northward trudge. "Wouldn't you agree, Meg?"

Prickly anger vibrated through his words, as did an offer of truce. Perhaps he felt it too, as she did—that sense of foreboding, the need to buttress uncertain alliances in the presence of deeper dangers.

She nodded. "To my cabin, then."

They arrived at Meg's dwelling by late afternoon, creeping through the woods like the fugitives they had become. Will eyed the single-room cabin. He hoped for dispassion, but he could not deny his curiosity in examining her home.

Timber-framed walls filled with waddle and daub protected a simple collection of rough furniture, including a freestanding cabinet, a rope mattress wide enough for at least two people, and a table and bench. A smoke hood made from waddle and covered with plaster hung from the rafters over a central fire pit. Woven mats of rushes covered the packed and swept clay floor.

In all respects, the cabin might be a fitting and anonymous residence for any tradesman or successful farmer—except for the laboratory.

Meg walked unaided, gracefully, to the laboratory and ran her hands along the top of a waist-high workbench. She fingered everything on its surface: an oil lamp on a freestanding platform, plates, numerous sealed containers, cooking pots of many sizes, utensils, a scale, and a mortar and pestle. She assessed them gently but efficiently. Her expression otherwise neutral, she wore the barest touch of a smile.

She had lost her sight, somehow, but if she lived in such a place, her sense of smell had gone as well. The stale air within the cabin reeked like damp garments left in a heap for too many warm days. Pungent chemicals, ever-present vinegar, and the heavy, cloying stench of manure assaulted his nose. Bunches of dried wildflowers lining the rafters and joists did nothing to alleviate the stink.

No matter his reluctant curiosity about Meg's life, he could not stay in that place. He ducked outside, surprised to be seeking the relatively pleasant scent of leaves and pine— although he still resented the canopy of skeletal tree limbs that marred his view of the sky. A burst of wind ripped tired leaves from the trees, bearing an urgent message about looming winter days.

Worn patches of ground surrounded the cabin, and a series of cultivated beds laid out to his right. Despite the animal stench, he could see no livestock and no pens.

Standing next to his cousin, Dryden covered his mouth and nose with the corner of a brown woolen scarf. "What a peculiar place."

"For a peculiar girl," Will said.

"What's the likelihood she knows half of what she claims to know?" Dryden asked.

Unnerved by his instant and defensive reaction to the question, he shrugged. "You saw her trickery with those woodsmen. Whether it's magic or manipulation, she won her point."

The mail Dryden wore clinked together as he crossed his arms. His shoulders pressed in an arc toward the ground, as if weighed by recent events. "I mislike situations where I'm unacquainted with the skills of my allies."

Monthemer nodded. "You and me, together."

"She wouldn't offer her assistance if such a bid would endanger her sister's release," said Will.

A tight smile dragged Dryden's face nearer to friendliness. "Shall I ask for more proof of her skills?"

Will grinned tightly. "Not unless you want your face blackened and your hair singed."

Meg emerged from the dwelling and walked across the bare stretch of ground between them. Her steps sure, her pace even and unhurried, she displayed no outward sign of her blindness. But her posture spoke to Will. She was not merely walking; she was walking and moving with the utmost control, fighting an unending battle against her impairment. Although betrayed by her body, she refused to admit a hindrance, let alone defeat.

He had assumed that the woodsmen feared her brash assertions and tricks. But her concentration, the mantle of detachment and isolation wrapped around her pale skin, held her apart from the world. No wonder a group of simple peasants shrank from her, holding fast to their superstitions.

"Did you find everything in order?" he asked.

"How do you mean?"

"In there. You appeared as though you were taking inventory."

"No, no," she said, rubbing her nose. "I was searching for the origin of that stench."

Dryden grinned, covering his mouth with a gloved hand, but Monthemer and Will laughed outright.

"What?" Her frown returned. "Did you think that was normal?"

Will angled his mouth near her ear. "Who can tell what is normal with a witch?"

"I don't live in squalor," she said. "Ada would've run away before living like this."

Dryden watched her closely. His expression barely composed, the nobleman lowered his glove and smoothed his close-cut beard. "Then what is the smell?"

"The niter beds, for a start. Do you see those trenches in the ground?"

Will eyed the line of deep furrows that stretched away from the cabin, like graves stripped of their corpses. "What of them?"

"We mix soil, straw, ash, and animal urine. The ferment creates potash, which aids in making fields fertile." She shrugged, as if explaining the obvious to a child. "We used to sell it."

"Before you turned to larceny and fraud," he said.

She tipped her head but ignored his dig. "If I don't turn the beds and add fresh straw, they begin to stink. But that is only half the problem. One of the jars inside the cabin was not airtight. The chemicals reacted with the air to produce that horrible sulfur smell."

"And the vinegar."

"Enough about the vinegar, Scarlet."

"And here against the wall," Monthemer said. "What is this?"

She turned to face the cabin. "The furnace?"

"I believe so."

"Earl Whitstowe offered my father his choice of gifts, thanking him for years of service." She stopped before a squat, circular clay dome about an arm's length from the wall of the dwelling. "Father chose to have the furnace constructed. It must have been very expensive, took months to build."

"But why?" Will asked. "What's its purpose?"

"Experiments, mostly." She knelt, swiping leaves away from the rough clay. "The temperatures can become much hotter than cooking fires or the village bread ovens."

"It must be expensive to run," he said. "Does it require much fuel?"

She dipped her chin. "It does."

"What was that look?"

"Money," she said, standing. "The reason why Ada began selling the counterfeit emeralds. We lived quite well selling the potash. It's a good commodity."

Realization rose to the top of Will's brain like bubbles

in yeasty dough. "But not enough to do what you want—your experiments."

She had the decency to appear uncomfortable, unable to squelch a very human, very unwelcome emotion: guilt.

Finally.

"Alchemy is an expensive pursuit," she said.

"Did you talk Ada into your scheme?"

"I convinced her to do this for me, yes."

"And now you feel badly for sending her out to make . . . to . . . so you can—I cannot fathom you. She's your sister. How do you treat people this way?"

"How?" She flung her arms wide. "How can I not? People have yet to prove worthy of my good opinion. You haven't, and neither has Ada."

He grabbed her wrist, bones fine and slender in his palm, and tugged her into the cabin. Blinking in the sudden darkness and wrinkling his nostrils against the stench, he struggled to keep hold of his slippery temper. "Are these her flowers?"

"What flowers?"

"Hanging from the joists and rafters, at this moment, are—oh, about three dozen bunches of dried flowers. They don't look like your handiwork because they're not on fire." He watched her fathomless eyes. "You had no notion of their presence."

"No."

Air shoving in and out of his nostrils like a wild mob, he stared at the ground. He could not look at her. Anger blotted her face and numbed the sting of regret—regret for having behaved as she expected. She expected disloyalty and lies. He delivered them with one hand, wielding a sword on her behalf with the other.

But no, anger was easier to tend and more comforting to feel surging in his blood.

"I thought I'd come between you and your sister, taking away your only family. I felt guilt and sympathy, both." When the sudden rush of honesty dazed him, he retreated to familiar ground. Anger warped into mockery. "Now, now I'm with you till the end, Meg. I want to get Ada back if only to see the two of you reunited. That will be precious."

"Meg?" Jacob stood in the entryway, lit from behind. "There's no more sugar."

Wrinkles scratched into the skin above her nose. "Even the underground stores?"

"I looked everywhere."

"You heard the boy, Scarlet. We need sugar."

Will could not swallow the foul taste of their argument. Frustrations ground together in his throat. "I admit it. I'm lost."

"Niter, when heated and distilled, creates an acid. Combined with sugar, that acid creates smoke. A great deal of smoke." Her condescending tone reminded him far too much of Robin. "The smoke may help us if we need to get into or out of places we shouldn't be."

"You're insane," he said. "But that's not a bad idea. Where?"

"The apothecary in Keyworth, I should think."

"But sugar is expensive," Jacob said.

Meg shrugged. "He's not wrong. You'll have to steal it."

Dryden followed Jacob inside, his shape blocking more of the gloomy daylight. "We should find horses too, if we're game for stealing."

"And Jacob can stay here to help me."

The young Jew glared at her. "Do you have anything he can borrow, Meg—clothes that don't shout Will Scarlet? Everyone knows him by the two scarlet lions on his tunic. He's worn them since his days with Robin Hood."

She walked to Will, a frown marring her face like indelible dye. She touched his tunic, pilfering his breath, his reason. He hardly minded losing the capacity to breathe, not in that stinking cabin, but he sorely missed the ability to think. She traced the outlines of appliquéd lions, missing nothing with her deft hands, not even the tiny embroidered claws.

"No wonder everyone recognizes you," she said, lips twisting. "And these have been on your tunic the entire time? How did I miss that?"

"You cannot see," he whispered. "And when the impulse struck, you seemed more interested in what lies underneath."

"You vain sod." She turned abruptly, waving at a molding trunk. "My father's clothes. Cloaks, hoods, whatever you need."

"Tomorrow, Dryden, we'll have errands to run." He coughed, eager to escape the cabin and inhale clean air again. "But saints be—tonight, I'm sleeping outside."

Chapter Twelve

So may we pass along the high-way;
None will ask from whence we came,
But take us pilgrims for to be,
Or else some holy men.

"Robin Hood and the Prince of Aragon"
Folk ballad, seventeenth century

"I don't trust him."

Meg tipped her head toward Jacob where he rummaged among her containers. "Who? And what are you looking for?"

"Scarlet," he said. "And the green vitriol."

She traced two fingers along the top shelf, edging Jacob aside and counting six jars from the left. Tapping the earthenware pot with the sharply conical lid, she said, "This one."

"Gramercy. And Scarlet?"

She skirted away. Already unable to keep the man from her mind, she did not appreciate Asher's son bringing him into their conversation, damaging her tenuous concentration. Never had she experienced such difficulty in stringing together the basic steps of a formula. A decent night's rest, a wash, and a fresh gown had done little to right her addled thinking.

"I don't trust him either, but he has reason to help." She found the double boiler and left the cabin. Jacob followed her to the furnace. "If what we suspect about the sheriff is true, Scarlet is a victim as well."

"That doesn't mean you should trust him."

"If I can keep him and Dryden from estranging each other, they'll each do their parts. And Scarlet has saved my life more times than I can count, already."

"He could have to serve his own purpose."

She slashed her jaw to the side, biting her lower lip. "We'll find Ada and that will be that," she said. "Please, hand me the vitriol."

Jacob placed the jagged crystals in her hands. She conjured from memory their frosty, variegated greens and blues, and the way light refracted through the glassy surfaces. She used to stare at the endless range of hues, imagining the sea, the way her father had described its froth-topped waves and rhythmic, shifting colors.

She pushed through the haze of loss and tossed several handfuls of the crystals into the larger pot of the double boiler. "Would you stoke the fire in the furnace? We need as much heat as you can manage for the sublimation."

Jacob collected armfuls of firewood to feed the hungry maw of the furnace. From Meg's vantage, a pair of paces back from the source, the heat rose and expanded from that earthen dome like the sun pulsing, pushing nearer the earth. She tipped her chin. The skin along her neck tingled and stretched beneath the power of that terrible fire. A smile blossomed.

But memory of Scarlet's angry chastisement ruined her pleasure. He had no cause to throw his outrage at her, not when her fires smoothed their escape—and not when he was as double-minded about morality as a man could be. That her weapon of choice happened to fascinate her did not mean she had acted rashly or without thought. Their lives were more important than a few shabby huts owned by ignorant, scornful peasants.

And if what she did knocked Hugo down from the petty kingship he had established with those gullible folk, all the better.

She inserted the smaller of the two pots into to the center

of the double boiler, nestling it atop the crunch of green vitriol. A large lid covered the outer pot. When the intense heat
of the furnace burned the delicate crystals, they would release
their mystery in the form of a gas. The gas would collect and
condense on the inside of the lid, dripping as salt acid into the
smaller collecting pot.

Upon setting the double boiler into the scorching furnace,
Jacob said, "Well, that's the first step underway."

"Now we wait."

Her words dropped like fat rocks into water. She waited for
more than the results of her alchemic process. She waited to
see whether Scarlet would return with the sugar, or whether
he would return at all. Maybe he was gone, long gone to parts
far from her shabby little cabin—a cabin filled with odors
and spells and old, nagging ghosts.

But perhaps that was for the best. She had believed as
much when she gave him an excess of wolfsbane, preferring
the woods to his aid or exasperating company. The only
reason she needed either man was because of Ada. One or the
other mattered not at all, as long as she played to their interest in helping her cause.

"I'm coming with you, of course."

"Jacob, do not feel obliged," she said. "This is not your
concern."

Near enough to keep watch on the boiler, Jacob sat beside
her. "You'd have me back at home with Father, mixing chemicals all day. Cruel woman."

She smiled. "But you're a brilliant scholar."

"I have no wish to be. What glory can be found in that?"

"I should find a great deal of glory pursuing alchemy," she
said. "Plenty for my life, leastways."

He laughed, a vaguely condescending sound she disliked.
"And there is the matter of a fair damsel to rescue."

"You're too good for the likes of my sister."

"Ada has not yet broken my heart."

She stood and stretched her legs, arched her back. The sublimation process would take time, and she did not want to spend those minutes discussing alchemy or Ada or Will Scarlet. Not with anyone. She wanted to watch the flames work their magic, but that was impossible.

"In that, Jacob, you're among a lucky few."

Will tugged the wool hood lower over his eyes. He pushed his back against the blunted sandstone wall of the parish church, edging around the corner.

The hamlet of Keyworth boasted no more than a few dozen haphazardly placed, rough-hewn dwellings, but its market married merchants' wares to peasants from the surrounding wood. Women in veils and tunic gowns dulled by long use crisscrossed two dusty cart paths, stitching a pattern of footsteps between the stands as they haggled and traded. Baskets woven of reeds and straw grew fat and heavy. An occasional horse and rider kicked smoke puffs of dry earth into the air, clouding the scene like fog across a lake. Voices melded with animal grunts, the blacksmith's clang, and forest sounds to give heady life to midday.

Beyond the town, encircling its heart like a cage of ribs, lay striped fields of oats and barley being picked clean of their annual yield. Villagers bent and broke and twisted their backs over the warbling furrows. Air painted with chill winds urged those backs, those calloused and practiced hands, to make haste.

Like long rows yet to be harvested, a peasant's days blended together with only ale and rough pleasures to blunt the toil. Will wanted none of it, the routine and hardship. He would not be shackled to the numbing, grinding rhythm of an ordinary life, nor would he sacrifice as he had during those wretched years of outlawry in Sherwood.

Having taken employment with the sheriff to avoid that exact village scene, he imagined days of comfort, early and late. Wealth, women, and song—nothing less would be compensation enough for doing Finch's dirty work.

But easy living and easy choices diverged like a road at a

fork. The inexplicable hex of a certain woman pulled him afar of steadfast goals.

Will shut his eyes, motives blurring. In an ideal sort of day-dream, he would rather bind his future to the first decent-minded liege to have him. But the only decent-minded liege he had ever known bore the name Loxley. Unless he wanted to creep back to Robin's service, he would be better to clear his name, ensure Marian's safety, and start again, maybe somewhere to the south.

All these delays worried him. How much time did he have before Carlisle and Finch would learn of Hendon's demise? How many days remained before they would make good on the threats against Marian and young Robert?

While pinching a measure of sugar from the local apothe-cary seemed at odds with good sense, Meg had him curious. The lye, the explosions in the woods—he honestly wanted to see more, if only to know the extent of her magic and per-haps, if he was lucky, to purge his growing infatuation.

And now he carried a little magic as well. In a bag at his waist, he carried a few dozen of the tiny exploding bundles she had used against Hugo's people. Inside pale twists of linen no bigger than the pad of his thumb, a combination of crushed rock, sawdust, and finely ground black powder gave the bundles their lumpy, nearly spherical shape. She had caught and tamed thunder.

Will would get her sugar. Come morning, he would drag her to Nottingham, if he had to, and be done with this night-mare. And Carlisle, milling among a small cluster of soldiers in the center of Keyworth, would only get in the way.

"What do you see?" Shrouded by a moth-eaten woolen cloak, Dryden met Will's quick downward gaze. Monthemer, alongside him, crouched low and pressed into the shadow of the church wall.

"Carlisle and six soldiers," Will said. "They stand in front of the apothecary."

"Do they have horses? Does anything show to our advantage?"

Will edged an eye around the right angle of the church wall. Innocent villagers interspersed with cluttered terrain. Too many unknown spaces could be filled with potential enemies. Disguised as humble pilgrims, their plan had called for stealth, not an open clash with Nottingham's soldiers—not in that unwise locale.

"Between them they have four horses and a cart pulled by a mule."

Dryden stood carefully, joining Will to watch the commotion. He arranged his cloak to cover all but the essential features of his face and the tips of his fingers. Clasping a walking stick much like Meg's rough branch, he rounded the corner of the church and waited against the front wall, head lowered. He almost appeared penitent.

Across the modest distance, Carlisle's words muddled to gruff, deep tones of impatience. Metal rivets along the seams of his boiled leather armor shone like silver coins among the dirt and dun of the busy market. He directed two of his soldiers, pointing with hands the size and shape of ham hocks.

The armored soldiers, draped in the sheriff's colors, dragged bulging linen sacks from the apothecary's large but shabby hut, to the apparent dismay of the apothecary. The bent, aged man clutched a pouch of what might have been his payment, but his mouth pinched into a tight scowl. He argued with the nearest soldier. They exchanged a vigorous volley of words, none of which traveled intact across the clearing.

The apothecary shook his fist at the laden cart, his face red. The soldier smacked him across the temple. Sprawling on the ground, the elderly man clawed at his head, his shoulders shivering with fear or sobs or unrelieved rage. Townspeople avoided the happening, ducking their heads and hurrying away.

Dryden turned to Will. "What is that they load into the cart?"

Squinting across the square, he shrugged. "Something they cannot obtain in Nottingham, obviously. Makes a body wonder."

"Is this worth the risk?"

"Of course not." A new and more vigorous headache threatened to blur his vision. He pushed against it and fought for a clear head. "But they must have had intentions when they murdered your families, working to create confusion about the perpetrators."

"And why does that concern you?"

"Until my name is cleared of your father's death, I am very concerned with Carlisle's actions. Whatever they want with those supplies may be connected."

Monthemer's pale face shone from within the woolen hood of his pilgrim's cloak. "We could rush them," he whispered.

"No," Will and Dryden said in unison. They glared at each other, then at the young baron.

"There are but five men." Monthemer stood hastily. Eagerness eroded his caution, threatening to expose them all. "We are three, and we have surprise to our aid."

Will restrained him with a forceful fist. "No, I say. Carlisle's no fool. He tucked Whitstowe's lead guard in his pocket. Who knows how many of these poor crofters he's bought?"

"He's right, Stephen." Dryden's usually calm voice spiked with irritation.

"No cause to make a scene here." Will pushed away from the wall and turned to the forest girding the rear of the church. He slapped the younger man on the back, urging his cooperation. "They'll travel back to Nottingham on the road."

Monthemer nodded, still far too enthusiastic. "What about the sugar?"

"Carlisle first. I would like to bid my former leader a good day."

"Hello, Meg."

She dropped a pewter bowl and spun to face the door. "Hugo! You filthy pig. You enjoy surprising me, don't you?"

"You know me to be a lazy man," he said, shuffling into the cabin with his strange, roundabout grace. "I find pleasure in effortless pursuits, and nothing is easier than surprising a blind woman."

She rubbed her upper arms. "Once I let a snake in my bed when I should have chopped it to pieces."

Closer now, standing on the other side of the broad work-table, he laughed. "There was no bed that first night. And the only thing you let me into was your tight cunny."

"Sweet words, Hugo." By all accounts, his nasty remarks should have made her flinch, but she felt only annoyance. And boredom. Their sick association had lasted too long. "I cannot wait to hear more, although I won't believe a one of them."

"You'd rather believe Will Scarlet."

"Hardly."

"Yet you think he'll help you find Ada."

"At present, yes," she said, rounding to the row of shelves and pressing her back into the wood. "Helping me serves his purpose. I intend to accept his aid for as long as he proves useful, but I do not trust him."

"You'll just take him between your legs. I understand. You have no good record of remaining objective when your body craves a man."

She shoved a clamor of voices into a dark corner of her mind. "Say your peace, Hugo. I have work to attend."

"Ah, yes, your precious work." He tossed a jar or pot onto the ground. Meg flinched. The pungent reek of tar rolled through the air. "It's nonsense, I say."

"Or you can leave."

"Why would I? You're a wanted woman. Word has it the sheriff is after you, now that he knows Ada is not an alchemist."

"Who told him? You?"

"You're notorious here in Charnwood. You know that. Maybe someone became a bit too bored, a little too hungry, and de-cided to sell their story. Maybe those poor sods whose huts you set ablaze. You've managed to evade notice for some time, but the forest hasn't given up its eyes and ears." He shambled nearer, standing side by side with her against the shelves. His whisper was conspiratorial. "Or . . ."

"What?"

"Ada. She's not the strongest girl in England, you know. Or the most dependable at minding your back."

"You would know."

"What makes you think she can resist, shall we say, rough questioning?"

His suggestion set her heart beating faster—not simply the idea of Sheriff Finch abusing his female captive. Meg should have been able to shut the door on Hugo and his malicious suggestion, but the festering thought remained: Ada could betray her. She had done before.

"And you would exchange me for a bounty, wouldn't you?" she asked.

"Me? Of course not. Meg, I thought nothing of the sort. Will Scarlet, however . . ."

Her skin went cold. "What of him?"

He played with the end of her sleeve, the one she had singed that morning. Not touching her. Trying to intimidate her. "You didn't hear much of the Robin Hood story when you were busy taking your very long nap."

"No," she said, yanking the sleeve from his fingers. "What I've heard since seems too outlandish to be real."

"You're probably right." He walked to the table. Meg heard the slush of an ale cask as he drank with noisy swallows. He smacked his lips. "Robin of Loxley married Lady Marian DuBois. They were quite in love. When Robin went off to war, Marian stayed behind with Scarlet, her valiant protector. A few months later, he left the manor. He's never been back."

She frowned, fitting disparate pieces together. "Why are you telling me this?"

"Rumor has it that if Scarlet doesn't relinquish you to the sheriff, Finch will set his men on Marian. Seems your boy would do anything to keep that woman safe."

She had no cause to believe the worthless thief, but her

heartbeat accelerated again. Her lungs worked at a furious rate. Since his rescue at the roadside, Scarlet had discovered a new excuse at every turn to stay with her. Emeralds be damned. The idea of his avarice stuck in her gut, as false as her shimmering creations.

But trudging through the forest to ensure the safety of his uncle's wife? *That* was a purpose foolhardy enough to suit Will Scarlet.

"You didn't answer my question, Hugo. Why tell me this?"

"I thought you would appreciate my warning, maybe reward me for being such a thoughtful fellow."

"The Devil you say."

He snickered. "Oh, come now. A little turn for old time's sake? But you'll have to keep those terrible eyes of yours closed. 'Tis daylight, after all."

She turned to the shelves and inhaled deeply. Willing her fingers to be steady, she emptied a container and faced him. "I have something for you. Take this and go."

He hesitated. "Is it false?"

"Of course, but in the right marketplace . . ."

"You're a thief too, Meg," he said, snatching the nugget of imitation gold. "Only a different sort."

"I never want to hear from you again."

He leaned over as if he was going to kiss the back of her hand. Instead he exhaled, raising goose bumps on her skin. She kicked hard and connected with his shin.

Hugo grunted, then laughed. "How fickle is woman."

Only when he was well and truly gone did she collapse to the floor. But she did not cry.

Chapter Thirteen

"And thou, Will Scarlet, take the lead of the others, for
thou hast a cunning turn to thy wits."
—Robin Hood

The Merry Adventures of Robin Hood
Howard Pyle, 1883

Carlisle ambled his gelding out of the tiny hamlet and away
from its sticky swamp-mud souls. He scarcely accepted his position in Nottingham, pale in size and grandeur when compared
to London, but trips into desolate little clusters of humanity like
Keyworth made him want to pluck out eyes—his or someone
else's, it mattered not.

The sooner he returned to the city fortifications with his
swag, the sooner he might indulge in the pleasures of the upcoming feast. And take a bath. He would return to the com-
forts of his residence, a sanctuary of luxury and far-flung
treasures that never failed to soothe his pride after bouts of
menial service.

Yes, life at the sheriff's behest proved advantageous. For
the moment.

However, Carlisle readily imagined a time when his association with Peter Finch would end. Abruptly and permanently.

The man proved surprisingly timid and much too cautious, despite the macabre plan he had instigated.

Since when did amassing power involve a girl magician? Successful men bought power, and when they could not, they pried it from their betters' grasp at the point of a sword. Chicanery and plotting ill suited him and wore at his patience.

No matter. Soon enough, and with the predictability of the morn, Finch would make a mistake. Carlisle simply awaited the moment when he might turn that mistake to his gain. Wealth. Leadership. A return to London.

Atop his mount, trailing at a casual pace behind the mule cart, he shined a bit of armor soiled by flecks of mud. He spent scant moments among those disgusting people, but the pungent stench of piss and wet loam grasped like the hand of a man in his death throes. He may as well have concluded his business in a mud hole, speaking in grunts and snorts with a herd of swine.

A sudden crack of thunder at the road's edge startled the lead horse. The animal screeched and reared, nearly discarding its rider. Two cloaked men, one with a sword and one with a bow, jumped from their concealments. Carlisle's mount shied and turned its neck to the rear. A third swordsman, also disguised by coarse woolen hood, strode from the foliage to complete a circle around them.

For the span of a finger snap, he awaited the petty outlaws' demands. But the cloaked men merely readied their weapons.

Carlisle almost admired their directness.

"Get them!"

The forward swordsman thrashed at Carlisle's paired foot soldiers—soldiers that could have been carved from oak for how promptly they responded. The assailant hacked with sure, rhythmic strokes. In a bloody, brawling rush, the procession of six dropped to four.

The two rear guards vied with their lone opponent. Swords flashed and clanged, an extension of arms and stretching, reaching shoulders. The lone man at Carlisle's back held off the mounted soldiers with quick, practiced skill. Only his cloak seemed to impede his abilities. He swished the lengthy garment behind him, revealing a full coat of mail.

He was no amateur bandit.

Carlisle's impatience burgeoned. His remaining men parried like inexperienced whelps, suddenly clumsy atop their steeds. He cared not for their fate but did not wish to squander the scant bodies between him and their adversaries.

The forward swordsman, his weapon dripping clots of red, came for him. He grunted, connecting his boot heel with his challenger's forehead. The sick thump of wood against bone brought a smile to Carlisle's face. The man stumbled back, then collapsed. The hood of his cloak flew away, revealing the blond head of Stephen, Baron of Monthemer. A crescent of skull and blood showed beneath the skin at his hairline.

Questions flashed as quickly as lightning. Carlisle knew Monthemer was a useless, eager madcap, but a spontaneous raid at midday was beyond the young nobleman's capacity. He turned, intent on discovering the identities of the remaining pair.

The archer, quiver indiscriminately strapped over his cloak, flailed at his back for an arrow. He missed once, twice, then pulled one free. Clumsy hands scraped the shaft. Flecks of white goose feather caught the wind, disappearing into the woods.

Sighting the mail-clad soldier atop the mule cart, the archer may have aimed true, but without the fletching for direction, the arrow flew wide. The driver snatched his reprieve from death and whipped the mule with frantic strokes. The cart lurched forward, finding momentum enough to roll over the arm of one of the limp bodies.

The lead soldier wrestled with the reins of his horse, spooked from the sharp noise that had precipitated the attack. He yanked hard, body straining, and swiveled the animal into an offensive position. Sword drawn, he swung his weapon at the archer, slicing through nothing but cloth. A flutter of wool fell to the ground.

Unscathed, the archer jumped free on nimble feet. He

rounded a tree, scampered atop a boulder, and aimed—not at his mounted opponent, charging fast, but again at the cart driver. Efficiency replaced clumsiness. At a hundred paces, his stance wide and relaxed, he smoothly slid an arrow through the thick forest air. Lethal steel punctured the base of the driver's skull, lodging in the scant inch of space between his mail and helmet.

The archer did not watch the man slump and fall. He turned his deadly aim to the useless horseman at the front of the procession. Another arrow flew. The soldier screamed and clutched the shaft where it pierced his eye. His body thrashed in spasms. Maniac screams redoubled, becoming forest-bred echoes. The terrified horse bucked and tossed the dead man from its back, running for the forest.

Looping the longbow over his shoulder, the archer watched the horse's undaunted flight. Sighting the target, he leapt from his rocky perch and landed astride the animal. He yanked fiercely on the reins. The steed reared and kicked, a vicious brawler, but it could not buck free of the unwanted rider.

Behind him, Carlisle heard a yelp. The other swordsman dispatched the first of two mounted foes. A gurgle of blood darkened the earth. Free of its rider, a horse ran in the direction of Keyworth. The remaining horseman swiveled his mount. Lashing hooves knocked the man to his hands and knees, his sword clattered free of his lax grip. Carlisle's last man raised his arm back, ready to slice with a downward arc.

Across the insipid remains of the procession, the archer drew his last arrow. Carlisle could not believe what he witnessed. Archers did not, could not aim from horseback. They stood on solid ground for a reason. But the man's arrow and uncanny aim found a chunk of vulnerable flesh beneath the soldier's raised arm. The last guard arched his back and screamed, succumbing to the arrow's deadly purpose. His sword clattered uselessly to the ground.

The archer, still mounted, tossed his bow aside and reached to draw a sword from under his billowing cloak.

Carlisle twirled his horse, futilely seeking aid but found

none among the corpses. An unusual taste of bitter fear coated his tongue. He wasted no more time assessing the loss or the odds. Kicking hard heels into stubborn horseflesh, he raced from the scene.

Will jumped free of his wild mount. Holding the reins against the horse's angry struggle, he tunneled his heels into the yielding ground. Mild nonsense words bubbled from his mouth, but nothing would soothe the crazed animal.

Across the road, Dryden stood and walked on wobbling legs. He ducked free of his cloak with stiff movements. Dizziness slid across his features. After taking a knee, he handed up the cloak.

Will looped the length of wool over the horse's head. The enfolding darkness quickly eased its frenzied fight. Moments later, the animal calmed and stilled, but a peculiar sense of unease came over him. Unlike horses, humans found no solace in blindness. In fact, blindness created shadows and specters out of the most innocuous words, touches, and sounds. Horses implicitly trusted their handlers, resigning their fates to cooler heads, but humans fought giving up control and held memory enough to lament their loss.

Annoyed to find reason for thinking about Meg—worse yet, to sympathize with her situation—he led his new horse to a birch. He securely looped the reins to a trunk layered in scaly white bark and fetched the other horse, tying it near the first.

Dryden pulled to his feet and stood over the soldier Will had pinned in the eye. "Good work."

"If I hadn't lost that first arrow, I could've taken Carlisle too, maybe to question him. But until yesterday, I hadn't held a bow in years."

"I cannot imagine your aim if you'd time to practice." Dryden pulled free of a leather gauntlet. "You have my thanks, Scarlet. You saved my life."

Will shook the nobleman's trembling hand.

A low groan startled them both. They turned to see Monthemer on the ground, clutching his mangled forehead. The young man groaned again and pulled his knees close, roiling in the dirt.

Dryden walked unsteadily to his cousin. "Have you decided to join us among the living, Stephen?"

They knelt next to the young baron. Mingled blood and sweat coated his face, tinting his pale blond hair an ugly, brassy orange. Will shed his cloak and used its tattered wool to scrape past the sticky mess. Dryden pried his cousin's clenched hands from his forehead. A crescent-shaped expanse of skull refused to rest modestly beneath muscle and skin.

Monthemer grunted, doubled over, then vomited. More a moan than language, he asked, "How is it?"

"I've had worse, and likely you have too." Will pulled his anlace from its sheath and carefully cut the man from his encumbering cloak. He wound strips of the wool around Monthemer's wound, purposefully blinding a second living creature in a span of minutes. He exchanged a concerned look with Dryden but kept his voice calm. "Meg will set you to rights. You'll smell of some curiosity, but you'll live."

Dryden wadded what was left of Monthemer's cloak into a makeshift pillow and stuffed it beneath his cousin's head. "Rest for a moment."

Will again eyed the man's trembling hands. "How did you fare? Injured?"

"That second horse of yours kicked me."

"He wasn't mine at the time. I take no responsibility for his disrespect."

Dryden grinned half-heartedly, standing once again. "Let us see what manner of plunder we've acquired for our troubles."

The pair found the patient, abandoned mule chewing a bit of scrubby foliage at the road's edge. Around the back of the cart, Will nicked a tiny hole in one of the two bulging linen sacks and gingerly tasted its contents. "Everyone has a craving for sweets today. 'Tis sugar."

Dryden passed him a frown. "What would they want with all that sugar?"

"Well, *we* want it. Carlisle thoughtfully saved us a second trip into Keyworth."

"Would anyone else know Meg's tricks? Maybe that sister of hers?"

Will bit back a laugh. "You think I understand the woman?"

"You've spent time with her, certainly," Dryden said. "Is she prone to lies?"

His laugh escaped, harsh and exasperated. "She would argue day is night if she thought deception would suit her aim. But your question remains. Why would Carlisle want sugar, or Finch for that matter? Not to make smoke. That makes no sense, no matter Meg's truth or lies."

"I am not partial to the situation."

"That much is obvious," Will said. "I'm hardly partial to the two of you, but at least we work toward the same end."

Dryden smiled, a look of such cold cunning that Will felt the urge to retract even the tentative trust he had mustered for the man. "I cannot claim to know your aims, Scarlet, but I wish Carlisle's head on a plate and served to Finch. At knifepoint."

"Well said," he replied, suppressing a shudder. But the nobleman's words sparked a sudden idea. "Wait, what day is this?"

Able to deliver only a blank stare and a shrug, Dryden tossed the question to his cousin. Monthemer moaned nothing useful.

"None of us knows the day of the week." Will shook his head, disgusted. "The forest is barbaric. Spend too many nights in the trees and we abandon all hope of civilization."

"Why do you ask?"

"When does the harvest feast begin in Nottingham?"

"This week, I believe. What are you thinking?"

Panic skimmed across his mind—panic and a distinct call to abandon the entire mess of the last few days. "You insist on looking to me for answers. Why?"

"Since you seemed apt to providing useful ones."

"A subtlety," Will said at last. "Perhaps they intend to make a subtlety for the feast."

"That fares well."

It did. The tradition of subtleties—sumptuous carved sugar statues presented for feast days—fit the timing of harvest. And such a boastful creation might suit Nottingham well if he intended to display his mounting influence.

He hoisted a sack onto his good shoulder and froze. Staring wide-eyed at what lay beneath the sacks of sugar, his questions piled high.

Puzzlement spread across Dryden's face. "What is that?"

"More's the question, what did Carlisle want with it?" Will passed quick eyes across the trees and the quiet thoroughfare. "I'll pose that question to a certain young woman we know."

Chapter Fourteen

[A]nd we shall hang all the trees with flowers, and we shall strew all the ground with flowers, and we shall dance with flowers . . .

Maid Marian
Thomas Love Peacock, 1822

Meg tried not to breathe.

She had long since acclimated to the unpleasant odors of her pursuits, but laboring within the niter beds tested her tolerance. Because Jacob had done more than his share, tending the furnace and watching the boiler, he was off practicing swordplay against the nearest offending trees. That left her to battle nausea as she leached the niter beds of their precious, foul-smelling liquid.

After collecting a large container's worth, she went back to the cabin where Jacob had placed the boiler to cool. She wiped hands on the lowest folds of her gown, searching for a scant inch of fabric left unsullied by the beds.

She held still, listening. Jacob's dull thwack of metal against wood sounded in the middle distance to the south. Otherwise, the forest was as still as she was, holding its breath in unison. She was alone. And for the moment, she convinced herself that solitude was a blessing.

Instead of tending the remainder of the formula, she approached the bench running parallel to the long eating table. Meals, experiments, studies—the table had hosted the mellow routine of her former life.

Life with her father. Life with Ada. Lives that no longer existed.

Bracing her walking stick on the floor, gaining traction with the soles of her boots, she stood slowly. The bench did not wobble. She reached high, searching through the open air. Edging farther along the length of the bench, she lifted a hand toward the ceiling. Sweat tickled the back of her neck and beneath her lowest ribs, but she continued.

Scarlet had to be wrong.

But he was not.

She grazed a flutter of petals as crisp as the autumn leaves. The flowers she touched, the flowers she pulled from the rafters and woven thatching, had been carefully dried. In the span of a few feet, she gathered six petite bundles. Crinkling petals tickled her fingertips and sounded like the last, quietest sigh of a dying fire. She tucked her nose among the neatly tied bundles but could find no perfume to distinguish variety.

She sat heavily on the bench. Scarlet said three dozen bunches decorated the cabin. Three dozen times, Ada had worked to preserve a collection of wildflowers. Three dozen times, she had used the table to fasten them to the ceiling.

And three dozen times, Meg had been too distracted to notice.

A ruckus outside the cabin caught her attention. Unexplained guilt stung her cheeks. She stood and turned, thinking of where to hide the flowers. Hide them in her own cabin. Hide the shame of having lived like a stranger with her own sister.

She found her father's fat, tattered book and opened its warped pages. Dozens of letters from his great-uncle Adelard of Bath, the famous tutor to King Richard's late father, Henry II, stuck out in disarray. She knew the feel of each one. She could no longer see the ornate scrawls of the famous scholar's handwriting, but she knew what they contained: observations, translations, theories about the natural world, and tales of Adelard's far travels.

Fingering the pages, she imagined the wonder of that distant relative, his travels and his marvelous ideas. Her father had read the letters to her and Ada like a balladeer, sparking curiosities and questions. They added to the undertaking with their own observations, ever expanding the scope of their family heritage.

And to that heritage, Meg added the flowers. She carefully pressed the dried bunch against the cured leather of the back cover and touched the flaking petals.

"They're pretty," Scarlet said.

She slammed the book closed and whirled. Dried petals gave way with a dull crunch. He walked to her, filling the tight span of the cabin with the distinctive tingle of his presence. She shivered.

"You climbed up for them?"

"Go away."

Hugo had stood next to her not three hours before, piercing repellent remarks through her defenses. But Scarlet set her senses alight, intimidating her with a different sort of menace. Even at a respectful distance, the heat of his body called to her. He smelled of sweat and leather and warm metal—primal, dangerous. She turned and gripped the thick binding of her book, keeping her hands from him.

"What is that?"

"'Tis no matter for you."

"And I suppose your sudden interest in dried flowers is none of my concern either."

A sudden awareness of how she must look and smell threatened a blush. She should have been happy to have the filth of the niter beds at her ready defense, but Scarlet made her unforgivably self-conscious, especially after his disgusted reaction to the unfortunate smell of her home.

She scratched a thumbnail across her lower lip, remembering Hugo's warning. By the Devil, she despised the idea of believing a man who lived to cause confusion and woe. But he was right. Will Scarlet was dangerous.

"Leave me be."

"No," he said. "We need your help with Monthemer. He's been injured. Dryden is retrieving him from the horses."

Pretending a quick inhale gave her courage, she nodded and pushed the smashed flowers from her mind. *Her* cabin. *Her* life. None of his concern.

"What happened?"

"Carlisle planted a boot heel in his forehead."

"Carlisle was in Keyworth?"

Scarlet sighed heavily, his weariness like a solid wall. "Yes, and the apothecary was none too happy to have his patronage."

Dryden and Scarlet dragged Monthemer to the pallet and recounted their trip and the ensuing skirmish.

Jacob returned from the woods. "Of course, I stay behind to boil rocks while your lot faces the sheriff's men."

Meg knelt beside the pallet next to Scarlet. He pulled her hands to Monthemer's forehead, helping her assess the extent of his injury. Warm blood slicked her fingers.

Dryden shuffled behind them in an anxious clatter of mail. "How will he fare?"

"By the saints, I believe Carlisle must have worn a blade on his heel," she said. "The laceration is deep. He'll require stitches."

"I can do them," Dryden said. "Do you have anything for his pain?"

"I do, milord."

Scarlet snuffed a bit of laughter but made no comment about the sedative. "Come with me, Jacob. You can help unload the sugar. No swordplay necessary, I'm afraid."

For an hour, Meg worked with Dryden to staunch the fast flow of his cousin's blood. She crushed wolfsbane flowers into a paste while the nobleman threaded a needle and laid the stitches. Their patient moaned on occasion, but he remained unconscious and still. She dabbed the completed stitches with a cleansing salve before wrapping his head in long strips of linen, leaving him to rest.

"You both do nice work," Scarlet said upon returning to the cabin.

Dryden sighed heavily. "I only wish I could've saved him the injury."

"Meg, you need to tell us: What purpose could Finch and Carlisle have for the sugar?"

She dipped her hands in a bucket of water and washed away the sticky blood. "With regard to alchemy?"

"Yes," Scarlet said. "Could your sister have told them of your spells?"

"They're not spells."

"Fine." His voice was like the tang of vinegar. "Could your sister have revealed any of your magic?"

She bit back a curse but considered his question. Yes, her sister helped note observations and read aloud portions of their father's ancient book, but her interest in alchemy only extended to the point of obliging Meg. She had always been more intrigued by the exotic languages contained within their book, not the facts and formulas.

"I think not," she said at last.

"Perhaps the sugar was intended for the harvest feast after all."

Dryden cleared his throat. "Did you tell her about the copper?"

"What copper?"

"This way," Scarlet said. Curiosity compelled her to obey. She followed him outdoors and toward the milling horses. A sharp clang spiked the air as something metallic tumbled heavily to the ground. "*That* copper."

Kneeling, frowning, she touched three slabs of smooth metal as wide as a man's body and half as long. Scarlet knelt beside her, the hard leather of his knee-guards creaking. "We found it in Carlisle's cart, concealed beneath the bags of sugar. What purpose would they have for it?"

She stroked the copper, trying to find imperfections with

her sensitive fingertips. The metal proved flawless, smooth, even at the corners and edges. "What is its color?"

"Shall I be poetic?"

"Merely descriptive," she said, shaking her head. Excitement and fireflies of apprehension made her giddy. "Can you see any variations in its color? Any streaks or flaws? Jacob—come help him look, please."

Jacob and Dryden joined the examination. Meg waited. Despite her concern, she amused herself by imagining their scrutiny, all three men hunched over the slabs. "Anything?"

"Flawless," Dryden said.

She nodded. "Cyprian, then."

"I would guess," Jacob said. "Although I've only heard of copper this pure."

"What does that mean?"

Scarlet's audible confusion fused with her fear, a fear for her sister's safety. Nausea lurched in her gut. She imagined an array of horrors, all in dazzling color.

"It means the sheriff has discovered a way to make Ada talk."

He split another log with a long-handled ax. Although his shoulder throbbed, protesting the strenuous labor and that morning's exploits against Carlisle, Will enjoyed the release to his frustrations. The strain of chopping enough wood for the furnace heaved breath after breath from his body, but physical pain was easier to bear than his perpetual confusion.

Jacob, returning to fill his arms with another load of wood, stopped near the chopping block. Black hair curled even tighter along his sweaty hairline, his face open and amiable as if sketched by an amused artist. He had been a fountain of inquiries throughout the late afternoon, peppering the air with requests for true stories of Robin Hood. Will humored him, intent on finding answers of his own.

"How did she go blind? Do you know?"

Jacob grinned widely, almost derisively, as if he had been

waiting for the questions. It bothered him that even an inexperienced boy like Jacob could fathom his purposes.

"You ask her, Scarlet."

"I'm asking you."

"Afraid?"

"I want a simple answer. I haven't the resolve for another fight today."

Jacob's expression sobered, reminding Will of the quick efficiency he demonstrated with the crossbow and his strange, curved knives. The calm killer wore a jester's mask.

"She grew ill about five years ago. The symptoms appeared no worse than a mild ague. A fever, chills, an intense sensitivity to light. Vile headaches began." Jacob paused, wiping palms along his breeches and squatting near the block. "I learned all of this after, of course, from my father. Eventually she fell asleep."

Will scowled and joined him, crouching low. "Fell asleep?"

"For six months, yes."

"Impossible."

He raised his hands. "I tell you true. When she awoke, she could not see, but neither could she remember anything."

Will suffered a disconcerting stab of regret for her. The trauma of losing her sight must have been devastating, and yet she endured. She created a life for herself in the woods, a life he had unsettled by seizing Ada. Guilt wove through his ligaments.

"She raved like an animal," Jacob said. "Ada stayed with her and talked her through those weeks, so she told me. Her memory returned, but rumors spread that she had gone mad, or worse, that she had been possessed by the Devil."

Mad Meg.

The woodsmen's frightened words echoed, bringing with them a shudder of understanding. To be completely cut from society because of an illness—he could not comprehend the damage she must have endured. She and her family both.

"And her father?"

"He began a quest to restore her eyesight." Jacob squinted and rubbed his eyes, like a child on the verge of sleep. "Ada said he had been the best sort of man. But after Meg's blindness, all that mattered was a cure—one he never discovered."

"Talking about me, Jacob?"

Meg stood a few paces away. Bathed in the deepening glow of early evening, she may as well have worn a veil for how little her face revealed. Impassive. Empty. Not even the set of her shoulders or the angle of her jaw indicated her mood. Upon finding herself the subject of still more talk, she bore the discovery as would a statue.

"Too bad, Scarlet," Jacob said, grinning broadly. "You haven't avoided that argument after all."

Whereas Will expected him to flee, Jacob simply and patiently filled his arms with another load of wood before departing.

"You could've asked me," she said.

Her cold tone dared him to fight. The sad, fatigued cast of her face—framed by a dark cowl and layered in shadows—nudged at a callous part of him. But he had been truthful to Jacob. The idea of battling her again wore a hole in his skull.

With more force than skill, he imbedded the ax head into the block. "I could have, but I asked Jacob."

She turned and strode back toward the cabin.

An old humiliation propelled her across open ground to the forest. Finding Scarlet and Jacob in conversation about her illness harkened back to the moment she had discovered Ada with Hugo. That sense of betrayal. That shove of disappointment. Her hands trembled, acknowledging how deeply the disappointment tunneled into her soul. She had no notion of being liked by Scarlet, but she suffered a disturbing need to be respected, perhaps because she had already behaved in ways that would banish any good man's respect.

He pursued, his long strides making a noisy hash of the

leaves around her cabin. Meg braced her body and mind, but she still flinched when he took hold of her upper arm.

"Wait, please," he said. "How fares Monthemer?"

"He's resting. Dryden has care of him."

Scarlet dropped his hand. "That makes me glad. He fought well today, if impetuously."

"Were you injured?"

She wanted to snatch the small question out of the air and smash it beneath her boot heel. His tenuous value to her quest did not justify the shadow of worry following her since his dawn departure for Keyworth.

He held still and silent. She felt how he scrutinized her, perhaps as surprised as she was by her concern.

"Gramercy, no," he said softly. "I made good use of the bow."

"Dryden said as much." A smile pulled at her lips, working against her foul humor. "He said you appeared as comfortable with the bow as if it had been your own hands."

"Dryden exaggerates."

"That is not in keeping with his nature. Either way, I should examine your shoulder when you finish chopping wood."

"Why?"

Because I enjoy torturing myself. Because I want to touch you.

She swallowed heavily. "To check for signs of infection."

"If you want me out of my tunic, you only have to ask."

"I should let it fester until your arm rots," she said, her cheeks on fire.

"That's hardly charitable."

"Better than you deserve."

He leaned closer, slowly, his breath warming her cheek. "Open your mouth."

Her lungs shuddered to a halt. "What?"

"I said, open your mouth. I have something for you."

"You're being absurd." Her heart was a terrified animal, shivering and demanding flight. But her feet refused to move.

"Trust that at this moment I have no notion of doing you harm."

The soft timbre of his voice nestled seductive images behind her eyes. She pinched them shut. "And why should I trust you?"

"I fear your ability to transform into a ball-twisting wench."

"You deserved that."

"Blessed be, woman, no man deserves that." He edged closer still, his hair tickling the skin of her forehead. He slipped a hand around the base of her neck, softly kneading and massaging her tense muscles. She may as well have been a kitten held by its scruff, so completely did he imprison her. "Open your mouth before I have to hold you down and pry your lips apart."

Every sharp retort and defensive reply shriveled to naught. She swallowed the pathetic whimper that wanted to beg for mercy, some reprieve from the onslaught. First Hugo and his hideous, baiting insults. Then Scarlet—the worry and guesses and vain attempts to understand him. Protecting against his influence was like trying to catch smoke. He was some powerful potion in masculine form, intent on driving her to madness.

"Open for me, Meg."

The intimate nature of his command shocked her. Dread flared, digging into her bones and settling between her legs. A throbbing ache blossomed, her body thriving on a spiteful blend of danger and curiosity. Heat licked over her skin like flames, setting good sense ablaze.

She opened her mouth.

He touched his finger to her tongue. An explosion of sweetness enveloped her mouth, nearly buckling her knees with the unexpected pleasure. Thought fled. She closed her lips around his finger and sucked, discovering every last crystal of sugar he offered.

Scarlet pulled his finger free. His breath was fast, strained, and very close. "More?"

She gave the smallest nod. He petted her lower lip, painting tiny grains along her thin, sensitive skin. She caught his finger again and licked the sweetness. The hand at the back of her neck tightened, near to pain. A combination of man and sugar swathed her tongue, slid down her throat, set her body on fire. Her breasts felt heavy and hot. A familiar hollowness opened inside her, aching to be filled. He offered more sugar. But she wanted more of him.

She swirled her tongue around his finger, sucking again. He moaned and shuddered. She could take no more. Burrowing eager fingers into a shaggy length of hair, she dragged his face to hers. Lips met in a heady explosion of heat and sweetness. His tongue thrust into her mouth. The syrupy remains of the sugar mingled with his own spice. His arms circled her back, deepening the kiss. Tight nipples crushed against the solid leather shielding his chest, arousing and frustrating her in turn.

Her hips found his. The insistent ridge of his erection offered proof of his desire. He groaned her name and arched her back, dusting quick, hard kisses along the length of her neck. She resented the high bodice that barred him from traveling lower, but flicks of his tongue wet a trail to one ear. He nibbled and suckled, threading his fingers into her hair. Lightheaded, she clung to his body as if a heartsick year had passed since she last held him, since he last held her.

Will.

And like a drowning woman finding a single gulp of air, she found herself.

Chapter Fifteen

How many miles is it to thy true love?
Come tell me without any guile.

"Robin Hood and Allin a Dale"
Folk ballad, seventeenth century

Sugar and Meg, softness and heat—their kisses were a fantasy come to life. She had held fast, bending and molding into his body, into his mind, until oblivion seemed a near and brilliant promise. And then she fled.

What went awry?

Minutes of stumbling through the moon-bathed forest brought him to Meg. She stood in the center of a circle of mature birch trees, illuminated by a waning crescent of light. Her slender arms wrapped around her face, clasping the whole of her head in a ferocious hold. She clenched fingers into her scalp, pulling hard. Her cries echoed like wild spirits through the woods, sending a quiver of fear up the muscles of his back.

He hated the woods, but her wails and whimpers made that otherworldly scene a nightmare.

Quieting, she lowered inelegant arms to her sides, shaking with manic force. An impatient gesture sent her dark green cowl to the forest floor. She lowered her head, tossing long hair until it fell like a waterfall of dark tangles and curls, from scalp to waist.

And she began to twirl. The filthy hem of her gown skimmed mud and grass. Her languorous movement followed the swaying trees, and the pale moon lit her lean features.

A little troubled by the pantomime, Will watched in fascination. Catching hold of her gown's full skirts, she swung from side to side. Swaying. Weaving. Twirling became spinning, spinning in full circles of frenzied energy. She moved ever faster until collapsing into the leaves. There she sat, panting.

A resigned sigh pushed into the evening air. He rolled his wounded shoulder, but a pain borne of more than his plaguing injury stabbed his brain. Huddled into herself, she appeared no more grown or brave than a child, trembling and abandoned. Yet somewhere in that pathetic creature lived a fierce woman.

"Why do you twirl?"

She jerked her head. "Were you watching me?"

He crossed to the center of the tiny clearing. Pushing his scabbard behind him, he sat beside her and crossed his legs. "Calm yourself."

"No, I will not. I cannot abide when . . . when I am—"

"At a disadvantage. Such as when you find Jacob and I talking about you."

"Yes."

"Forgive me. I meant no—I should have asked you directly." Careless of his shoulder, he flopped on his back. He groaned and settled into the yielding ground. "You have my attention. That is all."

She pulled at the flesh of a leaf, leaving only a stem and a few skeletal veins. "Once, when I was shaking the skirt of my gown and became dizzy, I thought—I thought I saw color."

"Have you since?"

"No. But I keep trying."

Forged of equal parts pain and hopefulness, her thin voice became a blade that slipped between his ribs. Her vulnerability dared him to resist the impulse to protect her. Antagonism melted like a shard of ice on skin.

"Be honest with me," he said. "Would you have admitted such a thing to Hugo?"

"No."

"And why not?"

"He would've ridiculed me for it."

"Remember that, Meg," he said. "Think twice before putting me on the same level as that low bastard."

He sat up, bringing his mouth nearly to hers. He could lean. She could advance. They could find an unlikely occasion to laugh. Any movement would bring them together. Again. The prospect fired his blood with a blend of anticipation and ire. He did not want to crave this woman, nor did he want to feel protective of her. But he did. He did with a fierceness that stole wit and reason. The need to kiss her again was a sore sweetness—sweet like the sugar on her tongue.

"Why did you do it?" Her whisper brushed his lips with humid warmth. "Working for the sheriff?"

Confusion and something akin to regret forced him to pull away. Such a complicated mess. And he hated every pathetic minute of it.

"Nottingham is corrupt," he said. "Openly so. I grew tired of living off moneyed acquaintances, but neither did I fancy a life of impoverishment. Finch pays handsomely for men who can uphold his version of the law."

"And what of Ada?"

"Carlisle told us that the sheriff sought a reliable alchemist. Any man who could provide one would be given a bonus and the chance to become one of Finch's personal guards."

She frowned, dark brows pulling together. "The chance?"

"That was my purpose along the Nottingham road." A shiver of memory climbed his neck, reliving the tension and disgust of those moments before the ambush. "I had been in Finch's employ for near on a year. I was to prove my loyalty as a member of his personal cadre, with Carlisle as our leader.

Now, I believe the entire test was a net to catch whatever dimwitted fool balked at Lord Whitstowe's murder—and pin the crime on him."

"You."

"Yes."

"You did all of this for money."

"Yes," he said heavily. "And there is no pride to find in that."

"You feel guilty?"

"Don't make me a saint, Meg."

Glassy eyes narrowed. "I wouldn't think of it, not when I'm buying your help with counterfeit emeralds. God's teeth, but I cannot understand you."

"Me? You—you're a puzzle for the ages. You're as fearless as you are afraid."

"I have good cause."

"Why, because you're blind? Do you really think this would be easier if you could see?"

"It could be." Discarding the remnants of a stripped leaf, she picked up another and started again. "Yes, it would be. Because I could see that you are looking at me."

"Who else would I be looking at?"

She dipped her head, looking nauseous. Realization hit him like a rock to the temple.

"Oh," he said. "This is about Hugo, isn't it? Hugo and your sister."

"How did you know?"

"When he kissed you, I overheard." He exhaled, his anger lifting high. "By my thrift, Meg, what did they do?"

Like a nervous bird, her eyes darted quick paths through the shadows. "He started to visit me at the cabin after Father died. After how I'd been treated, I enjoyed how he flaunted society's expectations, playing everyone for fools with his thieving. I had no one in the world but Ada, and then I had Hugo too. I was happy. We . . . eventually, he and I . . . because I wanted to—"

Choking, her voice died a quick death.

Will wanted two minutes alone again with Hugo, not even

so greedy as to require a weapon. Bare hands would ably mete the man's punishment. But bitterness followed closely on the heels of his violent fantasies. How had he behaved any better than the thief?

She rubbed her nose with the back of her hand. "He broke every rule, and I was fool enough to believe he'd make an exception for me. He would sit in the same room with my sister and me, smiling at her throughout. He flirted with her, and I couldn't see what happened right in front of me."

"How did you discover the truth?"

"I found them in the woods outside the cabin. They were *laughing* at me, at how gullible I was. Ada joined him in mocking my blindness. When I revealed myself, Hugo fled and Ada confessed to their tryst."

"She was remorseful?"

"She blamed me. She said caring for me resigned her to a life in isolation, that she may as well be blind too. That's when I convinced her to sell the emeralds for me."

Frustration pounded at his patience. She had played every possible sentiment against him from the moment of their first encounter, and still he could not decipher true emotion from manipulation. Apparently, she was not above treating her sister with the same base contempt and lack of regard.

Bitterness settled in his mouth like a canker. "Convinced? Or coerced?"

"She owed me! Don't slake your frustrations on me," she said, her words a snarl. "When you come to speaking terms with your uncle, I'll reconcile with Ada."

"Then you will be estranged for quite some time."

"So be it."

"But why trample across the countryside to save her? Why?"

"I love her." He began to protest, but she lifted a silencing hand. "She's all I have. I cannot trust her, I know, but I want things to go back to the way they were. Before Hugo."

"And you've pinned your hopes on that?" He shook his head and channeled his anger into bunched fists. "Hear me when I say life doesn't behave so courteously. Sometimes you cannot go back."

"And what would you rather me do? You, Will Scarlet—the man with a sure and clear understanding of his earthly purpose."

"What does that mean?"

After finding her cowl among the leaves, she stood hastily. "Do you or do you not have influential family who could intervene on your behalf against the sheriff?"

"It's not like that—"

"Instead, you shun their help," she said, tucking her hair into the headdress. "You take to the woods, which you *loathe,* with a blind girl, a Jewish boy, and a forest of people who'd have your head if not for a nobleman who tried to kill you. What answers do you hold to with such certainty?"

"I know you make this very difficult."

He took to his feet and led her back to the cabin.

"Will?"

At the first instance of his given name on her lips, he nearly stopped. But if he stopped, he would kiss her again. If he kissed her, this nasty new habit of making difficult choices would become a permanent way of life.

"Will, what were you going to say?"

"Caring," he said over his shoulder. "You make it very difficult to care what happens to you."

Into a waking darkness, Meg opened her eyes and gasped for a cool breath. Damp night air pressed into her mouth, drying her tongue. Try as she did to cleanse her mind of a dream, she found no relief. An imagined dance of limbs, hands, and mouths claimed her. Its fiery resonance coated her mind and slicked the insides of her thighs.

As her heartbeat slowed, she resented Will for the intrusion. But forgetting the heated pleasure of their encounter proved impossible. His voice, his scent, and every infuriating trait battered against her otherwise stalwart will.

And the kisses.

She wanted to run from him, but good sense had become mired in a sludge of passions. She could not even retreat to the privacy of sleep and the magic of dream fire. He followed her.

Sitting up quietly and slowly, she imagined the contours of the cabin's interior to orient herself. Somewhere near the door, Jacob slept heavily, snoring through his mouth. Will occupied a length of floor parallel to her worktable, while Dryden had constructed a makeshift pallet near his cousin's bed. He intended to minister to Monthemer's needs through the night.

Playfulness crept across her mouth, pulling her farther from the troubling, frankly sexual dream. Other than Jacob, she and Ada never had guests in the cabin. The room barely had space enough to accommodate a few bodies under and around the furniture.

Yet in her sister's absence, Meg accidentally hosted four guests. Four men slept under her roof. She should have been scandalized or terrified, but scandal had long since lost its teeth. As for the terror she ought to feel, surrounded in the dark by the drastically varied male creatures, she could not muster the energy for terrible scenarios. The previous few days had created predicaments worthy of a woman's worst nightmares.

And of those four men, only one truly frightened her.

A moan rattled her thoughts. She jerked toward Monthemer's pallet. For the barest moment, her fading dream pushed to the fore, bringing with it the memory of groans and whimpers. She dug into the skin along her temples, wanting to scrape the surface of her brain and erase those taunting memories.

She froze and listened for the next sound. Another moan? Dryden awakening? Dim echoes of once-hearty flames sizzled delicately in the fire pit. Outside, offering the first indication as to the hour, an ambitious lark began its tentative ode to the distant dawn.

Another moan from Monthemer's pallet.

"Milord?"

Her whispered call to Dryden barely disturbed the night-quiet room. No reply. She tugged a cloak over her shoulders and crossed the scant distance to Monthemer's side. The pale stench of blood and wolfsbane pinched inside her nostrils. "Milord?"

"Here."

She clapped hands over her mouth to keep from yelping.

"Sorry," he said. "I thought I should say something, rather than taking hold of your arm."

She nodded. "How is he? I heard him stir."

"You needn't concern yourself, Meg. I said I would tend to him, should he need care."

"He is patient to us both. I wish to know how he fares." She knelt and grazed a hand. "Yours or his?"

"What?"

"His hand, then."

Monthemer moaned again. She felt for fever, but his skin remained cool. He neither flinched nor roused when she found the strips of linen encasing the upper portion of his skull.

"I gave him more wolfsbane."

"Really?" She leaned nearer the unconscious man, again catching the sluggish scent of the potent flower. "To his wound?"

"No, by mouth."

She wondered if Dryden could see her displeasure, or whether his view of the cabin, encased in night, might prove as dark as hers. "I administered quite enough before you completed the sutures."

"He was moaning more fervently a few moments ago." An edge of impatience emerged when he said, "I've dealt with the plant before."

"Too much could slow his respiration to the point of death."

"Yes," Dryden said, sighing. "But just enough will permit him a restful sleep."

Meg sucked her lower lip. Even as she let the disagreement drop, she knew it would have worsened into an argument had Will been her opponent. But which reaction galled her more? Will's God-given talent to rouse her anger, or Dryden's inconsistent temperament?

Memories of sugar, kisses, and night confessions resurfaced. When she sedated Will and left him for the uncertainty of the woods, she did so against better judgment. Reflex had demanded that she flee the scene of her embarrassing behavior. She would have done anything to escape reminders of her vulnerability—one handsome and frustrating reminder in particular. Foolish, to be sure, but vital.

Now she felt that same urge to escape. Will Scarlet did not care for her. He did not want to help. Everything he did was a means of manipulating her. Perhaps for gain, perhaps to ensure the safety of his family, he would betray her to the sheriff.

And his kisses. Sweet pleasure. The fear of being exposed again for a gullible fool threatened to make impulsive decisions for her.

But no, reason was on her side this time. Circumstances had changed. She would not be navigating unfamiliar terrain by herself. Another ally stood ready to help her, one with far more potential for influence than Will.

"Milord, I want you to escort me into Nottingham."

"Excuse me?"

She straightened, toying with the hem of a long, loose sleeve. "You have the authority to speak to the sheriff and demand an explanation. He cannot ignore an audience with a nobleman."

Dryden shifted. "What about Scarlet?"

"He has reason to relinquish me to the sheriff."

"You're certain?"

"No, but I cannot take that chance."

"Negotiations are quite beyond my vision," he said. "Father handled those issues."

"You underestimate your abilities."

"And you are patient with me." Chagrined laughter twined into his whisper. His embarrassment resurfaced, as it had when discussing his behavior during Carlisle's attack. "Must be hard for you to believe I served my father with valor and distinction, for all the cowardice you've known of me."

Meg shook her head, uncomfortable with his contempt. "This is not a matter of cowardice or bravery. It's a matter of asserting your right."

Long moments passed. Another lark joined the first in welcoming the sun. Shortly, the world would reawaken. They would make for Nottingham. And she would leave Will behind for good. She sat waiting for Dryden to make her plans a reality.

He pushed the air from his nose. "My father took responsibility for you, and I shall as well. I have said as much, but I intend to make good on my promise."

She smiled with relief. "Thank you, milord."

"Thank me when your sister is returned. Now what do you propose for Scarlet?"

Chapter Sixteen

No greater thief lies hidden under skies
Than beauty closely lodged in women's eyes.

"In Sherwood Lived Stout Robin Hood"
Robert Jones, 1609

"I cannot say this is entirely unexpected," Will said.

He split his awareness between Dryden's mud brown eyes and the tip of the nobleman's imposing claymore—the one poised to remove Will's head from his body.

"I said, drop your weapons, Scarlet."

He knew better than to search Meg's eyes for explanation, but despite the weapon Dryden leveled. Will addressed his words to her. "Was this your idea?"

She found decency enough to appear embarrassed, tilting her chin to the roadside. Had she been able to see, she would have refused his eyes.

Will grinned, ignoring the sword. He would deal with Dryden momentarily. Instead, he watched Meg as she struggled and scraped within her own skin. Either she was becoming a better liar by the day, able to portray a woman in the throes of second thoughts, or attacks of conscience were finally getting the better of her inhuman reserve. And he felt better able to read her face. He had walked into her trap, but at least he could read her discomfort at having to face her accuser.

She pushed her lips into a grimace, fingering the skull-sized satchel she wore. "Does it change your situation? You wouldn't believe me, no matter what I say."

"Drop your weapons," Dryden said again. He inched the blade higher, his shoulders coiled for a life-ending strike.

"You're not wrong." Will scattered bitter laughter into the trees and unbuckled his scabbard. "I *don't* believe you. And I cannot believe I've come all this way, saving your sick hide more times than most people can count—and this is my treatment."

His sword clattered to the packed earth road. Daggers, a bow, and a quiver of arrows followed.

Dryden gestured with a flick of his head toward a nearby oak. "Sit at the base of that tree. Quick now."

Because wringing sympathy from a rock would yield better results than appealing to Meg, he petitioned his captor instead. "You know I didn't kill your father, milord. Would you leave me to the task of clearing my own name? With no witnesses to support my claims?"

A look of distress layered over Dryden's features. He swallowed once before proceeding to tie Will to the tree. "I'm obliged to follow through with the promises my father made to Meg. But I'll speak to the sheriff on your behalf."

"And if he's behind this plot?"

Neither answered his question, for they knew the likelihood of encountering another deception. Yet they eliminated him from the scenario entirely. Senseless.

Meg tapped her walking stick against the base of the tree and knelt. She dropped the stick and shrugged from under the wide leather strap of the satchel. Finding Will's head, she stroked the hair from his face. "All I want is to have my life back, such as it was."

"You have no notion of what you're getting into. Nottingham is a snake, his men are vicious, and that castle is a bloody labyrinth."

"Dryden will help me. He has influence."

"You're quite the mercenary, Meg."

"You would know."

"But you're a coward too. This has nothing to do with strategy. It has to do with kisses you enjoyed a little too much."

"I won't discuss it."

"Why not? When has my aid produced a bad outcome for you?" Bitterness washed through his mouth, withering his tongue. He wanted to spit but all saliva had dried to glue, coating his teeth.

Slowly, pushing tiny puffs of air from her nose, she pressed her smile against his mouth. A chaste kiss. Lips to lips, nothing more. But warmth oozed down his body, thickening in his veins and scouring his mind of thought. He held his breath as she traced trembling fingers along his jaw, down his abdomen—held his breath until his lungs turned to ash.

She teased him with the pale length of her neck. He could stretch forward and kiss that skin peppered with goose bumps, inhale its clean scent, bite it—but he stayed still. Her exploratory hands journeyed lower, to his torso and the outsides of his thighs. He expelled the breath he held and crushed his eyes shut against the sight of her head within inches of his groin.

She continued until no more of his body remained, stopping at his feet. A grin played across her lips in a smug look of triumph as she removed his tattered boots. That expression, mingling with the last remnants of his faltering good sense, tipped him to her intent.

"Devilway, Meg!"

But too late. She removed the lock picks from his boots.

Her grin faded as she pulled a veil low over her face. She stood, donned her satchel, and turned to her companion. "We're done here."

Dryden tossed the discarded weapons into the forest and shooed Will's horse. Without another word, they mounted their own horses and continued toward Nottingham. He watched the back of Meg's head, her veil catching a light wind like a sail. He watched, but he could not believe what had happened. None of his incredulity prompted her to pull the reins and turn back.

Cursing quietly, he tested the bonds. The rope only pinched deeper into his shoulders. His nagging injury shot a spike of agony through his limbs, a festering pain that would not abate. And his body still thrummed, eager for more of Meg's curious hands, more of her mouth on his. The laughter of a madman threatened to replace his foul curses.

How he wanted to be done with her.

In his fondest daydream, he imagined letting them ride away. He would never think of her again. Meg would do whatever fool thing she wanted to do, and she would drag some male creature, willing or otherwise, into her scheme. He would not help her, but neither would he turn her over to Finch. Both options involved being near her again—and nothing frightened him more, nothing tempted him more. Being tied to a blasted oak held more appeal.

He stretched against the bark, trying to loosen the ropes. The uncomfortable position festered an ache in his lower back. His shoulder throbbed as if branded with a deep, piercing iron. The same cool autumn wind that feathered Meg's veil brushed the gathering sweat on his brow, his hairline, and the soles of his bare feet.

Glancing to the east, he looked along the rough-hewn road parting the trees of Charnwood. Although no one appeared along the road's length, he admitted the truth: If people strolled past by the hundreds, not a soul would help him from his predicament. He suspected that even Marian, the only person to defend him unfailingly against slander and suspicion, would avert her brown eyes and stride past. For the sake of his hardscrabble independence, Will had burned every bridge with ruthless skill.

Regret brushed up his body. He counted to three, the number of years since Robin had thought well of him. Swallowing, he retreated from old blunders like a coward from a joust.

And *he* had accused *Meg* of pride and isolation—him, a man very much alone and tied to a tree.

Guided by a tether and trusting Dryden's guidance, Meg pinched her knees against the flaps of the saddle. Their horses' hooves clacked a hollow patter against the wooden bridge, high above the waters of the River Trent. Rushing currents nestled in her ears like the unending squawks of descending crows or the lurid gasps of a woman succumbing to the depths. She squeezed her eyes shut for good measure, fighting a tide of vertigo.

Strangling the reins with slick palms, she concentrated on maintaining her balance. The undertaking should have kept her from retracing her escape from Will, but the reverse proved true. Wandering thoughts only increased the difficulty of her task. She needed to stay seated, head up straight, and confident in the rightness of her decision.

But as her horse stepped onto solid ground, her assurance flagged. She felt conspicuous and vulnerable. In returning to the terror of an unknown blackness, the world constricted like a rope around her neck, stealing air and poise. She no more knew what she was doing than she knew the color of the leaves. At best, she could hazard a guess and hope for a lucky result.

Having partnered with Dryden, she expected certainty to erase the treacherous doubts. But her fears only increased. No matter his titles, his lack of confidence worried her.

"Do you need to stop for a moment?"

The nobleman's tentative question rescued her from a circle of insecurities. He might prove far less willing to help if he suspected her lack of faith.

She caught her veil against a building wind. "What was that?"

"I asked if you need to rest," he said, pulling the horses to a stop. "Perhaps to rest? You appear to be listing."

"No, I am well."

Time moved more slowly than the horse, needling Meg with the details of a nightmare she had constructed. Anxiety hastened her pulse as surely as would Will's sarcastic voice near her ear. That voice, perfectly conjured by a mean-spirited trick of the brain, taunted her. It repeated what she refused to concede: She abandoned the man who had saved her life.

Repeatedly.

Dangerous thoughts swelled. She licked her lips, half expecting to taste sugar, to taste him and the warm pressure of his sweetened tongue.

Two deep drags of air cleared memories of the river. She pulled her back tall, a tree seeking sunshine. Following Dryden was sensible. She would find Ada and return to her cabin, to safety. Because despite his gallantry, notwithstanding the times he had stood between Meg and danger, Will Scarlet held a knife blade to her heart.

A rush of words merged in a mash of English and French. Individual accents and timbres rose above the sea of sound, proclaiming their uniqueness before blending, fading. Women spoke like larks and men like bulls, moving over each other in layered harmonies.

People. By sea and sand—everywhere, people.

Dryden slowed their horses. "Welcome to Nottingham."

"Are we in the market?"

"No, the market is just inside these gates. We're waiting to enter."

Meg shrank from unknown, unseen bodies pressing against her ankles and calves. Her horse shied, stepping quickly to the side and magnifying her fretfulness. Dryden firmed his hold on the reins and steadily drew them through the crowd.

"Halt."

She stiffened. The guttural male voice raised hairs on her forearms.

"Let us pass." The surprising cool in Dryden's command, although appreciated, sounded out of character. "I am Gregory

Dryden, heir to the Earl of Whitstowe, and I have business with the sheriff."

Meg had thrown in with the nobleman because of his influence, and gaining admittance to the castle would be the first test. Blood beat in her neck as she waited.

"Forgive me, milord. Proceed, if you please."

The guttural voice continued to shout behind them, controlling the crowd and issuing orders. They passed through the gates. The jumble of bodies receded, but the sounds and smells only intensified. Grunts from autumn-fat pigs, slicing barks from dogs, and occasional whinnies from cordial horses mingled with the words of their owners. Tradesmen spiced the air with the noises of their professions, songs of metal and wood. Church bells added to the aural mélange.

Having grown up in the tiny hamlet of Keyworth before retreating to Charnwood, Meg had never known town life. The cacophony spun her imagination and tested her ability to interpret sound. Wonder battled with fear. She wanted to know more, to make sense of the wildness, just as she wanted to flee back home. Fond memories of her cabin had never seemed more comforting or more stultifying.

"Here we are."

Dryden stopped their horses and dismounted, his leather saddle creaking with the motion. He helped her to the ground with detached courtesy. She repositioned the satchel crisscrossing her body, thankful for the brief reprieve from men who intimidated or tempted her.

"The castle is to your left, encircled by the Norman settlements on Castle Hill," he said. "The older Saxon dwellings lay across the market to the north, at Weekday Cross."

The surface of her eyeballs dried, but the market did not appear—neither did the swirl of people, their clustered homes, the city walls, or the castle. She kept from asking Dryden to describe the scene for her, swallowing the pathetic plea. But she would have asked Will. And he would have indulged her with amused efficiency, snagging her in a trap made of words.

Frustration forced her teeth into the soft flesh of her lower lip. She bit hard. She would have busted her skull like a clay pot against a rock had the violence promised to scatter thoughts of him. Yet the thoughts remained. Guilt and doubt kicked her repeatedly, and she found no love for her budding relationship with those two encumbering emotions.

Dryden, smelling of horses and the wolfsbane he administered to his cousin, leaned close to her ear. "Entering the castle will not be as simple as riding through the city gates."

"I am ready," she said, filling the words with a certainty she might feel again someday. "Tell me what I need to do."

"If you can, keep from revealing your blindness. That will give you away to Finch's men. I don't want to spark an avoidable confrontation."

She arranged her veil, checking to ensure the thin linen covered her eyes. "Give me your arm and lead on."

Chapter Seventeen

My friends have fallen away from me in mine adversity
as leaves from an autumn tree.

Robin Hood and His Adventures
Paul Creswick, 1903

Jacob ben Asher's arms stretched taut and long, fighting
Asem for control of their pacing. He acknowledged the uselessness of his fight even as he continued his struggle. The dog
would not be deterred from his path, nose to the rotting autumn
leaves and legs pulling across countless acres of woodlands.

He wondered again at the wisdom of his decision to leave
Meg's cabin, but he could not endure being left behind. Wherever Will Scarlet went, trouble followed. The ballads narrated
tales of his adventures, tales that made Jacob long for a
chance at his own fantastic quest. Now Scarlet traveled with
a nobleman into the belly of Nottingham's most fearsome for-
tification, all the while shielding Mad Meg from villains and
her own strange impulses.

Jacob would rather miss the final twenty years of his life
than the awaiting confrontation.

A tiny twinge of guilt surfaced when he thought of the
baron. Monthemer, hardly older than Jacob, lay buoyed by

sleep and wrapped in an assortment of healing herbs from Meg's pharmacopoeia. He had to trust that the young nobleman would turn for home when he awoke.

The question of whether he would awaken at all niggled in Jacob's ears. He had knowledge enough to help the man, but the skills and potions he learned from his father held none of the allure of combat.

Asem, as fine an animal as ever Jehovah created, worked his massive shoulders, putting more and more distance between them and the cabin. The muscles of his haunches bunched and roped. His sides heaved. He did not bark or whine, but he held his muzzle to the unseen trail, presumably leading Jacob along the path Meg had taken.

But the giant mastiff did not find Meg. He found Will Scarlet—divested of weapons and shoes, lashed to an oak, and lifeless.

Or apparently lifeless. His head slumped forward and his spiky, straight hair cast shadows over his eyes.

"Scarlet?"

When the man did not reply, Jacob edged closer. The idea of Scarlet dying while tied to a tree, helpless and without the means to fight, struck him as particularly unfair. What manner of creature would behave with such ungallant menace?

Hugo, a name synonymous with dishonor and deceit, jumped to the fore of his brain. Meg's name followed closely behind. Although Jacob admired and feared her in equal measure, her schemes held no appeal. Her antipathy toward Ada also rankled his sense of chivalry. He would not put it past either trickster to force Scarlet into such a predicament.

Asem settled his haunches near the oak, sitting far taller than the bound man. A thunderous bark cleaved the woodland silence.

Scarlet's head snapped back, slapping the rough bark of the tree.

"For grace!"

"You're alive!"

Jacob dropped to his knees and produced his dagger, cutting the ropes with an efficiency he admired in himself.

"Yes, I am alive. At least she did not poison me." His grouse spoke of frustrations and weariness, but also sounded . . . *amused*.

"She? Meg, then?"

Scarlet shrugged free of the ropes and massaged the back of his skull. A smear of blood colored his lean fingers. "Yes, and Dryden with her."

"Shall we follow her to Nottingham?"

Upon standing, he idly scratched Asem behind the ears. The dog panted, a smile gracing his wide, sloppy jowls. "We?"

"I rescued you."

"You did, but I cannot let you accompany me."

"Why not? You've said yourself that I am skillful with a crossbow. Do not tell me I'm too young." He was horrified to hear his voice crack.

"I wouldn't dare." Grinning, Scarlet retrieved his weapons, arranging daggers, quiver, bow, and sword across his person. He transformed from a defenseless, bound man into a warrior— a warrior without boots.

"I was your age when Robin Hood aided King Richard," Scarlet said. "They besieged Nottingham Castle where John thought to usurp his brother's reign. I was in the thick of the morass, and I would've shot a man between the eyes had he said I was too young."

He swelled with admiration. "Then you'll let me come with you."

"No."

"Please!"

Scarlet picked up the jumble of ropes. "You have two choices, my young friend. You can take your beast back to Meg's cabin and do what you can for Monthemer, or you can take my place here in the woods."

"You would tie me up after I helped you?"

"Terrible, yes," he said, chuckling. Meg was not the only

soul in the forest gone touched. "I'm following the example of a rather unscrupulous woman we both know."

"Why can't I come with you?"

"Monthemer is a valuable man. Chance that may befall Dryden today, or any of us, Monthemer can bear witness to the plot—something he cannot do if he's attacked or killed."

Jacob stilled, excitement thrusting a rapid rhythm beneath his sternum. He loathed the mundane task of keeping Monthemer well, but he had not considered that the man might be a target. And soldiers yet traveled through Charnwood.

"You want me to guard him?"

"Precisely. Take him to Monthemer's family estate at Winhearst. We'll convene there." He smiled, gripping Jacob's shoulder and infusing him with the heavy, happy weight of his duty. "Now lend me your boots."

The young man disappeared into the deep woods. Renewed purpose and the pride of his responsibilities transformed mere steps into a saunter. Asem reluctantly trotted at his heels.

While he truly did appreciate Jacob's fortuitous rescue—disproving the notion that no one in the forest would offer Will aid—he could not permit the boy to accompany him to Nottingham. Odds against success demanded that he keep Jacob safe.

Not that he had a notion of what might constitute success.

But he would have given his left hand to keep from hurting the boy's pride. He had nothing but respect for Jacob's young dignity, not that his responsibility was a trivial matter.

When Will had accompanied Robin and King Richard against Prince John, he believed himself a grown, capable man. Robin's every attempt to coddle and care had grated against his youthful arrogance. Had he been so young, in truth? As young as Jacob? Had he been so in need of protection, from both himself and life's dangers? Perspective sullied righteous memories of those days, giving unwanted credence to Robin's blunt attempts to guide him.

He stomped his heels into Jacob's tight boots and tied the laces at his inner calf. Running shaky hands through his hair, he shrugged the tension from his shoulders. The half-full quiver settled at the center of his back. He hated to admit the truth, but taking up the bow again had proven gratifying. The easy rhythm of drawing and firing, the satisfaction of finding his mark—the weapon had reinvigorated a part of him that reveled in being skillful, proficient.

Spiting himself because of Robin made less sense than ever.

Anemic sunlight spread like a bird's wings across the steel-colored sky, approaching noontide. If he was lucky and quick, he could be out of the castle before dusk, his business with Finch over and done. His quick pace chewed lengths of road, infused with an unease he did not care to examine.

After crossing the Trent, he rushed across the bridge and out of easy sight. High walls made of imported granite eclipsed the city's southeast side, imported because the native sandstone was too yielding to create valuable defensive works. At the southeastern gate, dozens of merchants, farmers, soldiers, and revelers sought admittance.

The color brown, both functional and concocted from the dust and dirt of peasant life, outweighed every other shade. Amidst the ferment of people and their animals and wares, the occasional coat of silver mail or a brightly dyed tunic protruded like an oak in the middle of a sown field. With long hair following her as would a faithful pup, a young girl wearing a sky blue tunic nipped in and out of sight.

Will surveyed the scene, appreciating color as he never had. Meg's vexing influence spread to the very senses he employed to observe the world. She was a wind gathering before a rainstorm, an elemental presence, and she was in there somewhere.

From the quiver on his back, he removed a leather pouch. He could not imagine how a full-scale army would have used Meg's explosive black powder, but with it, thinning the glut at the gate might prove easier. He tucked a handful into the leather cuff of Jacob's boots and held the others at the ready. The drooping hood of his felted cloak would obscure his face from determined observers, even though it limited his field of vision.

He spotted a procession of four lightly armored warhorses within sight of the gates. Norman knights sat tall and impervious among the commoners, their blue and white tunics fluttering on a rising wind. The silver of their mail shone a dull gray under the overcast sky.

Sidling through the crowd, head low, he fastened his eyes to his objective: the lead horse. It pawed the stone slabs at the city's entrance, beset by a tide of people and merchandise. On the animal's back, the lead knight—an impressive collection of weapons and armor wrapped around a stick-straight spine—handled the reins with casual disregard.

After a quick prayer to the amiable saints who watched over fools, he jumped in front of the massive charger. He slammed a handful of the linen twists under its steel-shod hooves. A dozen sharp cracks burst forth like thunder on a clear day.

Mayhem erupted. The large stallion reared, its forelegs flailing in the air above Will's head. He ducked and flung his body away, running smack into the young girl in sky blue. Their legs intertwined, all knees and tangled fabric, until they careened into the dirt. Swathed by Will's faltering limbs, the girl promptly hurled a screech into the expanding mêlée.

The knight tried in vain to calm his crazed steed. Will tried to calm the screaming girl. He met her wide eyes. Sky blue. Like her tunic.

Impossibly, those eyes widened even more. She pitched her scream to curdle blood.

Over his shoulder, Will caught sight of what she feared: the half-mad stallion rearing above them. Hooves like flashing daggers raised high, exposing the animal's pale, bare belly. He wrapped the girl in his arms and rolled, rolled again, until dizziness and dirt soiled his vision. Free of the charger, he hauled the girl to her feet and pushed her against the city's outer wall.

"Stay here." Dust and adrenaline abraded his voice to a dull rasp.

The girl cowered, looking ready to dart without regard for direction or safety. Fear dulled her indistinct gaze. Her dirtied tunic blended with the stale brown of every other peasant. He caught her sliver of a chin. "Did you hear me? Stay here until this calms."

Weakly she nodded, granting the only permission he sought before making his escape.

Chapter Eighteen

He could not fight, he could not flee.
He knew not what to do . . .

"Robin Hood and the Beggar, II"
Folk ballad, seventeenth century

Meg pressed a flat palm to her belly, the tight tease of apprehension replaced by hunger. She had not eaten since before they left the cabin at dawn. The wafting scent of roasting meat, vegetables, and fresh bread made her dizzy with longing. Feasting revelers sucked and slurped with contented avarice. The noisy clutter of the overstuffed banquet hall disguised the sound of her rumbling stomach.

But she congratulated herself on having made a fine decision. Gregory Dryden, the presumptive Earl of Whitstowe. His name and presence opened doors. They had walked to the forward portcullis of the castle, her arm looped through his, and into the sheriff's fortified refuge as easily as they had entered the city.

She wanted food, but she dared not leave the wall where Dryden left her. Stranded like a boatman without oars, she urged her senses to drift across the massive hall. A hundred people, maybe more. A high ceiling, by the way the voices swirled and echoed, and lined with muffling tapestries. Every word repeated three times over, an aural sensation that fatigued her when she tried to follow conversations.

A hundred bodies and the hissing flames of a few scattered fires heated the room. Sweat dampened the skin beneath her arms, and the high collar of her gown chafed a ring around her neck. The humid, cloying heat, thrice-echoed words, and sumptuous aromas bullied her senses and left her disoriented.

But she could not leave that spot.

She rolled her shoulder blades into the wall, but having absorbed the heat in the hall, the stones provided no relief. She pushed harder until her bones chiseled deeper. The sharp bite of pain, the pinch of her skin between bone and rock, grounded her and focused her dizzied senses. She pressed her palm into the soft give of her abdomen.

Where had Dryden gone?

Perhaps she should have saved congratulating herself until after he returned with good news—that Finch had capitulated before the nobleman's firm command, news that Ada would be released as soon as the penitent sheriff found keys to his dungeon. She knew better, of course. But any fanciful thought was better than contemplating the possibility that Dryden had abandoned her.

Worse yet, she feared when he might prove half the man she left tied to a tree.

She could not leave. She could not find her way home. She could do nothing but remain pressed against the wall and wait for Dryden to keep his word. She slowly exhaled to release a rising swell of dread.

A commotion, signaled by the herald of two cornet players, began at the end of the hall. The scrape of wood over flagstones suggested the rearrangement of furniture. Shouts piled on laughter. Applause followed.

"'Tis the subtlety."

Bones and muscles leapt from her skin. Before thought,

she pounded a fist into Dryden, connecting with his shoulder. "Do not surprise me!"

"Forgive me."

She liked the genuine sound of his apologies. None of Hugo's cruelty. None of Will's teasing. "Did you locate Finch?"

"He's with an entourage at the other end of the hall, but I have yet to speak with him." Dryden took hold of her hands and curled her fingers around a fat slice of bread. "Here, eat this. I took it from a pantler."

"Gramercy." She lifted the fragrant piece of oat bread to her nose, inhaling the sultry, salty warmth. Her mouth watered, but she ate the offering with delicate relish.

"Shall I signal the cupbearer for ale or wine?"

Meg frowned. Although she appreciated his attention to her needs, she questioned his lack of acuity. They hardly needed to raise more of a fuss than they had by simply arriving. Yes, she wanted to eat and drink with everyone else, but this was not a moment for revelry. Dryden's lack of nerve niggled, forcing the need to question otherwise sound decisions. She wanted to push him, to force him into action.

"No, the bread will do," she said. "How goes the subtlety?"

"They are bringing it to the center of the hall on a cart. It stands several hands high, sculpted into the shape of a swan."

She raised her brows. "I wonder where they secured more sugar."

"And in time for the festival. I'm impressed."

"The sheriff has resources, apparently." She grimaced, remembering the purpose of their presence. "Makes me fearful of what we face by being here."

He grunted, a noncommittal sound that grated her thinning patience. "The steward has signaled to have the table linens changed, which means the entertainment will arrive shortly."

Before Dryden finished his sentence, the crowd burst into heady applause. Music filled the hall, the sounds of lutes and drums. "Who goes?"

"Tumblers first, with the mummers waiting for their turn."

An irrepressible smile touched her lips, recalling the spectacle of feast times from her youth. One spring, she had accompanied Ada and their father to Lord Whitstowe's castle for a May Day celebration. The tumblers wore parti-colored tunics decorated with samite ribbons, the gold threads of that silken fabric shimmering with every outlandish trick. Fools, masking their faces in gold and white porcelain, roamed the crowd in search of victims for their happy chicanery. With Ada at her side, she had hooted and cheered with the assemblage, just as the sheriff's reveling guests did.

Bitterness joined with nostalgia. Remembering how she and her family had been, years before, dug deep furrows in her heart.

Feasting citizens sang in rounds, filling the teeming hall with varied accents. High sopranos soared above resonant basses, as the tone-deaf struggled to find their way. Dryden turned his body. The pose and his lowered voice forced an awkward intimacy. "Meg, I have identified a member of Finch's entourage who concerns me."

"Who?"

"He is Gilbert, my father's youngest brother."

"What do you suspect, milord?"

"Should Stephen and I die, the lands of both our families would revert to Gilbert. That he dines with the sheriff within days of my father's murder makes me suspect an alliance. Finch could manipulate my uncle to secure a wealthy, landed pawn."

"Manipulate him? You do not believe him capable of the crimes?"

"Gilbert is . . . Gilbert is a dullard with certain . . . proclivities." A delicate lace of pain decorated his voice. "He has yet to think of an idea that does not involve perversion or vice. If he is happy and his appetites are satisfied, he would follow any strong leader."

"Then you are in danger, as is your cousin."

Hesitation stretched between them. "Yes. I had not believed such a possibility. Otherwise, to be honest, I would not have chosen to confront him directly."

Her hopes sank. The ally who possessed power enough to walk into Nottingham Castle not only suffered a humiliating lack of initiative, but he had good cause to flee the scene entirely. His authority would do nothing to free her sister.

Dryden leaned nearer. "But I'll attract less notice if I talk to Finch during the performances. This is an opportune moment."

"You insist on talking to him?"

He laughed softly, a sound of embarrassment she had identified before. "Not much of a champion, am I?"

"Milord, I said nothing of the kind. You have been a tremendous aid to me." But the blush burning her cheeks betrayed the truth, she knew.

"I've been reluctant, but I cannot abide this plot." A pale glimmer of outrage cloaked his words. "My father is dead, your sister is missing, and these men are ready to do worse. Some among these revelers stand to lose their security if Finch acquires an excess of power. He'll not act against me before a hundred witnesses."

She almost heard a question amidst his declaration. But ready to make an effort despite the perils he faced, Dryden stepped forward. At last.

The jester's body slumped into a pile of awkward limbs, his nose bloodied and broken. Will rubbed the knuckles of his right hand and mumbled his apologies to the insensate man, a man who garnered a beating solely because of his profession. He dragged the unconscious jester into a secluded alcove and assumed his colorful garb. The generous cut of the red and blue parti-colored tunic draped easily over his banded mail. An excess of fabric swirled around his knees, promising to trip him at the wrong moment.

Applause and shouts greeted the magnificent subtlety. Cupbearers continued to make their rounds with jugs of ale, while ewers provided basins of water for the guests to wash their hands. Within moments, even before the jesters finished their performance, the subtlety would be a memory, cut and served to a hundred gluttonous mouths.

Waiting outside the hall with the other entertainers, Will nervously stroked the edge of the mask he wore. Its sharp-edged porcelain delicately nibbled the pad of his thumb. He watched the mummers with the curiosity of a slumbering old man, bored by their silent patterns of motion and dance. Impulse and instinct urged him to find Meg.

What he would do once he found her . . . He found no ready answer. Doubts and conflicting desires tapped tiny fissures into plans that had been as firm as solid rock.

Nottingham had not changed in the mere days since his last night spent within its walls, and neither had it changed since his first weeks in Robin's band. Mineral-rich water, seeping through the city's sandstone foundation, advanced the tanning, dying, and brewing trades, elevating the local populace above that of a mere center for agricultural trade. The market attracted hundreds of people, augmenting the native population on a weekly basis and wringing currency and materials from the countryside, which each new sheriff invariably bled from the public. And he was looking at the gluttonous result of that cycle.

No, Nottingham had not changed. As he assessed the blasé manner with which its influential citizens indulged in the harvest festival, he wondered if it ever would. The peasants would not charge the gates and demand justice, not even when their families and friends stood threatened by the mounting power of another corrupt sheriff.

But he had changed. Gone was the indifference he had studiously courted and nourished. He shook his head. How had Robin managed to organize any means of resistance? How, without losing his mind in the face of such apathy, Will's included?

Securing his mask, he watched for his cue and bounded into the center of the long rectangular array of tables. Two other jesters in matched costumes feigned pushing the mummers from the floor. A fourth man jumped atop an ambry and juggled bread loaves, his madder red boots rattling the few plates stacked on open shelving. Set upon by the angered steward, the jester sprang from the cabinet and ran around the hall. Laughter chased him as doggedly, blurring the line between truth and farce.

Surrounded by fools, Will bowed overdramatically to all corners, searching for quarry and enemy both. He identified Finch and Carlisle at the head table, surrounded by a dozen well-armed sentries. Between bows, he found Dryden slinking toward the sheriff's party.

Tracing the nobleman's path back to its origins, he spotted Meg. She pressed against a wall, veiled and partly cloaked by a pair of overlapping tapestries. The hard angles of her shoulders revealed a woman locked in the grip of a cold fear. Likely, she was irritated at Dryden for not having delivered Ada already.

A jester streaked past, hauling a squealing mummer over his shoulder. He crisscrossed the interior of the rectangular tables, displaying a surprising measure of strength for his thin physique. When another jester approached him, Will set about mimicking the performer's every motion, from the angle of his wrist to the tilt of his head. The man grasped the diversion, and together, they increased the intricacy of their play.

His impromptu partner snatched the leg of a pheasant from a sallow young woman's hand and challenged a duel. "Have at me, knave!"

Will skittered back and chanced upon an empty platter, his mock shield. Shouts of encouragement skewered the air as they dueled. Each smack of the pheasant's chunky leg against the burnished silver platter echoed dully, like a skull hitting marble.

Repelling the man's silly, elaborate assault, Will jumped from side to side. He thumped the inside of the platter with his fist. "Is that all you have?"

The jester took his turn to play the mimic. He bounced from one foot to the other, the point of his cap jerking in opposition. "I have much more to give, but 'tis better saved for strumpets."

"This strumpet?" The juggler exchanged his baguettes for a squat, heavyset woman.

"Indeed!" Will's opponent tossed away his weapon and seized his new prize. "The night is for loving, not fighting!"

Indignation dyed her face red. The jesters paid no mind, twirling her amidst bawdy shouts. Another half dozen women, some willing and others dragged forcibly from their benches, joined the riot of farcical dancing.

With an eye on Dryden and Finch at the front of the hall, Will used the moment to escape his spontaneous role as an entertainer. He fled across the herb-scented rushes, bounding over a table to escape center stage. Because tapestries along the long north wall shielded him from observation, he removed his mask. The warm, cloying air within the great hall felt cool after so many minutes concealed by porcelain, his own breath doubled back on his skin.

Meg clung to the same location, adhered to the marble. She tunneled bone white fingers into the stones at both sides of her hips. She was panicked. Maybe frightened. Dryden had yet to return, and doubts appeared well on their way to gnawing her calm. To be stranded without an ally or a means of escape— even she could not stand tall in the face of such a nightmare.

Memories of the vulnerable woman he saw twirling in moonlight resurfaced, the woman who sought colors she would never again see. Sympathy and a grudging pride twisted knots in his head, in his joints and muscles. Stubborn, infuriating woman.

The familiar compulsion to protect her from an indifferent world—or, more often, from her own rash defiance—stood the wide breadth of Christendom away from his best interests. How easy, how painless his task? He only had to drag a blind woman past three dozen feasting mouths to Finch's seat and present his trophy.

Reaping the rewards, both his return to the sheriff's good graces and a guarantee of Marian's safety, should have been promise enough to compel him. Instead, Will wanted to put her hands to his face and make promises. Promises he would actually keep.

Chapter Nineteen

"That a duty which seemeth to us sometimes ugly and
harsh, when we do kiss it fairly upon the mouth, so to
speak, is no such foul thing after all."
—Will Scarlet

The Merry Adventures of Robin Hood
Howard Pyle, 1883

"A dance, milady?"

Meg jerked and slapped him, connecting with his forearm.
"Must everyone startle me? Does that amuse you?"

Will grinned. "Yes."

"Difficult man."

The talented minx nearly disguised her fear behind anger
and annoyance. He congratulated himself on being able to
hear the truth. She was finally coming clear to him.

"I would ask how you freed yourself, but I care not," she
said harshly. "You've arrived too late to spoil this."

"I doubt that," he said. "Are we ready to speak with Finch?"

She stilled, a cornered fawn. "Dryden already went."

Will tipped his head closer to hers. With an unsteady finger,
he lifted the corner of her veil to reveal a pale sliver of her
neck and jaw. As it had against the confines of the mask, his
breath radiated off her body, warming his mouth and raising

goose bumps on her skin. "Ah yes, Dryden. I saw him. The two of you seemed quite close over here."

"You watched us? Are you jealous or pretending in order to raise my ire?"

"I know not. Should I be jealous, Meg? Do you intend to turn your wiles on him?" He pushed the veil up and back, needing to read her expression. "You've proven capable of as much. You decided on his aid rather than mine. Will he take my place in every respect?"

"You have no place to take." She pushed him away, a hand flat to his face. He pursed his lips and kissed her palm. She wrenched away, tension making fired glass of her limbs—hard, luminous, and ready to shatter. "Leave now before someone recognizes you."

"They cannot."

He pulled her stone-bitten fingers to the jester's cap, amused by her frown. She explored its comical shape and ornamental ribbons, trailing lower to discover his oversized tunic. "What are you wearing?"

His smile widened. "For you, I play the fool."

"Granted."

"Your plan is proceeding masterfully, then?"

"You know nothing."

"Either your lies are slipping, or I am better equipped to read them."

"Nonsense."

"Ah, but let's see what we can see." He angled his head, peeking through the wedge of light between the overlapping tapestries. The fools continued their merry exploits, engaging half of the feasting guests in jests growing ever more vulgar. "Your man, Dryden—indeed, he's speaking with the sheriff. At least he honed nerve enough for that. Whatever did you say or do to bolster his confidence?"

Her fingers found the stonework again, gouging weak places. Crumbles of mortar pooled on either side of her boots. "He's being chivalrous, honoring a promise."

"You once admired Hugo's disregard for promises. I imagine you value chivalry now because it stands to benefit you."

She pinched her eyes shut. "And you benefit me none at all."

A flutter of unexpected movement caught his attention: Finch's guards mustered their armaments. As fastidiously groomed as ever, Carlisle pointed and shouted directions to the drones. An icy call of dread sounded in his veins. He checked the daggers strapped to his hips, the only weapons he had worn when he crawled through the castle tunnels.

"We have to leave. Now."

"Whatever do you mean?"

"They arrested Dryden."

She gasped, her eyes flaring wide. "Will, do not lie. Not about this."

"I am in earnest." He claimed her hands, pulling her along the makeshift corridor between the wall and the floor-length hanging tapestries. "Listen, Meg. The musicians have stopped. Listen to the room, how it has changed. They are taking him away."

Her expression became that of a sculpted idol as she concentrated, distant and elemental. Life returned to her features when she accepted the truth, life animated by equal parts fear and cold reason.

"What manner of villain is he? No one will have recourse, not if they can commit such an act in front of these witnesses." She pulled the satchel she wore around her body, resting a possessive palm on its fat contents. After a pair of flailing attempts, she found him with her other hand. She squeezed the muscles of his forearm, likely the nearest she would offer by way of a request for guidance.

"No time to worry about it now. We must go."

"Without Ada?"

"Have you another idea?"

He coveted a reply, a snappish suggestion of cunning and dubious morality—anything to deliver them to safety. She licked her lips, but plans and schemes sat silent in her mouth.

Carlisle and the shouts of mustering guards grew ever louder. Will swore. "Too late."

No. No. No.

She could not concentrate. The tedious word swallowed sound and every other thought.

Like Whitstowe before him, Dryden had been her promise. As a nobleman trained for combat, he should have been the man to release Ada. He wore influence like his family crest, a rare birthright that should have transformed hope into reality, despite his hesitant character.

Yet like his father and like Meg's plan, Dryden failed because of faith in his own authority. The Sheriff of Nottingham, that notorious title, exploited that faith and authority both. When he dragged her liege to the dungeons, Finch set fire to justice and rendered even the nobility vulnerable to his ploys.

Her champion stolen, she had no choice but to flee with the man whose greed imprisoned Ada in the first place—the man who had yet to fail her.

"Stairs! Down!"

She heeded his warning. Balancing with the aid of Will's hand, she severed thought from action. Instinct assumed command. She focused only on his voice, the information he hissed over his shoulder.

"Last one."

She stumbled only briefly, regaining her footing by the second step onto flat stones.

"Left. And left again." Instructions spun behind her eyes like a compass needle in search of north. "Duck. Careful."

On the other side of an archway, using a hand to outline its low camber, she struggled for a reprieve from the heady terror of flight.

Will permitted none. "This way."

Dizzy, disoriented, she gave herself into his care. He could drag her into a flaming pit or throw her to the sheriff's assembled

hoards—none of it mattered. Faith and pride splintered, winnow-
ing away like so much useless chaff. Her sense of direction fluttered in vast spirals, spinning and spinning until only Will
remained.

"You there," shouted a man with a deep voice. "Stop!"

"Meg, down!"

She dropped. The skin at her knees split, assaulted by the
twin demands of bone and unyielding flagstones. A sword's
deadly steel clanged when it slammed into a wall. Shards of
rock rained over her veil. Hearing only the grunts of a man-
on-man brawl, she could not recall if Will wore a weapon.
Had he relinquished his arms in favor of a jester's disguise?

She pressed against the sanctuary of the nearest wall and
fished in her satchel. Upon locating a particular glass vial,
she held it aloft. "Will!"

He snatched the vial without question. The glass shattered
and the other man screamed, his tinkling mail rattling to the
ground. The slither of steal pulled from a scabbard, a sound
too succinct to be that of a sword, etched the air. Will pounced.
The other man's life ended with a single nauseating gurgle.

Meg tried to stand, but trembling legs refused to sustain
her weight. "A dagger?"

"Two daggers, in truth." He sheathed the weapons, pushing
air in and out of his nose. "Lye?"

"Fermented urine, in truth."

"Do you create anything that does not stink?"

"Counterfeit jewels."

"Funny girl." He pulled her up, her knees throbbing. "Turn
to your right."

An endless labyrinth of turns later, he looped her waist and
pulled her flush against the hard length of his armored torso.
Bodies pressed into a tiny wedge of space, their limbs nego-
tiated the mysterious confines. The rumbling clatter of metal
and male shouts charged past.

Will panted, heating her temple. "Quiet now," he whispered.

For a bare moment, Meg relinquished her fear. She sagged

against him and sapped comfort from his arms. He tightened his hold, an enticing promise. He would defend her. No matter his lies or misdeeds, no matter the lengthy list of her own faults, he would defend her.

"I wish I could determine how much of this is to your blame," she said.

He pushed her none to gently against the wall, both hands on her hips. "Before you decide, let me describe my grand scheme to have Dryden arrested, and well before the end of his usefulness."

"Stop your foolery."

"I still wear my new costume."

"Will removing it put an end to your ill-timed wit?"

His lips were close, his words like a laughing sigh. "You and your obsession with removing my clothes."

Inches separated their faces, but the wide gulf furrowed by her pride would not allow her to taste him. Her hands hovered uselessly between their bodies. She wanted to hit him, push him away, deny his existence. Yet the possibility of touching him again became a temptation worthy of a bargain with the Devil.

"Where are we?"

"An alcove," he said. "A nice one, actually. Very secluded."

"You've already compromised my faith in your ability to find suitable cover."

"You would fault a man who was suffering a grievous injury at the time? Most unkind, Meg. But I assure you, this alcove is a wiser choice than that poor bit of brush."

"Good."

"How goes your plan now?"

His question provided a use for her hands: She pressed trembling fingers against her eyes, scrubbing her face as if the hard strokes would erase days, weeks of missteps. Grief welled behind her breastbone. Failure and hopelessness made her black world even more ominous.

"You truly abhor being wrong," he said. "Even now, you refuse to confess it."

"I will not."

"How I would enjoy if you made a habit of simply admitting to a thing rather than arguing." He placed a kiss to her forehead, but the hard hands at her hips, his insistent grip, laid bare the greedy tension beneath his teasing. "We would save many a wasted day filled with uncivil words."

She swallowed. Her voice, when it came, sounded deeper, more exotic. "I confess it. I mislike being wrong."

"Much better."

And he kissed her.

Masculine heat invaded her body. Taste and touch united in a quick surge. Her senses staggered beneath the swirling rush, rediscovering the textures of his tongue, his lips. Danger, thought, protest—all receded. Lethargic pleasure melted her bones. She leaned into him, reveling in the strength of his body. The banded mail he wore frustrated her, a barrier between her hands and the firm ridges of muscle along his back. Instead she found his face, cupping the line of his jaw, the strong column of his neck.

As Meg threaded greedy fingers into the straight, shaggy length of his hair, he raised his lips. "I have much to make up to you," he said gently. "Let me keep you safe."

"How can I know you speak the truth?"

"Because I have a confession too. I arrived with the intention of relinquishing you to Finch, yet here we are."

Some things about Meg had proven more predictable than the sun heralding the dawn. She weakened, she wilted, but she never backed from a challenge.

Will grinned, wanting to kiss her again, but she mashed pliant lips into a grim line. She went rigid in his arms. "Explain," she said.

Forcing calm, he related Hendon's bargain and his threats toward Marian. Days had passed, no more, but the strange confusion of that waning evening felt like an ancient memory. Much had changed, perhaps Will most of anything.

"I stood within thirty feet of the sheriff, there with you in the banquet hall, but I said nothing. I did nothing to betray you."

"Another attack of conscience? Or obligation?"

"There's more between us than obligation."

"Liars say pretty things too, Will." Her face remained stony and ghostly pale, lined by deep shadows. "You knew your bargain would not be upheld, not after Dryden's arrest."

"For grace, Meg! You looked like a lost child standing there."

"For pity's sake, then."

He twined fingers into her loosened plait. "Did you feel any pity in that kiss?"

"Every man has a price."

"That may be true, but I can only speak for myself. My price is you. I've surrendered friends and fortune. I've imperiled my family and my own life, but here we are. I'm not going to let you go now, not after trading away so much." He watched for any signal from her smooth gambler's expression. "Meg?"

"I believe you."

His heart thumped twice. "What?"

"Hugo came to the cabin. He said as much about your intentions, about Marian."

"When?"

"When you traveled to Keyworth for the sugar. Whatever his band of spies, he'd heard rumor of your intent."

A vice pinched beneath his ribs. "Did he do anything to you?"

"With regard to Hugo, I could become used to your gallant nature."

"Meg—"

"Enough, please. He did nothing." Her teasing smile wobbled and faded. "It was never about the emeralds, was it?"

"No."

"When you found me in the hall, I waited. You would either reveal me to the sheriff or . . . or not."

The vise eased, eased again. Wonder momentarily replaced fear. "You truly believe me. This is no performance."

"Christ save me, I do. Hugo would have sold me to the first peddler he met, but you . . ."

Before Will found words to object, had he wanted to, she grabbed fistfuls of hair and dragged his mouth to hers. Swift, hard, demanding. Her lips demanded of him a silent, binding contract. They would survive their tangled circumstances and live to explore each other anew, or he would betray her—at which point her promise would be one of vengeance. Either way, her gambler's kiss wagered everything on him.

"Meg, we should leave." His increased respiration had nothing to do with their flight from the hall.

She replaced a flicker of confusion with a resolve he had come to dread. "My intention remains unchanged. I came to free Ada."

"Refusing to give you to Finch and rescuing his prisoner are separate matters."

"We're here," she said. "I brought weapons to compliment yours. Why should we abandon her now?"

He labored to leash his temper and keep his words to a whisper. "She is not my sister, and she is a foul sister to you."

"I cannot leave her, and you put her in this place."

"By my thrift, do you have a cursed argument for everything? Is this how you wore Ada down, pressing her to do your bidding? I almost sympathize with the wench."

He expected retaliation. Maybe he expected violence or stinging wasps' words. But she gave him tears. Each tear, like a drop of acid, conspired to melt away good sense.

"Will, I cannot leave her, not with this great hollow between us. She is my sister, and I need to make amends."

"What you ask is impossible. You said yourself, if they can detain a nobleman before a hundred witnesses—"

"Then no one stands to help us." She dried the saltwater as soon as new tears streaked her cheeks. "This is *my* price. Please."

A large and sensible portion of him objected. And loudly. He still clung to a lovely picture, the dream that had landed him in such woe. Women. Song. A life of comfort, early and late. But Meg would haunt him. If he fled, his misdeed against her sister would only grow and fester, poisoning his peace. The promise of his life stretching ahead, having abandoned Meg and her tearful request, was a bleak one.

And she had said *please*.

"Well good, Meg. You win."

Chapter Twenty

The music struck up, and we all fell to dance . . .

"Robin Hood's Birth, Breeding, Valor, and Marriage"
Folk ballad, seventeenth century

Meg imagined her body becoming a shadow, fusing with dark gaps and hidden coves. She eluded detection just as vision eluded her. The swirl of music from a trio of lutes and a fife became her escape. She followed those lilting melodies into the open sky. Soldiers, common revelers—none would find her.

"Tuck your feet." Will pushed and prodded at her shadow self. His grouse rendered her solid again, mortal and earthbound. "Someone will see your gown."

"I find hiding a challenge when I cannot see our confines."

"We are behind the balustrade of a balcony overlooking the largest assembly hall." He pushed her hands along broad curves of carved sandstone, illustrating his words. "Stay tucked between this railing and the column at your back. The entrance to the dungeon is at the bottom of the stairs at the other end of the hall. I believe."

"You believe?"

His silent breath touched her face. The masculine scent of

him, animal and sweet, reminded her of their kiss, their
bodies sharing and fighting. "If you enjoyed our hiding place,
I should have left you there."

"I no longer believe your threats."

"And I no longer pay mind to your insults," he said.

"But only yesterday, you claimed to know this castle as
well as your own father."

Will chuckled. "If you live among the trees too long, you lose
a knack for sarcasm. I was raised by my uncle for a reason."

Sour understanding bathed her tongue. "When I've called
you a bastard, I was correct?"

"Yes," he said, cupping the side of her face. She stifled
the urge to curl deeper into the calloused warmth of his palm.
"But you cut deeper when you call me a pig. Save that for the
likes of Hugo."

"Done."

He shifted, rearranging his limbs within the tight confines.
"I was last here five years ago during King Richard's siege.
At great length, Robin made a point of reminding me of my
inexperience. I followed his lead and tried to appear compe-
tent, nothing more."

Her faith dwindled with his embarrassment. "You are truly
lost?"

"For the most part."

"*Most* of you is lost," she said. "What do you know for
certain?"

"We are yet within the castle walls."

"Edifying. Truly."

"And you would fare better alone?"

"Well done, Will. You have a better sense of direction than
a blind woman."

"I do enjoy being of use." She could picture the bright, sarcastic grin coloring his words, and her fingers itched to trace
its curving lines. "All that keeps us from the dungeon is a pair
of staircases separated by a great hall," he said. "The hall is
crowded with revelers in a chain dance."

She gasped. "Dancers?"

"Yes. I say we join the ring and dance round to the other side. We don't want to appear conspicuous." He pressed lips to the back of her hand. Grin, kiss, words—his mouth and its provoking talents pulled an anxious shiver from her belly. "A dance milady?"

"I refused you previously and with good reason."

"And I was a fool to accept your refusal, as is fitting with my stolen garb."

"No. I don't dance."

"Come, Meg. This is dancing, not escaping soldiers. What's the harm?"

She blinked uselessly. Will tempted her to make choices based on pleasure, not an avoidance of pain. But down that path waited only humiliation. "I've trouble enough walking across flat ground, let alone accounting for rhythm and grace."

"You walk by yourself, but you dance with a partner." His enticing words prickled the fine hairs along the back of her hand. "Do you remember, Meg? How we moved together? I am a good partner to you."

A crowd of fierce, insistent sensations demanded her attention: the peppery taste of his skin, the flex of his lean hips, the rough, rhythmic gasps near her ear. She licked her lips, tasting shared kisses and memories she labored to erase. Denying the intensity of their encounter had become a chore matched only by her efforts to disbelieve his valor.

But fear sat heavy on her shoulder, a fiend pushing talons into her muscles and ripping holes in her bravery. "I don't want to fall."

"I won't let you."

His promise. Never had he failed to keep a promise. Wretched soul, she could not deny the need for his assurances, his steady armor.

"For my sister, then."

"Of course."

He swathed her in the powerful mantle of his body, permitting no resistance. A covetous yearning for protection, one more powerful than physical desire, urged her closer. She found his neck with her lips, not kissing. Simply feeling. Connecting. Every moment spent in his presence thrilled her, like running through the darkness without guides or guarantees. The risk had naught to do with guards, plots, and villains, but with the potential for disappointment.

His whisper found her in the tight blackness. "Come now. Let's discover what mischief we can elude."

On hands and knees, feeling like a particular sort of fool, Will skirted the perimeter of the balcony overlooking the hall. He missed his sword, having stashed it before entering the castle, but was glad to be free of its noisy hindrance. Creeping silently along the balustrade required ample concentration without a length of forged steel tapping distress calls on the flagstones.

Meg crawled at his heels. The satchel she wore rested in the divot of her lower back. Somehow, she managed to keep her kirtle and skirt from hindering soundless progress. No matter the situation, she was ready to do the impossible. Had Will suggested they fly across the hall, she would have produced a pair of wings.

They reached the staircase and descended to the hall. The pulse of Meg's apprehension shoved against his back and kept time with his own heartbeat. At the last step, he turned her in his arms.

"Keep your satchel tucked close," he said, pulling the mask over his features. "Circle only to your left to follow me. Do not let go of my hand."

"Be calm, Will." She wrenched her veil into place. "This is dancing, not escaping soldiers."

"Well said." He tucked her fingers into his palm, judging the sway of the dancers until he spotted an opening in the ring. "Now!"

They hastened into the hall, linking hands with a circle of revelers. Feet skipped patterns of double beats in a galloping rhythm. The shrill call of the lutes and pipes urged movement, fast and primal. Laughter colored the air and layered the music of human voices atop the instruments. Heady motion blurred the great room into a smear of shades and smiles.

He squeezed Meg's hand and cast her a quick look. The veil had flown back, streaming behind her and waving with a spill of unbound hair. Eyes closed, lips turned up, she flowed and pranced as if she had never experienced a moment of fear. She appeared peaceful and happy, like when she twirled, like when he kissed her and she discarded her fearful pride. That cheer erased anger and distrust from her face, revealing the woman beneath. A stunning woman.

He finally found a worthy reason to keep her close.

The music carried them in a wide route around the hall. Nearing the stairs, Will recognized two of Carlisle's men-at-arms. They loitered in unadorned tunics, seemingly unarmed, but their eyes peeled over the crowd.

He cast his face back to Meg. "Dizzy yet?"

"No."

"Good. Another circuit, then."

She smiled broadly, perhaps like a woman enjoying herself.

Breathless minutes passed in happy revelry. Unaccustomed to Jacob's stiff, tight boots, his feet began to ache. Meg, however, showed no intention of slowing. She may have continued spinning around the hall in thoughtless abandon, holding Will's fingers as if to the top rung of a ladder, had the rhythm maintained its giddy pace.

But the musicians slowed. The pipes drew forth a melody of delicate longing. Two lutes quieted into a song of bittersweet sorrow, their harmonies coming together like lovers. Across the hall, men and women mimicked that harmony in lazy, swaying pairs. Groups of fond acquaintances raised mugs of ale and narrated long ago tales of love and adventure.

Will dropped the hand of the woman in front of him and

untangled Meg from the crumbling circle of dancers. She filled his arms with warm curves. Sweat misted her forehead, and a blush of exertion tinted pale skin a lively shade of pink. She gripped his bare forearms, testing the resilience of his flesh with distracting fingernails. He imagined those nails scoring his chest and stifled a groan.

"Are you lost again?"

"An insignificant detour," he said. "Nothing more."

"As you say."

He stared fondly and openly at her ingénue smile. The bitter-sweet tang of their recent kiss lingered on his lips, stirring his blood and creating a greed for more. As with good wine and food of quality, he wanted more—more than stolen kisses and her grudging reliance. But against nature, his need for her grew only more insistent with every taste. An unshakable hunger.

"What do you feel right now, in my arms?"

"Frightened," she said.

Her happy smile wavered and fell. He almost regretted the question, but he enjoyed her honesty. A single word. A word spoken with candor, stripped of pretense and guile.

Yes, he wanted more.

Will kissed her nose. "We'll get there."

"What do you mean?"

"When I hold you someday, I want you to feel safe like nowhere else."

"That will never be," she whispered. "With you, I am lost."

"No, you're not." He cupped her face, tracing her eyebrows with soft caresses. "Never with me."

She grinned. "With regard to direction, we have since established your limitations."

Greed overtook him. He wanted to steal her away from those dangerous halls—justice, honor, and her dubious sister be damned. Chivalry had never been a more tedious burden.

A familiar face in the crowd intruded on his daydreams. He tightened his hold on Meg's hips, edging her deeper into the mingling dancers. "Trouble follows you better than I do."

"What now?"

"Hugo."

She dropped her veil into place. "He's here?"

"Yes. With Carlisle."

"I suppose they'll have a better notion of my appearance now."

"For certain." Armed men circled the hall to flank Hugo and Carlisle. Their pairing struck him as unnatural. "Why would he follow you here? What aren't you telling me?"

She stumbled, her first misstep.

"Meg?"

"You trouble me. You cannot read my eyes or even see my face."

"But you're hiding something."

"Yes. Troubling."

"Tell me."

"When he came to the cabin, he said the sheriff had placed a bounty on my head. I wager he'd be first in line to seek such a reward. That and he demanded compensation for having offered us shelter."

Behind the mask, Will drew his lips into a sneer. *"Offered.* And what compensation did he demand?"

"Emeralds, of course. I gave him asem instead."

"Jacob's dog? That would be fitting."

"No, asem. A false alloy of silver and gold." Her explanation assumed that learned cadence, the one tinged with condescension. But he also recognized notes of excitement and wonder. "It's an amalgam of soft tin and white copper—melted, cast, and cleaned multiple times. Produced correctly, even artisans cannot discern asem from authentic gold."

"Nice swindle."

"But the quality of my materials was poor, which is why we hadn't traded it. At elevated temperatures, the consistency changes with any friction. Only a fool would believe those ingots had value beyond propping open a door."

"Perhaps that explains his face. I didn't give him those

bruises." Even from Will's vantage, the deep blue contusions mottled Hugo's complexion like evening shadows.

She laughed quietly. "You're making a habit of these sweet words."

"You couldn't appease him with anything less infuriating?"

"He wanted my body, but forgive me if I refused him that boon."

He gagged. "I forgive you."

"Sweet and gracious, both."

"Stop your teasing."

Hugo pointed in their direction. Carlisle nodded and drew his sword. The guards fanned across the hall, disrupting the dancers and stalling the musicians. A woman screamed. Men stepped between their partners and the soldiers, even as they eyed exits and slunk toward surreptitious escapes. Will did the same, positioning his body to better protect Meg, but he did not plan to flee—silly, stupid fool he had become.

"Hugo may be of use after all," he said.

"How so?"

"By providing us an alternate means into the dungeon."

"Stay where you are, Scarlet." Carlisle's rough command echoed across the hall's high rafters.

"This is our alternate means?" Meg whispered. "Has your outlook always been this hopeful?"

He flung away his useless mask. "Only when compared to yours."

"Drop your weapons," Carlisle said. "You are to be hanged for the murder of the Earl of Whitstowe. Is that the girl?"

At Carlisle's side, Hugo bobbed his bruised face. "That's her."

Meg threw back her veil like a warrior issuing a challenge. "Consider assessing the valuables on your person and around the castle. They've a habit of disappearing in that man's presence."

"Mad bitch." Hugo spat at her feet and crossed himself. "She carries the Devil's trappings in that satchel."

Will pulled his back straight. Having released the rich curves of Meg's hips, their dance long ended, he formed the fists he itched to use. Hugo's face was not damaged enough by half. "You and I are always at a disagreement, thief."

Hugo sneered, the distended flesh of one cheek bunched into a hideous knot below his eye. "Perhaps because we have the same taste in low women."

"She's rebuffed you repeatedly," he said. "You'll have to stoop lower."

"Can you spare advice for such a task? Noblewomen had been your sport, Scarlet."

"Enough!" Carlisle's rasping shout cleared the hall of its remaining citizens. He hefted his massive sword to reinforce his order. "Woman, toss me that bag. And Scarlet, I want to see those daggers on the ground."

Facing a score of armed men, Will felt brave and irresponsible in equal measure. A sensation of fear that bordered on glee saturated his brain. He grinned, a madman awakening.

"I think not."

Chapter Twenty-One

And why, Will Scarlet, not come to me?
Why not to Robin, Will?
For I remember thy love and thy glee,
And the scar that marks thee still . . .

"Robin Hood's Flight"
Leigh Hunt, 1820

The door grated shut. A lock clicked. Meg dropped to the ground and shoved anxious hands over the damp dungeon floor. Mutated by a ragged heartbeat, her frantic search sounded like the scuffling of rodents.

"Will? Will, speak to me."

"I'm here."

She found his hip, torso, face. "I heard you cry out. Are you injured?"

He grinned beneath her fingers. "You were worried?"

"Yes."

"Oh, sweet truth." Deep laughter filled the confines of their cell. He claimed the back of her head and pulled her near. A swift kiss embossed her lips with the feel and the taste of him. "That's my girl."

Possession, being possessed—the give and take fluttered in her blood. "Will, please."

"One of those bastards clubbed my sore shoulder, of all the foul luck."

"Is that all?"

"All?" His second laugh surrounded tinges of pain. "Woman, this grieves me."

"But nothing else? I thought you might have been stabbed."

"No, nothing else."

"Your shoulder is never going to heal if you keep doing it such abuse."

"Me? I didn't hit myself."

He shrugged out of his jester's costume. She found his arm and traveled up to his shoulder, burrowing beneath layers of cloth and leather armor. Smooth, warm skin stretched across bunched muscles.

He hissed. "Leave it be, Meg. There is no light here."

"I need no light."

Upon discovering the dressing, she checked for seepage or the tang of a wound mending abnormally. But dry bandages covered an unsoiled wound. She shook her head in amazement.

"How have you managed? You've fought time and again. The wound is not healed, but you persist. How are you doing this?"

He laid back and settled on the dungeon floor. "Maybe the lye?"

"And to me? How are you doing these things to me?"

"Doing . . . *what* . . . to you?"

She continued to touch him gently, stroking, wanting to massage those muscles until his tension dissolved. "I cannot think with you in my mind."

"Let me wager," he said in a whisper. "You ask yourself *why*. Why this? Why now?"

"Yes."

Releasing a long breath, he sounded bone weary. "The same questions plague me."

She stretched out beside him on the floor. They touched only where their fingers interlaced, holding hands in the dark.

But she confronted the possibility that she had misconstrued his intentions. He had followed her because of his concern for the safety of another woman. An uncomfortable twinge of curiosity was like a tickle in the middle of her back.

"Did you love her?"

"Marian?"

"Yes."

"Perhaps," he said. "Or perhaps I wanted to claim something of Robin's for my own."

"You worship your uncle, though you hate to. Small wonder you might covet all he has."

"Makes me nervous, what you know of me." He sighed and shifted on the hard floor. "Right from the first days among Robin's outlaws, she defended me—even when I had no desire for her assistance."

"Your poor pride."

"For certain. Until the weeks before I kissed her, I thought of her as an elder sister. Then our regard for each other . . . it changed."

"If God was kind enough to save you from an elder sister, you shouldn't contradict His purpose and create one."

He sat up, his low groan resonant with pain and oddly arousing. At the height of his pleasure, inside her, Will had groaned likewise. Those moments goaded and teased without relief, but they seemed like distant dreams. The wish to create that bliss anew throbbed across her senses until sound, touch, smell—all centered on him.

"Meg? I asked, was Ada that dreadful? Before?"

Sensual daydreams skittered away. Blame circled like a wild wind, to her sister and back to Meg. She wanted none of it. She wanted only Will and the freedom to make clean, fresh mistakes with him. Yet her spoiled relationship with Ada remained an affliction, an unhealed wound that crippled her more effectively than her blindness.

"Too much time has passed. I was a different person then, a girl really."

"You'll have the opportunity to set it right, if you wish to."

Close behind Will's reassurance lingered another, more dire possibility—that one of them would die before having that chance. The only way to keep that from happening was to complete her undertaking. And there in the dungeon, they were closer to Ada than ever.

"An escape, then," she said. "Tell me you have your lock pick."

He laughed, that teasing laugh like a breeze. "No, milady. Some harlot threw it into the woods, lost forever."

"Shall I add that to the tally of things for which I must apologize?"

"You keep such a tally?"

"I should."

"Acknowledging that you've spited yourself in an attempt to spite me—that will be apology enough."

"I'll think on it." She unbound her hair and threaded fingers through the snarls. "Have you anything else hidden in your boots?"

"Jacob's boots, actually. And indeed I do."

"Too bad about those principles of yours, Will," she said, plaiting her hair anew. "You certainly think like an outlaw."

"Principles, outlawry—I learned from the best."

Hugo strutted from the castle, tipping his cap to the sentries. Gold coins in his alms-bag composed a delicious ode to a most entertaining afternoon. He grinned, fondly recalling the bewildered expression on Scarlet's face when Carlisle and his men had overwhelmed the option to fight on. Contemplating that humiliation, not to mention the deadly punishment he yet faced, widened Hugo's smirk.

And then Meg. The mad girl. Losing her newest champion must have been a miserable defeat. Hugo had once admired her lawless methods, and convincing her of as much brought her willingly to his bed. A few kind lies softened her like tallow left in the sun.

He had hoped that Scarlet used her in a similar fashion. To watch her felled by another opportunist would have been satisfying. But because the gutless bastard had no intention of breaking Meg's spirit, Hugo would applaud when Scarlet hanged.

But his grin caused him pain. His cheeks throbbed. Memory of the beating he endured in Keyworth, attempting to barter Meg's shoddy asem, weakened his satisfaction like water added to wine. Identifying her to Finch merely resulted in her imprisonment. Her new lover would hang, true, but Hugo's doubling anger demanded more.

He strode to the base of Castle Hill. Stalls, tables, and wagons of wares had been cleared in preparation for the coming feast. Women cooked and ornamented the square, while a half dozen men started a bonfire. The common folk, like their betters within the castle walls, gathered to eat and drink a toast to the end of a growing season. Even the soldiers participated, smiling at the girls and accepting cups.

But word of the skirmish inside the castle had agitated the crowd. Hearsay decorated a plain festival with suspicion and worry. Men had not shed their weapons in favor of meat and mead. Women kept their children close, talking amongst themselves and invigorating the rumors with new details. Anticipation, like an arid haystack, awaited a single spark.

Hugo accepted a cup of ale from a half-grown girl, grimacing when she averted her blushing face. But he smiled past the inflamed pain of his bruises and eyed her fresh bosom. At the previous harvest festival, she had likely been running with the other children in careless games. But a twelvemonth brought her to the cusp of maturity. The temptation of that untried body dried his mouth and tightened his groin. A swig of young ale eased the parched tickle in his throat, even as his thirst for a different pleasure strengthened.

"Gramercy, miss," he said.

She kept her eyes to the ground and nodded.

"My dear, you needn't be ashamed of avoiding the sight of

my injuries." Blue eyes flicked briefly to his face and retreated. "You are curious what happened to me, I think."

She nodded again, her blush deepening. Innocence and interest warred with disgust, a combination Hugo found immensely arousing. And with her fair complexion, those pink cheeks would exactly match the color of her ripe nipples.

He took another long draw of ale. "I was beaten. Inside the castle, the sheriff keeps a witch as his prisoner."

"A witch?"

"Just so." He approached, catching her scent like a hound after a fox. "She is well-known in Charnwood for her spells. God cursed her, taking her sight because she would not repent."

The girl's eyes rounded, growing wide. "Is she hideous?"

"No," he said. "She is quite lovely despite her wickedness. Nothing to your beauty, my dear, but she uses her sweet appearance to deceive those who would be swayed to mercy."

"Why is she here?"

"Who can know? Whatever the sheriff's intent, surely he cannot justify keeping such a woman near good people."

"Of course not!"

"When I objected to her presence in our respectable city, the sheriff's men beat me. I scarcely made my way free. They pursue me still."

A mouth like a tight rosebud opened to an O of surprise. Hugo imagined pushing that mouth onto his cock. He swallowed heavily.

"Will you help me have justice, my dear?" He wove his fingers into the hair at the base of her skull. She flinched only a little and parted her moist lips. A tentative nod was his reward. "Then go. Find your friends and family. Tell everyone you know that a witch waits within the castle to cast her evil upon us."

She spun and fled, her skirts twisting about that nubile body. Hugo watched her bottom and downed the rest of his ale. She would be the first spark, spreading his tale until every reveler believed the sheriff held the Devil's own bride as his prisoner.

He exchanged the empty cup for another draft, grinning again despite a face full of bruises and the hard throb of unsatisfied lust between his legs. That girl would have quenched him, but worked into a lustful frenzy, any woman would do. He set off to spend his gold.

Will inhaled the earthy scent of Meg's hair. She fit him effortlessly, huddling deeper into his embrace. A humbling turn of events. For every minute they had spent in joy, they had spent an hour at each other's throats. Finding peace with her remained novel.

Experience taught him to doubt the durability of such peace, but he hoped against the odds. A stinging possessiveness burgeoned within him, leaving little room for doubt or fear or thought.

She stirred. "How long have we been in here? Hours?"

"It may be twilight by now," he said.

"What purpose could Finch have in detaining us without questioning us?"

"Perhaps he wanted us to share time alone."

She sat up, leaving him cold. "And this fits into his grand scheme how?"

"He hopes we'll gouge each other's eyes while we wait."

"That might have been true this morning."

Something akin to shyness colored her voice. He wanted a torch, any flicker of light to see her face and better read her expression. Realizing that she encountered such a challenge with every passing moment chilled him.

Rather than indulging in compassion Meg would find offensive, he opted for another insistent truth. "Now our only conflict shall be who relents first to use the privy."

"Do what you must," she said tightly. "I'll wait until it kills me."

He grinned and joined her in a seated position, rolling his aching shoulder.

"Will, can you see anything? Dance your fingers before your eyes—anything?"

As if doing so might change the result, he tried. Fingers fluttered, moving air against his face, but blackness swallowed all. "I can see shadows, motion. Nothing more. Why?"

"I've given our situation thought."

"Saints save us."

"Hush," she said. "Guards will arrive armed, as you said, and with torches."

"Yes."

"But when that door opens, you will squint and blink as your eyes adjust. I will not."

Her logic had resurfaced, but he could not decide if it was a boon or a curse. "What do you suggest?"

"Give me the explosives."

He clamped down on the impulse to refuse her. "And what would you do with them?"

"What we planned." She took his hands, resting them on her crossed ankles. "Especially after the blast, like staring into the sun, you'll be temporarily blinded."

"As opposed to you."

"If I can do anything without sight, I can find fire." Idly, she stroked the lump of scarred flesh at the center of his palm. "How did you get this? It feels like you were shot with an arrow."

Desire cooled. Defeat and old ghosts reigned as tyrants. "I was."

"What happened?"

"Robin," he said. "Robin happened."

"Your uncle did this? Why?"

"Because I deserved it."

She petted the humiliating scar as if trying to erase it. "You deserved being shot?"

He circled her hands to still her restless touch. "He accused me of cowardice, and rather than argue my point, I drew a knife and attacked him when he turned his back. He taught me that cowardice can make a man do terrible things. I would have done well to remember that lesson."

"Is he always right? Robin?"

"Certainly feels that way." The petulant child in his voice laid waste to years of life on his own.

"Does that mean you are always wrong?"

"I was wrong when he gave me this."

"Perhaps," she said quietly. "But does that resign you to behaving as his inferior at every instance? You could always try to see yourself as I do."

"You do not see me."

With lacey touches, she moved her hands up to his face. She straddled his hips. Will filled his arms with her body.

"I see you, and that scares us both," she whispered. "You are brave. You are good."

He gripped the soft flesh of her thighs. Blood spun from his brain in a dizzying rush and throbbed in his groin. "Are you seducing me, Meg, or only making your point?"

"Both." She smiled against his cheek. "I don't crave additional danger, but I'm right about this. When the guards arrive, keep your eyes shut until after the flash. Resist the impulse to play hero."

"*Play* hero? I was attempting the honest article."

"Release my sister and I from this place and I'll give you a hero's reward." Her breath kissed him before her lips touched his. More brazenly, she rocked her hips against his erection. He groaned. "Until then, let me do what I am able."

Once, Will had wanted to control her, to outsmart her, to merely understand her. But as laughter and longing burned his throat, as admiration and desire played games in his blood, he wanted only to survive her.

"You win."

She stiffened. "Good. They're coming."

Chapter Twenty-Two

But all in vain we have sought about;
Yet none so bold there are
That dare adventure life and blood,
To free a lady fair.

"Robin Hood and the Prince of Aragon"
Folk ballad, seventeenth century

Robin had taught him to trust his brothers in arms. Will had lived by that mandate for years, gathering the benefits of protection, spoils, and friendships forged in the heat of battle. Yet months spent teamed with corrupt soldiers and traitors and thieves had shaken that faith. And never had he thought to trust Meg, not like this. She was no one's ideal fighting companion, but she stood ready.

Will pushed the few remaining explosives into her hands. "These are for you."

She scampered away. A fog of detached purpose collected between them, blanketing the closeness they had fostered.

Footsteps sounded along the corridor. He could no more tell one striking boot from another, blending into a tangle of echoes, but Meg said, "Four men."

"Are you certain?"

"No."

He shrugged. "Fair enough."

Metal keys clicked against the outside lock. They scrambled into position. Meg pressed into the corner near the entrance. He crouched beneath the low ceiling, poised with his feet wide apart and his back to the entry. Anticipation throbbed in his veins.

He closed his eyes.

The tumbler turned. The door swung open and struck Will's back. The hissing song of a torch invaded their cell, sizzling at his ear. Thrusting, he gnashed his heels into the stone floor and trapped the guard's forearm.

"Now Meg!"

A thunderous crack split the air. The guard screamed. Sharp smoke singed Will's nose, but he kept his eyes clamped tight. He ground his upper back into the plank wood. His thighs burned. He pushed, finding scant purchase along the smooth dirt. Meg fled her corner and joined him, her back against the wood. The sickening crack of splintering bone and another scream proved their prize.

Will released the pressure, only slightly, until the guard yanked his arm out of the entryway. The door slammed closed.

"Can you see?"

He opened his eyes, blinking. The flickering tease of light from the guard's discarded torch played along the walls. The room began to materialize.

"Yes." Crouching, he grabbed the torch and pushed it into Meg's hands. She skittered away. "Ready for another go?"

A hard thump severed her reply. Will nearly lost his balance at that renewed assault, but he recovered and held fast.

Valuable moments allowed his eyes time enough to align the grays and oranges and shadows. Vision clear, he saw Meg huddled in a corner, knees pulled close and the torch in her outstretched hands. Flames obscured her face.

His legs trembled. The guards' onslaught against the door became rhythmic, two or three men fighting to open what Will kept closed. His teeth jolted together with every renewed attack. He bit his tongue, spitting blood onto the cursed dungeon floor. "Ready?"

"Yes."

He jumped away. The door crashed open, two guards falling into a writhing heap. Their swords remained concealed within scabbards, useless to everyone. Will stripped a man of his helmet and grabbed the torch from Meg. While a third guard hunched in the corridor, clutching his forearm, the last breeched the cell with a drawn sword.

She was right. Four men.

Tight confines permitted the soldier little room to wield his weapon. He swung the sword in a truncated arc. Will dropped low. Forged steel imbedded in soft, rotten sandstone. The guard tugged once before wrenching the blade free.

Will exploited the hesitation, springing forward. He clipped his opponent under the chin with the helmet and plunged flaming wood into his face. Screams ripped to life. The man dropped his sword and rocked backward. The stench of charred flesh layered with mildew.

One of the fallen guards tried to trip him, grasping an ankle. Will kicked him in the head and retrieved the burned man's sword. "Don't move."

He bounded into the hallway where the soldier with the crushed arm cowered. Will stripped his sword and poised both weapons. "Into the cell, now!"

Meg removed the other guards' helmets. As Will contemplated what to do with his unwanted wards, she chanced upon the keys and two sets of manacles.

"I think these were meant for us," she said.

"Scandalous, how these Nottingham folks behave toward guests."

"I shan't return."

He bound the guards and littered the cell with weapons.

Meg turned toward the clamor of metal. "You are leaving the swords?"

"I can only carry two. Better these remain locked in here than in the corridor for other guards to discover."

"Give one to me."

"Woman, you'll cut off a foot."

"They hardly know that. And I need a walking stick. Any-thing."

He sighed and handed her the most graceful of the weapons, one with a lightweight pommel and fullers running its length. "Careful."

She simply nodded and hustled from the cell, leaving him to lock the door behind him. His heart shook in a treble beat, but he could not afford to descend from the high of combat. Enclosed within the narrow dungeon corridor, he could no more stop and rest than he could kiss Meg again. He desired both to the point of pain.

Freedom first.

"We haven't much time," he said. "Your sister must be here."

She gripped his forearm, her expression intent. Trapped to-gether in the darkness, he had almost forgotten her eyes—not her blindness, but the skittering vacancy he used to find eerie. She was thinking again. "I noticed a single torch, yes?"

The need for action, for flight, pressed to the front of his brain. But he waited. "Yes."

"Did they bring it or take it from the wall sconce?"

He looked up and down the corridor. Illuminated by a dozen torches, the passage offered few concealing shadows, except for the well of blackness near their cell. One sconce was empty.

"From the wall," he said.

"Assess the passage and make a mental picture of what you can see." She blinked. She smiled. "Then put out the torches."

His head twitched involuntarily. He found no fondness for these new habits, stumbling in the dark and putting his faith in Meg.

"Trust me," she said, climbing into his thoughts. "Go now."

* * *

The last of the torches hissed and sputtered into extinction. Will cursed. He struck some manner of obstacle. "Such a!"

"How do you fare?" Meg made no attempt to hide her amusement, despite the danger.

"Poorly, and you are well aware of that. How do you daily manage this?"

His grudging compliment tempered her amusement. She tapped the slender sword along the wall to her right. Stone, stone, wood. She stopped, rapping her knuckles against the door. "Who goes?"

Minutes passed more swiftly than they did, sliding down the corridor without success. They checked each door only to find empty cells or other miserable wretches detained for some crime or another. The impetus to search every possible crevice for Ada, to move ever faster, eroded her calm. Her fingers flew over the damp stonework lining the passage, enduring nicks and cuts at every negligent movement. Dank air clung to the inside of her mouth. They could not have traveled so far only to fail. The few moments remaining to them seeped away.

Will caught her hand. "Be easy, Meg. We are lost if you cannot concentrate."

She inhaled deeply. Then the sound came to her unbidden. A call. Her own name.

"Listen."

He stilled. "To what?"

"A man. He calls my name. And yours." She leaned toward the call, then walked. "Dryden."

She pushed through the darkness with Will shuffling and cursing close behind. Counting, she made note of the four cells they passed without scrutiny. But they would free Dryden first. From two, they would become three people searching for Ada.

Tapping the sword again, she found the wooden barrier separating them from Dryden. "Here, Will."

"Scarlet! Meg! Is that you?"

"Quiet now, milord," Will said. "Hold fast."

She tucked the hilt of the sword between her knees and pulled the ring of keys from her wrist. The metal clicked with unnatural loudness in the desolation of the dungeon. She fingered the keyhole, judging the size and dimensions of the lock, and repeated the process to find a suitable key. Failure amassed on failure. Another key. Another turn.

Then a satisfying snap of release. The door swung inward. Will squeezed her upper arm. "Well good."

"Yes. Gramercy, Meg," Dryden said. "But we have no torch?"

She slid her wrist through the metal key loop and gripped her sword again. "It seemed a clever plan at the time."

"And it remains one," Will said. "My knees and toes are protesting, but we'll meet any attacker from the shadows, to our advantage. Dryden, are you injured?"

"No. Angered, outraged—but not injured. You are both well?"

A chuckle tinged with fatigue was Will's reply. "For the moment."

"And now for Ada," Meg said.

Dryden sighed. "Hours ago, I would've suggested that we confront the authority behind our imprisonment to effect your sister's release. But this is an abomination. I was naïve to think I could help you with titles and influence alone. We must accomplish this ourselves."

A rattling clamor at the farthest end of the corridor interjected. Alarm thrilled through Meg's muscles, but no one approached.

"We have but a few moments more," Will said. "Your sister cannot be far."

From down the hall, Dryden hissed their names. "She's here."

Meg rushed past two doors, bumping into Dryden. "My apologies."

"Listen," he said. A woman cried behind the wooden barrier.

"Ada," she whispered. "How did you know?"

"I heard soldiers near my cell an hour ago, and a woman's cries," Dryden said. "I thought to start here."

Another host of failed keys delayed progress until Meg finally opened the door. Dryden and Will stood at her back as she entered the cramped cell. Its tight, close walls pressed on her senses, every breath echoing without pause.

"Ada?"

"Meg?" Disbelief shaded the single syllable, the sound of a woman not daring to believe a dream. "You're here?"

"Yes." She found her sister, finally, and embraced the thin, trembling woman. Their reunion perforated years' worth of bitterness.

Ada cried, her sobs a heavy cloud. But hopefulness emerged. "Praise Mary! I've been released."

"No, no, we are yet pursued and in danger."

"I don't understand."

"We have no time for explanations. We must flee. Soldiers approach." She swept sweat-dampened hair from Ada's brow. "Are you injured?"

"I—" A strangled sob twisted into the air. "My feet. He cut me."

"Who?"

"The sheriff. Finch."

"Monster," Dryden said from the corridor.

"Who is that, Meg? Who's here?"

She forced lightness into her words. "I've brought allies for us. That is the Earl of Whitstowe's son and his companion."

A door banged open and soldiers' rough commands polluted the dungeon's unearthly quiet. Time had escaped them.

"Meg," Will whispered. "Stay in this cell."

She struggled from Ada's frantic embrace and found him

in the doorway. "So you can bumble in the dark? No. Being by myself will be more terrifying than fighting."

"To stay safe—"

"I will not."

Memories returned, those moments spent deserted in the great hall with no allies, no means of defending herself, no way to safety. Tears gathered. She wanted to touch his body, to latch hold of him, weaving into the metal and leather of his armor.

Instead, she choked on a mouthful of pride and whispered near his temple. "You said I looked like a lost child, there in the great hall. I felt that helpless. Will, don't leave me alone."

"You have Ada now. She needs you."

And I need you.

But she kept the words locked inside.

His quiet breathing filled the distance between them. "Hold fast to your blade," he said. "Stay with your sister. She seems of no mind to tend herself. Dryden and I shall dispatch this lot."

"Simple work?"

"Of course. We'll make our escape through the tunnels I used to enter—where we'll need you, Meg." He hesitated before kissing her gently on the temple. "Until then, let me do what *I* am able."

"Ideas?"

"None."

"Here," Will said. "Have the second sword."

Dryden took the weapon, secreting among the many shadows. "I am weary of this nonsense. Shall we end it?"

"Probably not today. But I am keen for the opportunity and your assistance, both."

A quick look into the cell, barely illuminated by approaching torches, reassured him of Meg's compliance. She huddled in the corner with her bedraggled sister, stroking the woman's hair. The sword glinted at her feet.

Guilt chewed his conscience like a rabid animal. He had separated them—unknowingly, yes, and certainly without the intention of injuring Ada. But he had helped bring this day into being. To set events to rights, he would keep his promises. And Meg's anger be damned, he needed to know she was safe from harm.

His choice was abrupt but necessary. He pushed the door shut, locking the sisters away from the impending clash. The heavy oak almost concealed Meg's screeching outrage.

Man after man pushed through the dungeon's entrance. Heavy chunks of armor and curtains of mail clattered as boots descended four shallow steps. Frenzied flames colored the walls, but as many shadows remained as patches of light.

Opposite Dryden, backs against the corridor walls, Will counted the opposition. Eight, nine—he lost track as man and shadow walked together, appearing as twice the threat.

"Farther into the shadows," Dryden whispered.

"We cannot hide forever." He scowled, unsympathetic to Dryden's hesitation. "And more will come if we wait."

Determination—a pale cousin to the ruthless purpose rallying in Will's muscles—stole over Dryden's features. He swallowed and nodded, raising his sword.

Inhaling once, Will held the air until it seared his lungs. He clenched the hilt until the bones in his fingers threatened to snap. Spots patterned his vision. His brain stumbled and eddied in a suffocating fog. When he could endure no more, he spat the poisonous breath into the corridor and attacked.

Chapter Twenty-Three

So they fell to it, full hardy and sore,
Striving for victory . . .

"Robin Hood and the Shepherd"
Folk ballad, seventeenth century

Ada flinched and shrank into her sister's arms. But no embrace could quiet the rattling echoes of deadly armaments. The vicious clash of swords invaded the cell as if the door remained wide and welcoming.

"What is this? Where is the earl? Meg?"

"Hush now. Listen."

She unwound her limbs from Meg's stiff hold. Confusion and anger festered behind her breastbone. Because confusion too closely resembled fear—the fear she had lived and breathed for weeks—she concentrated on anger.

"I will not," she said. "I demand to know what is happening!"

"And I'm trying to hear that."

She whipped her head. Meg had never spoken so sharply, her words hissing like a snake.

A body slammed against the other side of the wall. Both women jumped. In the passage, a man ground out a hard cry. Meg gasped. The need to reassure her, in turn to allay her own worries, returned to Ada like an ancient instinct. "We will endure."

"I pray, yes."

Another clash of bodies and swords shook the oaken door. A sword imbedded in the wood. A thump. Another man cried out. "Halt! We yield!"

"Meg, who is that who spoke?"

"Dryden." Her sister stood. The sword she held scraped like a claw along the floor. "He has surrendered."

"What does that mean for us?"

"I know not." Another set of keys jangled outside. "Get to the back of me."

Ada arose. The soles of her feet ached. Hobbling on her heels, she put no pressure on the dressings wrapped in irregular rolls around the arches. She found her sister's raised forearms, the muscles bunched to support the weight of her sword.

"Stop, Meg. Please. If the earl's son has surrendered, what hope have you?"

"None." An unexplained sob cracked the word.

The door swung open. Sheriff Finch stood silhouetted in front of a cache of weapons and torches. Ada shrank back. Her feet blazed in pain. She stumbled. Only meeting the sandstone wall with the sharp bones of her shoulders prevented a fall. "Get away from me!"

Meg hefted the sword. "Who is it, Ada?"

"Ah, you must be my uninvited guest," the sheriff said.

The milquetoast quiet of his voice erased the last vestige of conflict from the dungeon. Only he remained, weaving a soft threat into the air. "Ada, you must tell your sister that in Nottingham, introductions are never made across drawn weapons. Such barbarism shows poor manners."

"Please, Meg," she whispered. "He'll kill you."

She hitched the sword higher. "No, he won't. He needs me."

Finch smiled, a serpent readying his strike. "She is no simpleton. No coward either—unlike some participating in this botched escapade."

Ada looked behind the sheriff, briefly meeting Dryden's gaze. A sickening blend of shame and disgust covered his features. He turned away.

"But she does not know me like you do, Ada," Finch said. "She does not know how convincing I can be."

"Please!" She did not know to whom she begged: Finch for mercy or Meg for good sense.

Finch stepped into the cell. Had Meg been able to see, she could have taken off his head with one slice. "You are right, my new friend Meg. I do have need of you. But you will drop the sword. Now."

A foursome of helmeted guards entered the cell and flanked Finch. A man wearing a tunic slashed with blood stepped away from the others. He pinned Ada to the wall with a hand to her neck. He raised the blade and laid it gently against her skin.

"Meg," she whispered. *"Please."*

She closed her eyes although she had no need. She could peel back her eyelids and slice them with a knife, all without a whit of difference. But she closed them. She needed to concentrate.

Ada fairly trembled at her side. The fear pulsing from her stooped body roiled against the walls, turning Meg's stomach into nauseous twists. Whatever Finch had done to her sister proved he could make good on the threats he delivered with calm grace. Other men cluttered the cell, their panting breaths like horses penned in a stable. More waited in the passage.

And Dryden had surrendered. He must be there too.

But Will. She could not hear Will. The temptation to call his name stabbed the inside of her mouth.

"Be a clever girl," Finch said. "Release the weapon."

She frowned, working his intonations in her mind. Menace. A tranquil menace unlike any she had ever heard. A shiver skimmed the bared skin at the back of her neck. But she would not be trodden under by this man. A thief and a bully, only his station separated Finch from someone of Hugo's ilk.

She opened her eyes and her fingers, both. The sword clanged to the floor. A soldier scraped it along the floor as he retrieved it.

"Gramercy," Finch said.

Meg lowered her chin. If Will was dead, their survival depended on her success in maneuvering the sheriff. She cleared her mind of fear and a surprising stab of grief. From deep in her blood, she found the strength to submit.

"My apologies, my lord sheriff. I shall offer whatever cooperation I am able. Please release her."

"What an agreeable sister you have, Ada. Far more than you were at our first meeting. Did you tell her about your feet, perhaps?"

"Yes." Ada's voice rasped a bird's broken wing dragging in the dirt.

"She is brave and a quick learner." Finch touched Meg's chin with gloved fingers. "Such qualities must explain her proficiency in the ancient arts."

"Release me! I demand an audience with Finch!"

Her knees bowed. Her heart jumped to life.

Will! Will lived!

But secrets might bolster their chance of escape. The only secret Meg concealed was her altered feelings for the man who had once been her adversary.

"Get that man away from me," she said with a snarl. "He is a liar and a traitor."

"Meg, Meg, no cause for insults." Will's mocking tone said he agreed with her strategy, a pact written between them without forethought.

"There most certainly is cause," she said. "You lured me with the promise of my sister's release, and yet you locked me in with her! Let me out at once."

The guards ushered them into the passage. Ada clung to

Meg's arm, whimpering in obvious pain. "Meg, you came here with Will Scarlet?"

"And with Dryden, I did."

"But he's one of their men! He kidnapped me these weeks ago and left me to Finch's whims."

"I have no whims, Ada," the sheriff said. "I have *intentions*. And I intend to have your sister work on my behalf."

"She's here thanks in large part to my dedication," said Will, dragging what sounded like heavy manacles. "I shall collect my reward and be on my way."

"Hardly, Scarlet," said Finch. "You killed two of my men here and at least as many in the great hall, not to mention the list of crimes for which you've been hunted. What was the first? The Earl of Whitstowe's murder?"

Ada squeezed Meg's arm. "How could you?"

"The story is a long and tedious one," she said. "Just as my captivity with this man has been long and tedious."

Will laughed, a sound like a sneer. "My joy is boundless now that I'm free of your mad prattle."

"I had no intention of slinking into Nottingham Castle to cause trouble," she said. "The fault is his. I wanted nothing but my sister's safety."

The sheriff stepped nearer. She felt his eyes boring into her face, testing her, measuring her resolve. "Are you willing to make an exchange for your services?"

"Of course."

"Before this ridiculous pantomime of violence, I was prepared to offer you a choice."

Fiery anticipation licked her from the inside. "What choice?"

"In exchange for your services, you may choose who will go free—and who will be hanged."

Speech and reason fled with equal haste. A deadly ice storm doused her fire, leaving her to shiver in an unearthly cold. Will said nothing. Ada said nothing. But the words in Meg's mind screamed, railed, and sobbed.

He stroked her cheek. "The choice is yours, Meg. Will Scarlet or your sister."

Will's head throbbed where a guard had set him to crash into an unyielding stone wall. He tugged against the manacles, struggling to regain the few minutes he lost to unconsciousness. All he knew was that bickering with Meg had become a demanding task.

She clenched her jaw. "Your pardon, my lord sheriff?"

Finch crossed his arms and cast Will an insipid grin. He wanted to shake the man's head from his neck. No weapons. No tricks. Just limitless frustrations focused on a single slimy individual. "By the way you and Scarlet danced in the hall upstairs, I would have thought you at quite the crossroads."

"Meg, you danced with him?"

She flinched but ignored her sister's revolted question, concentrating on the sheriff as surely as if she stared him in the eyes. "I cannot choose."

"But you will," Finch said. "That is part of my enjoyment. And that is my price for letting one of them free."

Relish danced merry circles across his face—a face Will was glad she could not see. Meg would not have held her temper, or he hoped as much. He could have used a dose of her sparkling anger. Flanked between Finch and her sister, she seemed incapable of standing straight.

The dungeon door banged on its hinges. All heads turned to see Carlisle stride down the four steps. Another dozen men lined the passage behind him. Will shot Dryden a foul look. The man cowered between two guards, his head lowered like a man at prayer. Had the nobleman any mettle, any backbone at all. But no. They were well and truly trapped.

Carlisle joined the knot of guards and prisoners. "Scarlet."

"Carlisle."

The sheriff stepped closer to Meg. She sniffed, wrinkling her nose—Meg, the girl who toiled among the foulest smelling compounds in England. "And if I refuse?" she asked. "You cannot make me work for you."

"You know very well that I could send both to their ends, without question or protest."

"I cannot."

Ada began to cry. "The sheriff tortured me! And you ponder whether to free the man who sent me here?"

Will listened to Ada with great interest. She spoke to her sister with the shrewish insistence of a woman used to being obeyed. Meg shrank with every word, a willow tree drooping beneath a gale.

"Why are you even contemplating this?" Tears streaked Ada's grimy face, her eyelids rimmed in red.

"We both know why I might be tempted," Meg whispered.

It was Ada's turn to flinch. "You would punish me still? And so harshly? Have you enjoyed thinking on my suffering, sitting in this cell?"

"I would not be here if that were true."

"You have no notion of the trials I have endured."

Meg raised her head. She shrugged from her sister's hold. "And you have no notion of mine."

Will suppressed a grim smile and caught the daggers Ada threw with her eyes, hurling them right back. She hardly merited the arduous path Meg had traveled to that bleak dungeon, and she fostered an inhuman quantity of guilt in him. Aiming his frustrations at her entailed no hardship.

"I grow impatient," said Finch. "Make your decision. We have time yet this evening to display your less fortunate friend to the crowd outside."

Meg paled, her features turning to granite as she faced Finch. "I shall do what you ask of me, Sheriff Finch. Please release my sister."

He smiled. "To be sure, this is the less interesting decision. I had been prepared to strike a more personal bargain with Ada for her release, but such as it is."

Dryden shifted his weight. "And what is to become of me?"

"Now you think to speak up, coward," Will shouted, pulling against the guards who held him. The chains at his wrists rattled. "A blind woman held her sword longer than you!"

But Dryden ignored the taunt, looking to Finch with expectation of a dog awaiting scraps.

"Meg, you chose interesting companions for this foolhardy quest," the sheriff said.

"I had little choice, seeing as how your men killed Lord Whitstowe."

His painted grin did not change. "We already established that your friend Scarlet was responsible for that debacle. That is correct, yes, Carlisle?"

"Of course. And for that he'll hang."

Will sneered at his former commander, noticing Meg's satchel slung over Carlisle's shoulder. He cut a cold glare between his adversaries, Dryden included. "Shall I have company?"

"Alas, no," said Finch. "Hanging a nobleman is a tricky matter—far more so than disposing of a bastard piece of rubbish such as yourself. I have detained him long enough." The sheriff turned to Dryden and signaled a guard to release him. "Take Ada out of Nottingham. If you hold your peace about what occurred here, we shall have no further involvement."

Dryden nodded, his face sodden with sweat and pale beneath his shadowed beard. "I beg your pardon, Meg, please. I, I cannot—"

She interrupted with a quick cut of her jaw, lips mashed together. Strands of hair escaped her plait and framed the ire on her face. "I appreciate all you have done in your father's stead, but you have begged my pardon one time too many. Get my sister to safety and have done."

Chapter Twenty-Four

The day's example proved
That grateful love esteems
No sacrifice too painful—none too great.

"Robin Hood: A Fragment"
Robert and Caroline Southey, 1847

The guards jostled and prodded their prisoners out of the dungeon. Well ahead, a half dozen men escorted Dryden and Ada from sight. Meg received no apology from her sister, no thanks, no backward glace. Will crushed his teeth together, briefly contemplating which of the two freed prisoners he disliked more.

Guards loomed at his back, but he coaxed a haphazard path to Meg's side. "Are you injured?"

"No. Are you? I heard you hit the wall." Glass and steel were softer than her expression.

"I saw stars, apparently long enough for Dryden to surrender."

"Are they away?"

"Yes," Will said. "Ada is safe."

"But you are not."

Resignation crept on stealthy paws, walking over his plans for the future. Unless he brought about some miracle, he would hang. And Meg almost sounded sorry for that.

Coming into the grand hall, a guard pushed her from behind. She stubbed her toe and faltered, falling to her knees and crying out. Will dropped beside her, his fettered hands gripping hers. Tears glittered in her pallid blue eyes.

"Meg?"

"Up, you," Carlisle said. He and a second guard hauled Will to his feet.

Another man lifted Meg, his arms encircling her breasts. She paled and struggled. Will saw red. He pulled at his restraints, but unyielding metal snagged his wrists. "Leave her go."

Carlisle released Will to a pair of soldiers and wiped his hands on his thighs. "Be more concerned for your own neck, Scarlet."

"Because the fate of my neck is already sealed, I say again, leave her go."

The guard spun her around and kissed her. He gripped the back of her head and her bottom, gloved fingers gouging her curves. Carlisle and other soldiers laughed. Even Finch raised an eyebrow, almost amused.

Meg squirmed, pulling, arching away, but her attacker would not relinquish his hold. His tongue pushed between her clamped lips. And she bit down.

"Bitch!"

The guard roared in pain, blood dripping onto his chin. He drew back his fist and landed a hard blow. Her cheek split. She screamed and dropped to the floor.

"Meg!"

Will pounced, landing atop the guard. Momentum propelled them to the floor, his ankle twisting at an odd angle. He pushed manacle chains across the man's windpipe. The guard gagged, his face a deep, fiery red. A trio of soldiers yanked Will up, hurling him to the unforgiving floor. Familiar stars spun before his eyes. He doubled over when the hard toe of Carlisle's boot connected with his gut.

"Enough, Scarlet," Carlisle said, propping beefy hands on

his hips. He unlocked a manacle cuff and nodded toward a distant corner of the hall. "Get him up."

Limp, moaning with every graceless movement, Will was wrenched to his feet. Soldiers dragged him to a low strut angling between the wall and a support column. Carlisle looped an end of the cuffs over the beam and refastened them, leaving Will to dangle there. His toes scraped the ground. Metal bit his wrists.

Carlisle slapped him on the cheek, amused. "He's yours to have, Smithson."

The guard stepped forward, rubbing his windpipe and grinning. Blood tinted his chin like madder root. "Can I kill him?"

Finch denied his request. "I want him alive enough to hang on the morrow."

Smithson nodded. Without hesitation, he burrowed a fist into Will's middle. Then his kidneys. Then his face. Another punch. Another groan. He fought unconsciousness, stretching past the pain, looking beyond the blur of color and motion in search of a weapon. The only weapons he saw were trained on him.

Dreamlike, from some distant place, Meg screamed for them to stop. The screams multiplied and broadened. Shouts and calls. Voices. Voices upon voices clamored in his brain, digging at his ears like a crow's razor beak.

But he was not mad. Others heard it. Wary guards shifted their eyes away from the beating Smithson dispensed. Finch crossed to a window slit overlooking the castle's courtyard and peered into the evening darkness illuminated by the eerie orange glow of festival fires.

Across the wide hall where Will and Meg had danced, dozens of angry fists pummeled the pair of locked oaken doors. The doors shook. The hinges scraped and rattled.

Carlisle flashed the sheriff a hasty glance. "Finch, what goes?"

"A mob."

"What do they want?"

"Listen."

The room stilled. Ears trained on a hundred livid shouts weaving into a distinct and bloodthirsty demand. One syllable, over and over.

Panic seized his breath. He looked to where Meg sat, her legs sprawled on the floor. Except for the blood flowing between trembling fingers, her rigid face was ashen. She, too, heard the call—a single chanted word.

Witch.

And the doors ripped open.

Meg could not see the anger and terror, but the fusion of voices communicated plenty. The cry infected the air with fear. Boots and bare feet slapped on the flagstones, running. But she could no more fight her accusers than she could see them. She could not run as they did. And struggling—she had grown too weary for struggle. When hands hoisted her into the air, she found nothing. No strength. No surprise.

She would succumb to the mercy of the mob, and Will would hang if the soldiers did not beat him to death first. His frantic shouts failed to rouse the passion she needed to fight. Too many years of suspicion and fear made such a fate inevitable. She hid in the woods. She practiced those ancient arts in secret. But fate found her and dragged her into the courtyard.

Fingers ripped her hair and gown. A chilly evening wind whipped around her legs as they spun her. Wide-eyed, she looked for color and tried to imagine the sky. Did clouds obscure the moon? Would the stars watch as these fearful, frenzied people put her to death?

The mob righted her body and pushed her against what may have been a maypole. She tried to stand, instinctively, but her boots slipped on unsteady logs. With lengths of rope, men tugged her arms backward and secured her to the pole. Perhaps girls had danced in circles that afternoon, weaving colorful ribbons around its length. She imagined the ribbons fluttering over her head, watching her as the stars did.

And then the fire.

She smelled it first, the smoke and the torches. Flames laughed and shushed, eclipsing the incensed shouts, soothing her. The pungent odor of burning wood and cloth wafted skyward. Heat warmed the leather of her boots.

She stood atop an island of fire. Soon the flames would consume her. Its power, its ancient mysteries would render her body to ash. She would drift into the air as smoke until nothing of pain and bitterness and betrayal remained. The crowd would become ordinary citizens again. They would wander home before dawn, able to sleep a little more soundly—their fears lessened, her fears gone altogether.

She closed her eyes, licked her lips, and remembered Will's kiss.

"Burn her!"

Hugo.

He did this. She knew him; she knew his dark thoughts. He had rallied the mob. And he was murdering her as surely as if he slid a dagger across her throat, smiling and taunting her across the long minutes of a slow demise.

"Burn her! She's a witch!"

Rage awakened the passion that the thought of death could not. She would not die with Hugo by to watch and laugh.

Her resignation gone, the flames turned against her. No longer soothing, no longer laughing, the fire grabbed at her. Smoke contaminated her lungs. The leather of her boots ignited. She kicked with her heels, stamping the unsteady logs. And she screamed.

Will wound his left wrist, the smaller of the two, within the manacles. Yanking, twisting, the skin flayed away from muscle. Red trails streaked his forearms. He lifted his knees and used the weight of his body to pull down on the restraints. Iron carved deeper furrows. Blood slicked and slipped between the metal and his skin. He bit the inside of his cheek.

A grand shout from the courtyard snatched his attention. The sinister orange glow intensified.

"Damn you, Finch!" Sweat wound tiny rivulets down his forehead. "After all this, you'll let her die? Your precious alchemist?"

The sheriff recoiled. Alone in the hall except for Will and Carlisle, he turned his eyes from the spectacle beyond the window. "No one can stop them now. My men would have to destroy half the town to get to her. We'll find another."

Will caught sight of the satchel Carlisle still wore. "I can stop them. Turn me loose."

"I'll not lose two prizes in one day," Finch said, eyebrows knitted together. "Better that my guards protect the castle and the allies in these walls."

Another shout from the crowd. And Meg's scream.

"Fiend!" He pulled again with brutal force. The beam above his head creaked.

"Secure him, Carlisle!"

The burly soldier strode forth. As if awaiting a fellow animal in a baiting pen, Will watched. Sweat blurred his vision. Pain scrambled his senses. But when Carlisle stepped into his realm, he kicked him under the chin.

Carlisle reeled. He spat broken splinters of teeth and a spray of blood. "Scarlet!"

He grinned, his lilting voice only half sane. "I must admit, Carlisle, I never liked you."

Magnificent shadows danced across the hall, irregular measures of orange and black. Carlisle's sword glinted in the light. He charged.

Will connected with Carlisle's hand, kicking the sword in a high arc. He winched his knees into the air and swung forward. He clasped his attacker around the neck with his calves. They wrestled and tugged, every motion imbedding the manacles deeper into his wrists. He bellowed, fueled only by rage. With a twist of his hips in opposition to the swift snap of his ankles, Carlisle went limp.

Thighs shuddering, Will kept hold of the man's hanging body. He yanked against the manacle encircling his left wrist, using Carlisle's weight and his own. A bone in his thumb shattered. He roared as agony flared through his body. His wrist slipped free. The manacle flew over the beam, attached to only one arm. He smashed to the ground and landed atop Carlisle's inert body.

He caught the fleeting sound of Finch's boots running up the wide staircase at the front of the hall. But the villain could wait. Meg could not.

Rolling off Carlisle's lifeless mass, his left hand refused to respond. It lay limp at the end of his arm. He retrieved Meg's satchel and slung it across his shoulder. The sword, however, he abandoned. He could not restrain the dangling manacle while brandishing a weapon, not when his left hand was useless.

At another of Meg's macabre cries, he tore through the hall and into the courtyard. A strengthening wind shot sparks into the night sky and challenged the brilliant stars. Smoke mingled with shadows along the castle walls, dancing like wraiths. Chanting and urging the flames to do the foul deed, tenscore citizens circled a blazing pyre.

Silhouetted, Meg stood bound at its center. She screamed and kicked. Each strike of her boots against the smoldering wood whirled a new puff of sparks around her legs.

Hefting the loose cuff in his right hand, he tested its weight and cinched the chain, forming a makeshift mace. He sprinted through the courtyard and swung the manacle around a guard's ankles. A quick yank sent him to the ground. Will stomped the man's hand and pilfered his shield.

Looping the shield over his left forearm, he bullied past, through, and over the mob. The thrashing manacle cleared whatever path the shield did not manage, connecting with random heads and limbs. Taken aback by the madman in their midst, the hysterical citizens of Nottingham cowered.

He dropped the shield facedown onto the stones near the pyre and withdrew the weighty bag of sugar from the satchel.

He spilled it into the basin of the shield. The satchel came next, atop the sugar, where he smashed it with the loose manacle cuff. More of Meg's black power exploded. Acids of all sorts bubbled with the sugar, forming a thick blanket of smoke.

People fell back, screaming. Will tackled a man and stripped him of a short sword and cloak. Smoke blackened the air. He hunched over as a cough wracked his body, the smoke spiking his lungs and setting off spasms.

"Stay! This is the work of the witch!"

Will whipped toward a disgustingly familiar voice. Two hundred people gathered around that pyre, but only two interested him.

Meg. And Hugo.

But Hugo could wait.

He doused the pilfered cloak in a barrel of rainwater, then draped the sopping cloth over his head. He tore past Hugo and scrambled up the pyre. "Meg!"

He expected her to be senseless. He expected her hysteria to match that of the mob. He expected her to be someone, perhaps, other than Meg.

But she was herself and spitting mad.

"Hugo did this!"

"I know."

Flames licked his legs with hot scrapes of pain. The short sword made quick work of the smoldering ropes, freeing her hands. He pushed a length of wet fabric against her face. Four bounding steps later, they burst through the fire and onto the courtyard flagstones.

Free of the pyre, she collapsed on hands and knees, chest heaving. Her head hung low. Will slapped her gown with the cloak, extinguishing a dozen tiny fires. He draped the singed wool over her body and urged clenching fingers to take the short sword. "Stay here. I'll return."

He swiveled and ran back to the pyre.

Hugo clutched at his failing supporters. "She must burn! This smoke is her sin!"

Turning frantic circles, he spun right into Will's fist. The dangling metal cuff hit Hugo in the forehead. Blood exploded from his nose. The satisfying crunch of bone goaded Will with the need for more. Finch, Carlisle, even Dryden the coward—not one of them mattered. His frustrations found a home in the shaggy, miserable thief.

Hugo produced a dagger from his tunic, but Will jumped free of the petite blade. He stumbled on a log at the edge of the pyre and fell. Embers stung the backs of his thighs. He saw the smoldering shield to his left. Rolling away from the pyre, he took a flaming piece of timber with him. Hugo swooped down with the dagger and just missed his neck.

The shield's strap had melted beneath the onslaught of mingled chemicals. Will shook his disobedient left hand, to no avail. With his adversary at his back and no way to use the shield, he could only kick the hunk of metal. Hugo side-stepped the flying shield and pounced.

Spinning, Will smashed the fiery log into the back of the thief's head, catching his cap on fire. The dagger glanced along the outside of Will's forearm, but pain was a memory. Every new sensation blended into a numb pulp.

He spun and hurled his weight into Hugo's torso, driving him down. The man's skull bounced off the flagstones with a sickening thump. Hugo shrieked as his hair ignited.

"Scarlet!" He bucked and struggled. Flames slithered across his head. "I beg you!"

Will ground his knee-guard into the thief's forearm and snatched the blade. "You'll never hurt her again."

Fire consumed Hugo's face. Ending his life was a mercy he hardly merited, but with a quick jab of the dagger, Will did the deed.

Chapter Twenty-Five

I have a sudden passion for the wild wood—
We should be free as air in the wild wood—
What say you? Shall we go?

The Foresters: Robin Hood and Maid Marian
Alfred Lord Tennyson, 1892

All around her, people ran and screamed. Burnt wood and reeking sulfur layered the evening air, as did the blistering tang of salt acid. Will must have made smoke. She swallowed a mouthful of foul phlegm, coughed, and vomited.

Dizziness vexed her, but she crawled away from the flames. A hand forward, then a knee. Drag the sword. Again. Steady motions. The task required her full attention. Will told her to stay still, but she needed the safety of a wall or an alcove. Huddling beneath the scorched cloak offered no protection.

The earth tilted, so disoriented had she become. But then, an obstacle. Scraping her fingertips on the rough sandstone, she outlined a circular opening in the courtyard wall. A stench more disgusting than the smoky sulfur assaulted her.

A sewer entrance.

She tugged on slack metal rods barring the entrance. The grate jerked free and she wiggled inside. She pulled the smoky cloth over her back and head, the short sword waiting

patiently in her hands. Nearby screams rammed into her ears.
Soldiers ran through the courtyard, their mail announcing
every action. All she could do was wait, hoping they would
ignore the knotted mass of her body, hoping Will would come
for her. Again.

He had braved the fire. Meg chose her sister, but he had
come for her.

Another wave of dizziness swam on currents of emotion,
flooding her brain and laying siege. Tears borne of fatigue
and fear and gratitude wet her face. They mingled with the
ash on her cheeks to form a sticky paste. She wiped and
wiped, but the tears ran fast and hypnotic.

"Meg?" His frantic shout snapped her from that fog.

She poked out of the tunnel. "Will! I'm here!"

He gathered her into his arms. They knelt together, em-
bracing, clutching. Chaos claimed the courtyard as its
domain, but Will held her.

"A much better hiding place this time," he said.

"I strive for improvement."

He kissed her temple. "Hugo is dead."

"You save my life and offer me a gift." She wound greedy
fingers down to his scalp, pulling, trying to drag him into her
brain. See him. Keep him. "I do not deserve you."

"You will," he said. "Come now. We still have to escape
the city."

"I never would have thought you one to long for the forest."

"I am wherever you are, Meg. This way."

"No. Here."

He hesitated. "The sewer?"

"Why not? It will lead us to the river. The weather has been
fair. The water level should be low."

He cupped her cheek. His skin smelled of ashes and chemicals and blood. "You? And the river?"

She shook her head, a violent swipe. "Do not remind me.
Not now."

He returned a moment later with a torch. Meg flinched at

the sound of the flames, fearful of fire for the first time in her memory. "Here," he said. "Take my arm."

Hunched low, they edged into the entrance. They exchanged the disorder of the courtyard for a tight, reeking tunnel that led to the most powerful river in the Midlands. She exhaled shakily. "Do we have any other weapons?"

"I have only Hugo's dagger, but I stashed my bow and sword by the river."

"Then you should hold this sword, yes? Will?"

"Just take my arm and hold the sword for safe keeping." Misery and a flicker of dread lined his words.

When Meg gingerly took his left hand, he hissed. She explored the damage with unsteady fingers. His thumb drooped at a repulsive angle. Swollen and sticky with blood, the raw, mangled skin of his wrist pulsed, unnaturally hot.

"What happened?"

"I escaped my manacles." He rattled the chain still clinging to his other hand. "Halfway, at least."

Her stomach curled, revolted by hideous imaginings and the very real stink of the sewer. "Which is why you cannot hold both a sword and a torch?"

"With that hand, I cannot hold a thing," he said. "When these daring rescues are behind me, I'll need a long and lovely rest."

"And I shall join you."

The words sighed from her mouth before thought, before apprehension or pride stalled their birth. Boldness and vulnerability iced her body beneath a layer of fear.

He turned, his question tickling her ear. "Truly? You'll refrain from fighting me or poisoning me—"

"—or tying you to a tree," she said, unable to keep from smiling. "Yes. I will refrain."

"Then, yes. You should join me." He clutched her hand, a promise. "You can tend my injuries after our long rest."

"And a bath."

"Dear God, yes."

* * *

The torch he held dwindled to a low nub, offering a meager flicker of light. His back ached from stooping in the tunnel, a place dominated by shadows and fetid rot. A fouler smelling place existed nowhere outside of hell. Sharing few words, they breathed through their mouths. Meg marched behind him in a hazy quiet.

No one followed them, at least. A hundred soldiers and ten times as many angry peasants might wait for them where the tunnel emptied into the Trent, but for the moment, they were safe.

Will heard the rushing river long before he could see it. "Not far now," he said. "Can you manage?"

"If you can abide the woods, I can abide the river."

"That is no strong assurance."

Meg passed a shiver from her hand to his. "Why do you mislike the woods?"

"Will this shape into another fight? Because I haven't the strength."

"No, truly. I am . . . you make me curious."

Perhaps fatigue prompted his honesty. Perhaps their growing closeness did. But the words came easily and without the urge to stop them. "My grandfather evicted my mother from Loxley Manor when she got with child. My father was some useless bit of human rubbish who refused to marry her. She hated living in our woodsy little village and raised me on bitter stories of the privilege she'd once known."

The tunnel sloped down, tipping the sewage to the river and making their sloppy walk precarious. The current of refuse at his ankles accelerated. "When I was twelve, I killed her paramour. He'd beaten her to death. Instead of facing the law, I fled to Sherwood and lived in hiding for months."

"Alone?"

Between his cloying memories and the stench, Will fought for air. "Yes, until I found Robin and his men. We knew naught our relation until some weeks later, after which time he made my upbringing his special endeavor. I was quick to anger and wanted nothing of it."

He slipped, just enough to make his pulse jump. Meg held firm, lending her lesser weight and strength to keep him upright.

"If you go, I go," she said, gasping. "So do try to keep to your feet."

"But if we slide to the river, we'll get that bath."

"I'll give you a push, if you like."

He grinned. It was either smile or collapse, and he refused to expose any more of his body to the muck than was necessary. "Generous to a fault, Meg."

"Are Jacob and Monthemer yet at my cabin?"

Exhaling, he was happy to leave behind their conversation about his youth. "I should hope they're not. Jacob was the one who freed me from your ropes."

She offered something close to a laugh. "I thought you used an extra ploy I hadn't discovered."

"No, no such tricks," he said. "I asked him to take Monthemer back to Winhearst."

"And he agreed? I would've believed him too eager for exploits."

"He agreed, but that offers no guarantee. I suggested that if we three failed in Nottingham, Monthemer would be the only one left to explain what occurred. Keeping him safe must have seemed a charge worth fulfilling."

"Stephen, Baron of Monthemer, escorted by a Jewish alchemist's son. This enterprise has created a few unusual alliances."

"Ours not excepted."

Meg faltered, her foot slipping forward. She clutched his arm. Will dropped the torch to catch her at the waist. Glimmers of light fell to black.

"Was that the torch?"

"Yes."

"Sorry."

"If you go, I go." He rested his forehead against hers, briefly, eyes closed. Fatigue and the irritation of the smoke stung the backs of his eyelids. The terrible stench wedged an unreleased sneeze in his nose.

"Will?"

"Hmm?"

"Can you forgive me?"

He frowned. "For the torch?"

"For the choice I made," she whispered.

He lifted his forehead and resumed their onerous trudge. Pushing his right shoulder into the tunnel wall, he stretched that arm to feel a way forward. Meg crept behind him, holding onto his debilitated left arm. Check, step, slide—their process slowed like a river icing over.

"The choice Finch gave you was no choice at all," he said at last. "Would you have sent Ada to the gallows? Or have her make an unholy trade with Finch for her freedom? I'm flattered you gave the matter as much thought as you did."

"Ada was not."

"You are a wayward girl, Meg. I hear you smiling."

"Now you know how I manage, always listening."

"A dreadful nuisance."

The insistent sound of falling water interrupted. Stretched far, Will's fingers found stone, more stone, and then air. He stopped. Meg staggered into his shoulder, nearly toppling him forward. But he smiled when fresh air greeted his violated senses.

"Hold fast, now," he said. "We're at the brink."

She turned her back to the tunnel wall and molded her spine to its curve, her feet braced against the current. Will mimicked her stance and gripped the lip of the tunnel with his good hand, edging his head outside.

The moon tilted low in the sky, offering little light. He looked up and down the river. Barren oaks and beeches stood as silent sentries. No one waited on the opposite bank. The water raged some six feet below, a wall of liquid refuse spilling straight into the Trent.

"By the best."

"What? Will?"

He pulled his head back into the tunnel, hungry, exhausted, and in pain. "Someday, I hope to say the worst is behind us."

"Not today?"

"No."

"What do we need to do?"

"Jump."

She threaded a hand through her hair, combing wet tangles from her forehead. Deeply shadowed in the moon's slanting glow, she swallowed heavily. She shook her head—side to side, again and again—in a wordless objection.

"You can do this, Meg."

"I cannot see! I cannot swim!" She clanged the sword against the tunnel wall. "Stab me and be done with it!"

He caught her upper arm with his good hand, squeezing until she winced and cried out. "You *must,* do you hear me? This place is not fit for a rat."

Her eyes pinched tight. "Will—"

"I won't let you drown," he said, calming. "And we shall have that bath, at last. Do you hear me?"

Nodding once, she tossed the sword into the river current with a fierce shout. It sailed over the lip of the tunnel and out of sight. The dagger Will held soon followed.

She clutched his good hand, weaving her fingers into his. "If you let go of me, I'll find that sword and cut off your head."

He glanced his knuckles against her cheek. He could feel her skin, even if his fingers refused to move. "Ready?"

Breath exploded from her body. Instinct demanded a breath to take its place. She inhaled, gagging on a ripe mouthful of the river. Will's fingers slipped free.

Terror replaced instinct, or perhaps amplified it. She kicked and thrashed, finding no purchase. Only more and more water. The current mauled her sense of direction. She could not find the surface. A second tide invaded her mouth. Her foot struck a rock. Another rock bit her thigh. Cold dissolved her skin, seeping into her muscles. Her strength melted away.

But the colors.

Colors danced in her brain. Dazzling colors. A passive observer, she watched pieces of rainbow and starlight, floating, twirling. Her limbs slackened. Warmth returned.

And then peace.

Chapter Twenty-Six

I got me to the woods; love followed me.

"In Sherwood Lived Stout Robin Hood"
Robert Jones, 1609

She struck another obstacle, one that wrapped unfailing arms around her middle. Will towed her upright, bringing her head above the river's wild plane. She gasped. The water in her lungs rebelled against the invading air. She coughed and retched as he hauled her over his shoulder.

"Meg? Speak to me, girl."

As air returned to her starved brain, Meg thought the pleasant blur of his voice a fair trade for the vanishing colors. She would have admitted as much, but coughs overwhelmed language.

"Meg? Your gown is drenched. I cannot carry you."

Her feet connected with soggy earth. Land. She collapsed into a grateful mass of sodden cloth and trembling limbs.

"A little farther," he said, arm still banding her waist. "We need to find a place to rest."

"How about here?"

"I never took you for a sluggard. Come now. Stand up."

Righting her face, she tried to allay the spinning blackness. Fear still tingled at the base of her skull. "You endure a great deal to keep me alive."

"I do."

"I can walk on my own, at the very least."

"Yes, you can."

She toughened her knees and stood. The heavy hem of her dress and kirtle dragged behind like an inert body. A chill set into her muscles. She trembled and staggered, but she would not relent, not when Will had already done his part. Nothing could have kept their hands joined, not against the force of that impact, but he had not forsaken her to the river's cold mercy.

"Here," he said. "An outcropping."

She crumpled to the ground, Will sprawling next to her. "Always the cozy little caves."

"Naught but the best."

"We should tend your wrists," she said, finding his left hand. "Whatever we walked through will hinder your healing."

"No lye."

"No lye. I promise."

"Sleep first, Meg. Come sleep."

She had never coveted anything more than curling into his hard planes and firm muscles. She did, weary and safe. The only warmth in England existed where her body nestled along his.

Will awoke to a pale, cold light. He could not decide if dawn or dusk greeted him with gentle illumination. Hunger jabbed at his gut, as did a nauseating sense of disorientation. He lay on his back on a pallet of fresh straw covered by a rough woolen blanket. It smelled old but clean. A thatched roof topped daubed walls. Gathering in a thin haze, moist smoke lingered near an opening at the apex of four beams, beams decorated with dried flowers.

Meg's cabin. Yes, they had made it.

She swished past, oblivious to his return to consciousness. Scrubbed clean, her dark, unbound hair trailed past her waist. She wore a deep brown gown in the style of others she had ruined, having pulled the lengthy sleeves to her shoulders and tied them behind her neck.

The sure and easy way she navigated the one-room dwelling hypnotized him. She did not knock against furniture or trip over the rushes. But she did touch every item several times— locating, identifying, working busy fingers over jars, pots, and cookware. He never would have believed such skill from the way she bumbled through the uneven wilds of Charnwood, clutching his hand.

At the squat worktable, she crushed something gritty in a pestle, adding to it with measured pinches from other bowls. She dipped two fingers into the mixture and touched her tongue. Nodding with an expression of approval, she began to hum something quiet and tuneless and halting. Would she perform the song if she knew he lay awake? The question made him uneasy, observing her in secret.

Her task finished, she poured what looked like ale into a wide, shallow bowl, bringing it and the pestle to his bedside. A second trip to the shelves yielded two tiny jars, one of oil and another of a dark green paste. She knelt at his left side, the skirts of her chestnut gown covering the fringe of straw at the pallet's edge.

Will caught draft of her scent, sweet and exotic. A hideous purple bruise marred her cheek, a sliver of split skin at its center. Memory of the guard's brutal punch excited a killing rage, but an unexpected tenderness accompanied his protective anger. He anticipated her touch, welcoming the powerful need to pull her across his body.

Her touch tickled him like a butterfly, tall grasses, the wind. She found his jaw, fingertips against stubble, and rested her palm on his forehead. A thumping pulse gathered at his groin. She trailed lower to the expanse of his collarbone. His skin prickled. The fine hairs on his forearms stood upright. A flash of nervous tension stiffened the muscles of his back, even as he worked to keep his respiration slow and steady.

Nudging aside the blanket, she touched his chest. No matter how he managed to control his breathing and his body's wild urges, he could not calm the hard beat of blood in his veins.

And she noticed. The smallest grin turned up her lips.

"Have manners. How long have you been awake?"

He moved to sit up. The blanket slipped, revealing that he wore only breeches. "How long will you keep me half nude?"

"You developed a fever. I did you a favor."

"That doesn't answer my question." He frowned at her curt reply. The woman he had fought, loved, and saved knelt before him like a stranger. "Have I been asleep for long?"

"The three days since we arrived."

After emerging from the river, they had recovered well enough to walk. Fatigue made them clumsy, but the fear of pursuit kept them moving toward the seclusion of her cabin. A dangerous combination of his broken hand, an ax blade, and Meg's blind aim freed his wrist of the other manacle cuff. She had been proud of the results, but the half dozen attempts terrified him more than jumping into the Trent. He was lucky to have a hand, let alone one that worked.

She dipped a rag into the shallow bowl and wrung it between slender fingers, her demeanor cool and detached. A practiced nursemaid, nothing more. He disliked losing their newfound closeness and teasing repartee. He might even prefer a bit of earnest bickering to her aloofness—anything to light a path back to the Meg he knew.

"What are you using?"

"Ale to rinse away the caked blood," she said.

The sting of the cleansing ale pricked raw skin at his wrists. He relaxed and absorbed the ache, studying Meg as a distraction. She used both hands, the left navigating the split skin the same way his eyes followed her progress, and the right dabbing with the rag. Ale swam in lazy circles around the shallow bowl, the nauseating tinge of blood deepening its color to a dirty red.

"What next?"

She dried her fingers on the kirtle poking from beneath her gown and picked up the pestle. "A mixture of crushed shell, salt, and dry mustard to scrub the wound. The mustard fights infection. When we cover it in oil, the ingredients form a soap on the skin."

Gently scouring the thin scabs, she spread the salt and shell over his wrists.

"Here." She offered the tiny jar of oil. "Drizzle this over the wounds. Coat it thoroughly."

"And now?"

"We finish with the green salve and bandages."

He eyed the jar. "What is it?"

"A paste made from fir needles to keep the new scabs intact." She painted the salve onto his skin, her fingertips beset by a fine tremor.

She's shaking.

At last, he had a sign. She was not unaffected by his presence, stubborn thing. Reclining with a smile, he relaxed and appreciated the cool, soothing paste on his wrists. He decided to regain his strength and wait for the moment when she would lower her defenses again.

Meg patiently wound strips of linen around his wrist, her head tilted. A long spiral of hair fell over her shoulder. Shining clean, textured like a loch when storms bluster its surface into choppy waves, those deep brown strands stretched toward him. His blood raced, and his mind followed to wild realms of clutching and inhaling. He swallowed that sudden thickness like dry bread, nearly suffocating on a heady charge of lust.

Waiting would be a new sort of torture.

"Thank you, Meg."

"Returning the favor, as you well know," she said, blushing. He looked again, but yes—she blushed. "I am worried about your thumb. Can you move your fingers?"

He raised his left hand and curled his fingers, one after the other. All of them responded except his thumb. It smoldered deep inside the joint and refused to move. He had been contemplating Meg's hair dancing toward him, and before that, the peace of sleep buoyed him against his injuries. He disliked the shocking contrast between those pleasures and the stab of pain.

"The other fingers are sound."

"We'll make a splint after supper." She stood and nudged logs in the central fire pit with an iron poker.

"Let me do that for you."

She turned, her gaze landing somewhere over his shoulder. "If I cannot accomplish tasks within my own home, I should've asked you to leave me on that pyre."

Meg crossed her arms, tucking fidgety hands from his view, keeping them from the potent summons of his skin. He had made promises. So had she. Expectation borne of their imperiled closeness at the castle lingered, but devoid of threats and potential harm, she could not broach her embarrassment. What part of her feelings had been desperation? And of his?

Stillness draped the cabin. They ate together, sharing broth from a large bowl. Picking at a boiled hunk of greasy dried venison, she appreciated the quiet noises of his eating. He had to be hungry, nearly as ravenous as when they arrived, but he did not slurp or chaw. That simple nod to politeness allowed her to focus, instead, on the persistent temptation of his nearness. She did not need to touch him or hear him speak to be affected by his steady presence.

Trying to speak, she cleared her throat twice before the words would come. "Thank you for the help."

"My, we're civil now."

"Shall I try for acerbic?"

"No, I could become accustomed to this."

She reached for a piece of barley bread. Dipping it in the

broth made the burnt crusts palatable. She had not attempted to make bread in years, and the results were disappointing.

"You manage that quite well," he said.

She raised an eyebrow, hoping to appear caustic rather than hurt. "Eat, you mean?"

"Dipping the bread. I would drip, maybe miss the bowl."

"That was a compliment, yes? Not a slight?"

His fingers grazed hers, then gripped. "I thought we were past that."

"What?"

"Your fear. Of course it was a compliment."

"Sorry." She dropped her forehead into her palm. A heavy pulse beat beneath the thin skin. "This is strange."

"For me as well."

Four quiet words lessened her apprehension. He behaved oddly, likely as confused by their rapid, hectic swing from lovers to enemies to partners. "What are we going to do?"

"Share a meal?"

"Coward."

"Witch."

"You try," she said, chewing. "Close your eyes and take a bite. Think about the spaces between the bowl, the plate, and your mouth."

"Meg." Her name emerged as a single, dubious syllable.

"Try." Reaching across the table, she found his face and rolled his eyelids closed. "After all, I will not be able to witness your mistakes."

He flattened her hand to his mouth, kissing her there. His teeth sank gently into the pad of flesh at her thumb. Surprised, she rounded her fingers to cup his jaw. The rough growth of stubble prickled her palm, and his heavy sigh radiated up her wrist.

She shivered. Doubt disappeared.

Pushing higher, she wound her hands into his hair, pulling, leaning over. He met her halfway, their lips coming together. She dragged him nearer and opened her mouth. She sparred with him, accepting the rough texture of his tongue, fanning and feeding the delicious heat. He tasted of broth, smelled of pine, felt like fire.

Even the pain in her cheek added to their urgency. Memory of that painful blow reinvigorated the danger they barely escaped. She moaned and deepened their embrace, pulling roughly at the hard, bunched muscles of his upper arms. The kiss seared her uncertainty and revived every sensation she had experienced with him—the fear and yearning, the safety and panic.

Will shoved aside their supper and pulled her to sit on the table. He urged her back, back, until her head bumped wood. She bit his lower lip. His harsh grunt cut into her brain, settled between her legs—possessive, aroused. He slid his body to cover hers, demanding more. She arched, offering more. He molded his hands to the swell of her breasts and the curve of her buttocks, gripping. A thrust of his hips. Another low moan.

Discovering a treasure, she found his bare torso. He wore no tunic. She clutched the sinewy muscles of his upper back, her fingers digging deep. Sweat slicked his skin. The solid weight of him settled into the cradle of her hips. She succumbed to the hysteria of sensation, reeling, his hungry mouth at her neck. He kissed, bit, suckled her earlobe. Arching again, she struck the table with her foot until entangling skirts freed her ankle. She wrapped her calf around the backs of his thighs. Their gasps and groans mingled.

She remembered this. She wanted this. Now. More.

"Yes, Will. Please."

His mangled hand stilled at her hip. The other released a fistful of her unbound hair, smoothing her temple. His rasping breaths slowed, nestled into the curve of her neck.

Panic of a different sort scratched at her. "Why did you stop? Will?"

He knelt and moved off her body, pulling her upright. Rejection slapped her in the face, but he merely stroked the backs of her hands. What should have been a comforting gesture felt like consolation.

"When I cannot see your face, I am left to hazard your thoughts," she said, angered by her shrillness. "What of your expression can't I read? Revulsion? Pity? Tell me."

"Shall I ever cipher you?"

She jerked her hands away. "Me? How do you mean?"

He exhaled forcefully and stood, filling two mugs from the ale flask. He drank but she left hers untouched on the table.

She waited. Either he would explain or he would leave. She refused to beg, no more than her body already had.

"You flit between roles, Meg," he said at last. "One meek, one manipulative, and one brave enough to match ten men. Yet you expect cruelty."

Her body still hummed and pleaded. Her heart shrank in sick fear. But with what remained of her mind, she listened. His words eased her like a balm.

"But I wonder what is at your core." He laid a hand on her bare foot and sidled closer. "More of the same weakness, or something stronger?"

Her foot twitched, ticklish. "I doubt I know anymore."

"What if I hadn't stopped? What if I bedded you and betrayed you, like Hugo? What would you do?"

"Hate you. And myself."

"But you would endure. I know you would."

She jumped from the table. Her skirts whirled in a confusion around her legs. "Is that what I have done for years? Endured? Because I want none of it. This living is like pacing a cell. I cannot breathe!"

He pursued, easily cornering her in the tiny cabin. She fought, but he trapped her within the strong, gentle cage of his bare arms. Muscles overpowered her anger, landing them both on the floor. He pried her fists open and stretched her flattened palms against his cheeks.

"What do you read here? Here on my face?"

She shook her head and tried to pull free. His fingers knitted with hers, refusing any demand for release. Linen scraped her wrists. Bandages covered the wounds he had suffered to save her life.

"Answer me," he said roughly.

The fight drained from her, through her pores and into the scented rushes. Taut muscles liquefied. "I can count on one hand the number of faces I've touched since my illness," she said. "I can no more read you than I can read my father's book."

"Shall I tell you, then?"

She nodded.

"Fear, Meg. Fear and love."

Her body trembled. "Why do you say fear?"

"Because I nearly lost you—to the fire, to the river, and likely a dozen times to my own foolishness. Because we are both too stubborn for much other than spite. And because you may yet refuse me."

She pressed her lips together, his thick words drawing tears from her eyes. She petted his cheeks, the grim set of his mouth. "Why do you say love?"

He offered a tremulous grin and pulled her hands to his mouth, kissing her knuckles. "What I feel can be described by no other word."

"Yet you pulled away. Why?"

"I refuse to be like him, like Hugo—a knave who takes what he wants and offers broken promises."

"What would you offer instead?"

"My heart," he said. "And my hand, if you'll have it."

Chapter Twenty-Seven

His shoulders they were broad and strong,
And large was he of limb;
Few yeoman in the north country
Would care to mess with him.

"Little John and the Red Friar"
Bon Gaultier, nineteenth century

The pounding on his door matched the pounding in Tuck's head. His beard itched, as did his naked backside. He scratched both with abandon.

Saints be!

He rolled over, caught around his stout middle by a pair of shapely female legs. She slapped him square between the shoulder blades. "Quiet! I am abed."

"Aye, that you are." Tuck grabbed a handful of her fleshy bottom and squeezed. She squealed. "And stay abed, Agnes love. I'll see who disturbs our slumber."

"Bring me an ale when you return." Drowsiness covered her voice just as a haze of disheveled hair covered her oval face.

The pounding intensified, a spade to cleave his brain. He spat at the trembling door. "By my bugles, I'll chaste the daw who wakens me!"

"Open, Tuck."

"Robin? Merciful Christ, hold the order of ye."

He snagged his cope, yanking the voluminous brown robe over his head. From a cask as large as his forearm, he swigged a last mouthful of ale and wiped his lips. A rosary around his neck and a dagger at his hip set him armed.

Tuck pulled the door wide. The moon graced a tall masculine form, silhouetting his features. On his back rested a quiver. "On God's half, Robin! I thought you to be in France yet."

The man stepped into the cabin. A weak tallow candle shone brighter than the waning moon, lighting his face in an orange glow.

"For shame, Tuck, mistaking me for my uncle," said Will Scarlet. "He would be long to forgive such a grand insult."

He laughed to mask his surprise. "As will you, I hazard. And wearing a quiver no less. You suss my blunder, lad."

Will shrugged, a casual gesture at odds with the intensity of his stare. He caught sight of Agnes where she draped half nude across the pallet. He raised his brows but offered no other reaction. "I apologize for the lateness of the hour."

"You did not make the hour late, but you did choose to blight my bigging at this inhospitable time."

"Your pardon, Tuck. I have come to beg a boon."

"And what could you want of me? I'll not be party to skulking under Robin's nose."

Will frowned, hands behind his back. "Your loyalty to my uncle is hard earned and well deserved, but I mean no mischief."

Tuck squatted on a low stool. His long clothes draped between knees spread wide. He stared at Robin's only nephew, disquieted by the likeness. The soul of an impetuous youth had once shared place with a brigand's brain in a warrior's body. Yet there he stood, a man matured. He spoke with an authority Tuck had only heard from Loxley's absent lord, an authority that persuaded wayward souls toward obedience.

But from young Scarlet? He crossed himself, per case of the Devil's trickery.

"Have out with it, then. What boon do you seek?"

The lad flashed a hard smile, some manner of private jest. "I ask that you preside over my wedding. Tonight."

"Wedding? To whom?"

"Meg."

Tuck stared at the entry and rubbed the scant hair ringing the back of his head. He stopped, scowled, then crossed himself again.

Looking like an angel and a witch, both, a blind woman tapped a hushed path through the door. She wore a dark brown gown with a woad kirtle beneath. Her hair draped loose about her shoulders, unadorned and uncovered. Not even the tallow flame's golden flicker much altered the fair hue of her features, blemished by a sickening bruise.

Will took to her side, offering his arm and settling her on a bench. Only then did Tuck notice the mass of bandages at the lad's wrists. Spots of dried blood marred the sallow linen. Another dressing wrapped his forearm.

"Tuck, this is Meg. Meg, meet Friar Tuck."

Her eyes focused on nothing distinct, but she mimicked the angle of Will's face. "How do you do, friar?"

"Well, gramercy." He stood and backed a step. "Excuse us please, miss? I wish to speak with the fellow."

"Of course."

Tuck shuffled to the pallet and draped a blanket over Agnes's body. She roused briefly. "Who goes, friar?"

"Pay you no mind. Sleep now."

Amenable girl, she shrugged and rolled over, eyes drifting closed. Tuck turned to his guests in time to see Robin's nephew rise from where he knelt, kiss his woman on the forehead, and whisper in her ear. She smiled and nodded.

Will crossed to the near side of the fire pit. "We'd be better served to step outside if you wish her to remain ignorant of our words."

"I'll not go with you into a night woods," Tuck said. "As ever I ate bread, you're a slippery knape."

"Suit yourself."

"Set me to rights. What goes here?"

"The details should be of no importance. You only expect the worst of me." The lad's fixed stare dared Tuck to disagree. "See me safely married and you can rest assured I'll not bother Marian again."

"I'll grant no such certainty." In plain sight, he gripped the hilt of his dagger.

"You know me capable of desiring another man's wife," Will said. "The jump is not wide to believe I could betray a wife of my own. But I shall not." He tossed a quick glance to the rosary hanging over Tuck's fat belly. "If you're any holier than the rest of us, tell that to God."

"You love her."

The lad nodded, rubbing an unsteady hand over his eyes, his mouth. Shadows and candlelight marked the contrast between pale linen and murky blood at his wrists.

"What troubles have you endured, my boy?"

"Much," he said. "Will you do this, Tuck?"

"Aye. I am curious to gather how your ballad concludes."

"Ah, yes—because I yearn to hear more foolery bearing my name."

He slapped his young caller on the back and chuckled. "No ballad of yours will bear your name. Whether for masteries or misdeeds, I hear the first line now: Brave Robin Hood's dear nephew did traverse the merry wood."

Will shook his head and matched a rueful grin. "You're not mistaken."

"Let's have done with this, Master Will," he said, sidling his eyes over Agnes's lush curves. "I have the Lord's work to attend."

"And you toil at it happily."

Dipped in darkness, the cabin appeared an apparition, a hulking black animal squatting low in the woods. Silhouetted trees moved like creatures in the wind, tossing their arms against an ink black sky in a macabre pantomime. A shiver decorated Will's skin with prickling hairs, so ominous did Meg's dwelling appear in the waning light of the moon.

Married. He was married. *They* were married, although his new wife had recited her vows with closed eyes and fingers gripped into tight fists. The words she dutifully repeated at Tuck's command had been a far cry from the vows Will had meant.

He pressed his hand into the hollow of her lower back, nervously tracing her valleys and hills. Even touching, touching, he could not convince himself of her presence, so thoroughly had she withdrawn into her dark world. He wanted the mania of his affections returned. He wanted some acknowledgment of all he surrendered, all for her. Yet he wanted more than she might ever decide to give. She infected him with reckless, insane compulsions—something like love, he suspected, and something like obsession.

But he hated her home. The wind shivered around him.

United, no longer enemies, they crossed the threshold to embrace a new dreamlike life, if not each other. A different manner of nervousness overcame him suddenly, as he stood alone with his bride. His tongue swelled. He swallowed, eager but anxious. "Here we are."

Meg only nodded, walking deeper into the tiny cabin and standing before her worktable. She stood cast in halves of shadow and light. Splaying both hands against the chafed surface of the table, she leaned into her palms and tucked her chin to her breastbone. Weariness, and maybe a nervousness to match his, shaped the awkward bent of her shoulders.

"Tell me—are we by candlelight? Moonlight? In darkness?"

He inhaled and closed his own eyes. Imagining only the sinister specter of the forest at night, he censored those descriptions. And while ballads and poetry did not rush to his tongue, he found details. He found the world she could not see and offered it to her. A marriage gift.

"The moon is at half, but low. It hides in the branches. Here, the corners are masked by darkness, and Ada's flowers cast long shadows. We have only this torch from the friar. The flames make the room move."

She smiled. No chastisement. No sarcasm. She simply raised her slanting dimples for him to see, blessing him with those crooked, smiling lips. He would have studied ballads and poetry through his remaining days had she promised, for all time, to offer that smile in exchange for mere words.

"I always loved how, when illuminated by flames, even the most ordinary things appear fascinating."

Another shudder twitched his limbs. He wished she would open that tightly guarded inner refuge, but what she revealed often startled him. "After what we endured at the castle, I have no fondness for fire."

She raised her eyebrows like a shrug. "We cannot help who or what we love."

"Even still? That nightmare did not cure you of your fascination?"

She crossed to her pallet and sat with less grace than a falling tree branch. He joined her.

"My father once asked if fire was alive. At first, I thought *no*. Of course not." Her fingers danced intricate steps, plaiting her hair and unwinding it again. "But fire is born. It consumes and grows. It gives heat like a body. It moves, reproduces, and dies. I said, yes—yes, it is alive."

"And? What did he say?"

"He said it is energy, nothing more. Miraculous and valuable, but it does not live."

Will shook his head. Fire was fire—useful, dangerous, and commonplace. That he might find love or even affection from a woman whose perspective differed so greatly from his own seemed laughably naïve. "How old were you?"

"Five or six," she said. "No more."

He grinned. "You were strange even then."

"Earlier than that and stranger than you know."

He searched her familiar face, reading the pull of muscles beneath her skin and the slope of her neck. Her eyes told him nothing, but every clue to Meg was there to read, near enough to touch, to embrace, if only he found the patience to learn her language. "You didn't believe him, did you?"

"I accepted his explanation, but I thought he must be wrong. It *is* alive."

She leaned back on her elbows. Hair like a waterfall swept back from her face. A pair of dark crescents beneath her eyes revealed her fatigue.

"When I was ill, I dreamt of fire. I cannot recall the last thing I saw because the illness overcame me suddenly. Perhaps I saw my father, my sister, the ceiling—I know not. But for six months, I dreamt of fire. It kept me warm and intrigued with life. It pulled me back from death. And it spared me at the castle."

Will chuckled. "I had a hand in that, I believe."

"Yes, my brave champion," she said like a breeze, touching his face. "I never expected to be shy around you."

He shuddered and closed his eyes, savoring the tease of her fingers. She ventured to the cap of his good shoulder, kneading tense muscles. His own fingers clenched and released in a pattern of restrained need. "Why are you shy?"

"We're married!" Shadows and flames did nothing to disguise the rose red blush on her cheeks and the bridge of her nose. "This . . . this is awkward."

He wanted to ask if she would regret their hasty union, but the question skittered away from his tongue. Will had no faith that he would appreciate the answer. Instead, he traced the cat-like curve of her mouth. "Have I told you how much I adore your lips?"

"No."

"When they are not set in a frown, they curl up here, at the corners." He dipped the pad of his forefinger into a dimple before kissing her there. "Even when you aren't, you look like you are smiling at me."

She kissed him in return, the touch of a feather. "I've had reason to frown at you."

"No more," he said, his voice sounding deep and unfamiliar. "No more, Meg."

He turned into her body and wrapped an arm around her waist. Despite taut resistance, the firm set of her back, he pushed her onto the pallet. She smelled of smoke from the cook fire, the scent of night terrors and tragic endings. The urge to protect bore down on him like a tempest, ripping his past to tatters. To protect her from harm was to protect his own heart, the place where they had united.

But Will's body reacted with another sort of instinct, pressed against her, molding to her. His mind demanded that he protect his woman; his body demanded possession. He held her closer, shifting to settle into the promising basin of her hips. He filled his arms with curves and filled hollows with his hands.

He kissed her. Only a moment passed, the span of three nervous heartbeats, before she joined him in earnest exploration. Hard urges fought with tenderness until only the rushing heat of mouths and tongues remained. He relished her flavor, an exotic wine, dark and deep. Currents of need blended time and taste, weaving their limbs into an unending embrace.

Breathing became as difficult as flying. He pulled from the kiss. Dizziness and pure passion blurred. He rested his forehead on hers to regain his equilibrium, uncertain of ever regaining it—not when she claimed the power to tilt him sideways with a word.

"Do not dare, Scarlet." She yanked him against her body, fighting with his tunic until she stripped him bare. "I married you, and I expect no more of your clever delays."

He took hold of her backside, kneading the full, yielding flesh. "Making an honest offer of marriage was a delay?"

She untied his breeches. Hot fingers stroked his rod, stealing his mind.

"Yes, yes," she breathed. "You are a chivalrous man. Now make good on what you started tonight."

Will had learned her body once before, and memory of that

heated encounter twisted into the present. They had endured much together in the dreadful days since, and rediscovering her nearly surpassed the joy of their initial exploration. The thrill of having her hot and eager beneath him, so very vital, spun his brain like a miller's wheel. He wanted more. More kisses. More skin.

"I want to see you," he rasped.

She came to her knees and worked to remove her clothes, untying the laces at the bodice. Will pulled thick handfuls of wool past her hips, over her head. After tossing the gown to the floor, he threw the kirtle atop it. His breeches followed.

She lay prone on the pallet, the sight of her nude body ripping loose a shuddering breath from him. Skin like a pale moon covered graceful limbs, a taut belly, and gently curving breasts that rose and fell with every quick breath. A rapid pulse fluttered at her throat. Her hair spread into a dark pool around her face.

"Will?"

"I'm here," he said thickly, sliding a forefinger between her breasts and down. Her belly quivered. "Just looking."

"I want to look too."

"My pleasure."

Slender hands circled his neck and pulled him near. She dug deep into the muscles of his upper back. Taunting nails tested his skin. At times petting, at times scratching, her fingers rolled over his body like a storm. She found his hard length again, squeezed, stroked, robbing him of control. He hissed and gasped, groaning her name.

"Touch me, Will." She spread her knees, welcoming.

"Sorry, my love," he said against her mouth. Between their bodies, he found her sensitive nub and began to pattern rhythmic circles. "I have but two hands. And one of them is in shambles."

She moaned. "You have a mouth."

"Yes." He bit delicately at her lower lip. "Right here."

"Lower."

"Where?"

"Where your fingers are."

He chuckled, a low and throaty sound born of her surprising demands. The cadence of his fingers sped, intense. "Greedy wench."

"Please, before I have to push your stubborn head down there."

He kissed her deeply, drawing her tongue into his mouth. Sucking. Biting. He intended the kiss to be a brief good-bye before complying with her demand, but she stiffened beneath his vigorous, rhythmic assault. Release rocked her. She thrashed and cried out.

Patience shattered. Will snatched his hand from between her legs. With a sure movement, he plunged into her shuddering body. He dragged one of her thighs higher and jerked his hips. She whispered his name, a panting hymn.

Carried by the sound of her voice, possessed by the blaze in his blood, enveloped by her slick warmth, he gave himself to paradise. Mindless, questing, every thrust took him closer to fulfillment. Nothing remained but the white heat of his climax. He shook, groaned, then collapsed.

Chapter Twenty-Eight

And I pray thee let me follow thee
Any where under the sky,
For thou wilt never stay here with me,
Nor without thee can I.

"Robin Hood's Flight"
Leigh Hunt, 1820

"That was . . . colorful."

Will raised his head. "Colorful?"

"Very." She swiped at heady tears. Although she lay still, her body still trembled in the moments after release. "Has been from the first."

"Interesting," he said, lazy fingers fondling her nipples. "Must explain why you find me irresistible."

"Like when I twirl, I only want you for the color." She cupped his face, feeling his grin. "But mind you, I saw rainbows when I was about to drown."

"You'll agree this is much safer. And more pleasurable."

"For certain."

Those lazy fingers became more insistent, tugging her nipples. "Now, as an alchemist, would you recommend we attempt to create the experiment anew?"

She gasped, arching slightly. The slick skin of her inner thighs slid with the softest friction, hot and wet. She rubbed them together, wanting. But the void remained unfilled and unsatisfied. Enjoying him with her eyes closed, her heart closed, her body open—only then could she truly indulge in the man she had taken as her husband.

She welcomed the return of that sharp physical need, staving off the reality of their hasty marriage. Agreeing to his proposal had been an impulse. Because Will refused to lie with her until they married, the solution was simple. Her body craved his—that much she would never deny—and he kept her safe from all manner of physical harm.

But the rest . . . she would not think of it, not when his hands on her breasts offered the most mindless sort of distraction.

"For certain," she said. "First results can never be trusted."

"Does the process need to be duplicated exactly?"

"Perhaps only the end result must be repeated."

"I can aid you in that."

He dipped his head and took a firm peak into her mouth. His tongue softly laved the sensitive skin. Each wet, lingering caress sent shivers of fire to her sex, as did the soft sounds of his lips stroking her, licking her. Her breasts swelled, aching and full. Again, more—she writhed under his patient attention. Fiery color played behind her eyelids.

With the same maddening care, he moved to the other breast. One hand molded the soft flesh in a rhythmic massage. He squeezed, bringing a rigid nipple to his warm lips. He kissed, the simple touch of skin to skin. He sucked. Hard. His tongue flicked endless patterns over the sensitive tip. Gentle teeth tugged and caressed. She gasped, shivering as he nibbled and nipped.

His hair tickled her skin, yet another caress. She delved into those thick bunches and savored the straight, silken texture. Color blazed in the darkness, spiraling in beautiful patterns of light against the familiar black.

She pulled his head from her aching breasts. "What color is your hair?"

He laughed, the sound rippling through his strapping body. "I've been inside you twice but that remains a mystery to you."

"Indulge me." She slipped her hand between their bodies and clutched his thickening shaft. "And we'll make it three times."

He shifted on the pallet, raising above her, muscles taut. She caressed his length with insistent strokes and spread her thighs, guiding him. He tried to thrust but she gripped harder, restraining his eager need. She savored the unusual texture of him, softest skin and hardest flesh. She slid her palm over the firm head, finally pressing it against her most sensitive nub, rubbing her there.

He cursed, a harsh whisper. "My hair is brown."

"You can do better." She sucked at the hollow where his neck met his shoulder.

"Meg—"

He groaned, his hips flexing convulsively. He claimed her mouth in a demanding kiss. The tightness of his muscles and the rough push of his tongue told her how hard he fought for control. But he played her game. He let her take her pleasure. His submission thrilled her, left her wet and flushed. She kissed him in return, taking the hard thrusts of his tongue and nipping, tasting, fighting him.

He broke the kiss and whispered against her lips. "Light brown."

"Better still."

"Like ripened wheat."

"Good," she sighed, smiling. She allowed him the slightest entrance. A scant inch of him pressed between her wet folds. "And your eyes?"

She fanned through the possibilities. Blue. Hazel. Black. She could imagine them all, just as she could imagine the feel of him sliding fully into her. But still she waited. His hips begged for entrance with tight, truncated thrusts, and his pulse throbbed beneath her curious fingers. He pushed her breasts together, hands trembling, his mouth dancing from one nipple to the other.

"Tell me," she said.

"Green." Warm breath washed over her wet skin.

"More."

"Green," he rasped. "Like your emeralds."

She sighed and removed her imprisoning hand. He filled her. Their moans wove together. She pushed her hips to meet his, accepting the sweet invasion of his quickening thrusts. Muscle, skin, breath—she lost hold of the world until only his body remained, above her, penetrating her.

She whispered his name, or maybe she only imagined the word. Will, her husband. Will, with his hair the color of wheat and eyes of emerald. *Will.*

Pleasure crashed over her. She arched and rode the tide of her release, bucking her hips to take him, take all he could make her feel. He groaned and stiffened, burying himself a final time in her trembling flesh.

Groggy minutes passed. Will lay collapsed atop her slack body. She petted the sides of his face, combing the hair back, imagining wheat fields ripened beneath the autumn sun. But she would never know its color, not beyond her thoughts.

A bittersweet tide swelled beneath her tenuous happiness.

"I wish I could see you," she whispered. She cringed at her ragged vulnerability. "I want to catch your eye and share this closeness across a distance. I want to see your smile."

"And if it's not as beautiful as you imagine?"

"It would be." She traced his lips. "It is."

"But I'm relieved."

"That I cannot see? Why? Why would you say that?"

"Calm yourself." He lifted his head from her breast and snuggled her nearer. "I mean nothing by it. But you save me much embarrassment."

"Embarrassed how?"

"I watch you all the time," he said, his voice deep and hushed. "My pride would not survive if you knew to what extent."

"You and your pride."

"With you, I have none." He pushed fingertips over a few

disobedient tears, blending them into her cheeks. "Meg, I would do anything, *anything* for you to see again."

"Don't say that. You cannot. The quest to restore my sight drove my father mad," she said. "It cut him from the world."

"How?"

She nuzzled into the hard surfaces of his body. "When I took ill, he consulted Jewish scholars and women thought to be witches. The people in Keyworth believed I was possessed, and his inquiries did nothing to ease their suspicions. But he persisted. He'd never encountered a question without an answer. He sought refuge here in Charnwood. Earl Whitstowe was his only contact with proper society."

He tightened his arms when she shuddered. "When Father died, he left no way back to a time when people accepted us. Ada hated it."

"Your illness took more from you than your sight," he said. "It took your family."

She nodded, a dark and silent mourning.

A long breath pushed free of Will's powerful body. The vigor and strength in those muscles ignited a new heat in her blood. To fight and to love this man tested her, made her weary, made her stronger in turn. And more fearful than she had ever been.

"I've never felt more helpless," he said. "Not like this."

"And I haven't felt the need this badly, not for years." She tried a wobbling smile. "I blame you."

"A deal, then. To atone." He sat up, pulling her across his lap and bringing her hands to his face. "Touch me, Meg. Whenever you're lost inside yourself, scared—I'm here. You don't need to ask permission. I give it to you now. Simply touch me."

Tears wobbled at the corners of her eyes. She wanted to hit him across the mouth for leaving her that exposed, for finding where her desires hid. But an irrepressible, foolish part of her jumped at the chance he offered.

"No excuses? No preamble?"

His slashing smile pressed beneath her palms. Her skin tingled.

"Think of it as seeing," he said. "I don't need permission to look at you. I take that freely—my privilege. In return, I give you this."

Laughing and weeping, both, she clung to him as if to a rock face. He held fast, arms and hands and murmuring words working hard to ward off her dread. Wrapped tight to Will's body, the loneliness of her dark world peeled away, even if the new world he offered was wider, farther, more terrifying than she could have imagined.

He moved to kiss her.

She smiled. "You missed."

"The torch has gone out."

"You cannot see me?"

"No."

Meg sighed and arched against him. This was easier. Loving him was easier, their bodies together. His mouth and hands on her, his lean muscles naked and hard beneath her fingers. She kissed him deeply. "Then it's your turn to explore in the dark."

Nights and days passed without thought.

As evening dwindled, Will stared at the ceiling where silhou-ettes of Ada's flowers fluttered. Heat from a small fire did nothing to ease the chill snapping at his nose, a foretaste of the frigid winter to come. Beneath a mantle darned with fur, he molded Meg's nude curves to his body and smiled. Their arms and legs wound together like the twigs of a bird's nest, the beginnings of a home.

He flexed his left hand, heartened by the resurgence of power and elasticity there. His fingers worked in concert. Even his thumb was on the mend, still bound by a splint. The skin at his wrists itched beneath the bandages, healing.

He was healing.

Kissing Meg's hair, he inhaled deeply. His eyes slid closed, floating on their steady heartbeats. The cadence increased. The noise intensified.

He bolted upright. "Meg!"

Bleary and dazed, she rolled onto her back. "What is it?"

"Listen."

"Horses?" She jerked to her knees. "Armor?"

He jumped from the pallet and donned his clothes, mail, and boots. Meg dressed and tied her hair beneath a cowl.

He retrieved the quiver and bow from next to the pallet and fastened the scabbard at his waist. A compliment of daggers circled atop the scabbard's leather strap. He pushed the handle of a deadly blade into Meg's hands. She took position, crouched on the side of the fire pit farthest from the door.

Better than most, she would be able to determine the extent of the odds they faced. She listened.

"How many?"

Face ashen, she said, "Hard to tell. More than a dozen."

He tightened his left hand. "I cannot fight that many."

Meg crossed to a wall and pulled a torch from its sconce. "Use the niter beds. They're flammable, but likely these men do not know that."

"My clever girl." He took the torch and dipped its head in the fire pit.

"We'll have but little time once they burn."

"After I secure a horse, we'll make for the woods," he said. "Like old times."

"Be careful."

He circled to the door, cursing himself with less mercy than would the Devil. Happiness made him lazy. He should have known Finch would pursue them, but the existence of her cabin was known to few. Hugo was dead, and Will counted as allies the men who knew its location. Yet soldiers approached. Someone had betrayed them.

Pushing his back into the wall, he studied their attackers. From the northwest, the direction of Nottingham, men circled around the cabin. More approached and stayed to the rear. Horses grunted beneath their armor, the rhythm of their hooves made irregular by the wooded terrain and darkness. They shied and whinnied. The men atop their backs urged speed.

One man's bellow sounded above the others.

Carlisle?

Impossible. But he listened again, hearing the soldier's shout cleave the night.

After throwing a prayer to heaven, he charged outside. Four men on horseback with torches of their own circled the yard to the abandoned barn, setting the structure alight. Like teeth on a comb, the niter beds spanned the distance between the barn and the cabin. Errant flames rained down. The barn fire would do the deed—but sooner than he had planned.

He tossed his torch and retrieved his bow.

Although her soul refused to doubt, Meg prepared as if Will would not return. She stashed the dagger in her belt and pulled from the shelves an assortment of jars, satchels, and bottles. She arranged the collection in a rough circle on the floor near the fire pit. There, panting, she tracked the chaos outside her home: a taunting cackle of flames, a horse's foul shriek, and ever more hoof beats.

Regardless of the outcome, nothing of her old life would remain come dawn.

Her mind flicked through the cabin to fix her bearings and envisage an escape. Instead, she remembered her father's book. She raced once again to the shelves and retrieved the heavy tome, its familiar, dusty leather scent tickling her nose. After emptying a large satchel of its salt, she stuffed the book inside and angled it across her body.

Crashing down the door, the soldiers invaded. She dropped to her knees and scrambled to the fire pit, torch in hand.

Will—

The soldiers circled their horses around the cabin, Carlisle at the fore of the offensive. He swung a massive battle-ax in a low arc. Will could do nothing but run to escape its deadly turn. He sprinted past the heavily armored foursome, to the barn. Drawing an arrow, he touched its shaft to the flames. The horses circled in pursuit. Working against the pain in his thumb, he aimed, fired, and caught a soldier through the front of his neck. But two more arrows flew past their targets.

Horses closed the distance. Shouldering the bow, he drew his sword. He jumped into the barn and ducked behind a wall of burning timber. The ax smashed through the wood, unsettling the structure. Smoke seared his lungs and blackened his vision. He took hold of a flaming plank and fought free, inadvertently slamming the forelegs of a horse. The animal reared, bucking and trampling its rider.

Fires skated across the beds, each igniting on a quick path to the cabin. Time was short. He needed a horse.

As Carlisle bore down with the ax, Will ran backward to the beds. He stopped. He stared the hulking man in the eyes. Dropping, rolling, he swung his sword under the horse's exposed flank. An equine scream punctured the night.

Carlisle dropped his massive weapon in order to restrain his pain-crazed mount with both hands. The animal stumbled in the soft earth and pitched into a niter bed. He flailed beneath the wounded horse and screamed as flames ate a greedy path across his body.

Will retrieved the ax and imbedded it in the fourth horseman's leg. The man bellowed and sliced down with his sword, catching nothing but the ax's shaft. Will caught his arm and yanked hard. Although the soldier held fast to the pommel, still mounted, his helmet fell free.

Springing away, Will pulled the bow from his back. He drew the bowstring taut. The bones in his left hand gritted like a pestle in its cup. He released one arrow, then another, and caught his opponent between the eyes.

He snatched the horse's slack reins, mounted, and swiveled in time to see the cabin explode.

Chapter Twenty-Nine

With quiver and bow, sword, buckle, and all,
Thus armed was Marian most bold. . . .

"Robin Hood and Maid Marian"
Folk ballad, seventeenth century

Meg's head pounded. She felt fire. Heat swelled around her body, scorching skin and cloth and hair. A mad wind whirled where the walls had been and showered her with sparks. Sounds blurred and mashed together, muffled like her ears were stuffed with tar.

"Will!"

Smoke crammed into her throat, exchanging poison for valuable air. She coughed, pressing the singed hem of her gown over her mouth. She could not call for help, not again. But how she wanted to. Her sense of direction had gone up with the explosion. Fear choked her like the poisonous smoke.

Twisted at a strange angle, her ankle smarted. The dagger waited at her waist. Her bodice hung open, singed like the hem. A hunk of hair had been scorched clean away, as had the strap to the satchel.

The book.

She shuffled to her knees and searched the floor. Rushes

burned under her hands. After spitting on her fingers, she persisted. Another fit of coughs claimed her. Her head sank into thick syrup. She panted through a drape of wool and sank onto her side. Doubling over, she caught something hard with her knees.

The rim of the fire pit. But where on the circle?

She smacked a flicker of fire at her wrist. Colors twisted before her eyes. Terror climbed her spine like a ladder. The pyre. The river. And now she had much more to lose.

One last attempt yielded the book. Clamping it close to her chest, she tried to stand. Dizziness washed across her skin like a hot wave. Not dizziness—fire. A wall of fire. She ducked, collapsed, and caught flames in her hands. A paralyzing scream mingled with fire and ever more smoke.

"Meg!"

Will shoved his heels into the horse's flanks and raced across the yard. He dipped to the right, leaning well to the side of the saddle. Narrowing his lids, he snagged the hilt of the battle-ax and yanked it from the earth. All around him, the forest glowed and men scattered into the night. But he rode into chaos.

At the scene of the explosion, he made a quick circuit in case Meg had gone free. With no sign of his wife, he shrugged free of the bow, quiver, and his tunic. After ripping off a sleeve, he wound the tunic over the horse's eyes and secured the giant animal to a nearby oak.

He stuffed the sleeve into his mouth, freeing his hands to heft the ax, and tore into what remained of the cabin. Odors other than wood polluted the air. Sulfur, vinegar, the black powder Meg concocted—whether by accident or intent, the flames worked to destroy her laboratory. A roof beam angled to the ground. The other three creaked and swayed. The thatching burned to ash, while timber and daub smoldered in every corner. A black wind sucked angry sparks skyward.

He dropped low and crawled, dragging the ax. He wanted to call her name but did not dare. Smoke tore at his eyes and mingled with stinging tears.

And then he was staring into her eyes.

He faltered, mistaking her gaze for the unseeing eyes of a dead woman. But her lids trembled, stretched wide. Her lips moved without sound, her body curled tight like a fist.

Ripping the sleeve from his mouth, he called her name. Coughs claimed him. He replaced the strip of cloth and fought his body, calming the spasms. Meg, however, offered no response. Waving away a thick cloud of smoke, he caught sight of a rivulet of blood trickling from one ear.

Will touched the side of her face. She mouthed his name and flailed, her expression a study in terror. He pushed hard against her shoulders, signaling her to hold fast.

The fallen joist barred her escape. He hauled on the heavy beam, unable to move it. With frantic power, he hoisted the ax and swung it down. The force of landing three massive blows clawed his injured body to ribbons. Smoke suffocated him. He landed the ax again, again, finally splintering the beam. Shouting, angry now, he kicked hard against the flaming wood. The remaining beams scraped and groaned above their heads.

Time slowed and trembled, gathering around him and stealing his strength. He dropped the ax and grabbed her shoulders. She clutched her book as she would an infant.

Will swung her into his arms and picked over the smoldering debris. He kept his eyes stubbornly fixed to the black night beyond the flames, his heart thumping, breaking, his lungs drowning in smoke. But he would not look at her. Not until they were clear. Not after seeing the charred skin of her hands.

Dawn broke at Loxley Manor. The sun lightened the sky but could not pierce the thick mantle of clouds. Marian dressed and ate without fanfare, preparing for the day's many tasks. Excitement branched through her veins, infusing every bend of her body with giddy energy. Anticipation made sleep nigh impossible.

A messenger had delivered word of Robin's forthcoming arrival. By providence, he would be home in less than a week. She wanted the entirety of their holdings in fine form for his return. She enjoyed the challenge of the estate's myriad tasks, and with her many aides, she had weathered Robin's long years abroad.

His homecoming would mean a reunion with her husband— her lover and partner—but also a restoration of her customary role as mistress of the manor. More complicated matters such as mediating disputes and meting justice would revert to his domain. While part of her enjoyed the idea of relinquishing many of her chores to his care, she would miss the thrill of those responsibilities.

Trepidation, too, littered her thinking and banked her fierce, eager longing. She had not seen him or held him in nearly three years. Three years of warfare. And neither had he seen young Robert in that time. The changes they had yet to negotiate intimidated her.

A clattering uproar at the main gates startled her from the half-wakefulness of sunup thoughts.

Robin? An intruder?

She quickly secured a headband over her veil, tugging the white linen to cover errant twists of thick, dark hair. She strapped a leather belt at her waist and a sheathed dagger. Although many guards protected Loxley Manor with undying loyalty, old habits refused to pass into history.

Running down the stairs, Marian reached the entryway where, rather than abating, the commotion had escalated. Six armed sentries barred admission to a man. Their shoving bodies obscured his face, while profane and frantic shouts punched the quiet dawn stillness.

A single shout stopped her breath. "Marian!"

Disbelief ran through her first. Confusion and dread followed close behind.

He bellowed her name again.

"Will?"

Pushing forward, she stayed the angry jostle of well-intentioned guards. The crowd at last divided, permitting clear access to her unexpected visitor.

"Will! Saints save us!"

Ash and sweat streaked his contorted face. Grime dulled the twin scarlet lions embroidered on his tunic. A sleeve was missing. In his arms, wrapped chaotically in a half-fastened kirtle, draped a filthy, bloodied woman.

"I need your help, Marian."

Surprise stole her questions, but the pain in his plea fired her to action.

"Alice!" She whirled from the entryway and forced the gaping guards aside. "Make way! Find Alice! *Now*."

The men scattered. To Will she said, "Come with me."

They climbed the main stairs, Marian leading the way. His coarse breath chased behind her. They strode along a corridor and reached the nearest guest room. With the tenderness of a mother setting her babe abed, Will placed his insensate charge on a newly-made pallet. The woman moaned but did not move or open her eyes.

Marian knelt to evaluate her terrible condition. The soot-covered skin along her hands and arms puckered. Blister after blister blended into angry red welts, disfiguring her limbs. The stench of fire and other, more astringent smells clung to her. Thick masses of brown hair had been singed, curling un-evenly in short, matted clumps.

"What happened?"

"We were attacked at her cabin. Sheriff Finch's men."

"Will, who is she?"

"Her name is Meg." Anxious eyes swathed the woman. His voice grated with unshed tears, the sound of boots grinding broken glass. "She's my wife."

Marian stilled. A bittersweet but profound happiness pulsed in her blood.

Meg. Will's wife.

She touched his shoulder, feeling nothing but hard tension beneath her fingers. "I swear to you, we shall do for her all we can."

Her personal maid, Alice, swept into the room, a formidable flurry of twirling skirts. Behind her trailed a pair of young girls, both of whom carried an array of medicinal remedies. Blankets, hot water, and fresh clothes arrived shortly thereafter as more of the household mobilized for the woman's care.

Marian managed to drag Will from the deluge of helpful hands, but only as far as a corner of the room. His face appeared waxen and stiff beneath the grime, and his gaze never left his wife's inert form. Charred remains of matching bandages hung limp at his wrists. Another concealed a wound on his forearm.

"You're hurt too."

He shook his head, wild bunches of straight hair falling across his brow. "I could do with a drink."

She snapped her fingers and sent a young maid to the kitchen.

With that ground-glass voice he said, "Forgive me for coming here, Marian. I didn't know—"

His suffering tore at her. She stepped nearer, raising her hand to touch him again, to absolve his moment of vulnerability.

But forestalling pity, he hauled his severe green eyes from the pallet and regarded her directly. He stood to his full height, forcing Marian to crook her neck higher. When he adjusted his broad shoulders into a dynamic stance, he suddenly reminded her of Robin, powerful and certain.

Words that had choked from his mouth became clear and sure. "I didn't have anywhere else to go. If you wish me to leave, I shall. But please, let Meg stay."

She pushed a shaky palm against her forehead and sighed. An abiding guilt pressed back, just beneath the skin. "You should not have to work this hard to come home, to ask for help from your family. And for that—for that, Will, I ask *your* forgiveness."

Arched eyebrows pulled low and his mouth flattened into a rigid line.

"Stay," she said. "She'll need you here."

"You are certain?"

"Of course. You cannot leave the manor until you tell me everything."

He nodded and crossed his arms. Already his focus had returned to Meg, a sweep of his eyes like a dismissal.

"I'll return as quickly as I can manage." She turned, reaching the door.

"Marian? Where is Robin?" A sentinel, he watched Alice and her assistants minister to his wife's countless burns. The sharp planes of his face and the tense angles of his body spoke of nothing but pain that yet echoed at his mention of Robin's name.

"On his way home."

Will permitted Marian to tow him to the kitchen. Reluctant to leave Meg's side, he needed something in his stomach other than a sickening combination of ale and worry. The respite provided a moment to calm, a moment when images of singed flesh would not demand his obsessive focus. But even after Alice concealed those wounds with salves and bandages, and even after kitchen scenes replaced those of the guest room, he could not forget the tormenting sight.

A maid brought two mugs of warm broth. Marian slid gracefully onto a bench across from him at the table. She removed her veil, swiping errant curls from her brow. For a half hour, she listened as Will recounted everything from that distant day on the Nottingham Road to the attack, fire, and explosion.

"I am surprised at you."

He grimaced. "Why?"

"While I understand the need to prove your worth, to make your own way, I cannot imagine pursuing material ends by that callous means. Working for the sheriff?"

"Not so valiant, am I?"

"No, not that. I am surprised you believed your conscience would give you leave." Soft brown, deeply set eyes watched him. "But how would the sheriff have known the location of Meg's cabin?"

He yawned and stretched the stiff muscles running the length of his backbone. A new headache threatened—or more likely, a rejuvenation of the same pain he had endured for weeks. Loving Meg had briefly dispelled it. "I cannot figure, honestly. They could not have followed us, not four days on from escaping the castle."

"And surely not the friar."

"No, not Tuck. But someone. I—God, I simply cannot think straight."

Marian smiled, a gentling gesture where the corners of her eyes curled to match her lips. "Don't think ill of yourself for it. This ordeal must have been a great trial for you."

He could not help but reply with a rueful chuckle, welcoming a return to easy camaraderie with his uncle's wife. "You have no notion."

"Oh, but I do. You remember the terrible hardships we endured to correct the injustices in Nottingham." She paused, her expression at once hesitant and wistful. "And falling in love with Robin was not an easy matter."

Camaraderie floated away on the smoke of the cook fire. His bond with Marian would never be solid and easy again, not until he mended a number of ramshackle fences with Robin.

"You had no help from me," he said grimly.

She lifted her gaze. "I share in the blame for those months, as does Robin. None of us knew a clear path. I certainly did not."

"I kissed you." He ran a hand across a jaw made rough with too many days' stubble. "I was using you to strike at him."

"Was I any different? Did I not invite your attentions?"

"How do you mean?"

"Robin was in London, bound for France. I was a new mother. Certainly I could no longer think of myself as a maiden." Laughter and embarrassment mingled in her words. She took a sip of the broth. "You reminded me of those months of adventure and danger. I would speak falsely if I claimed your interest wasn't . . . tempting."

"You asked me to leave."

"I had no steady feet beneath me, but I knew enough to keep temptation at bay."

As if sorting the memories of another person, a younger and more reckless man, he remembered their kiss. He had come across Marian alone in the secluded garden courtyard, her angular, elfin face illuminated by the palest shades of moonlight. Tears pushed down her cheeks. Her beauty had lodged in his imagination like the stab of a knife, a knife like jealousy.

He had not asked why she cried, taking her upper arms in his rough grip and claiming her lips. Had he given any thought to her comfort or her desires, two years' worth of reflection might have caused him less shame. But for his own pleasure, to assuage his abiding resentment of Robin's success and happiness, he had taken. He reveled in being bad when his uncle had proven nothing but worthy and good.

And Marian had met his punishing mouth with abandon.

Part of their shared past shifted, the events and emotions standing in a new light. Shock buzzed in his ears. "You kissed me back."

"I did," she said, her blush raging. "And I had no notion of forcing this much distance between you and Robin."

"Did you tell him?"

A swift breeze of surprise fluttered her features. She cast an anxious gaze toward her lap. "In a missive? What would I say? No, I never could find the words."

Will smiled then, fully and with a feeling of unexpected

hopefulness. "Seems we both have matters to discuss with your dear husband when he returns."

Marian returned his smile. Rounded cheeks pushed upward, tapering her wide eyes at the corners. "And he'll turn right around for France."

"If he won't stay and fight for you—"

"Milady!" One of Alice's assistants, a young girl with trailing braids, skittered into the kitchen. She searched beyond the hanging pots and ran between the cooks, sliding to a stop next to the table. "Milady, she's awakened!"

Chapter Thirty

Shall I not soon, Heart's Dearest, good-morrow to thee say,
And kiss thy lips of kisses forlorn for many a day?

"Robin Hood's Good-Night"
Nora Chesson, 1906

Will took to his feet before the girl finished speaking. The brief moment of levity faded like a kind dream, leaving him the bleak candor of reality.

Meg. Meg in the fire. Meg in danger.

He took the stairs three at a time. The broth he drank pressed against the back of his tongue. He swallowed convulsively. And he prayed.

"Will!" Her terrified screams reached him before he found his way, briefly confused by the many rooms along the corridor. "Will, where are you?"

Bursting through the door, he scattered the trio of maids trying to restrain her frightened thrashes. He gently caught her upper arms and slowed her fight.

"Here. Here I am," he said roughly. He pressed a kiss to the damp skin of her forehead. "Meg, I'm here."

"Will? Where are we? What happened?"

Tenderly, keeping the bandaged limbs from tangling with

one another, he crossed her arms over her abdomen. "Do you remember? At the cabin?"

Her chin quivered. "The fire."

"Yes."

"My ears are ringing. The explosion?"

"Yes, was that your doing?"

Folding the skin of her forehead into parallel ripples, she frowned. "The soldiers charged in. I thought to— My book!"

"Easy, my dear." He smoothed an unsteady hand across her forehead, calming her. "Your book is fine."

Appearing exhausted after only a few moments of wakefulness, she leaned her head into his palm. "Good."

But as Meg relaxed, his frustrations boiled. "I saved you from the witch-burning, but that wasn't danger enough for you, was it? You had to risk yourself for that thing."

"It is a record of our research—my father's, mine. Everything. I could not lose it."

"Meg." His anger gave way to torturing fears. A quaking sob wracked his shoulders. "God, Meg, I could have lost you."

"Are you crying?" She reached to find him and grimaced when her linen-wrapped fingers bumped his face. "Wait— what's the matter with my hands?"

"They were burned."

Panic marked her features like a jagged stretch of lightning. "I cannot feel you."

"Calm, Meg, please. These are bandages. Do you feel?"

Ever so softly, he turned her hands and rubbed bound fingers across her face. She ran the length of each forearm along her cheeks, finding the edges of the bandages where they extended past her elbows.

"And will they heal?"

"Of course. Of course they will."

"Scarlet, you've not lied to me in days."

He had almost forgotten how quickly she could rip away the vulnerable charm to reveal forged steel beneath. "We have to wait."

"We?" She shifted subtly and turned a keen ear toward the bulk of the room. "Who else is here? Where are we?"

"Loxley Manor."

"Your uncle's estate?" She smiled past her fatigue and worry, her dimples toying with his heart. "'Tis the sweetest deed you've yet performed."

"Stop. You embarrass me." He turned and ushered Marian to join him by the pallet. "Meg, this is Marian. Robin's wife."

Her blue eyes lolled toward their hostess. "I'm happy to make your acquaintance, milady. I wish the circumstances were more cheerful."

Marian stared, her eyebrows raised in question, as if she had not truly believed his description of Meg's blindness. But her poise quickly stifled any discomfort or surprise.

"Oh, but they are," Marian said. "I wish you both joy. And I'm glad to provide you shelter and a place to recover."

Meg nodded, but her head bobbed without finesse. Weariness ebbed around her in a sluggish tide, pulling her back from consciousness. He kissed her forehead and whispered, "Sleep now, love. I'll be here when you awaken."

Will!

She thrashed to waking. Sweat soaked her brow and dampened the clean kirtle wrapping her torso. Strands of hair, chopped short to remove the singed ends, clung to her neck. Restless legs itched. Panting, listening past her banging pulse and the damage to her hearing, she fought for bearings. The room whispered with quiet night voices. No birds filled the air with song. Will lay beside her on the pallet, his feet tangled with hers.

Loxley Manor, yes. And the manor was still.

But sadness engulfed her, a wringing sense of hopelessness. The nightmares would not relent. Confusions muddled together as she relived the dreams she had experienced during her illness. Except this time, the fire consumed her, hurt her.

She raised her arms and urged her heartbeat to calm. With a precision born of three days' practice, she touched enshrouded fingertips to her mouth. Bandages imprisoned the ruined skin of her hands. Her lips felt the touch, but beneath the burns, her hands remained numb. Nothing. Not even pain.

Although she wanted to curl into Will's arms, she lay rigid. Her shoulder nestled alongside his. The passion and understanding they had barely discovered taunted her, lost in the fire. When he touched her, he soothed and held, speaking quietly like a man afraid to wake the dead with an incautious word.

And she could not touch him. She could no more appreciate the textures of his body than she could comb her own blunt hair. Streaks of saltwater trickled down her cheeks, wetting the hair at her temple.

At last, birdsong filtered through the night air. Dawn would arrive soon, but the scope of her day remained the same. She was bored and scared, already missing what she had known only briefly, even though he lay beside her.

"You should be asleep," he whispered.

She turned her face to his. "I cannot."

He shifted on the pallet and drew her into his arms. She rested her head in the hollow of his shoulder. For long moments, he held her in silence, stroking her bare upper arm. His heat pressed into her scalp, the skin of her neck.

A manic burst of sound pushed from her mouth.

"That was almost a laugh," he said. "What about?"

"Us."

"Oh?"

"Our hands. What a sorry pair. How do yours fare?"

"Marian's nurse fashioned another splint for my thumb. She's warned me to keep it immobilized for some weeks. Otherwise, I am better." The lazy rhythm of his touch and the soft rumble of his words calmed frayed nerves. "I sent missives to Bainbridge and to Monthemer's estate at Winhearst yesterday. We'll have word from your sister shortly."

"Thank you, Will."

He flexed his arm, muscles bunching at her cheek as he pulled her closer. "You are troubled. Tell me?"

For the briefest moment, she considered a lie. Hiding would be a comfort after so much time spent opened to him. But she doubted her ability to deceive him any longer. And lying to him would disgrace all he had offered.

"Upon the advice of his uncle Adelard, my father studied an alchemist named Al-Rhazi, an Arab man who lived hundreds of years ago and well beyond Christendom. He organized the world alchemy into categories he called bodies: acids, vitriols, salts, stones, and metals. As my father read from the texts, I willed myself to be metal."

He trembled with a soft chuckle. "I would never mistake your body for iron, Meg."

"Not my body, but my core," she said. "Al-Rhazi wrote that metals can be hammered and shaped. They can be sharp or smooth, always malleable. I wanted to be that, something to endure. Now I feel like a stone, something that when hammered—it does not bend, but shatters."

He rolled from under her and braced an elbow beside her head. He stroked her cheek, rubbing at the salt of her dried tears. "That's how you see the world, isn't it? With your ideas and questions?"

"I have no other way."

"You put objects into categories, expecting the same results time after time. Regularity," he said. "You look for patterns, even for yourself."

"It doesn't work with people, does it?"

"No. You don't shatter, Meg. You bend and change. I've seen it already." He closed the inches between their mouths and kissed her, a soft caress. "And you of all people are without category."

From the rooftop sentry, Marian walked to stand beside Will. He likely wanted his privacy, but she did not intend to let him wallow in a head full of turbulence.

Habit stretched her gaze over the manor grounds to the east. Half of her wanted Robin home, home in her arms and able to guide his troubled nephew through dark hours. But the part of her made timid by cowardice wanted her husband safe . . . but well away. A selfishness borne of three years of loneliness resented these complications. This was not going to be the happy reunion she had long envisioned.

"How fares young Robert?"

She inhaled the bracing air and chastised herself. People she loved dearly needed strength, not selfishness. "He's already abed. You exhausted him."

"He'll do well to see his father returned."

Throughout the afternoon hours, Marian had watched Will carry her son about the gardens, swinging him and chasing. Their play tensed a fist around her heart. Yes, she took comfort knowing the unlikely cousins, separated by a generation, enjoyed their sport. And smiling, laughing, Will seemed nearly without care, a happier shade of the young man she remembered from distant days.

But the man laughing with her son should have been Robin.

In many ways, from the timber of his voice to the cut of his shoulders, Will resembled Robin. The strength of that likeness fascinated her. Had he changed? Or had she simply come to understand why he once turned her head? She missed her husband with a longing made more brutal by Will's return, making her realize how much she adored Robin. Only Robin.

"I have a missive for you," she said at last. "A rider only just delivered it."

He turned and arched his brows. A bluster of hard cold ruffled his hair. He received the flutter of parchment from her hands and clutched it against the wind. After breaking the seal, he said, "'Tis from Dryden. At last."

"Read it?"

His eyes flitted over the page. "I was heartened to read of your safe arrival at Loxley Manor. Please know Ada is safe and recovering in my custody. Come for her when you are prepared."

"Meg will be pleased with that news."

He nodded, but a black fog shrouded his mood. Beneath the slate October sky, his narrowed eyes shone like chips of an exotic jewel. The wiry tendons of his clean-shaven jaw tensed. He shoved the parchment into his belt and pulled his furred cloak tighter.

Although he wore no armor, he was a man doing battle.

"Will, how does she fare?"

He chafed his face with unsteady hands. "The ruined skin has come away. What lies beneath appears sound, but raw. Her healing will be lengthy."

"Any fever? Infection?"

"No," he said. "The book she salvaged contains more than a record of her family's research. It also served as a pharmacopoeia. Alice complains about heathen potions, but the medicines from that book are staving off infection."

"Has feeling returned?"

He shook his head. Glancing at his bandaged wrists, he said, "These remedies are not kind, Marian. Trust that I know. But she has yet to flinch. Alice and I can change the dressings and apply the salve while she sleeps. I can make no sense of it."

"And her humor?"

His head twitched, a wounded dog snapping at a kind touch. Green eyes shuttered.

"I beg pardon, Will," she said. "You know my enthusiasm to offer aid can make me discourteous."

He grinned tightly. "I used to hate when you stepped between Robin and me."

She blushed and turned her face to the wind, unused to feeling chastised. "I meant well."

"Yes, you did," he said. "Far be it for a headstrong boy like me to recognize that."

"But I have no right to ask these questions. Forgive me."

"This is your home, Marian. You have no cause to ask my forgiveness. I value your concern, truly."

"Then what troubles you?"

"I'm losing her," he said, words like a plea. His pain was a palpable pressure against her skin. "She hardly speaks to me. When she does, melancholy is consuming her strength."

Head bowed, she curled a fist to her mouth. His new wife impressed her with a sense of strength, even while injured, but she could not adjust to Meg's ambling eyes, how they skittered and rested on nothing. Her reserve, her rigid demeanor—she would not be an easy woman to know. Marian hoped for time and familiarity enough to overcome her wariness, because Will had discovered a woman worth loving.

She caught sight of the white linen at his wrists and the splint bracing his thumb, the visible proof of his devotion. "Why did you marry her?"

He scowled. "What?"

"I only wonder about the suddenness of your wedding. Do you love her?"

"Yes."

"Does she love you?"

He skewered her with a stare hard enough to unnerve a battle-hardened knight. But Marian found the strength to return his glare, keeping her eyes level. She knew him almost as well as she knew Robin, no matter the years since his departure. And like Robin, Will was a very stubborn man.

He forced a pale breath into the cold. "I cannot be sure."

"What did you hope from such a hasty thing?"

"I thought my affection would bridge the distance between us."

"Or her gratitude would."

He pinched the top of his nose. "I wanted to do what was right."

"Because that's what Robin would do? Because your father forsook your mother?"

"Saints be, Marian. Enough!"

"No, not by half. You forget what I know of you."

He turned troubled eyes to the horizon. "You think I wanted a reward for . . . for . . ."

"Giving up everything for her? Yes, I suspect you did."

"I made the mature choice."

"No, your heart made the choice. And hearts are notoriously selfish." She shook her head, shivering when the autumn wind twisted her cloak and skirts at her ankles. "But this is about *her* now, what she needs to be well again."

"Which is what? I would fight anyone to keep her safe, but this—I don't know how to reach her."

"Keep with her, Will. Fight her if you have to, and don't play fairly." She stepped between his hard eyes and the horizon he watched. Her hands around his, she tapped the splint and offered a smile. "You're unaccustomed to helplessness, I know."

"So is she."

"Wretches, the both of you. But give her time."

He exhaled again, visibly shrugging from beneath his anger. He softly kissed her cheek. "Thank you, Marian."

"You're welcome."

With a quick spin, he twirled her to face the east, setting her eyes toward rolling glades made dull by the first frost. Galloping into the afternoon sun, six riders bearing the Loxley coat of arms topped a knoll. "Now go attend your husband."

Chapter Thirty-One

'If thou be feared, thou William Scarlet,
  At home I advise thee be.'
'If you be angry, my dear master,
  You shall never hear more of me.'

"Robin Hood's Death"
Folk ballad, fifteenth century

In his lifetime, Robin of Loxley had seen two angels.

Once, on the plains above Jerusalem, he looked across the barren wastes of the Holy Land. An apparition took flight against a severe blue sky, fleeing the chaos of armies' violence in the valley below. Whether a messenger from God or a faithful soul newly departed, peace washed over him at the sight. Gone were the hard winds and stinging sands, the endless blood and brutality. He understood that although he was as far from home as a man was from heaven, he would return to the place he loved, to his England.

The second angel flew at him across the dells of the Loxley estate. Atop a steed, she could not have been a mortal woman. With the falling sun at her back, her face silhouetted, she rode with reckless skill. Dark hair raced behind her in fat plaits. Animal and angel galloped ever closer, never touching the ground. They dared to fly.

But unlike the sensation of peace he had tasted in Jerusalem, he felt only anticipation at the sight of this unearthly creature. He wondered why he would be blessed with such a vision now. When he arrived at the manor, he would have to ask Marian if all was well—

Marian.

The angel materialized into a woman, his woman. She raced with the impulsive abandon of a girl, one without worries or heavy years. A grin as broad as the valley animated her features.

"Robin!"

Never had a more glorious sound touched the world.

To his second he called, "Ride on, Hargrave. We shall arrive shortly."

The riders in his entourage continued their steady, tired trek to the manor, passing their mistress with courteous nods. Her eyes never left his, barreling closer. Robin vaulted from his steed. Marian soared into his arms. They collapsed in a commotion of limbs and laughter.

She kissed him. Like a blessing, his angel kissed him. And he could only say her name, a chant, a plea to God to make his dream real.

Victory, hardship, and long, long years melted into the grass. She stretched across him, hands frenzied with the need to touch. Her curves and sighs hardened him with a quickness to leave him gasping. His armor kept her distant. He wanted to pull her to him, tight, flesh to flesh.

"My love," she said, at once breathy, at once laughing. "My love, you are home."

Joy trampled him. He dropped his head to the soft earth and sighed. "Our Lord be praised, yes—I am home."

His joy reflected in her eyes, eyes bright with tears. She petted his face. "I don't trust what I see."

"I'm here," he said, pulling her to his mouth again. Tasting her made her real. In his dreams, he had never been able to taste her, no matter his desperation. "And for wont of a few more trees, I would claim you."

She grinned, a sinful tease. "You are considerate of my virtue, husband."

"Until we're indoors."

"Then let's away."

A horse neighed. Robin glanced at the pair and laughed. "By the way you rode that animal, I would have sworn it was a champion steed to carry the finest warrior into battle."

She tossed a quick look to the bareback plow horse and shrugged. "Once I saw you from atop the lookout, waiting for my own horse to be saddled seemed a torture. I climbed atop the nearest I could find."

"You're not the angel I imagined," he said. "You're a wicked fiend."

"Let me prove it to you."

She caught his lower lip between her teeth, pushed her hips to his. The groan he heard must have been his, but his conscious mind seemed far removed from the man whose wife straddled him in an open field.

"Marian," he gasped. "Enough, please."

Her breasts pushed against the ornate embroidery at her bodice. With a last kiss, a gentle good-bye and a promise for more, she sat up. The cold wind frosted her cheeks to a ruddy pink. She smoothed wayward curls from her face. "Just as well," she said, calming. "Your armor is a nuisance to lovemaking."

"You may help me remove it."

He climbed behind her on his steed and pulled his fur mantle across their bodies. Marian nestled into his arms. The second horse loped behind.

"Robin?"

"Yes, my love?"

She hesitated. "Will has come home."

Cold invaded the mantle. "Will Scarlet?"

"Yes."

"He's come back?"

"Yes," she said. "Some days thence."

"I did not expect that." Emotion thickened his words.

Sudden, sharp pain sliced at his contentment. A conflicting sense of disappointment and failure poisoned those tiny cuts.

Will Scarlet. God protect him and damn him.

"Why? What does he need?"

"You're right to suspect that he would not return without strong motivations." She straightened but did not meet his eyes. "He is married."

"What?"

"I was surprised as well," she said. "Of late, there has been trouble in Nottingham from the newest sheriff. Soldiers attacked them at Meg's cabin. She was badly injured, and Will came here for aid."

"You admitted him."

She fixed him with a prickly stare. "Of course I did."

"And he offered no explanation for why he left?"

"Do you think I required an explanation before offering care?" Holding her was like holding a tree branch.

"No, but answers from him would be courteous."

"Robin, his wife lay unconscious in his arms. He came for her sake. I thought nothing of your grudges, nor did I behave to spite you."

"Where is he now?"

"Probably with Meg." She hesitated again, the wind teasing strands of hair from her plait. "She is blind."

"Because of the fire?"

"No. She has been for many years."

The horse took them nearer to the manor, toward the stables, but Robin held the reins carelessly. He shook his head. "Will returned and married a blind woman. I've missed a lifetime."

She wove cold fingers into his hair, massaging the tight muscles of his neck. "It feels that way."

"I suppose I'll have to speak with him tonight."

"'Tis evening," she said. "Let them rest. You, come and rest. We'll have time enough for reunions tomorrow."

Her optimism offered no relief. The prospect of bridging the gulf separating him from his disloyal nephew held no charm. The distance may as well have spanned Christendom. That Will had abandoned Marian and young Robert—the knowledge twisted in his mind, a betrayal of trust he could not forgive. Enduring anger tempted Robin to burn whatever bridges remained.

But he held his wife in his arms, safe, warm, and right. The evening stretched like a marriage bed before them, replete with promises. Whatever conflict stood between him and Will would wait until the sun returned.

"Yes, in the morning," he said. "Now where is our son?"

Her deep brown eyes met his. She banished all misgivings and smiled, stealing his heart anew. "He's sleeping. His room is on the way to ours."

From a chair in the corner, Will watched a narrow band of light move over his wife's face. She slept, peaceful and calm for the moment. The clouded dawn tinted her skin a pale pink.

A small fire burned in a cauldron, shaking the chill from their room. But he shivered. He knew no peace, no rest, because Meg still suffered. And Robin was home.

He had watched from the lookout as Marian tore across the knoll to meet her husband. Her happiness shone like a beacon, a ward against evil. Their reunion, a sweet collision of lovers long separated, covered his eyes with unshed tears. He had wanted to greet his uncle at the gates upon their homecoming. Instead, he slunk into the manor, his cowardice returning in force.

Morning dissipated the cowardice but a little. He would face his uncle like a warrior. But like a boy, he wanted to lean on the man who had taken up the role of his father. He wanted to confess his worries and deeds. The threat of rejection made a laughingstock of his childish wishes, just as pride demanded that his uncle look upon him man to man.

When Alice gently rapped at the door, he permitted her entrance to administer Meg's morning treatments. "Shall I stay with her, Master Will, while you break your fast?"

"I thank you, Alice."

"She's no trouble to me," she said, kneeling with her tray of remedies and fresh bandages.

He kissed Meg on the forehead. Standing straight, he tugged into place the tunic Marian's tailor had fashioned for him. A deep breath later, he left Alice to her ministrations and strode down the main staircase. Loxley Manor buzzed with the excitement of its entire household, all smiling and adding an extra zeal to mundane chores. Their master had returned safe and whole. Will envied their pure regard for Robin.

He combed fingers through his hair and made a silent vow. He was a man, not a boy, and he would not back from obligations to his family, to the truth. And he would not give Robin any more cause to despise him than he already possessed.

You are brave. You are good.

A smile touched his mouth. Mad, strange witch that she was, he placed his trust in her regard.

His shadow in the doorway stalled all conversation within the dining hall. A dozen sets of eyes turned in his direction. Robin dropped his gaze and the bread he held, but Marian smiled.

"Good morrow, Will," she said. "How is Meg?"

"Sleeping, thank you. Alice is tending her."

A flick of her dark eyes dismissed the servants. She ushered him to the table where Robin took to his feet. They stood as would adversaries, arms stiff. A tension Will had never seen in his uncle warped the slope of Robin's shoulders. New wrinkles scored his face.

Cold blue eyes met his. "Hello, Will."

"Robin," he said with a nod. "I'm glad to see you safely returned."

"And I was surprised to learn of your homecoming."

"Marian has been kind in offering her assistance. We shall trouble you no longer than Meg's care requires."

"Meg. Your wife, yes?"

"Yes. I await the opportunity to make your introductions."

Robin caught sight of the bothersome splint binding Will's thumb. "And you've had trouble with the new sheriff, I hear tell."

His jaw clicked. "Nothing beyond my measure."

Although he appeared unconvinced, Robin did not contradict. His wife glanced between them and mumbled an excuse to smooth her departure. They settled at the table, alone, and the wall between them thickened.

They ate in silence. The bread dried his mouth and made a chore of swallowing. Every sound echoed in the hall and aggravated the open wound between them. After a long swig of ale, he found words to break their silence. "You were at Châlus with Richard when he died?"

"Yes," Robin said, his mouth a grim line. "Senseless. All of it."

"And you wonder why I didn't volunteer."

Robin leaned back from the table, arms crossed. "I do, rather. You knew your duty."

So this will be our field of battle.

"Are you speaking as my uncle or my liege?"

"Both."

"This has naught to do with my refusal to go to France." Anxiety tingled the backs of his legs. "This has to do with why I left Loxley Manor."

Robin drove his fists into the table. Broth sloshed from shallow bowls. "I trusted you! You promised to stay, to look after the manor in my absence. Instead, you disappeared. You left my wife and son vulnerable."

Will took to his feet, slowly, glaring. "Marian is not my wife. Robert is not my son."

"I was called upon by the king. I had no choice."

"You of all people taught me that we always have choices."

"You were a coward."

"And I just made another choice." He jabbed a finger at his uncle's tunic. "I'll keep my fists off your face."

Robin caught his wounded forearm and twisted, pulling them into an awkward dance. "You walked away from your family."

Will yanked his arm free and backed away. "I walked away from Marian, you fool! And that was one of the noblest things I'll ever do."

Blue eyes turned to lead. Robin blinked, mouth ajar. "What does that mean?"

"Ask your wife. Mine needs me."

He crossed the floor, the sound of his light strides absorbed by heavy woolen rugs. Pacing, prowling the bedchamber, Robin awaited Marian's return. Through linen windowpanes oiled to near translucency, white afternoon sunlight shone at a low angle, creating long, misshapen shadows.

Bone weary, he wanted only to rest, to hold Marian in his arms, to undertake the future he had delayed by obeying Richard's call to arms. But an undeniable restlessness covered his skin, poisoning thoughts of peace and home.

Part of his dissatisfaction stemmed from his return to a life free of warfare and battlefield sacrifices. The other portion began and ended with Will Scarlet. He would not know peace until he ended their long disagreement. But how Marian figured in the dispute, he could not figure.

The worst scenario, that Will and Marian had become lovers, afflicted him like a cankerous sore. But the possibility rang false, even in his darkest imaginings.

Will and Marian? He could not believe it of either. He would not.

"Husband, you are distressed."

He turned to find Marian standing in the arched doorway.

Lit by that ghostly white light, her skin glowed with the radiance of silver. A wide, embroidered neckband displayed the elegant curve of her collarbone, the slender length of her neck. Silken ribbons twisted around her hair to form four long ropes, but a gentle halo of unruly curls teased him. Beneath the finery was the wild woman he cherished. He yearned to let loose her plaits and glory in his beautiful maiden.

"Robin?"

Will. He wanted to talk about Will.

But Marian . . . he needed her.

"I am distressed," he said at last. Striding to the cauldron, he took up a poker and nudged the coals. The small fire could not banish the autumn cold. He shivered, pulling his fur-lined cloak more tightly around his body.

She touched his shoulder. "What troubles you?"

"More like who."

"Will? What has he done?"

"I am to ask that of you."

She nodded, regarding him with a look he could not interpret.

As if eternally trapped in the terrifying moments before a battle, his knees weakened. The question pounded against his temples with repetitive strikes. Robin cleared his throat, willing the courage to hear her reply.

"What happened between you both, before he left the manor?"

He silently pleaded for Marian to slap him, to shout and rail over the absurdity of his accusation. Instead, she stepped away. His stomach shrank into a lump of ice.

"He kissed me."

The ice melted, replaced by molten fury. "I'll kill him."

He twirled away from the cauldron, those embers mild and pale compared to the flaring heat of his anger. Keen eyes caught sight of his sword, his bow, his quiver of lethal arrows. He gathered all three before Marian's pleas reached his fevered brain.

"Robin! Robin, please, stay your ire and talk to me."

Will Scarlet. His own nephew.

"You did not tell me?" His shout circled the room like a feral wind. He dropped the weapons with a clattering crash, making her flinch. He wanted to see her flinch again, to injure her in return.

A tiny furrow etched between her brows. "I was ashamed, Robin. Ashamed. Please understand. I feared what you would think of me."

"But he kissed you." The distinction seemed important, the only thing left for him to grasp before hurtling over a waterfall. "The fault is not yours."

She shook her head slowly, sending shivers through her wrapped hair. "You blame only Will. In that, you are mistaken."

"You returned his feelings?"

"No, and nor do I now." Her body leaned toward his, but she stayed rooted like a tree. "He paid me a lovely compliment, one that I enjoyed too much. Because I valued our future, yours and mine, I asked him to leave. For good."

He said her name on a rough exhale.

"Robin, I wanted a life with you, and I still do." Two tentative steps closed the distance between them. "I love you."

"I thought I knew that."

Tears leaked from the corners of her eyes, tears she did not seem to notice. "Forgive me, Robin. Please."

The sight of her crying, the tremor of fear—he could do little to resist her. He drew her into his arms. Her body sagged against his, overwhelmed by sobs. Robin pet damp wisps of hair from her face. "I can do naught but forgive you after all I've asked you to bear."

He cupped her cheeks. "But . . . Will?"

She pulled from his embrace, shoulders tight. Her voice toughened. "I half wonder if you would have reacted differently had he been anyone else."

"Nonsense."

"He is a man, Robin." Dark eyes still beset by tears shone with a fierce and unexpected fire. "Through your guidance and tutelage, he has become a fine man indeed. One to be proud of, to respect. And the only two people on this earth who cannot see that are Will Scarlet and you."

She fled, her words stinging like a nest of hornets. He hung his head. An ache of unreleased tension pulled at his neck. No encounter in his life left him as defeated.

An undeniable impulse to release his anguish jerked through his veins, powering his body without thought. Pain and instinct determined his actions as he took up his sword.

Chapter Thirty-Two

And about, and about, and about they went,
    Like two wild boars in a chase;
Striving to aim each other to main,
    Leg, arm, or any other place.

"Robin Hood and the Tanner"
Folk ballad, seventeenth century

Marian wiped at stubborn tears. The agitated ticking of her boot heels on marble echoed through the corridor. She found Will as he stepped from the room he shared with Meg.

He frowned. "Marian? What is it?"

"Stay away from her!"

They turned at once to find Robin striding down the hall. His face contorted into a mask of rage and hurt, one so unlike the man she loved. He wielded a broadsword.

"Robin! Put that away!"

"Out of the way, Marian. I have business with my nephew."

"I shall not."

"Taking his side?"

She touched her gaze to the sword in Robin's fist. Panic pushed at the back of her tongue. "Yes, if your business entails attacking an unarmed man."

Metal clattered on the marble, making her jump. Will's

dagger slid to a halt against the wall. "I'm unarmed now," he said.

Robin sneered. "Are you refusing to fight?"

"I shall defend myself, if I must."

A dangerous current flowed between the bellicose men. Marian backed away, a shaky hand at her neck. "Robin, please. Not like this."

"Stay clear."

Eyes intense, never leaving those of his opponent, Will nodded. "He's right, Marian. Do not come between us, not now."

"You're fools, both of you!"

Robin attacked, swinging his deadly blade in a high arc. Will leapt back and landed on his side, grunting. The sword struck a column. Without pause, Robin lunged. Will rolled clear and kicked, catching his uncle around the ankles. His shoulder slamming into the wall, Robin dropped the sword but stayed on his feet.

A door opened along the passageway. "Will? What is happening?"

Marian hastened to Meg's side, holding her clear of the fight, but not before her voice distracted Will. Robin propelled his foot into Will's gut, his face. The younger man grunted and doubled against the attack, blood spurting from his mouth.

Meg grew paler with the sound of every sickening blow. "What is this? Will!"

"Get her out of here, Marian!"

But Will's bellowed command only strengthened his wife's resistance. She fought to pull free. Marian tripped her and pulled her to the floor, crouching together along the corridor wall. "Hold fast, Meg. They—"

The silver glitter of a blade caught her eye.

"Robin!" She abandoned Meg and seized her husband's arm, staying the deadly direction of his aim. "Have you gone mad? This isn't you!"

"Stay out of this, I say."

"Look at him!"

Clutching his middle, Will struggled to his feet. Blood coated his face and the front of his tunic, but Robin was not swayed. He shrugged free of Marian's grip and shoved her into the wall. She cried out.

Will exploited the moment and punched Robin in the ear. He kicked high, striking Robin's hand with paralyzing force. The sword dropped. Another heavy right blow landed between Robin's eyes. His head smacked the wall, then his body hit the floor.

Marian's first instinct was to throw herself on her husband, to come between him and more pain. But Will gave her no cause. As soon as Robin sagged, all fight gone, Will backed away. At some time during the fight, he had taken up the dagger; it dangled from his belt.

She knelt beside her husband and watched Will, wary, but no aggression shone in his green eyes. Rabid emotion had blinded Robin to the dangerous man his nephew had become—dangerous, but judicious.

"Enough now, Will," she said. "Please."

He continued to watch Robin. "I have enemies, Uncle. More than I care to consider. But you are not one of them."

Robin spat. With a voice made nasal by his broken nose, he said, "You are worse than an enemy—a traitor in my own home."

Will nodded, shoulders low as if he were the defeated man. "I pray you can forgive me of that, because I am tired of fighting you."

"Get out of my sight."

"I'm going." He found Meg where she huddled on the floor and urged her into their room, closing the door behind them.

Marian stood. A shuddering breath ripped free. She could not trust the stability of her knees, but neither could she trust the malicious words building in her mouth, words meant for her husband.

"Marian?"

"End this, Robin. For all our sakes."

"And if I cannot?"

The agony in his voice had naught to do with physical injuries. She turned and regarded him, her chin wobbling but her eyes finally clear of tears. "The man I married can."

Will shed his tunic and pressed the linen to his nose and mouth. His face swelled, and he gingerly tongued his molars to find one loose. But he harbored Robin no ill will. His uncle deserved a release to his anger, but he suspected the shame would become a far greater burden once Robin sobered from the exchange. Maybe then they could begin to forgive.

But Meg . . . Following the fight, she merely returned to her pallet, a listless rag. He knelt beside her. Eyes, mouth, expression—she offered no path for reaching her.

"What do I do?"

She turned to his question, those curled lips unsmiling. "What?"

"Tell me, Meg. Tell me what to do for you."

"Were you fighting about Marian?"

He blinked. Did Meg harbor jealous thoughts of Marian? But no, her tone was distant and emotionless. She could have been inquiring after the weather.

"In a way," he said. "Marian confessed to our kiss. Robin is having a difficult time of the news."

She nodded, still listless and far away. "Do you regret marrying me?"

"What? Meg, what is this?" He bracketed her face in his palms. "You will heal. This is not permanent. Do you understand me? You cannot think that way."

She scrambled from him, pulling back into the lonely darkness. "Do you know how long I waited? My father told me he would find a cure. I stared into black and looked for any shade or glimpse of color. I became mindless for it."

Her sob tore at his soul. But Saint Mary, at least she was talking.

"After a year, I thought surely God had tested me enough. I was not embittered; I was hopeful and good. I did everything father asked of me, every remedy and cure. And I suffered travel into town. I bore it all. And after a year, nothing. Still more black."

The agitated memories left her quivering. Sweat salted her brow. "You say my hands will heal and I shall feel again, but I do not—I *cannot* believe. I don't have the strength to be disappointed again."

"And you think because you cannot believe, that I don't? That I'll abandon you?"

"Our life together will be hard enough," she said. "You married a blind woman. Did you take time to imagine the difficulties of raising a family? And if I cannot use my hands? I'll be an invalid."

Perhaps days of apprehension loosened his tongue, or maybe the fight against Robin still swam in his blood. But he spoke the truth, no matter how painful. "When you talk like that, Meg, you already are."

"How dare you?"

"I dare," he said. "Nothing I say will dent the pity you've wrapped around yourself. But I won't let you use this to undo what we vowed."

"I don't want to undo it! I want to live as your equal, not some dependent child. Not a sickly little creature who needs your constant attention. These past days, you've become a nursemaid. Is that how you want us to be?"

"No. But it won't be this way forever." He sank his knees into the straw pallet, his thighs trembling. He rubbed the length of her upper arms, anything to touch her. "Enough, all right? I loathe being angry with you. If I could pick a fight with your pride and leave you be, I would."

But she pushed from his hands and the comfort he offered. "Go, Will."

"What?"

"Send Alice tonight to tend to me. And find another room for yourself."

Rejection and anger doubled his heartbeat. He stood, his muscles as stiff as bones. "You are not in earnest."

He witnessed the return of the hard, cold woman he first met in the forest. That woman needed nothing and no one, not even her new husband. "I am."

"I misjudged you, Meg. You're not as strong as I thought you were. And that breaks my heart."

Three hours before sunset, Will prowled the corridor outside of Meg's room. The closed door mocked him, urging his frustrations to a higher pitch. Every hollow strike of his boots agitated him like a woodpecker wearing at the bark of a tree. He wanted to smash through that door and break through his wife's cloying melancholy, through the fear and doubt and pity she had yet to conquer.

He directed some of his anger at his acquiescence to her demands. He never should have agreed to leave her to her own dark company. He never should have agreed to allow her solitude, not when isolation was her most paralyzing fear.

He stopped his anxious pacing for the fourth time and glared at the wooden barrier that separated them. If he believed it would change her cheer, he would break down the door. He would litter it with arrows and hack it to pieces with his sword. But she remained hidden from him. Even if that door burst wide, even if she stood before him in the glaring brightness of midday, she would hide.

Alice ascended the stairs bearing a tray of supplies to change Meg's bandages. The plump, red-faced woman caught his eye and smiled shyly. She dipped a tiny curtsy. "Would you like to take this in to her?"

"No. She wants you."

Alice smiled with more assurance. "We both know that

isn't true, Master Will. If ever a girl knew naught of what she truly needs, your Meg would be her."

He moved to open the door for Alice but stopped.

Maybe Marian was right. He had married Meg in the hopes of receiving her gratitude, even more so than her love. Rescuing her had marked the end of easy choices and dreams of a carefree future. Loving her required that he set aside selfish habits, and he had wanted a reward for his sacrifice.

But that was past. He needed only Meg—safe and well and able to love him in return. If she wanted to.

He pushed unsteady fingers through his hair, squeezed the back of his neck. The extent of his loss threatened to fell him more surely than any other grief or betrayal. Not even his conflict with Robin caused more pain, and his pain tempted him with the worst possible option: to give in to her. But abandoning Meg had never been an easy task. Loving her made it impossible. The notion of allowing pain and grief to fester, obliterating their new life before it really began, was simply too terrible.

Fight her if you have to, and don't play fairly.

"Forgive me, Alice," he said. "I ask that you keep those supplies for another time."

"Your pardon, Master Will?"

A determined grimace pulled the muscles of his cheeks. "I've business to attend with my wife. I'm afraid your good attentions will have to wait."

For a moment, Alice appeared ready to ask questions. Knowing her strong hand with the other servants and her status as Marian's favorite, she may have thought to protest. But a quick glance at his face kept her silent. She walked down the stairs without a look back.

He took hold of the latch and pushed the door open. The metal handle was neither cool nor warm. He felt nothing. Every action lacked grace and timing, as if he had rusted from the inside out. But at least he knew what he needed to do.

Meg lay on her pallet, eyes closed and dressed in a kirtle.

Her skin glowed with the same pale whiteness of the bandages she wore. Will remembered the first time he saw her on the Nottingham Road. She had been terrified, yes, screaming and fighting, but she had thrived. Atop a burning pyre, life had pulsed from her. She was forged of strength and defiance. Now she lay like a broken doll, tiny, fragile, and unwilling to lift her head, let alone fight or defend herself.

Recognizing the contrast reassured him. He was making the right decision.

Three long strides brought him near. He leaned over, a tree above the forest floor. Short, unbound hair snuggled around her slack face like clumps of autumn leaves. Thinking that way, Will knew he had spent too long in the forest.But the image of Meg and trees and wild nature blended until the woods no longer loomed like some heinous place.

"Enough of this, Meg. Get up."

Her eyes fluttered open. She tossed blue irises around the room, searching for the location of his face.

"I say, get up."

"Will? What are you doing? Where's Alice?"

He mashed his lips and found her borrowed blue gown draped across the chair. With a smooth motion, he snatched the garment and knelt by her side. "I want you on your feet. I want you dressed."

She shook her head and continued to do so as he pulled her into a sitting position. He fastened the neckline of her kirtle, doing his best to ignore the lush swell of her breasts near his shaking fingers. After another steadying breath, he brought her to her feet. She wavered. He caught her under the arms and dressed her in blue. Only when he delicately drew her bandaged hands through the sleeves did he slow and soften.

"Will, why? What are you doing?" Wariness clouded her face like silt and sediment churned in a river.

"Your convalescence is over, Meg." He pounded stiff boots onto her feet. "You're coming with me."

"You have no right to do this."

The grim set of her jaw spoke measures. But he wanted even more defiance. "I am your husband, and I am claiming the right."

He hauled her up and over his good shoulder, closing his ears to her sputter of outrage. Flailing elbows pounded between his shoulder blades and bare feet futilely kicked the air in front of his face. She wiggled, screamed, and twisted, but he held tightly to her struggling body, wrapping his arms around her waist and upper thighs.

"Will! Let me go!"

He grinned. The heavy weight of worry blew apart like clouds after a storm. Thinking past Meg's writhing and fighting, he could not remember a recent moment when he had known more certainty. That certainty brought peace.

He tightened his strong grasp and headed for the stables.

Chapter Thirty-Three

"I am none of your delicate Norman maidens who can
only broider and mayhap ride a-hawking with the help
of the men."

—Maid Marian

The Foresters: Robin Hood and Maid Marian
Alfred Lord Tennyson, 1892

High above the ground, perched indelicately on the saddle,
Meg balanced using the strength of her thighs and spine. She
tucked both hands beneath her arms, unable to grasp the
pommel through her bandages. Any incautious movement
would send her hard to the callous earth, a fall that promised
pain and humiliation.

"Get down." Standing near the horse's head, Will spoke
sharply. She hardly recognized his voice as that of her new
husband.

Resentment and confusion gurgled in her mouth, building
toward a scream of frustration. But resignation glazed her
tongue. Apathy muffled any sound. She barely cared what
would happen next.

"I am waiting, Meg."

"Why are you doing this?"

"Because I am a very tired man," he said. "I've grown
weary of tiptoeing around you and your injuries, afraid you'll

fly apart. This pathetic *thing* you've become, sitting in our bedroom for a fortnight—this is not my wife. I want her back."

The horse whinnied and shied at his strangled declaration. Meg lurched across its mane, barely steadying herself with elbows on either side of the animal's neck. Carefully, crouched low, she used gravity and luck to slide a leg over the saddle. She expected Will to offer support—a hand at her waist, the strength of his body to lean upon—but he stood fast. A sullen snarl crawled across her mouth. She bared her teeth to the late-afternoon breeze.

Both feet planted, she turned to her tormentor, her husband, and willed her knees to cease their trembling. "And what if that is impossible?"

"This is your chance to find out."

"What do you intend?"

He stepped away, dragging the obedient horse with him. Meg felt the absence of its heat.

"Your walking stick is here. I'm leaving you in the woods." An obscene smile twisted his voice. "I'm going back to the manor."

"You lie."

"If you're angry, come find me." A few more steps took him out of arm's reach. "If you're strong enough to be my partner, come find me."

"Will, stop this." More steps encumbered the woods with the sound of thrashing leaves. "Will? Will Scarlet, get back here!"

"Come find me, Meg. Five hundred yards. Due north." Shouting now, his words echoed through the creaking trees and faded.

"Will? Don't do me this injury."

No reply.

"Oh God," she whispered. "Will?"

The October wind pushed leaves from their homes. They fluttered softly, whispering to the ground like the gentlest rain. Overhead, swaying branches composed an eerie and lonesome song.

She stepped back. A twig snapped beneath her boot heel. She jumped and whirled, blood fast in her limbs. "Arrogant pig! Useless, hateful man!"

Still no one.

Extending her arms, leading with the backs of her hands, she eased across each foot of forest. Racing heartbeats urged a fearful escape. Lungs pumped air out of her open mouth. Her body wanted to run when she could manage only slow, deliberate paces.

Despite her caution, she struck her forehead on a low-hanging tree limb. "God's teeth!"

The harsh syllables rattled into the sky. Following the limb, she found the trunk of the oak and pressed her back against its sharp bark.

"I don't believe you, Will! I know you. I know how you think. You're watching me out there. You cannot leave me!"

She kicked a space free of jagged acorns and slid to sit where the trunk met the dirt. The shelter of that massive tree hardly eased her anxiety.

"I'm not moving from this spot. Do you hear me, Will Scarlet? I am not moving!" Tears threatened. Her throat ached as fiercely as when she had inhaled nothing but smoke, surrounded by fire in what remained of the cabin. "Will, please. You know how afraid I am. Don't you?"

A magpie squawked in flight. Squirrels chattered and scraped their claws along the bark. Meg closed her eyes. She drew her knees in tight and hugged them, huddling until she imagined her body bowed round like a wheel.

How long would he make her sit there? How many minutes would she wait?

And if she could forgive him, how many years would she need?

Will passed the horse to a groom and climbed to the lookout tower, his eyes to the southern woods. He stared into the bleak, dense tangle of limbs and leaves. In his mind, he urged and cursed his wife, wanting nothing more than to see her trailing out of the forest. She would scowl and spit and hate him, but she would come.

Any minute now.

Marian stood at his side. Free of a veil, tightly curling hair haloed her head. Lines of tension creased the skin near her eyes. "You're taking quite a risk, are you not?"

He crossed his arms and banished his frown. "I'll return if she does not appear in a few minutes."

"No."

"No?"

She narrowed her dark eyes, an expression alluding to her skill for strategy. Will had not seen that calculating look in years. "You have the right idea. That is, if she's as strong as you believe. I worry, however."

"As do I, which is why I'm waiting for her."

"Oh no." Her smile transformed into a confident smirk, one more arrogant than any he or Robin might have conjured. "I worry she'll outlast you."

And more often than Will or Robin, she was right.

He nodded, a sharp jerk of acquiescence. "What do you suggest?"

Meg wrenched to wakefulness, thumping her head against the tree. Cursing, she rolled her aching shoulders. A chill shook her body. No warmth from the sun invaded the forest's dense shade, making her attempt to discern the hour impossible. She may have slept for minutes or half the night.

"Will?" His name croaked into the silence. The gritty feel of fatigue and unshed tears chafed her eyes. But she was still alone.

He left me.

Betrayal stained her every thought. The man who had vowed to become her husband, the man who had promised never to let her fall—he left her stranded in the woods. Again.

Shock followed betrayal, for she never believed he would leave her. Fear marched closely behind.

How would she get to safety?

But anger drowned that pitying, whining question. No matter the pain of her injuries, she wanted to wrap her hands around Will's neck and squeeze until he begged for the freedom of death. She needed to hear him plead for forgiveness, although she could not imagine granting him such a generous boon. Yes, anger would do nicely. She toughened her vulnerable emotions like donning armor.

If you're angry, come find me.

She would.

Seething, she pulled a wrist to her mouth and caught the end of a bandage in her teeth. She tugged and twisted free of that linen strip until she bared her raw flesh to the cool air. After freeing the other hand, she gently touched her palms to her cheeks. Scabs and patches of skin covered plentiful raw blisters, but none of the wounds wept as they had a week previous.

She wrapped her right hand in her cowl for padding and found the walking stick. A deep breath buttressed her against the daunting dread of her hike.

Struggling to orient herself, she tapped her way back to the oak and gingerly assessed the trunk. Rough, biting bark scored her fingertips until she found a patch of moss. Knowing moss grew only on the north faces of trees, she circled and aligned herself toward the manor.

Five hundred yards. Due north.

At every new tree, she felt for the telltale moss and checked that she walked in the proper direction. She even used her cheeks, petting sensitive skin against the moss when numb hands failed her. Raw palms bled. She ached to draw in air untainted by fear, her head vibrating with a concentration bordering on pain.

But she would not stop. She could not.

Sweat matted her hair and glued the kirtle to her torso. Her legs stung from the whipping strangle of twigs and brambles at her knees. Had there been a trail to travel, she had long since strayed from it, forging ahead with only the faltering faith in her own abilities. Every step worked to banish her fear, swinging a sword in angry circles and driving it to distant corners of her mind. Despite the logs, undergrowth, and stumbling, halting progress, even her anger ebbed.

If you're strong enough to be my partner, come find me.

She stopped. Frowned. Breathed.

The feeling of betrayal transformed into shame. Embarrassment feathered over her face and built into a fierce blush. She imagined the moping little girl she had become since the fire.

"On God's half, he's right." Whimsy pulled the corners of her mouth into a tiny smile. "The damnable swine."

She was still going to haul Will Scarlet over hot coals by his hair, but at least she understood his purpose.

Minutes blended into an unfathomable span. Riddled with fatigue, her muscles cramped and complained. A scuffling noise like boots on brick wrenched her from the mindless absorption. "Who goes?"

"Meg, are you well?"

"Milady," she breathed.

Marian caught her when she faltered. "You're bleeding."

"My hands. I'm well, truly." The need to finish the trudging journey on her own conflicted with the abject pleasure of leaning on a supportive arm. Agitated butterflies fluttered beneath her sternum. "Tell me, milady, did Will truly leave me to the woods?"

"By a manner," Marian said. "He wished you safe, but he did not trust himself to let you make your own way."

Her quivering belly calmed. "And you've watched after me all these hours?"

"Yes."

"Thank you, milady." Relief sluiced through her body, melting bones into useless, molten puddles. "Now where is my dear husband?"

* * *

Robin heard the curses before he entered the garden. Arms crossed, he leaned against a white limestone column.

Poised with his feet wide, bowstring drawn taut, Will trained his eyes on an empty archery target a hundred paces distant. He had covered the bandages at his wrists with protective leather cuffs. In a half-formed fist, the splint on his thumb jutted over the fingers he wrapped around the bow shaft. The hemp string snapped and flung the arrow wide into a hedgerow.

Will bit hard, bunching the muscles along his jaw. A scowl ruined the line of his brow. He sighed, shoulders square, and drew another barbed arrow from the quiver at his back. He slid a thumb and forefinger over the fletching, lined up the shaft, and fired again. Still wide.

"For grace!" He kicked a splatter of gravel and hurled the bow in a high arc, missing the target by a great span.

Robin pushed away from the column, hoping for a casual air but feeling only stiff wariness. And shame. He had returned from war, but he had escalated the conflict within his own home. His behavior crippled his pride.

I'm tired of fighting you.

He hoped Will meant those words. Having eschewed the bow and arrow as a matter of protest, the fact he held a bow at all raised Robin's expectations. Watching his nephew's storm-cloud expression, he sought any crack in the door closed between them—even if he had to be the one to knock.

"Your thumb grieves you," he said.

Will glowered. "Say what you wish. I know you want to."

"Can you try again?"

Eyes narrowed, Will regarded him with no little suspicion. Anger lurked in that stare, as did the dark glimmer of an old, old battle. A pattern borne of countless years reemerged in the garden: Robin offered advice, and then his nephew pitted pride against a yearning for knowledge and skill. He never knew which way the scale would tip because Will, often as not, shunned advice in favor of spite.

But not that day. He nodded, a single movement to buoy Robin's hopes.

Will retrieved the bow. He checked the nock carved out of horn and the braided string. Yanking another arrow from the quiver, he readied his stance and raised the bow high. His green eyes pinched to slits.

Instead of allowing the wounded thumb to form an awkward fist, Robin positioned the splint wide, away from the other fingers. He stepped away and waited.

Will maintained his grip, fingers trembling with the effort to stabilize his aim. But he plied surprising stores of patience against the task. Slowly, he eased the tension from his shoulders and relaxed. The line of his back limbered.

The arrow pierced the target two foot clear of the center, but a sight better than the hedgerow.

Will spat and shook his left hand, grimacing. "How's your nose?"

"Broken."

"I lost a tooth."

"Better than your head."

"Small mercies, Uncle."

His smile grew. "Is your wife well? I should finally like to meet her."

The brief flash of levity drained from Will's face. "And I should like you to meet her, if that's possible."

Before Robin could ask for an explanation, his nephew loaded another arrow, cocked his thumb away from the grip, and fired again. Nearer the target. But the tension from his body nearly hummed like the singing snap of the string. He exhaled roughly and stamped the bow into the ground.

Footsteps pulled their attention to the central archway. Marian wore breeches and a tunic, bow and quiver slung across her back.

"Marian? What on earth—?"

She led Will's new wife into the garden, a sight to shrivel Robin's question. Blood and frayed bandages drew a grisly pattern over the woman's hands. Grass stains and mud covered her gown. Thorns chewed its ragged hem. But in spite of her appearance, she wore an expression of calm. The smallest play of a smile touched her lips.

"Here we are, Meg."

Pushing free of Marian's assistance, the woman nicked a long, bare branch across the walkway, scattering uneven clicks into the air. She tapped a slow path forward. Will appeared outside of himself, watching her, his face stony but oddly hopeful. He took her free hand. She dropped the walking stick and Robin stepped away, joining Marian.

Delicately, slowly, she stroked Will's head, petting back his hair. Streaks of blood marked a path across his skin. Robin felt compelled to look away from that private embrace, but could not, so engrossed was he in their silent drama.

Will leaned into her touch, his mouth finding the center of her palm. She clutched damaged fingers into a fist and yanked a hard handful of long hair, snapping his head back.

"Saints be!"

"Bastard."

She balled her right hand and landed a solid punch. Knuckles cracked against his cheekbone. He grunted, staggered, then found his balance. To Robin's bewilderment, Will laughed. The tension that had distorted his posture and stiffened his stance dissipated.

Will caught her wrists and tugged her near. Their hips flirted. "Glad to have you back, Meg."

"Glad to be back," she whispered.

The energy between them pulsed and heightened. Robin did look away then. Marian played with a catlike grin.

The woman angled her face near where they stood. "Forgive us, please. We shall retire for the evening."

"You've walked far enough today," Will said, scooping her

into his arms. He kissed her forehead and smiled against her skin. "Allow me to escort you to your room."

Robin picked up the discarded bow. "I'll bring your weapon to the house."

Will stopped at the threshold of the garden and nodded. "Thank you, Robin. Perhaps we can practice again tomorrow."

With Marian at his side, Robin watched the odd pair enter the manor. One wore a splint on his thumb and favored his right shoulder. The other wore half the forest and more blood than good humor. But something crackled between them, the firm strength of a shared regard.

"My poor husband," Marian said, her laughing eyes on him. "What happened here?"

"I only half understand, myself. But I suspect we'll meet Meg tomorrow, both of us for the first time."

He grinned, looking her up and down. "I haven't seen you dressed for the woods in years."

She cast a quick glance down at the close-fitting outfit, all shades of green and brown. "I had no need for it, in the end. Meg made her own way."

"Target practice?" he asked, hefting Will's bow.

"For what stakes?"

Robin leaned close and whispered in her ear, placing a gentle kiss along her collarbone. She smiled, nodded, and drew an arrow from her quiver.

Chapter Thirty-Four

There, you may kiss my hand, Will, and I will take you
for my man . . .

Robin Hood and His Adventures
Paul Creswick, 1903

Behind the closed door of their shared room, untangled
from each other's arms, they retreated to opposing corners.
Will expected a lashing, either physical or verbal, and did not
trust his ability to keep from crushing her to his chest. His
blood surged hot and menacing in his veins, a turbulent combination of tenderness, desire, and profound relief.

She was out of the woods, literally, but whether she would
forgive his ploy remained a secret for the future.

"Meg, let me see your hands."

"No, no you don't." Her voice, although sharp, revealed the
depths of her exhaustion. She sank onto the pallet, tucking
bloodied hands into the folds of her gown. "I've had enough
of your commands."

"Let me see them. Please," he said, kneeling before her. He
opened clenched fingers and examined her damaged palms.
"You opened the scabs."

"I feel like every tree in the forest took a piece from me."

He grimaced. "Nearly."

"Ow." She winced and yanked her hands away, protectively wrapping one inside the other.

"That hurts?"

"Yes." Her amazement fluttered between them. A smile like the sun broke through billows of fear and fatigue. "Yes. It hurts."

He matched her smile of wonder. That she could feel anything at all, even pain, boded well for her recovery. Despite scars and clots of mangled skin, she might regain the feeling in her hands, given time.

"Here, carefully." He pulled her hands and wrapped his face in her trembling palms. "Can you feel me?"

She grinned, laughing and flinching at once. "Through the splintering pain, yes."

"Good," he said softly. "Good."

She tightened her hold and dug jagged fingernails into his cheeks. "Do not ever do that to me again."

"Do not make me."

"Agreed."

In a most languid homecoming, the air between them slowed and thickened. They drew together for a kiss. Captured by Meg's clasped hands, he angled his head and better fit his lips to hers. He caught the base of her skull and imprisoned her as surely, catching her little whimpers in the cavern of his mouth.

Inch by inch, she lay back. Bit by bit, he followed her enticing lips, joining her on the pallet. "Close your eyes," she said.

"They are closed."

"I don't believe you."

Repositioning her hands, she pressed shaky fingertips over his closed eyes, completely obscuring the pallid light of early evening. Surrounded by Meg, joining her in darkness, Will feasted. He savored his remaining senses, catching the salty scent of leaves and sweat on her skin, tasting her tongue.

Braced on a forearm, he relished the feel of her warm and supple flesh beneath his own. Like sun-baked stone emitting heat into the cool of evening, her body warmed him. The

insistent press of her lips to his, hot and needy, fanned hungry
embers. He grazed a thumb across her lower lip, enticing from
her a sigh. She bit down, tearing small teeth into the pad.

Blood that had simmered with impatience flared to a hard
boil, urging him to take and bite and demand. But neither did
he want to hurt her, not after what she endured. The most patient of sinners, he kissed gently, protecting her from the
brunt of his urges.

"Will," she whispered against his mouth. "You won't
break me."

A groan of happy frustration ripped loose. She may as well
have skulked into his brain and brought his thoughts to the
light. "Perhaps you've made me more cautious than I like."

"You always have been."

"I don't want to take chances with you. No more." He
kissed the bridge of her nose before journeying lower, nipping along her jaw to her chin. Carefully, mindful of her injuries, he removed her fingers from his face and opened his
eyes. "We'll just have to keep your hands out of the way."

"Out of the way?"

He nuzzled her skin, the earthy scent of her body shoving
aside thought. "Put them over your head."

"Do you intend to be gentle with me?"

"Not if I can help it."

"Good." Voice rough, eyes closed, she curved reddened
lips into a smile to suit both angels and devils. "Because I've
missed you."

She complied, loosely draping her wrists above her head. Her
breasts strained against the bodice of her gown, a sight to steal
all moisture from Will's mouth. He caught her lips again, harder
now. She arched. He moaned. Hunger and passion blended in
their kiss as each crawled more deeply into the other.

Quickly, abandoning caution and grace, he tugged the ties
of her gown at the neckline. A stubborn knot drew from him
a pitiable curse. "Forget the gown," she gasped.

He stood and shucked his clothing. On the pallet below, Meg

lifted her hips and gingerly slid tangled skirts to her waist. That done, she dutifully returned her hands above her head. The combination of submission and wanton invitation froze the breath in his lungs and throbbed in his straining erection.

He rejoined her in a heartbeat, filling his hands with ripe curves. He whispered her name, nestling his face to the side of hers, and took an earlobe into his mouth. Suckling hard, he reveled in her surprised gasp.

Meg, unable to touch him, nuzzled her cheek to his and kissed the patch of skin where his hair met his temple. She arched again and ground her bare pelvis into his, urging him closer. "You owe me," she whispered.

"That I do."

Meg pushed her head deeper into the pallet, the fresh, sweet scent of straw twining into her nose. She closed her eyes and floated along the most languid dream. Her ankles slid over Will's calves in a restless dance. His humid breath bathed the bare skin of her abdomen. He bit the inside of her thigh, teeth etching her skin. He suckled the flesh of her thighs, delaying and urging her higher. Liquid heat licked where he did.

With a hand on the inside of each knee, he urged her knees higher, wider. His tongue found her core. He kissed her. He sucked and nibbled with greedy abandon. She wanted to clamp her thighs around his head and hold him there, pressed tight, but he fought the push of her legs. His hands held her legs open to him, to his torturous mouth, and licked her wetness. She shivered at the thought of her vulnerability. Gasping and arching, she allowed her body to beg.

Will sat back, stealing the warmth but leaving the madness. He kept her wanting, wanting him closer. He cupped her sex, nestling his thumb at the apex of her need and wrapping his fingers to her backside. He flexed. She jerked, a streak of pleasure running through her body.

"Am I your husband, Meg?"

"What?"

"Do you love me?" He circled his thumb. A whimper escaped her control, a whimper that pleaded for more. "Do you need me as fiercely as I need you?"

She could not breathe fast enough. She could not think. The steady, mounting pressure of his circling thumb stole all she had. "Will, *please.*"

"I love to hear you beg, my dear."

She groaned. "Because you want me to succumb?"

"No, because at the next opportunity, I know you'll treat me in kind."

Licking her lips, she smiled. "You have my word."

"And I want your answer," he said. "Otherwise I'll have to prolong this all night."

"Decisions, decisions."

She wound her ankles over his shoulders. Crossing her feet, she used her legs to pull his head closer. He kissed the skin of her inner thigh, then settled alongside her body. The insistent pulse of his thumb never faltered.

The warm slide of his tongue at her jaw made her shudder. Warm breath feathered over wet skin. "No jest now. Did you mean your vows?"

"What does it matter? I said the words."

"Can you deny what I know of you? I've seen how you show people whatever face they care to see. But I won't be one of those fools," he said. "I'm in love with you."

His thumb threatened her sanity. He gently bit her earlobe, pulling a gasp from her arid throat. "Perhaps you're the bigger fool."

"Perhaps." He kissed her mouth. His lips matched her own trembling. "Do this with me, Meg. Be the bravest and the most reckless you've ever been."

"And if I will not? If I cannot?"

The insistent madness of his thumb against her sex slowed, stopped. He placed a feather soft kiss atop her head, twisting tears from her eyes. "My wife, my love, how long has it been since someone cherished you?"

A sob leapt free.

"Let me try, Meg."

Yes. Please, yes.

She melted into his muscles and skin and warmth, burrowing her lips into the crook of his neck. Kiss, breathe, be.

He pulled from her desperate embrace and dipped his mouth, replacing his thumb with his tongue, replacing tenderness with renewed passion. But he did not offer release. As good as his word, he prolonged her pleasure, drawing out every caress, every nip of his teeth. She writhed and fought, clenching her hands despite the shivers of pain.

"Help me," she rasped, thrashing her head.

With a last lick, he raised his mouth. "You know what to do, Meg. But mean it this time. I'll hold you to it, whatever you say."

The smile in his voice melted her defenses. Fears had piled onto one another like dirt thrown atop a coffin. No joy could come from such a life. But Will showed her a way clear, giving her a reason to fight, a body to crave and prize. He saved her. The champion she never dared imagine—he helped her come back to herself. Peace settled over her, a warm blanket.

She freed her smile, marveling in the pleasure they shared, seeing only what she needed to see. "I love you, Will. My husband. I love you and I need you."

"You're a good girl."

Half crazed, she giggled. "I haven't been called that before."

"And good girls earn rewards."

He closed his mouth over her sex, creating an insistent rhythm. The cadence of his suckling lips and his throbbing tongue shredded all reason, all restraint. She clasped her knees and ankles, holding him her prisoner just as he claimed her. The strength of her climax left her dizzy, floating, flying. She cried his name, grinding into the source of her torment.

"Watch your hands," he said, urging her to turn over.

He fondled the curve of her bare backside, sustaining her arousal. The sensitized skin of her nipples scuffed the material of her bodice. He gripped the bones of her hips and pulled her to her knees. She rested on her forearms, too dazed to resist, too lost in him.

His thrust demanded another gasp. Long, rigid, he stretched and filled her with every powerful push. He moaned. Her body rocked. Knowing hands wound around her body, again finding her aching nub. Will matched the timing of his thrusts to the pinching, insistent clutch of his fingers. He leaned low over her body, biting the thin skin at her neck.

The rasping sounds of his breath, so harsh and hard near her ear, washed Meg into another place as sweet as paradise. She arched and spun away on a spray of bright colors. Will wrapped powerful arms around her middle, holding her tight as he sought his own pleasure. He drove into her once more, and again. A violent spasm claimed his body. Her name became a cry and a plea.

Withdrawing, turning Meg in his arms, he guided them back to the warm embrace of the pallet, his muscles quaking as badly as hers. Wrapping her forearms around his neck, she left battle weary palms face up. Long, quiet moments passed as their twinned breathing slowed.

"I'm sorry," she said quietly. "I lost myself for a few days. Maybe longer than that."

"I'm sorry too."

He pushed hair from Meg's face, inhaling the musky scent of her sweat. A scatter of goose bumps dotted her slicked skin where he petted her arm. "Let me tend your hands."

"I thought we'd finished with you playing nursemaid."

He unraveled their limbs and crossed to the fire cauldron. After adding a few logs to ward off the evening chill, he looked back on Meg—prone, limp, ravished. And dreadfully dirty.

"You have to trust me," he said, smiling. "You don't want anyone else to see you."

"That bad?"

"Oh, you are a thoroughly loved mess."

"This one last time, then."

He dressed and fetched water, bandages, and medicines from Alice in the kitchen, avoiding her meaningful looks. Feeling like a scurrying rat, desperate only to avoid Robin and Marian, he returned to the bedchamber within moments.

She lay dozing with her gown rucked around her thighs, tempting him anew. But the raw wounds of her hands stayed his yearning. He had hoped and gambled, and she rediscovered her strength in the forest, conquering the melancholy that hindered her recovery. That she returned to him whole in spirit made him all the more eager to heal her body. He needed her well and safe and his. They had undergone too many trials to waste more time, more happy time together.

Kneeling by the pallet, he dipped a cloth into warm water and washed her face. She smiled from beyond the haze of sleep, a quiet purr in her throat. Careful, patient strokes cleared away the grime and blood to reveal the luster of her skin. The fire's placid glow bronzed every newly cleaned inch, a pagan goddess made flesh.

He circled the cloth over the balls of her feet. She roused, eyes fluttering open and skittering. She giggled and flinched. He trapped her ankle, working the cloth up each supple leg. Blood thumped with a heavier weight, more insistently, as he worked toward her torso. A few bumbling tries finally freed her from the knotted strings at her bodice, baring pale flesh to the golden light.

After returning the cloth into the water, wringing it, he paused. He thought she should wash between her legs; the chore was too intimate, even after what they had shared.

"Almost finished, Scarlet."

He licked his lips, his mouth dry. "For certain?"

"Yes," she whispered, a little flushed.

He stroked the cloth into Meg's dark curls, crossing a barrier between washing and petting. She sighed, eyes closed, body asking for more. But her hands remained untended. Will finished the cleansing as quickly as his shaking hands could manage, intent on healing her before enjoying a resumption of their pleasures.

Legs tucked to the side, she sat up and presented her hands. He opened them tenderly. Tears sliced her cheeks as he washed. She hissed softly.

"Sorry."

"I'm not," she said. "I can heal now."

He touched her lower lip, then kissed her there. "We both can."

Every application of the remedies tore a cry from her, a whimper, sobs. Every application wounded him too. But soon the injuries were clean, salved, and bandaged.

She released a shuddering breath and crawled nude beneath the coverlet. "What now?"

"I can read to you from Al-Rhazi," he said, climbing in beside her.

"You've taught yourself to read Arabic in a fortnight?"

"Arabic?"

"The things you do for me," she said. "Now I won't have to ask it of Ada."

"Maybe another scheme to occupy our time." He cupped the soft curve of her breast.

"I meant our future, in truth. Our lives."

"We didn't plan this very well, did we?"

She nuzzled her nose into the arc of his neck. "Maybe not."

He stared at the light sparkling on the ceiling and listened to the crackle of a comforting fire. The difference between that tiny blaze and the flames they had battled—he could not make sense of all they survived. He wanted no more of it. He wanted only Meg, there in his arms.

"Robin and I shall be speaking again come tomorrow," he said.

"Truly? All is forgiven?"

The brief moments he had shared with Robin in the garden

teased him with hope. Stomachs full of pride, they ground a few stilted sentences into being, but it was a start. The morrow would offer another chance, a chance he intended to take. "I believe so, yes. We can leave him and Dryden to administer Finch's punishment."

"You want no more of it?"

"Do you need revenge, Meg?"

She lay silent. A spray of short brown hair concealed her face where she rested on his chest. "Let justice have them," she said at last. "I need you. And Ada. I must find a way to explain this to her."

"To reconcile?"

"If you can manage with Robin, I can reach Ada. That was our deal, yes?"

He smiled, remembering the near and distant times when he had gloried in provoking her. The people they had once been seemed so lost and heartbreaking. "Well good," he said. "We shall begin there. Tomorrow, we can travel to Bainbridge."

"Tomorrow."

"Yes."

She dragged a knee higher, brushing his phallus, his belly. She kissed his neck and sucked. "Many hours from now."

"Yes."

Chapter Thirty-Five

Thou hast been traitor all thy life,
Which thing must have an end.

"Robin Hood and Guy of Gisborne"
Folk ballad, fifteenth century

Meg lazed in what threatened to be the last clement day before winter's final push. On a garden bench, she tipped her head toward the sky. The sun, although listless, convinced her skin of its warm shine. A lassitude borne of too little sleep and a great deal of pleasure softened her bones, making even the gentlest of tasks formidable.

At the archery range, Will and Robin did their best to eviscerate each other's pride. The sound of their gruff bickering and competitive insults rang with a good humor to gladden her heart. And later that day, they would travel to Bainbridge. She would see her sister and make all things right. Contentment slipped over her, sneaking into her soul and stealing the last of her bitterness.

A scatter of footsteps intruded, bringing the sound of armor. Will cut his latest barb midsentence and called a greeting to Monthemer. Meg straightened, her back stiff and her inner thighs sweetly aching.

Will offered her his arm and made the necessary introductions. Once Robin excused himself and returned to the archery range, the trio took position on a pair of benches. "Glad to see you, Monthemer, and in a better condition than at our last," Will said. "How do you fare?"

"Healing. I thank you both for the attention you provided."

Meg tipped her head, wondering at the grave timbre of his words. "Our pleasure, especially considering the aid you offered."

"What brings you here?" Will's question emerged as a serious one. He must have heard the same weighty inflection or saw more clues on Monthemer's face. Contentment slipped like a fish from her hands.

"I came to ask whether you've heard word from my cousin, Dryden. He has yet to return the missives I sent to Bainbridge."

"I received a note from him some days ago," Will said. He quickly related the nature of their escape from Nottingham and Dryden's departure with Ada. "As the matter has it, we were readying a journey to Bainbridge this afternoon."

Meg frowned. "Milord, do you suspect violence against him? Should we have reason to fear for Ada's safety?"

"I know not what to suspect," Monthemer said. "The male members of my family have been imperiled these weeks, and his failures to reply leave me wary."

"Perhaps you should inquiry after Gilbert," Meg said. "Do you know his whereabouts?"

Monthemer inhaled sharply. "Gilbert?"

"That was his name, I'm certain. In Nottingham Castle, Dryden identified his father's youngest brother, Gilbert, as a member of the sheriff's entourage. He feared for his own safety and yours, being that Gilbert would inherit your families' lands should you both die." She hesitated. The air snapped with tension. "Am I mistaken?"

Will's hand on her arm tensed, a pulse of unease running from his body to hers.

"Yes," Monthemer said. "His name was Gilbert, younger

brother to Earl Whitstowe and my late father. And yes, he would have inherited at my death and that of my cousin." He sighed, the sound of a man accepting defeat. "But Gilbert has been dead for three years."

"That cannot be. He—he—" Realization and a keen sense of outrage climbed from her toes to her scalp. "He lied to me. He stood by and created a fiction, because I could not see to contradict him."

"Meg, there must be an explanation," Will said.

A memory hit her, strong enough to make her flinch. Suspicions aligned like the most sinister of puzzles. "The night before we left for Nottingham, there in my cabin, he took the responsibility to tend you, milord. The quantity of wolfsbane he administered—I felt concern enough to question him."

Will's words held all the warmth of a winter wind, rubbing a nervous hand along her back. "Milord, had you died in the second roadside attack or because of your wounds, who would inherit Winhearst?"

"Dryden."

"But we assumed this was Finch's doing. He instructed Carlisle to lead the ambush where Lord Whitstowe was murdered. And Finch's men likely struck your entourage, milord, disguising the attack as the work of outlaws."

"We have to assume they were in league," Monthemer said, his voice grating like the squawk of a crow. "I feel a traitor to say that against my own kin, but the coincidences have been too many, especially with his financial difficulties."

Meg swallowed. "What difficulties?"

"Lord Whitstowe was near bankrupt. He had been supporting Arthur's claim to the throne over that of King John, and quite enthusiastically."

"Saints be," Will whispered.

Robin's footsteps crunched gravel, approaching from the nearby archery range. He cleared his throat. "Pardon the interruption."

"What do you know, Uncle?"

"In his final days, Richard confided that he worried about Whitstowe's influence in the Midlands," he said. "The earl supported Arthur's bid for the throne because John was intent on continuing the warfare in France, demanding armies and tributes from the nobility. Whitstowe wanted none of it. Arthur would've stayed in France with his holdings and let the English barons have their sway."

"But my cousin was never the political sort," Monthemer said. "He wouldn't care one hand or the other who became king."

"Perhaps his motives had nothing to do with influence or politics." Will hunched low and scraped hands through his hair. "Why settle for a paltry inheritance when you can secure much more?"

"That explains their pursuit of an alchemist, and why he was keen to escort me to Nottingham." She felt like her skin was made of boiled leather, stretched across inflexible features. "We assumed he acted out of cowardice when his father was murdered—"

"—and in the dungeon," Will said grimly. "By the saints, I saved his life when we clashed with Carlisle. I should have let his deceptions catch him out."

Meg gripped his upper arm. "What did he write in that missive?"

Will sat away from her and pulled it from his tunic. The sound of that parchment unfolding filled the expectant silence. He cleared his throat. "He wrote, 'Come for her when you are prepared.'"

"Sounds nearer a challenge than an invitation," Robin said.

"That it does." Will sighed, his back bowing.

"But he planned this? All of it?" Her heart pinched beneath her ribs. "And we gave him Ada."

Will held her and absorbed her shuddering tension. She did not cry, but her body trembled. "We'll find a way past this, Meg. I promise."

The look of anguish on her face cut him to the size and strength of a child. He did not believe his words. Neither did she.

"Oh, Will, I apologize."

He frowned. "In truth?"

"I—Dryden. I trusted him." She shuddered and cupped her elbows in bandaged hands. Short, dark hair bobbed around her chin. "I knew better, but I trusted him. I placed more store in his station than in your actions."

"You write history anew, Meg. I gave you little cause for trust."

She jerked to her feet as if pulled by strings. "We *gave* her to him."

"We had no way of knowing. And Finch offered you a poor choice."

"This is my fault," she said. "From the start, I pressed Ada into our scheme. She complied out of guilt. Now—dear saints, how she must despise me."

Like a thin layer of new ice over a lake, her skin had a sickly sheen. Red edged her lids, making pale irises even more ethereal. She pushed linen-covered hands into her eye sockets, grinding.

He curled her into his embrace and kissed her head. "We'll come to that when she is free."

"But how? Dryden fooled everyone, and he'll be awaiting our play. We cannot simply walk into Bainbridge Castle and ask for her . . ."

The desperate cadence of her words trailed into silence. "Meg?"

"Ada's only value is as a hostage," she whispered, her expression distant. "If Dryden seeks an alchemist this badly, he'll trade for me."

Fear stabbed his gut, then more fear. Anger flooded the wound. "Absolutely not."

"Why? The decision is mine to make."

"Hardly, *wife*," he said. "I won't permit it."

She stiffened. "Will Scarlet, I have not had cause to argue with you in hours. I relish the opportunity."

"Enough of it, Meg." The fear and anger poisoned his manners, coarsened his tone. "Dryden will not play fairly. Either he'll be desperate to hide his actions, particularly the murders, or he'll flaunt his superiority over the law. Think now," he said, grasping her arms, shaking once. "You have to know that."

He almost regretted the hard words that drained hope and fight from her face. But neither would he play fairly or gently, not when the prize was her safety.

"Then what do we do?"

"Come with me."

He walked her through the gardens, into the manor. Guards that had regarded him with suspicion or contempt only days before offered their fair greetings. He nodded absently, weaving through the corridors and halls, until he found Marian working at an embroidery panel in her chambers. Robert played nearby, holding Alice's apron strings like reins to a horse.

"Marian? Pardon the intrusion. Will you keep my wife company?"

She raised an eyebrow. "Of course."

"Watch her," he said. "She's blind but crafty. Tie her to a tree if you must."

Meg stayed his retreat. "Where are you going?"

Marian's eyes watched him. Meg listened. But only Will knew his thoughts, thoughts hewn of desperation. He had used his pride like a shield, a defense as he sacrificed hopes and selfish dreams in favor of honor. With Meg he had discovered something more dear, the strange manner of regard and trust they agreed to call *love*. And to keep her safe, to correct the wrongs committed against her sister, he would lay down that shield.

Where he needed to travel, his pride could not follow.

"Excuse me, Meg, Marian," he said. "I must speak with my uncle."

* * *

Robin sat at the wide oaken table, a litter of parchment and ledgers scattered over its surface. Although he worked to become acquainted with three years' worth of manor history, he could not concentrate. The trouble with Will, Dryden, and Finch tugged his thoughts.

He wanted to help. Duty and title demanded that he, the Earl of Loxley, aid in ensuring safety for the people within his sphere. And an old, innocent, insistent cry gathered inside him. He could do no less than fight for justice.

But another sort of call urged him to wait, one of a more personal character. Will had stumbled into this trouble, although quite by accident and through disreputable means. But the fight was his to conclude. Robin could not stomp into his nephew's fight, nor could he abandon his responsibilities to the people under his care.

What that left for him to do, he could not decide—other than the small, anticipatory choice he already made.

Sighing, he turned back to the ledgers. Marian had kept impeccable records of the manor's work receipts and productivity, as well as testimonies for every dispute and judgment. Her fine hand touched every sheet, curled around every detail. Touching a finger to the long-dried ink, he imagined the life she must have led in his absence, the responsibility and the waiting—and a loneliness to match his. At each turn, she behaved on behalf of their lives together.

Even with regard to Will, he finally admitted.

"Robin, may I speak with you?"

Will stood in the doorway.

"Devil be," Robin mumbled to himself. The muscles along his torso tensed of their own accord. He gestured to the chair opposite his desk. "Sit."

"Gramercy, no." Stance wide, hands behind his back, he maintained the posture of a man ready to do battle. "I shan't be long."

Robin lamented the circumstances that brought them to enmity, but looking at the boy he had guided and raised filled him with pride. Marian was right, which came as no surprise. Will had matured into a man of worth and goodness, ever seeking but never asking for the validation Robin long withheld.

"What is it, Will?"

"Dryden is unpredictable. He is dangerous. A threat to order throughout the whole of the Midlands."

"No argument there. You found a hornet's nest and pried it wide."

He expected a quip, some manner of crass reply. But Will's face remained stony. A battle fumed inside him, permitting no levity.

"I cannot—" His voice splintered. His cheeks reddened. He adjusted his feet in that arrogant stance. "I cannot brave him on my own."

He stood and averted his eyes from Will's embarrassment, half out of respect for the man's pride and half out of hopeful expectation. "That surprises me," he said, trying to keep his words level. "Your entire life, you've tried to do everything on your own."

"Not this." Will dipped his head and swallowed. "I hardly escaped Finch with my neck. In doing so, I put Meg at risk. I am—I am not endowed with experience enough to defeat him."

Robin poured a hasty glass of ale. He required a few swallows before admitting the last and thorniest impediment to offering aid: He wanted Will to ask. The dictate struck him as petty and selfish, but neither could he suppress it. Somewhere during their association, Will had stepped to the fore. He was younger, stronger, more daring and thoughtful, and now he was more determined, more disciplined. Robin's dominance waned, and he was prepared to act more like a friend than an uncle. But he required an invitation. He wanted to know that in Will's eyes, in the eyes of his most fruitful and frustrating undertaking, he was still a man of value.

Facing his nephew, he looked into those eyes. And waited.

"Robin, I need your help."

Chapter Thirty-Six

Then Robin Hood blew on the bugle horn,
He blew full loud and shrill,
But quickly anon appeared Little John,
Come tripping down a green hill.

"Robin Hood and the Tanner"
Folk ballad, seventeenth century

Will's throat clenched around the request, as if pride alone could drag the words back inside. Accepting assistance when offered—that was one consideration, however galling. But asking outright and admitting his deficiencies leveled him.

Too late. He had asked. And he awaited his judgment.

Face unreadable, a man of strategy and power, Robin placed the mug of ale on the desk. He turned and left through a rear door. Will stood there, his plea hanging in the air like a noxious stink.

His hopes plummeted. He had done too much damage. He had waited too long. And in doing so, he had failed Meg.

Anger surged past hurt and his sore pride. This was greater than Will or Meg or Robin of Loxley. This was about justice and the need to make right a dreadful set of wrongs. His uncle's refusal to answer a humbled call for assistance pushed Will's teeth into a gnashing rhythm.

Mistakes and bitterness aside, how could he shirk his duty?

That Robin placed more importance on their paltry arguments than on the greater good, that he denied the very principles he preached, struck Will in the heart. He whirled and smashed his fist into the arching stone doorway. Blood seeped from his knuckles. Tears threatened.

Robin Hood, his hero laid low.

"Ay, Scarlet! You'll need that hand."

He spun. Ducking beneath the rear doorway, a giant bear of a man emerged. Furs doubled the width of his massive shoulders. Wild hair and a beard large enough to house a birds' nest nearly concealed his face. Narrowed eyes danced a merry jig.

"John," Will breathed. "Little John."

The man laughed, stepping aside to permit Robin's return. "You daft bugger," John said, his happy insult banging through the room. "Did you think we'd let you have all the fun?"

Will blinked and looked again, tempted to rub his faltering eyes. But there they stood, the heroes of his youth and as great as ever. A grin insisted on peeking past his surprise. "You can have your fill of it, old man."

John clapped Robin on the back, a hearty smack that sent the smaller man forward a pace. "What is this place, Nottingham, eh, Rob? Every passel of years, we need to scrub that pisshole clean."

"Right on schedule with your baths," Robin said.

Passing his pale eyes between them, John sobered. He shook his giant mane. "It's set me sad, Will—you at a jangle with Robin here. Glad to have you home."

He accepted the burly man's hand, still disbelieving. John drew him into a massive embrace, cracking his back and laughing. The sour scent of pelts and musky sweat overcame him, watering his eyes. Or maybe that was simply relief.

Upon his release, choking for a bit of air, Will found himself face to face with his uncle. The span of a handshake separated them. Robin extended his hand, his gaze direct, respectful, and proud. "You have our aid," he said. "We are brethren, howsoever it stands."

Will accepted his hand and the embrace that followed. "By God's half, I hate you still," he whispered.

"And you are a stubborn menace to my health. Welcome home, Will."

John clapped them both on the shoulders. Will winced. Robin stumbled. They exchanged a quick glace as the un-washed stink of their giant ally assailed them equally. "Now bring me to the point," John said, his voice like an armored horse at charge. "We'll 'venge this menace yet."

Night shadows clustered in thick bunches along the high stone ceiling. When the wind spiked, invading from unseen cracks, the thick tapestries fluttered with stiff movements. Fire warmed their bodies and ornamented every surface, every corner. Will rested against Meg's side, feeling a light-ness and hopefulness he never dared imagine.

He could do this deed. He and Robin, together.

Meg had received the news with relief but with no undue sentiment. She simply held him, stroking his hair—fine and fitting praise for a difficult afternoon. But her own restless-ness, borne of a distress he could not identify, made her a prickly body to hold.

"I need your help," she said.

Will said those same words only hours before, and he glo-ried in being on the receiving end of a request. And for Meg, even the impossible was easy to grant.

"Anything. What?"

"This could take most of the night."

He raised his brows and kissed her neck, her collarbone. "You have my attention."

She stilled his advance toward her bosom, catching the sides of his face with stiffly bound fingers. A petite smile lined her lips. "The sooner we accomplish this, the sooner you can resume your journey."

"What is it?"

"My father's book," she said. "I would like you to help me read a passage."

He sat and donned a billowing undertunic. "If it's French, I might be able to help. Marian too. She's very good with letters."

She joined him, sitting up and partly dressed. A wild thatch of short brown hair haloed her face. "Part of the text is in French, yes. But not this."

Dubious, he found the book among their meager pile of belongings, mostly weapons and borrowed clothes. Meg's fire-eaten boots were fit for a rubbish heap. As soon as they dispatched Dryden, he would need to find a means of income. Dreams of wine, song, and a life of ease had been replaced by the necessities of home.

Taking the weighty, chaotic book back to the pallet, he angled it toward a small oil lamp. "What am I looking for?"

"Find the first entry that appears written in a child's hand."

As Will delicately burrowed into the meat of the book, pages crinkled and puffed dust into the air. Every diagram, every passage in a foreign code sang of ancient puzzles beyond his understanding.

"Here," he said. "Uneven, large, but a few lines. The first word is fire. Then *fue*—in French, yes?"

She nodded. "My first observation."

"And beneath it?"

"*Ignis*, in Latin. *Narr*, in Arabic."

He chuckled. "Your father gave you a page in his book and you wrote about fire."

"Ada wrote it, actually. She was a year older and already obsessed with language. I was too taken with burning leaves and strips of cloth to care about recording what I discovered."

He shook his head. The woman he loved was as unknowable as the mysteries in that book. She frightened him just a little. "How old were you?"

"Eight."

"Eight years old?" He grinned, sliding a hand up her leg. "You don't want to know what I had done by eight years."

"I do, but not today," she said. "Look at the word in Arabic, then sort through the unbound letters to match the symbols. That is what we seek."

"The Arab word for fire? And I shall read it to you before bed?"

"No." Her mouth pulled tight and her brows drew together. "You can help me make the weapon to take down Bainbridge Castle."

"What weapon?"

"You'll know, betimes. Find that passage and we shall translate the formula."

He grimaced. "A letter at a time, likely."

Across the long scrawls on each letter, he pushed his gaze over bewildering symbols: boxy Greek letters, more familiar Latin ones, and the strange, slanting wisps of Arabic. Hours of tedious study cramped his shoulders and settled an ache in his bones. His eyes throbbed and grated, covered with dust and dulled by a fruitless search. Meg tended her injuries, washing and applying medicine to her hands. Will watched those hands, coveting a long, deep massage for his aching back.

He rubbed the rough bandage of his splint over closed lids. Then, eyes open, he saw the word. He checked again.

"I found it. I cannot make sense of it, but I found it."

Meg smiled and climbed into the pallet beside him, one hand free of the bandages. She touched the frail parchment with a fingertip, the blisters and damaged skin making a hash of her ability to discern texture and detail. The page she touched could have said anything, maybe a formula to distill urine into a solvent, but she trusted Will. She petted the page, smiling a gentle greeting to her father, her great-uncle, and Al-Rhazi long before them all. Will would help her use their ancient, long-guarded knowledge to defeat Dryden, to rescue Ada.

Hope and confidence finally loosed her tongue. "I want to go with you," she whispered.

"No."

She flinched. "I'll stay out of danger, well behind the archers' line."

"No."

"You want me to wait here, wait for news of your fate?" Pain seized beneath her ribs and robbed her of air. "I cannot—I, this will kill me."

"The answer is no, Meg," he said, touching her cheek. "You know that."

She closed her eyes and pulled away from the symbols she could not see. Refusing to leave the cabin had protected against such a moment, when her impairment would leave her behind. But the pain was short-lived, surmounted more quickly than she feared. She could not handle a sword or fire an arrow or charge the ramparts at Will's side, as Marian would next to her husband, but she could understand the book he held. She could make those symbols into potent magic that would aid in the fight.

"Yes, I know."

"Keep this with you," he said, curling her bare hand around the hilt of a dagger. He kissed both cheeks. "Just a little something to augment your natural fangs and claws."

She laid the dagger and the book aside and dove into the shelter of his embrace. He grasped her fully, pulling her to the pallet. His arms crisscrossed her back, binding her close. Through the pain shooting across her palm, she touched his face, his dear features, memorizing him. That pain paled beside the gaping terror she felt. She had feared loving this man, and now she only feared losing him.

All fight faded, leaving a nightmare in its place. She wrapped her arms around his neck and held, hugged, and cried.

"You will come back to me?"

"I swear it."

* * *

Despite how Meg's concoctions stirred frightened rumors among the household staff, they did as she instructed.

Will journeyed back to the forest, collecting Jacob from his father's cabin and supplies based on her requests. He also ensured the servants' compliance. Obeying the dictates of a former outcast, a purported witch, and a half-grown Jewish boy tested the obedience of the Loxley staff, but Meg was engrossed in her work and hardly noticed the nervous rumors. She studied and practiced, failed and started anew, until she produced a substance fit for the Devil's own armies.

Inform the archers, she had said.

Other allies assembled too, including David Fuller and a ragtag band from Charnwood. Little John brought a merry company of men. Fletchers, iron workers, and men skilled with bows and swords. They came from surrounding holts, bringing with them a thirst for justice, a rowdy willingness to fight, and a sense of camaraderie Will had not experienced since his boyhood. He greeted each face, whether familiar or fresh, with humbled thanks.

Days later, Will and Robin rallied the men. Two barrels of Meg's potion burdened a pair of horses—horses the forest folk avoided. Across the stables teeming with men and animals, Will caught sight of Marian standing alone. She wore a sad expression and a beautiful gown, not armaments for fighting. He led his mount by its reins and came to her side.

"I thought you were set to accompany us."

She turned her deeply-set eyes to him, gracing him with a soft smile. "I thought to, but I cannot leave Robert. The chance . . . if—he needs one of us to survive, should the worst happen."

"No more adventure and danger?"

"My son needs me, as does this manor. Meg and I shall keep company."

"Thank you for that." He matched her bittersweet smile,

saying good-bye to the wild woman he had known. The mistress of Loxley Manor stood before him, and she knew lessons of steadiness and sacrifice he had yet to master. "Does Robin know?"

"Yes." She flicked bright, sharp eyes over Will's shoulder to where Robin mounted his horse. "We've said our farewells."

A heavy sense of responsibility weighed on him, the dangers he asked so many to bear. But the task had grown larger than him, larger than Meg and her sister. Again they stood ready to unyoke Nottinghamshire from injustice.

"I shall bring him back to you, Marian."

"Both of you," she said. "No less."

He kissed her hand, bowed, and faced the men. "Take to your horses! On to Bainbridge!"

Chapter Thirty-Seven

And once again, my fellows,
We shall in the green woods meet,
Where we will make our bow-strings twang,
Music for us most sweet.

"Robin Hood Rescuing Will Stutly"
Folk ballad, seventeenth century

Will Scarlet hated trees. Any trees.

And Sherwood Forest, most of anything.

But at least he did not crouch among the oaks, wondering at his purpose and the allegiances of the men beside him. He traversed through Sherwood with Robin, Little John, and threescore men, covering the distance into Barnsdale Forest by early evening. Clouds thinned and dispersed when they dined at midday, but storms fiercely fell near sundown.

He tightened his short cloak and drew the hood over his head. Although the leather lining provided some protection from the rain, droplets chased by hard winds lashed his face. He tipped his head toward the saddle and presented the hood to the worst gales.

Miserable.

But his boots were sound, his horse showed no signs of fatigue or ill temper, and he could trust the men at his back. A fair change, indeed.

Robin rode beside him, looking like the hooded outlaw of fame and fable. A gleaming bow hitched over his shoulder and a quiver of arrows with goose-feather fletching promised a wealful attack. He welcomed the opportunity to relinquish leadership to his experienced uncle.

"What are your plans?"

"Me?" Robin raised an eyebrow. "I made ready to ask the same of you."

A sluice of panic drenched his skin more thoroughly than the rain. "You jest."

"Not in the least. This is your gambit, Will. The lead is yours."

"But you let as though you had ideas. I haven't the experience to mount an attack of this scope."

"Now you think to admit your lack of experience?"

"Yes, and aren't you proud?"

His uncle grinned. The years-old tension banding Will's chest eased at last. Apprehension about the pending attack pulled at his attention, yes, but he would not be alone. Robin no longer bore him ill will, and their easy, renewed camaraderie made him smile. A fresh start.

"Mounting an attack is different than understanding your enemy," Robin said. "What do you know of Dryden? What can we expect of him?"

Will frowned, lips tight. Dryden's thorough deception still rankled. "He acted a part. While he fought me initially, he behaved differently when he met Meg. As soon as he discovered her abilities as an alchemist, he demurred. We believed him a coward or a man reluctant to assume leadership."

"But circumstances suggest he is neither."

"Correct," he said. "He was biding time, I wager. If not for Hugo's mob capturing Meg, Dryden would have had both his alchemist and a dupe for the murders."

"You?"

"Yes, and all without revealing himself as the perpetrator."

"We shall reveal him this day, no matter how else we fare."

He shivered, eyes on the forested horizon. "That won't do, Rob. My aim is Ada returned safely."

His uncle's expression turned grim beneath the shadow of the hood. "Once Dryden discovers that we have no intention of trading or compromising, he'll have little reason to keep her alive. Have you considered that?"

"I have."

Robin adjusted his hold on the reins, gloves sliding on the wet leather. "Has Meg?"

"Possibly."

Closing his eyes for a moment, Will clung to the memory of their good-bye. Desperate, rough loving. Mingled tears. Promises made and made again as they willed fate to be kind. Meg had stripped her bandages, endlessly touching his body and his face. They had endured too much to be bested at the final hour, but both understood the looming danger.

Night had vanished like a flashing spark. Holding fast to each other, the gathering daylight offered no reprieve. They could not forestall the inevitable.

"Our parting was . . . difficult," he said. "I felt no cause to make the moment more dire by discussing bleak scenarios."

Robin offered a tight nod. "I understand entirely."

Thinking of Meg, of Marian, of home and safety—they would only distract him from the trials they faced. He forced the grief to a distant corner.

"Dryden sent that message to the manor," he said. "He knows we shall come for him. Stealth may be of little use."

"After what Meg showed us of that potion she created, stealth seems the last of our options. Your wife is a dangerous woman."

"You're one to talk."

"Robin!"

His uncle turned to Little John's rumbling call. "What is it?"

"We've arrived," the burly man said. "Time for plans and action, not words. What say you?"

Robin flashed eyes of blue ice. "What say *you*, nephew?"

Will scowled, hardly the expression of a confident leader. A few dozen armed woodsmen—some of whom had been intent on hanging him weeks earlier—turned to him in a glade overlooking Bainbridge Valley. He had avoided responsibility for half the span of a man's life, always wondering why Robin withheld his trust in difficult scrapes. The answer stared at him now. Asking Robin for aid was not the most difficult aspect of his venture; leading was.

"John, you and your men will come with me to the gates." He found a sodden mop of curling black hair among the mass of armed men. Jacob, armed with his crossbow and curving knives, stood at the ready. But whereas Will had always resisted leadership and the advice of his elders, Jacob proved an able learner with a reluctant but firm grasp of his limitations. A man could not ask for a better fighter at his back, no matter his youth and heritage. "You too, Jacob."

"Such a small envoy?" someone asked.

The faceless doubt irked him. He had no faith in his own command, but no one else needed to know. "We'll take a small force to the castle, secretly. Keep as many people as possible out of the way of the archers' arrows."

The men in charge of tending Meg's potion stood with a swath of leather draped across the openings of two watertight barrels. Another man removed a wide tub from the back of a donkey and turned it to the pouring rain, while a fourth pried the lid off a drum of sand, leaving the wooden slats to rest loosely atop it.

Robin edged his horse nearer to Will's. His face unreadable, he addressed his corps of archers. "To make ready, dip an absorbent arrow into the solution and then into the water. As much as possible, keep water out of the barrels."

"And separate them," Will said, gesturing to the men guarding Meg's concoction. "Put the barrels at either end of the line."

Robin nodded. "We'll hold fire until Dryden proves unreasonable."

"Only two or three minutes, then," John said. Raindrops beaded in his tangled beard and rimmed his eyelashes. "At least let us get to the castle gates, Rob."

Will and his entourage slunk around the shallow valley dipping between the fringe of Barnsdale trees and the moat surrounding Bainbridge. Rain sluiced across the field, blurring his view of the earth and timber palisade. Atop the mound, a single gate bifurcated a wood and stone defensive wall. A lone turret made of granite lifted above a keep that was hardly larger than Loxley Manor, but battlements offered high shielding for Dryden's archers.

Little John grinned. "If that be a castle, Robin needs to call his pittance as much."

"Not big enough for you?" Will asked.

"Just right for our purposes, I wager."

"Agreed."

Although hidden at the base of the mound, Will felt the stir of countless eyes on him, from above, from behind. He kept his back low, legs pulling him up and up. Bow, sword, and daggers hung ready for use. The nearer they could get without initiating a fight, the farther they could push with full quivers and limbs unburdened by fatigue.

Watching for movement, he skipped his gaze across the parapets. The strengthening rains made walls of granite appear to move. Specters and shadows trembled in the murky evening light, concealing their stealthy advance but shielding any enemy threat.

Will signaled his entourage to hold fast. Twenty yards away, up the hill, two armored men stood guarding the half-drawn portcullis, pikestaffs crossed.

"So few defenses?" Jacob whispered. Crossbow at his back,

he shifted black eyes in a nervous pattern: walls, palisades, gate. And again. "Like they expect us to take sup with them."

"Likely a trap."

"You're not wrong," John said, joining them. "But Robin has our backs. If you trust him and your woman's potion, I say we push on."

Will nodded and pulled an arrow from his quiver. Little John did the same, his large frame belying the grace with which he handled his weapon. Though the rain made a misty mess of aiming, they drew back their bowstrings, silently counted to three, and fired in unison. Both men at the portcullis dropped.

"Now!"

They raced up the mound, closing the remaining distance in a matter of seconds. High above the gate, wooden hoardings opened. A score of archers appeared from under the galleries, bows trained on the advancing party. Someone inside the gate struck the release rope for the portcullis, for the raised grating screeched in a plummeting descent to the ground.

"Inside!"

Will ran and rolled beneath the falling portcullis. John, Jacob, and a half dozen others heeded his urgent command. But trapped between the gate and a hail of arrows from the hoardings, men on the outside huddled into tight corners.

"Come now," John said. "Robin will do his job, right sure. We do ours."

Will shook his attention from the trapped men and charged into the courtyard.

Ada sat in the center of a chapel in Bainbridge Castle, her heartbeat like a gathering storm, growing stronger. Feet tied, hands tied, her limbs numb, she searched her mind to determine why Dryden had changed her accommodations. Nothing short of a gentleman since escorting her from Nottingham, that terrifying place, he even supplied medicines to heal the lacerations on her soles. He told her that a missive had been delivered to Meg, but her sister had yet to make contact.

The delay set her on edge. She could not shake the outrage she harbored since that day in Nottingham. When offered the choice between Ada and Will Scarlet, that vile wag, her sister had wavered and waited. If history was any indication, he held Meg under some manner of delusion, as Hugo had. Every day spent separated from her would make their reconciliation more difficult. Until then, she dwelled on her aversion to Scarlet.

But worries about her sister came to an abrupt end that afternoon. Following the midday meal, a pair of his guards dragged her from the dining hall, tying her to a heavy oaken bench.

A mistake, surely—her first thought. Ada screamed for Dryden until her voice lost its luster and the echoes threatened to destroy her hearing.

A punishment, perhaps—her second thought. But what had she done?

After fighting the restraints with no success, she calmed to conserve her strength. The chamber was empty. While not as bleak, the circular chapel with its high ceilings and tall, narrow stained glass windows may as well have been a cell in Nottingham's dungeon. It offered no more freedom. She sat at its center, bound, frightened. And angry.

Behind the locked door, guards began to shout. Their weapons rattled but they did not turn toward her place of captivity. Sounding ready for an encounter, the men ran through the halls and bellowed confused orders. Had the sheriff grown bolder, having decided on an open confrontation with Dryden?

A key chafed the rusty lock and turned.

Clad in his customary black, Sheriff Peter Finch stood in the doorway. Daylight matched his eyes and nondescript brown hair. In his hand, he held the jewel-encrusted dagger.

She screamed.

* * *

"Prepare your weapons!"

Robin pulled a special arrow from his quiver. Instead of barbed metal, the head was made of tightly wound and knotted wool. More like a slender torch than an arrow, he drenched it in the gelatinous solution. The man in charge of that barrel quickly dropped the leather cover back in place, keeping it clear of the rain.

He marveled at the magic he witnessed. Each drop of water landed upon the coated shaft and sizzled. When he dipped the saturated wool into the open drum of rainwater, it burst into flames. The downpour did nothing to extinguish the fire and, in fact, strengthened its mysterious heat. All around him, he heard his men—sound men of long experience in battle—wonder and fret about the unnatural blaze.

But then the hoardings opened. Dryden's archers began their assault of Will's team.

He watched the trap unfold, neither surprised nor discouraged. At least Will and a few of his accomplices made it inside the gate. "Archers! On me!"

A line of men stood ready, wielding the flaming arrows no water could douse.

"On the hoardings! Ready! Fire!"

Curving over the shallow glade, blazing arrows glowed against the deep gloom of the evening storm. While a few flew wide in the wind, most of the points met their mark and imbedded in the wooden galleries that shielded the opposing archers. The arrows burned and burned. No amount of water quenched their hunger, until even the rain-soaked wood fell victim to the tremendous heat and caught fire.

"Again!"

Another round of arrows like torches found Bainbridge's fortifications. From beneath their shields, the remaining men trapped by the portcullis fired up with standard arrows. Men fell from the hoardings, some of them ablaze, all of them screaming as they plunged earthward.

"Look, Robin! As if the rain weren't doing the job already!"

He looked where Hargrave pointed. Dryden's soldiers threw buckets of water on the hoardings. The flames increased. He grinned, amazed. Never had he seen a marvel so contrary to nature.

"Your directions, Lord Loxley?"

"Some of the men outside the gate yet stand," Robin said. "Likely, they are not being attacked with arrows from the other side of the portcullis. Will and John must have pushed through. Continue the assault."

But from the left of the line came a fierce roar of pain. Robin whipped around his head to see two men engulfed by flames.

Chapter Thirty-Eight

> "Set on foot with good will,
> And the sheriff will we kill."
> —Little John

> *Robin Hood and the Sheriff of Nottingham*
> Anonymous, fifteenth century

"No need to be frightened, my dear."

Ada watched Finch through a film of tears. He played with the dagger, teasing the luminous blade across his palm. Fire slashed behind the stained glass and cast cuts of colored light across the chapel. Flickering shadows of his negligent posture warped over the circular walls. Another flash of fire plummeted from the roof, streaking down the length of the narrow windows.

"I'm here to help you," he said.

"Where is Dryden?"

"Doing battle with Robin of Loxley." A slow, serpent's smile curved his lips. "He has little time for you now. Does that upset you?"

"*You* upset me." Tears lumped in her throat. She could not look away from that nightmare blade.

Finch eased forward—no sudden advance, but every stealthy movement liquefied her courage. It seeped through her pores, evaporating into air thick with rain.

"Dryden has no further use for you, not now that your sister has found allies with teeth."

Meg?

"Dryden took care of me," she said, sounding as feeble as she felt.

"You were of use to us, but no longer."

"Us? You were in league?"

Shrugging with grace enough to suit a woman, Finch knelt at her bound feet and lifted her skirts. He petted the length of one calf, rhythmically, gently. Ada wanted to scream, but her voice died in her mouth. Terror soaked up the sound.

"Yes, my dear, and now he wants me to kill you. Can you imagine? He wants to have done with you, as if you have no further value." Beads of sweat dotted his brows and temples. His hand at her calf became bolder, sliding past her knee. Bile collected on the back of her tongue. "But you and I have become attached, haven't we? Dryden, for all his ambition, never had the opportunity to know you as I did."

"Get away from me!"

He gripped her cheeks in a slender hand. Soulless brown eyes drifted nearer, swirling as if she had consumed too much ale. "Understand this, Ada: Dryden wants you dead. I want you for myself. And despite how intimately involved you are in the outcome, you have no say."

Finch sliced through the ropes at her ankle. With the tenderness of a lover, he straightened her knee and touched her sole, smoothing bare skin against bare skin. Ada shuddered.

He smiled gently. "Has Dryden helped to heal your wounds? What a generous sort. Other than his lack of regard for your life, we should be pleased by that turn. Such a gift to start anew, you and me. How we began."

He brought the dagger to her sole. The world of circular walls and decorated shards of light swam in a hazy pool, coating her eyes. The gleam of metal sapped her sanity. He petted and stroked, never cutting. She could not turn her eyes, mesmerized by the sick rhythm of his caress and awaiting the inevitable pain.

A crash of fire shattered the windows. Flames and stained glass fragments like slivers of colored ice pelted the chamber. His body between Ada and the windows, Finch turned in time to catch the shards with his eyes and cheeks.

She screamed, her terror finally let loose.

The sheriff leapt to his feet and staggered around the room. He clutched his ruined face, a blinded and bellowing animal. Echoes chased around the chamber. Wild flashes of lightning stitched the night sky. Silhouetted against the dark and the unnatural light, he ran headlong into a wall. His body hit the marble with a heavy thud.

The rain persisted. Ada breathed and breathed. She watched where Finch slumped against the wall to her right, but she did no trust that he was dead. The flaming torch that splintered the window lay burning a few feet away.

Using the foot Finch had cut free, Ada pushed the floor with her heel. Her newly healed sole protested. Pain coiled into her skin. She pushed again, budging the heavy bench back toward the lingering flame. Another push, another few inches. Sweat covered her forehead. Her heart beat like the wings of a bird trapped inside a satchel.

Finally, she reached the torch and dangled the ends of the ropes binding her wrists. She waited for the rope to catch. Across the chamber, Finch stirred. His groan dragged her fears higher, leaving her lightheaded. Pulling, leaning as far as she could, she dipped the ropes nearer the fire.

The hemp sizzled and caught. Ada squeezed her eyelids shut, again awaiting an inevitable pain. She pulled hard on the ropes. Heat climbed ever closer until the fire touched her skin. Her eyes watered and the hairs on her forearms smoldered. She whimpered, her body shaking and rebelling against her mind's steadfast purpose. The ropes gave a little. She pulled again, gaining momentum as she rocked. A final tug and a maddened scream threw her free of the restraints, sprawling on stone.

Ada flung the ropes away and checked her wrists. Charred hair and hemp, singed skin—they conspired to turn her stomach. She swallowed a heavy lump. But another smell caught her attention. Standing on shaky legs, she found the torch—an arrow, really—that had punctured the window. She gingerly sniffed the blazing wool at its head.

Naphtha. Greek fire. Meg's doing, surely.

Meg had come for her after all.

Relief washed over her like the rainwater pouring through the ruined stained glass.

Finch stirred again, his groan a promise of future nightmares. Ada whirled on her captor. He turned his face to the ceiling. Glass perforated his skin. Blood flowed where his eyes had been. He called her name.

She found his jeweled dagger and drove it into the thick vein in his neck.

Will dropped his stance, leveling the weight of his torso over relaxed knees. The man he faced in the main hall of the keep was half his size. Their contest began without thought. One moment they stood still and wary. The next they fought. Neither smiled nor spoke to set off the contest. The massive soldier lunged, wielding a sword as large as his leg. Will watched his eyes, not the massive claymore, and read his intent just before the ferocious thrust.

Able to roll clear, he swiveled on his heel and hurled a dagger, catching his opponent in the calf. The man fell, wailing. Will jumped atop his back and drove a second dagger into the base of his skull. The blade carved between bones to release a gurgle of blood. Although covered already in the offal of other slain combatants, he turned, doubled over, and retched.

"Are you well?" Jacob tugged at his belt, dragging him back to straight.

He wiped his mouth and nodded.

Little John simply laughed, a laugh like a growl. "I thought you'd have guts like a rock of late, Will."

"I am not impervious to—"

"Look out!"

Jacob's warning spiraled across the hall. Will dropped, rolling again, readying his bow and an arrow. He jerked his gaze up the stairs where Meg loomed over him, clutching a jeweled dagger of her own. Blood blackened the front of her gown.

"Ada! No!" Jacob yelled.

Will blinked. Not Meg.

Ada.

She launched forward. Too stunned and disoriented, Will let the arrow fall slack. He caught Meg's sister around the waist and grabbed the hand with the dagger. Both fell to the floor. She snarled and screamed, struggling to free her hand.

"Ada," he said, straining against her vicious attack. "Ada, we're here to help you."

"Liar! What have you done to my sister? Where is she?"

"She's safe." He grunted. Instinct demanded that he protect himself from the blade slashing near his face, but he could not hurt Ada—not and live with himself.

"I'll kill you for what you've done!"

She bit the back of his hand. A spasm of pain jerked his fingers wide, freeing her. She reared back with the dagger, but a pair of monstrous arms yanked her clear.

Little John plucked the blade from her petite fingers like petals from a flower. He subdued her, his grumbling laugh still filtering through the cavernous hall. "Against an army, he is well good. Against a single female, he is useless."

"And I know it," he said, rubbing the teeth marks on his hand. He approached John's flailing charge and caught her wild gaze— keen, wild eyes of a deeper blue than Meg's. "We came to 'venge you against Finch and Dryden. We mean you no harm."

"But I meant *you* harm, Will Scarlet." She drew pale lips back in a gruesome smile. "And Finch is already dead."

Will flinched, shocked by her vehemence. "Get from this place. Meg waits for you. Jacob, this woman is your responsibility now. Can you manage?"

The young Jew nodded. Taking Ada from John, he clasped her upper arms and repeated her name until she held his eyes. "Stay with me, Ada. Look here. Stay with me. We have to get clear. Can you listen?"

She dipped her face, the smallest acquiescence. Jacob looped an arm through hers and hoisted his crossbow, drawn and loaded. With a quick look back to Will, he pulled his addled charge toward the portcullis.

"The rest of you, on me," Will said, retrieving his bow. "We must find Dryden."

"Right here, Scarlet."

At the top of a wide staircase, Dryden stood flanked by a trio of soldiers.

The barrel nearest the two burning men tipped on its side. Solution burbled over the sodden ground, igniting in the rain. Flames ran across the clear gelatin, nestled inside the barrel, and exploded. Robin ducked and shielded his face with the leather guards on his forearms. Two men covered in fire rolled on the ground, to no avail. A glade full of allies disintegrated into a morass of confused shouts. Terrified of the mysterious fire that would not die, archers fled.

"Hargrave! The sand!" Robin and his second ran to the drum of sand. He signaled to a nearby pair of archers. "I want swords on those two. Make them hold still."

He and Hargrave whipped the cover from the drum and lifted it between them, grunting. The weight pulled at the joints in his arms. They hoisted it higher still, balancing it on their shoulders. The burning woodsmen writhed and rolled among the soggy leaves, but the water only exacerbated the flames they wore. Two swords aimed at their necks hardly restrained their agonized thrashing. They screamed and begged.

Robin and Hargrave tipped the drum. Muscles strained to control the flow of sand, to keep it from spilling too quickly or chaotically. Sand poured and doused the men until the fires fizzled. Rank flesh and chemicals mingled into a repellent stench. Witnesses covered their mouths and noses, crossed themselves.

"I want medical attention for these two," Robin said. "Save what remains of this sand. Get it covered. I want no more accidents!"

Astonished warriors edged away from the second barrel of solution.

"You have orders, men. Archers! On me!"

Robin eyed them each in turn, but terror held them firm. He had never encountered a situation where his men feared their armaments more than they feared their enemies.

Despite uneasiness droning in his ears—for he misliked Meg's brew almost as much as his men did—Robin pulled another torch-like arrow from his quiver. He strode forward and saturated the wool, willingly shaking the hand of a dangerous ally. Dipped in the water, the arrow ignited. He stood, aimed, and fired. A flaming arc of light touched upon a distant hoarding. He repeated the process, a single archer wielding the Devil's own brimstone.

"I will not stand for your cowardice!" His bellow shook the trees. He punched an angered fist at the castle gates. "And I will not stand for leaving those men stranded, without cover."

Hargrave was the first to shake free of his shock, taking up his bow and nodding grimly to Robin. Another man followed. And another.

"Ready!"

"No, wait!"

Robin pulled his attention to Hargrave, who pointed toward two figures emerging from the castle gate.

* * *

With John and a pair of loyal woodsmen at his back, Will sprinted up the stairs. Dryden appeared taken aback by the decision to charge. He stepped to the rear once, only once, before leveling his sword and aiming it at Will's climb.

"You won't escape this place," he shouted, smiling.

The trio of guards barreled down the stairs in advance of their liege. Will stopped and fired an arrow at the rearmost of the three, piercing him in the thigh. The man doubled forward and clutched his wound. The momentum of his descent pitched him forward, onto the backs of his cohorts. Will sidestepped the tumbling bodies.

"Cover me, John! I'll meet you on the outside."

He charged again, discarding his bow in favor of a sword. Meeting his opponent at the top of the stairs, he drew strength from his advantages. Ada was free of the castle. John and Robin had his back. And no way under heaven was he letting Dryden best him at swordplay a second time.

"Yield now," he said. "You lost your prize, and I do believe she killed the sheriff."

The nobleman flinched. "You must be disappointed."

"Not at all. He was my second favorite villain."

"No matter," Dryden said, hoisting his long claymore. "Finch was expendable, just like you and Carlisle."

"And your father? Your cousin?"

He smiled, that unassuming grin that had duped them all. "Of course."

Dryden held the higher ground, hacking downward and catching Will's sword. Will focused on maintaining his stance. He shifted his weight in wary dance of waiting. After another deflection, he climbed again. And again. In a matter of heartbeats, forcing aside his fear, he stood level with his opponent at the top of the stairs.

"And you wanted Meg's emeralds to support a coup d'état?" Will asked. "Was that your intent?"

"Here."

Will caught the palm-sized rock thrown his way, quickly

defending against another onslaught of blows. He jumped
onto a bench, jumped over a chopping blow, jumped back to
the floor. Edging away from Dryden, he glanced at the rock.

"What's this?"

"You wanted answers, Scarlet," Dryden said. "My father
owed Arthur more than our estate was worth. But those emeralds of Meg's—Finch sold them for real gold."

"That was your aim? Paying your father's debts with coun-
terfeits?"

Dryden grinned. "You understand why finding an alchemist like her was a priority."

He shook his head, chagrined. "Finch, Carlisle, me—all of
us driven by greed and thinking you worked for some higher
purpose."

"Amazing what faith people place in the nobility."

"No, people simply assume a son wouldn't have his father
murdered for a bit of coin."

Dryden laughed and shuffled away from another strike.
"Don't be high-handed, Scarlet. You've found redemption but
that doesn't mean the rest of us have need of it." He attacked
again, swinging the sword.

Will formed a semicircle with his torso, bending over the arc
of the blade and dropping the nugget. He twirled and brought
his own sword down with a two-fisted grip. He and Dryden
stood, weapons squealing, mouths mere inches apart. His
thumb ached. His shoulder trembled. He grunted, pushed, spun
away—and caught sight of the gold nugget.

No, two nuggets.

Laughter bubbled free, a wellspring of fatigue, rage, and
glee. "Seems someone thought very little of Meg's emeralds."

Dryden checked his advance with a quizzical expression.
"What?"

"Mad witch that she is, my new wife told me a little something about metals, rocks, and hammers." He turned the blade
of his sword to the ceiling and knelt, driving the pommel into

one of the nuggets. It shattered. Golden dust floated around his face. "This is a rock."

The nobleman looked ready to spit. His face glowed an angry red beneath his beard. Will took the advantage and leapt forward, but Dryden veered left through a corridor and out of sight.

As he slunk nearer to the palisades, crouching low, Robin watched Bainbridge Castle burn. Fires from the inside met the flames he and his archers sent to its outer walls. A massive blaze lit the night. Rain did little to quell the strengthening inferno, but it soaked through his cloak, his tunic, every scrap of clothing.

Midway up the mound, he met the wiry Jewish lad where he crawled through tall grasses. The woman he guided was covered in blood, marred by soot, and trembling. Her eyes would not focus. For a moment, Robin thought of Will's new wife.

"How goes? Where are the others?"

"The men trapped outside the portcullis pulled it open," Jacob said. "Ada and I came free, and they went to join John and the others."

"Did our men set the fires inside?"

Jacob shook his head and glanced at the woman. "I think she did."

"And Will?"

"No notion, milord."

He nodded, quelling his worry. "Get her to safety."

Squinting through the rain, he waved back to the line and signaled escorts to aid the refugees. Hargrave, however, pointed to the castle roof. Robin angled his head high, looking past the walls of flame.

No!

Silhouetted against orange and the black, Will dueled with Dryden. The men shuffled steps along the topmost rampart. Flames licked at the walls supporting the platform on which they fought. Every lunge met a parry. Every retreat spawned an advance. Matching and clashing and surging anew, their swords jerked as if pulled by a puppeteer.

He tore his eyes from the scene. Ushering Jacob and Ada back to the safety of the line, his mind and heart bellowed desperate questions.

What is Will thinking? Where is John?
Why am I down here?

Robin tossed the wool-headed shafts to the sodden ground and grabbed a handful of arrows tipped with barbed steel. He climbed near the top of the mound. Sparks shot from the burning structure. Walls trembled and bowed in odd places. A few soldiers yet fought, but most abandoned the ruined castle in favor of distant trees.

Watching the duel in the sky, he was momentarily transfixed. His nephew fought like a warrior, a true and brave warrior. No hesitation dogged his steps. No fear tainted his technique. But Dryden stood taller and had not suffered Will's injuries. The nobleman swiped and stabbed with practiced ease, never giving Will the opportunity to cast a fatal blow.

Robin could stand no more. He drew back the bowstring, aiming at the torso of their enemy. The arrow flew. Dryden swung his blade. Will teetered on one foot, his balance a casualty of his last-ditch defense, and lunged a final time. The arrow hit its mark, but too late.

Like a flutter of leaves, two bodies whirled to the ground.

Chapter Thirty-Nine

[She] who took Will Scarlet by the hand,
Quoth, "Here I make my choice."

"Robin Hood and the Prince of Aragon"
Folk ballad, seventeenth century

Meg sat at Marian's side in the dining hall, sharing a brittle tension. They exchanged meager words—a request for salt, an offer of more wine. Servants remained silent at an indiscernible distance. The waiting crawled under her skin, like grubs wiggling and gnawing beneath the bark of a fallen tree.

Night had been a torture of sleeplessness and restless, stilted pacing. But come morning, she donned a brave demeanor. Marian sounded fatigued and unnaturally cheerful. Neither of them spoke of the horrors they likely conjured in tandem through the night, and her hostess was kind enough to ignore the telling circles Meg felt puffing her lower lids.

Will would be well and home and whole. And Ada. She would have Ada returned to her.

Soon.

Following a stilted morning meal she could barely chew, she walked with Marian in the garden, arms linked. The rain gave way to another killing frost. Grass crunched beneath her boots. A half dozen soldiers followed at a near distance, their clattering metal weaponry and mail shaking animals from the trees. She imagined noisy ghosts haunting the paths they walked, spirits whispering the words she and Marian refused to say, to think.

They walked and waited. Anxiety built inside her joints, lacing through muscles and tendons. She hitched her cloak more securely around her shoulders, but bandages caught and tugged against the brooch.

"Saints be!"

She shrugged from Marian's arm and tossed the cloak to the ground. With teeth, with her patience in shreds, she tore off the bandages of one hand. Marian caught the other hand and helped strip the linen, baring damaged flesh to the chilly air. Both of them laughed like madwomen.

Marian pulled the cloak over Meg's shoulders and fastened the brooch. "We'll rebind them when we return to the manor. A little freedom will do no harm."

"Gramercy." The bracing cold spread a tingle over her skin. She flexed her hands, slightly, feeling the painful pull of scabs and blisters.

Marian placed a hand on her upper arm to resume their walk. "The differences between you and Will are rather incredible."

She swallowed a gasp. They could not talk about Will, not if she wanted to hold back a wave of tears. But Marian's words made her curious. "How so?"

"Please regard this as a compliment, Meg: You have a face for gambling. Between your eyes and your expression, you hardly give away a thought."

"And Will?"

"In a crowd of men he stands apart, always holding something in reserve. His expressions say more than he does. That you've been able to communicate at all impresses me."

Cultured and precise, her words also held a warmth of affection. Meg almost envied their long association, but she appreciated Marian's candor.

She swept short strands of hair away with the backs of her forearms. "Perhaps that explains the rough time we've had in coming to an understanding. I needed to find a different way inside him."

"I wager you've found pieces of him no one else thought to discover."

And he of me.

She stopped. She heard it more clearly then, the fast approach of distant hoof beats. "Who comes?"

"I cannot tell."

"Milady," said a guard. "Let us return to the manor, if you please."

With the men-at-arms flanking them in a circle of fretful metal, they came to the manor gates. The sound and feel of yielding, frostbitten earth beneath her boots gave way to stone, then marble. Another guard ran into the foyer from a rear doorway. "Milady, a Jew requests entry to the stables. Says his name be Jacob."

Meg said his name on an exhale. News. At last.

Marian tensed only briefly, a quick flex of fingers on Meg's arm. "Grant him admittance. Show him to the main hall."

The man hesitated.

"*Immediately*, I say."

Minutes later, a bustle of noise and footsteps overran the manor. Servants and guards moved with equal haste in a flurry that set Meg's head to turn. When at last she sat on a padded bench, she dug nails into the brocade. Pain lanced her palms. She dug harder.

"Meg!"

She found Jacob's voice, if not his face. "What news, Jacob? Tell me true."

"I brought someone for you."

"Meg? There you are!"

"Ada!"

The sisters dove into each other's arms, Meg sitting and Ada kneeling. Relief sluiced through her body, dissolving the hard armor she had worn since Will's departure. She touched and touched again, reassuring her mind of the truth. Ada was free, safe.

"Are you well, Ada? Tell me how you fare."

"I am . . . I am well." She laughed with the uncertainty of a person waking from a dream. Smoke and blood wafted from her clothes and hair, a sharp, nauseating pang. "I set a dozen fires. Thought you would be proud of that."

"Ada?"

"'Tis true. I set Bainbridge alight. And then I killed the sheriff." She sounded unlike herself, a warped imitation of her sister.

An unnamed fear spun in her veins. "You killed Sheriff Finch?"

"Yes, with no regrets," Ada said. "But saints be, I couldn't get that ramskit Scarlet."

Marian gasped. Meg flinched, her body drawn taut.

"She took a dagger to Will," Jacob said, pulling Ada to her feet. "I stopped her and brought her on ahead, hoping tempers would cool."

"Tell us, please." The tone of Marian's voice was soft enough to tame wolves. "Do you know what fates befell the others?"

"No, milady. My apologies."

"Come then. Let me see to your care."

They departed, leaving the great hall barren save the sisters. Meg stood, her knees shaking. "Now you can tell me, Ada. What exactly did you do?"

Meg wore a borrowed gown of deep green, one more fashionable than her unusual clothes. But she had foregone a veil, that ridiculous bit of stubbornness, unmindful of people who gawped at her eyes bouncing in loose, useless circles. Brown hair hung short to her chin. Ghastly red blisters covered her hands.

And her expression. Only once had Ada seen an expression

to match the one on her sister's face: when Meg had discovered her with Hugo in the woods. She had transformed into a statue, never fully returning to flesh in Ada's company. In the great hall of Loxley Manor, she turned to stone again.

"Will led your rescue, but you sought to do him harm?"

The heightened terror of battle resurfaced, bringing a tremor to her hands and sweat to her brow. She pushed those horrors in a box and closed the lid. "Of course. He sent me to that place. Places I cannot bear to recall. I shan't discuss this, Meg."

"He risked his life to redress his misdeeds." Her voice scratched like a shard of flint.

"I say—enough, Meg. I am dreadfully tired."

"You're not the only one who has suffered these weeks."

"And I'm sorry for your hurt." Ada glanced at her sister's mangled hands. The sympathy she dredged for Meg's injuries was like donning a mask. Underneath her words, she felt nothing of the sort.

"Will suffered too."

"For mercy's sake! He can roast in hell fires alongside Finch for all I care!"

Her echoed words flew like bats around the hall, but Meg's stony face never altered. Ada wanted to shake her and pinch her blistered fingers just to elicit some vulnerable reaction.

"You don't believe that," Meg said.

"Don't tell me what I believe," she said. "But I am willing to proffer forgiveness, so long as we depart this place and put the whole lot behind us."

Meg laughed, a statue coming to life. "And where would we go, sister dearest? Our cabin is a ruin. Our livelihood burnt."

"Good! If I never have to hide in the woods or tend those stinking beds, I'll come away from this in a better circumstance." She led her sister to a bench. "Let's away, Meg. We can go to Toledo like we always wanted."

"Like *you* wanted."

Frustration tightened her throat and made her words shrill.

"You would rather stay here? Stay in the forest where all who knew you ridiculed you?"

Meg snatched her hands away. "Traveling to Castile would not prevent my being ridiculed, not if you are my companion."

"Back to that?"

"No, in fact." She shook her head, short brown locks forming an impromptu veil. "I know about your flowers, the ones in the cabin."

Ada sat hard on the flagstones, vulnerable, as if her sister opened her soul to grope around inside. "What of them?"

"Why did you keep them from me? Why the secret?"

"Because you would have been the one to ridicule," she said. "You would have thought them frivolous and childish."

"I know. And these weeks have taught me to try, at least, to understand how life must have been for you. I was too involved in my own disappointments to notice or care. But I love you, Ada. I want to know you again, once all of this is past." She paused, brought her head up. Unshed tears glittered over pallid eyes. "I withheld my forgiveness because without it, I knew you wouldn't leave me. You would stay and try to make it right. For that I'm—I am sorry."

She studied Meg, looking for any hint of mockery or falsehood. "You've never admitted to being in the wrong."

"Not to you," she said. "But I've had practice of late."

Ada smiled. She petted loose hair back from Meg's face. "Then we *can* start anew. We can put this behind us."

"We can, yes. If you can forgive Will."

She leapt up, skirts twisting around her legs. "You make that a condition of our reunion? Why do you defend him? Even in the dungeon, you vacillated when offered the choice between him and me. Why?"

"I love him, Ada. He's my husband."

The two blunt sentences hit her, a snowstorm gale. She stepped back. "No, no—this cannot be."

"I tell you true, Ada."

"This is madness! He arrested me and put me in that place!"

Meg stood, her expression direct despite her unsteady gaze. "He saved my life and yours."

"Gratitude, maybe. An infatuation. But you cannot love him."

"Don't tell me who I love."

Dizziness spun into anger and disbelief. "And you keep that mocking tongue to yourself! I'll not have this, Meg. I won't!"

"Which part? My being married?" She laughed a little, color suffusing her cheeks. "Because that is well and done. Or are you frightened that I am standing for myself?"

Outrage painted crimson blotches over her vision. "You're not standing for yourself! You've merely found another person to prop you up."

"You're wrong, Ada," she said, almost too softly to hear. "I assure you of that."

"Enough!" She burrowed her fingers into tangles at her temples. The imaginary box she had used to contain her nightmares burst open. Wild visions of fire and blood and pierced flesh wrapped around her mind, ravaging her peace. Like her sister. Meg gave her no peace. "You've no need for two fools leading you through this life, if Scarlet yet lives."

"Ada!"

"And I'm curious what choice you'll make now."

Meg paled, the useless creature. "What choice?"

"You cannot guess? I'm asking you to choose, sister dear: your husband or me."

Will's head throbbed. His back felt gnarled like an old oak. Sharp teeth bit into his lungs where bone ground against bone. But he lived. He breathed, despite the anguish.

That he slumped in his saddle, feeling as vigorous as a sack of barley—well, some rewards proved worth the aggravation. He would bear any manner of hardships if it meant reuniting with Meg. But fewer such hardships in years to come would be his aim.

Shouts and happy cries echoed over the valley. Maybe

Marian's eagle eyes from the high tower had witnessed their return. Robin dismounted and helped Will down from his saddle. Pain shot from head to heel.

"Have you your feet?"

Will nodded but cut the motion short. Faint, he gripped the pommel and his uncle's shoulder. "You simply couldn't wait, could you? Taking a shot at Dryden?"

"Only offering the aid you requested, although that meant wasting a perfectly sound arrow. The sword imbedded in his gullet meant you'd already seen to the job."

"Serves you for doubting me."

"Never a doubt, Will. I was greedy for a piece of that louse." Robin's gaze held fast, blue like a summer sky. "And I wanted you safe."

"Robin!"

He and his uncle turned to find Marian fast approaching.

Robin grinned, a mischievous sense of play fully mending their rift. "One day I would like to return to the manor without these elaborate homecomings."

"You enjoy it." He stretched and looked for Meg, but dizziness trounced him afresh. His knees trembled, threatening to give. "A favor, Rob?"

"Anything."

"Ward off eager females?"

"They'll be too much for your likes, true," Robin said, his arms suddenly full of Marian.

Will trampled his tongue and averted his eyes. He waited without complaint, despite how he desired his own happy conclusion to the harrowing attack. But his reserves of patience dwindled, flickered, extinguished.

He cleared his throat. "Milady?"

"Hmm?" She looked up from her husband's fierce hold, eyes bright and lips slightly swollen. Decorum demanded a blush at the very least, but she revealed no such modesty.

"Marian, where is Meg?"

Her bright smile dimmed, a flicker of hesitation. "She quarreled with her sister."

He grimaced, fingering the row of teeth marks on the back of his hand. "As did I."

"Their argument became rather heated, I fear."

"Heated? Why?"

She frowned, a little flustered. A halo of dark curls swirled around her face despite the thick plait at her back. "I know nothing of the particulars. Meg has not confided in me."

He closed his eyes and brought a fist to his lips. Blood raced through his ears. Foolish man, he had aspired to erase the errors of his past and deserve the love he discovered with Meg. But whatever the reason for their quarrel, she would bow to the sister she fought to save, as she had in the dungeon, shrinking to a shadow of her true bravery.

Concerned faces watched him. He wanted no such concern, but he pushed his temper deep. Robin and Marian deserved none of his frustrations. Buttressed not even by anger, the wind chaffed his skin. He felt colder now. His injuries throbbed without hope to salve the ache.

"She's waiting for you at the manor," Marian said gently. "And likely set to claw you to pieces for dallying."

"That I can believe. If you'll both excuse me?"

A last burst of energy, one promising to be the death of his worn, abused body, propelled him atop Robin's horse. He galloped over frosted glades, the sun glimmering off every blanched blade of grass. Meg stood framed by the wooden double doors of the arched entryway. Her lips turned up at the corners, waiting.

Will exhaled, dismounted, and held her. Graceful feminine arms encircled his neck and dragged him closer. Words of welcome and relief whispered merry songs in his ears.

"You're home," she whispered. "You're safe."

"I am. I'm home."

"And Dryden?"

"Dead. He won't hurt anyone again."

She kissed him, a hard plundering of his mouth, a turbulent contest. He absorbed her anxious energy and savored the sting of salt and sweetness. His bones, his muscles—every inch of him ached, but her embrace eased deeper hurts.

"Wait, wait." Uneven breaths filled the tiny space between their lips. "What happened? With Ada?"

"I asked her not to be rash, but she insisted."

"Meg, you're not making sense. Can we talk to her?"

She shook her head, tucking her quivering lower lip into her mouth. "No, she's gone—gone with Jacob. Bound for London."

"What?"

"She was hurting, I know, and confused by all that happened. I begged her to stay till her temper slaked, but she refused." She offered a rickety laugh. "And she always accused *me* of stubbornness."

"With good reason."

"Now—now I . . . everyone fought to free her. How can I explain to them?"

"We did battle for more than Ada. There would be no justice in Nottingham with Finch and Dryden in control. Do you hear me?"

She nodded, her expression drawn and tired.

"Besides, you said Jacob is with her. I wager he'll keep her safe." He gathered her body close and petted up and down her back. "But why did you argue? What brought this about?"

Tears slipped onto her cheeks. "She demanded that I choose between the two of you."

His muscles seized. "Choose?"

"Like the sheriff did: you or her. I told her she was behaving in error, but she insisted." She found his face with bare, scarred hands and cupped his jaw. "I chose you."

"Which is why she left? Meg, I had no intention of coming between you again."

"I chose you, but the decision to leave was hers. It was different today," she said, her voice stronger. "There was no danger. I couldn't deny you a second time or turn away from our new life. Here in your arms, Will. This is where I belong, where I'm safe."

He smoothed away the last of her tears, not surprised to find his hands shaking. "You humble me."

"No, I *love* you. And I love the woman you've helped me become. Ada . . . she needs time to find that for herself."

A glimmer of sun found a path through the clouds, perhaps the last temperate rays until spring. She tipped her face to the sky, her smile bittersweet. He followed the direction of her thoughts, to the southwest, to London, and held tight when she shivered. "Will you regret your choice, Meg?"

"No more than you'll regret saving a blind woman on the road to Nottingham."

Crossing the glade to the welcoming walls of Loxley Manor, Robin and Marian arrived with Little John and their ragtag band that had brought Dryden low.

His family, with open arms and glad greetings. His family returned to him.

"Meg, my love," he said, kissing her hair, breathing her in. "You saved me too."

A thing impossible to us
This story seems to be;
None dares be now so venturous;
But times are changed, we see.

A True Tale of Robin Hood
Martin Parker, 1632

Author's Note

A person named Robin Hood might have existed, but the extensive legend bearing his name has been forged from bits of fact and centuries' worth of creative license. No matter the truth, I like to think that Will and Meg's story adds to that tradition, blending history and myth.

Many of the ballads, plays, and poems quoted in this book were collected and edited by Francis James Child in the fifth volume of his *English and Scottish Popular Ballads*, published in 1860. Online, you can find collections of Robin Hood literature at the Internet Sacred Text Archive (www.sacred-texts.com) and The Robin Hood Project hosted by the University of Rochester (http://www.lib.rochester.edu/camelot/rh/rhhome.stm).

Will Scarlet first appeared in one of the oldest surviving Robin Hood ballads, *A Gest of Robyn Hode*, and no other character in Sherwood has undergone the same radical shifts. From foppish dandy to cruel thug, from trusted sidekick to lovesick paramour, Will has filled the narrative role that writers and moviemakers required of him. Only his stormy loyalty to Robin is a constant.

The scholar Adelard of Bath traveled extensively during his life. What he learned of Arab culture and language made him a celebrity at Henry II's court. He wrote to his nephew—a man I imagined to be Meg's grandfather—on diverse topics, such as his hypothesis that the Earth was round. His knowledge of chemistry included all of Meg's creations: hydrochloric acid, healing balms, gunpowder, false gems and metals, and naphtha, an ancient Greek forerunner of napalm.

I based Meg's illness on meningitis, which was first described in the eleventh century by the Persian physician Avicenna. People have survived the disease without treatment, suffering comas, memory loss, and visual impairment, but permanent blindness is rarely an outcome.

My website contains additional facts, links, and resources on these topics, as well as details about my upcoming projects. I invite you to stop by!

Wishing you all the best,
Carrie
www.carrielofty.com

Richly written and compelling historical fiction
from Carrie Lofty. . . .
Here's a fascinating sneak peek
at her next book,
coming from Zebra in 2009 . . .

Toledo, Kingdom of Castile
Spring, 1201

Ada of Keyworth stared at the poppy pod, the one the apothecary rolled between his skeletal fingers. "What would you have me do for it?" she asked him in Arabic.

Seated, Hamid al-Balansi lolled the pod in his palm, around, around. A halo of sunlight from the doorway at his back left his aged, bearded face in shadow. But she could see his voracious eyes and the arch of his rank smile. "When was your last taste, *inglesa*?"

Englishwoman.

She licked chapped lips, darting a glance to his wide pupils. "Two evenings ago."

"Ah," Hamid said, his grin widening. "Without your ration, I do not envy your suffering come nightfall."

"Then don't make me suffer. Give me the tincture."

"The question is not what I would have you do for it." His sharp voice held none of the pity she sought. "Instead, I should ask what you are *willing* to do."

The cramped alcove at the rear of the apothecary's shop pressed closer around her. She cringed, the tapestry-lined walls threatening like ominous sentinels. Angled rays of intense afternoon sunshine illuminated the ragged edges of the tapestry covering the doorway, shining around it like a corona, polluting the air with the stench of heated wool. Seated on a scatter of worn brocade pillows, Ada hugged her knees and concentrated on the pale green seedpod.

"Please." The plaintive word grazed the parched tissue of her throat. "I have no money."

"Worse than that, pretty one. You have debts. Bad debts to unsavory men."

Panic caught fire in her chest, at war with the chills. "My debts are no concern of yours."

"Oh, but they are. If I give you the tincture for free, I keep you from asking for another loan." Hamid teased one of the pod's seams with a ragged thumbnail, releasing a drizzle of milky liquid. "Your creditors won't appreciate my taking business away from them."

"Do they have to know?" The grotesque little whisper hardly sounded like her.

"They always know. These people you owe, they are the eyes and ears of Toledo—not the high-minded courtiers you count among your patrons." He raised a bushy white eyebrow. "Why haven't you asked Doña Valdedrona for the money you need?"

"She is at the Alcázar in Segovia with King Alfonso, and most of the household with her," Ada said. "But even if she was here, I could never ask such a favor."

"And you have nothing else to sell?"

She thought of the scrolls, the ones she had pilfered from amongst the belongings of Daniel of Morley, her mentor. The English scholar had helped her and Jacob find patronage with the Condesa de Valdedrona, then spent the better part of a year

tutoring Ada in the half dozen languages of Iberia. A ragged
bit of her conscience had not let her bring the man's scrolls.
They sat in a satchel in her room. Now she wished she had.

"No. I have nothing."

He laughed without mirth, the squawk of a crow. "More's
the pity. We shall have to come to an agreement, you and me."

His fingers steady and sure despite his age, Hamid picked
up a bowl from the squat table at his knee and placed the
poppy inside. With a mortar, he crushed the fragile, unripe
pod until nothing remained but moss-green filaments bathed
in creamy resin. He added two more pods, pulverized them,
and sluiced wine over the mash. Deep burgundy muted to a
paler shade, swirling around the bowl. After draining the
liquid to a flask, he added pinches of cardamom and cloves.

Ada absorbed the scene, taking in every familiar movement. She imagined tasting the foul, stinging tincture, feeling
the blissful release of the opium. Relief washed over her.
Soon. Soon, she would be free of the wicked torture of unending dreams, that terrible nightly spectacle.

The only remaining matter was what Hamid would ask of her.
She closed her eyes. A distant part of her mind—the part that
hovered above the pain and the insatiable cravings—recalled a
very different life. Ada of Keyworth, the scholar. The translator.
The woman from England who had once lived for reasons other
than opium. But what had those reasons been? She could no
longer recall, a failing that only added to her despair.

And what would Jacob do when he found out? He had
asked her to make one promise, one ridiculously harmless
promise for her own safety. And she could not keep it.

Hamid capped the flask. The liquid sloshed as he shook it
vigorously, the fluff of his shabby white beard shivering with
the movement. Watching, waiting, Ada faced an unassailable
truth. She lived in that bottle. She would do anything to have
it, devil take the consequences.

"And now the small matter of my fee," he said.

"Whatever you ask. I'll find a way to pay."

His rodent grin sent frissons of fear up her arms—or was that the sickness? Anything but the sickness of withdrawal.

If need be, she would stab the grizzled apothecary in the neck and steal his goods. She had killed once before, and memories of Sheriff Finch's bloody end revisited her nightly. Finch's ornamented dagger still dangled at her waist, the last item of value she possessed. But she would never part with the macabre souvenir, a talisman against those who would do her further harm.

Tension curled in her muscles. She clutched the hilt, patterns of inlaid jewels and raised scrollwork gouging her damp palm. One quick strike and Hamid would fall dead. One quick strike and she would steal every poppy pod in his shop.

Movement at the curtained doorway caught her attention. Two giant men in black robes swished the tapestry aside, blinding her with a stab of bright sunshine. She released the dagger to shield her eyes. When they dropped the faded wool into place, the burly guards stood at either side of Hamid, his bony limbs and parchment skin.

And the flask was gone.

"Where did it go? The flask? You said we could come to an agreement!"

"But our agreement had naught to do with murder," he said, the dark pools of his eyes alighting on her dagger. "I felt you were liable to become unreasonable."

Fingers, hands, arms—she could not stop shaking. "You know I need it."

Hamid removed the flask from the folds of his white linen robe. He removed the cork and set it on the table at his knee. "Keep your peace, if you would. A hasty move might upset the table, and then your tincture will be no more."

"Please!"

Once she had been able to read people very well. Particularly men. She had read them like her beloved languages, knowing just what they needed to hear. But all she heard was a watery streak of hysteria in her own voice.

"Now here is my proposition," he said. "Will you hear it?"

Struggling for a breath, she looked up at the stern guards, their impassive faces and broad shoulders. One wore a massive mace at his hip. They made the tiny alcove seem even more confining. Backed against the rear wall, she would not be able to leave without their consent.

But she had no desire to escape, not without the tonic.

"Yes, I'll hear it," she said flatly. "Name your price."

For the first time, pity washed over the old man's withered features. His toothy grin faded. With steady hands Ada envied, he gestured to the open flask. An invitation.

She snatched it from the table. Greedy swallows bathed her tongue in bitter, spiced wine, trailing a path of fire to her gut. The warm wash of opium soothed her tattered spirit and quelled the shakes. Warm. Floating and free. The price he would demand, how she would satisfy her next, inevitable appetite— none of it mattered.

As the tincture enveloped her senses, she smiled and retrieved the dagger from her belt. It was no use, holding onto that grim reminder. "For you. My payment."

"Keep your blade, *inglesa*," he said. "Where you're going, you will need it."

Hands clasped behind his back, Gavriel de Marqueda followed two other men from the Order of Santiago. They walked deep into Toledo's underbelly where the sun lost its way among dark holes and labyrinthine streets. He concentrated on the journey and eschewed the need to inquire after their destination. His novice master, Gonzalo Pacheco, revealed nothing before he was ready to do so, and novices who asked questions only raised his ire.

No, he would know soon enough. Working to dispel his unease, he breathed steadily through his nose despite the littered foulness of the alleyway. Returning to any city, especially one as large as Toledo, filled him with dread. An undercurrent of vice, sin, and violence spoke to him in a language he had struggled to forget.

He belonged to the Order now—at least, he would after completing Pacheco's final assignment.

Listening to footsteps in triplicate, he allowed the monotonous parade of sound to drown his misgivings. His place was one of submission now, and in submission, he would find peace.

Someday.

"I understand your gloom, brother," said Fernán Garza, a fellow aspirant. He eyed the dank alley with his usual mixture of disdain and amusement. "To return to life fettered by these robes—I cannot bear it, not when we're within reach of women and wine."

Gavriel pulled the white linen of his hood to one side, glaring at his companion. "You would rather partake in the sin than rise above it?"

"Yes. And I'll believe you a decidedly less interesting creature if you disagree with me."

"I disagree with you," Gavriel said.

"Ah, but what am I saying?" He rolled his eyes skyward and shook his head. "At Heaven's door or in a beautiful woman's arms, your foul temper would never abate. You're an example of all that is tedious about our, shall I say, profession."

Pacheco glanced back through the half-light of dusk, never breaking his powerful stride. "And you're an example of why noblemen should keep from having more than three sons."

"Master, my feet ache," Fernán said, his voice that of an ill-mannered child. "Shall we have a brief respite?"

Stopping at the top of a stairwell, Pacheco's white robes roiled around his legs. The red emblem of Santiago—a fleury cross tapering to the point of a sword—decorated the left side of his chest. He nodded toward an entrance at the foot of the stairs. "We shall take our rest down there. Inside."

Gavriel eyed the scarred wooden door as he would an armed combatant. Whatever lay beyond that portal would serve as his final trial. One more task and he would prove himself worthy of the Order. Failure would mean expulsion. Expulsion would mean a return to life with De Silvas, or his revenge against them. He shuddered as sweat beaded at the base of his neck.

"Lead the way, Gavriel." Pacheco stared from beneath his white hood. "Unless you would rather forfeit your obligation."

Accept. Submit. God's will.

He nodded and descended the rough, crumbling steps. Splinters of shale slid beneath his boots, as did human refuse and slippery garbage. He scraped his palm along the stairwell to find his balance. Moist patches of rotting mortar gave way beneath his fingertips.

"Fitting you should lead us, as this place seems in keeping with your disposition," Fernán said. "Though when we've concluded our ministering, I should like to visit some happy place of love and verse—in keeping with *my* disposition."

Gavriel turned at the base of the steps and threw back his hood. Two days of Fernán's prattle on the road from Uclés would wear a hole in the patience of a saint, patience he worked hard to maintain. "Brother, I have taken a vow to abstain from violence—"

"Or else you'd likely cut out my tongue, I know. God grants small mercies."

Pacheco angled his head of cropped silver hair toward the door. "Proceed, both of you."

Fingers tensed on the rusted iron latch. Gavriel breathed deeply and prayed for fortitude. He knew this place. Rather, he knew places like this. Hidden from sight. Shrouded in lies and crime and hopelessness. Rife with temptation.

He pushed open the heavy door, and the brothel inside confirmed his darkest fears.

"Well, well," said Fernán, peering over his shoulder. "Perhaps this is my sort of destination after all."

Illuminated by meager torchlight, a score of women in varied states of undress lounged on pillows and sloping chairs. Men lingered with the harlots, ducking beneath low, irregularly spaced beams. The shadowed mess of garish colors contrasted with the dark streets outside, but finery and incense could not mask the underlying stink of unwashed bodies and sex.

At the far end of the wide, windowless room, a man stooped on a raised platform. An olive-skinned girl wearing only a kirtle stood at his side. The man spoke in a clipped mash of languages—Castilian and Mozarabic, the vernacular of the underworld—and espoused the girl's virtues. She had no family, no disease, no debts. Neither did she have her virginity, the man disclosed, but patrons lined the platform anyway, gold and morabetins in hand. Eyes closed, the girl swayed on the verge of collapse.

Merciful Lord. An auction.

Six brawny guards surrounded Gavriel and his companions, an offensive maneuver for close-quarter combat. He watched for weaknesses but found none in their formation. With the exit at his back, he felt confident in his ability to make a hasty escape—except for Fernán pressing close and whimpering.

The largest of the six men drew a lustrous, engraved sword of Berber origin, barring their entrance. "What business have you here, Jacobeans?"

The blade glinted beneath the torchlight. What Gavriel would have given to grip that sword. But his hands were empty and his vows heavy. He was an aspirant to a sacred order, an obstinate fact that had been much easier to remember while secluded in Uclés. Before any manner of belligerence, he was defenseless.

Pacheco pushed forward and addressed the lead guard. "Salamo Fayat is expecting us."

The words were a key to unlock the human gauntlet. Five of the armed men dispersed, blending with the shadows, tapestries, and patrons. The lead man sheathed his sword and offered Pacheco a curt bow. "This way, honored guests."

Gavriel exchanged a quizzical glance with his fellow novice. Fernán smiled and said, "This is a greeting more befitting the Order, don't you agree?"

"At a brothel?"

"Pacheco has influence enough—and the Order has gold

enough—to ensure everyone finds a happier afterlife. No wonder they welcome him."

"I am curious," Gavriel said with a heavy sigh. "Why would the owners of such a place want their clientele redeemed?"

"What would it matter to them? Sinners are easy to come by. Tomorrow there will be just as many eager to gain entrance." Fernán grinned, his pale skin shining with sweat and oil and his eyes wide to the room's delights. "Oh, that I could be one."

Weaving a narrow and careful path between the harlots and their patrons, edging nearer the auction platform, Gavriel followed the burly guard. He wished he had kept his hood in place, for he felt curious eyes walking over his face, his neck and hair, while his own curiosity swelled like a gorging tick. Waiting. Waiting for Pacheco's decree. The brothel's ominous temptations and worries about the upcoming test crushed against his breastbone. The air vibrated with currents of lust and greed, the laughter of the damned.

"Stay near the platform," Pacheco said before slipping into the crowd.

Gavriel lost sight of the slender man's silver hair near a rear alcove. Minutes passed, leaving him no choice but to confront the auction proceedings. The girl in the linen kirtle had been replaced by a young Moorish boy with skin like oiled wood, dark and smooth. He wore wrapped breeches and a neck manacle, his skittish eyes the size of eggs. A handful of murmured bids later and the boy was sold.

The hands Gavriel clasped at his back tensed and released, almost of their own accord. He stilled the anxious rhythm and fought a quick surge of nausea. Sweat slid between his shoulder blades, pressed on all sides by the heat of torches and bodies and wild memories. The urge to flee was nearly as strong as the urge to fight.

"You are to choose one," Pacheco said at his back. "Each of you."

Gavriel turned to him, questions stuck in his mouth. But Fernán found no difficulty bridging the silence. "I have dearly missed the luxury of personal slaves since leaving my parents' estate. Very thoughtful, master."

"This is your trial, Fernán, just as you are mine." Pacheco's black eyes narrowed and swiveled between his aspirants. "These souls are in desperate need of redemption. You will work with one to provide spiritual guidance. Turn them toward the Church. Redeem them of their wicked ways and you will pass your final test."

A year spent within the confines of the Order and living by its doctrines had taught him not to disagree with Pacheco's commands. His word would determine if and when Gavriel would pass his novitiate, the period of penance and trials before being accepted into the brotherhood.

But how he wanted to disagree.

The lines on either side of Pacheco's mouth deepened into trenches. "You fear this challenge, Gavriel. Why?"

Because I am not ready.

For once, he wished Fernán would intervene with some inane drivel, but the man was busy assessing the next slave standing at auction. Gavriel exhaled through his nose and forced tense muscles to relax. He toughened his lies until they became the truth.

"I have no fear, master."

"Then choose one," Pacheco said quietly. "It's quite intimidating, I know, to look upon a sea of depraved faces and know that you can give such a gift to only one. How do you choose?"

Fernán rocked back on his heels, that idiot grin stretching his lips. "I, for one, will choose some terrible good-for-nothing. No sense busting my hopes on a near miss."

Pacheco scowled. "You will regard this challenge with great sincerity, or you will not be returning to Uclés."

"And how is this a threat?"

"Your father has indicated that you are no longer welcome at your family estate. As of last week, the retreat at Uclés is your one and only home. Treat it with the respect it deserves."

Fernán's features drained of their scant color. He used a wide sleeve to mop the sheen of sweat from his forehead. "Well then, that changes my standards considerably." He turned toward the bulk of the room and addressed its seedy occupants. "Are there any virgins here? Virgins with an inclination toward study and prayer? And perhaps rudimentary husbandry skills? Anyone?"

Gavriel tugged on Fernán's arm. "Stop it, you fool."

"This isn't working. Should I try speaking in Mozarabic?"

"You should try behaving as if you wear the Cross of St. James," Pacheco said with unmistakable menace.

"Master," Gavriel said. "What if the one I choose does not wish to accompany us?"

"This is a slave auction. What choice will they have?"

"You intend that the Order will own them?"

"Of course," Pacheco said with a shrug. "Gavriel, you of all people should know this is no ordinary brothel. Make your selection and let us have done with this place. Now that our business in Toledo is concluded, we will return to Uclés tomorrow."

Fernán nodded toward another Moor on the platform. "I'll take him then. One's as useless as another."

Pacheco placed the appropriate bids and purchased the slave. The stooping auctioneer led his most recent sale down the steps. Fernán looked the young man up and down, his expression twisted in a distasteful sneer. "I wonder if he even speaks Castilian."

"You could ask him," Pacheco said.

"Oh, the hassle this will be."

A woman with fair skin followed the auctioneer to the center of the platform—a woman to stop the breath in Gavriel's lungs. The muddied sounds of the brothel faded. Fashionably dressed in a deep blue linen gown decorated with fine embroidery, she surveyed the crowd of buyers with a placid look. No fear tainted her shadowed eyes. No tension contorted the muscles of her body. No bitterness twisted the smile from her mouth. For all the world, she embodied the peace he had yet to find, this woman on the verge of bondage.

She rolled her eyes shut and licked her lips, head falling back. Unbound hair the same red-brown of ripened dates stretched to the shapely curve of her waist. Gavriel imagined digging his hands into those silky strands, bending her body to his, tasting her white flesh. Mouth dry, he choked on the image of transforming her look of peace into one of desire. Desire for him.

A quick glance revealed that animal hunger mirrored across dozens of faces. Fernán bathed her with a look of abject lust. "Can I change my mind?" he asked.

The muscles in Gavriel's arms and torso tensed. The nameless woman inspired more thoughts of sin than he suffered in a month. Lust. Envy. Wrath. He closed his eyes, breathless, but dark imaginings would not leave him be. Squeezing his fists until he thought his fingers would break, he prayed for strength—strength enough to hold his temper until she was gone, until temptation passed.

A loud commotion of shouts and drawn swords clamored from the entrance. Heads turned. The same six guards materialized out of the shadows, barring entrance to a young man with black, curling hair. Patrons around the auction platform backed away from the disorder, cramming bodies against bodies. One man elbowed Gavriel in the stomach. A woman screamed.

And so did the man at the door.

"Ada!"